It was then, for Felix, it began. The hatred for the briefing officer had expanded to include his superiors, the captain of the ship, the commanders of Fleet itself, and finally the thick-headed idiot humans who had undertaken something as asinine as interplanetary war in the first place. The hatred blazed brightly, then vanished. From somewhere inside came a shock of all-consuming rage, the nova-like intensity of which startled even him. But then the rage was gone, too. It seemed to shoot away like a comet. What replaced the loathing and fury was something very different, something cold and distant and . . . only impersonally attentive. It was an odd being which rose from Felix and through him. It was, in fact, a remarkable creature. It was a wartime creature and a surviving creature. A killing creature.

The Engine, Felix thought. *It's not me. It's my Engine. It will work when I cannot. It will examine and determine and choose and, at last, act. It will do all this while I cower inside.*

You are
What you do
When it counts.

     —The Masao

ARMOR

John Steakley

DAW BOOKS, INC.
DONALD A. WOLLHEIM, PUBLISHER

1633 Broadway, New York, NY 10019

**To my beloved father,
first (and foremost) John William Steakley—
and to Eagle,
first (and foremost) pal,
this book is gratefully dedicated.
Every single day I love them both.**

DAW Book Collectors No. 605.

First Printing, December 1984

6 7 8 9

PRINTED IN THE U.S.A.

PART ONE

FELIX

He drank alone.

Which was odd since he didn't have trouble with people. He had always managed to make acquaintances without much effort. And, despite what had happened, he still liked people. Recently, he had even grown to miss them again. Yet here he was, drinking alone.

Maybe I'm just shy, he thought to himself and then laughed at such a feeble attempt at self-delusion. For he knew what it was.

From his place at the end of the long bar he examined the others in the crowded lounge. He recognized a handful from training. Training was where it had begun. Where he had felt that odd sensation descending upon him like mist, separating him from all those thousands of others around him in the mess hall. It was a dull kind of temporal shock at first, a reaction reverberating from somewhere deep within him. He had somehow felt . . . No, he had somehow *known* that they all would die.

He shook his head, drained his glass. If he was in the mood for honesty he would have to admit that his chances were no better. No better at all. . . .

He paid the credits for a full bottle and then paid the extra credits to take it out of the lounge. It was strictly against orders on a battle cruiser to have a bottle in one's personal possession. But on the night before a drop a lot of things were possible. And as the hour for the drop grew nearer, he noticed that his fellows were beginning to take their drinking more seriously.

Outside the lounge wasn't much better. Lots of bottles had been smuggled out tonight. The ship wasn't exactly a giant party, but there were enough get-togethers here and there, and enough legitimate crew business here and there, to make it almost impossible to find a quiet place to sit and think. After a while he had settled into an idle rhythm of walking, sipping, smoking, and hunting.

After most of an hour of wandering about the corridors of the immense ship he found himself standing beside the center template strut of Drop Bay One. Drop Bay One was the largest single room in the ship and, since the *Terra* was the largest warship, the largest single room in space. It was over a hundred meters long and sixty wide. Around him in a checkerboard style were the little square spaces for drop assignment. From here it all began. Thousands of men and women would go into battle from this room. At the same moment, if necessary. The overhead was ten stories above him, criss-crossed with the immense cranes that lowered the equipment of war into position. A hell of a big room, he thought. Bigger even than the Hall of Gold back home where he had first stood at age ten beside the boys and girls of the other nobles and watched the coronation. He and the other children had had a tendency to giggle, he remembered, and so had been placed at the far end of the Hall, away from the throne.

Enough of this, he said to himself. *That's over for me now. It's far, far away . . .*

He sighed, shook his head. He perched himself atop the center strut and lay down on his back and stared up at the distant overhead and didn't see it.

"Enough sentiment," he said aloud. "It's time for brainwork. Time, in fact, for a cold logical assessment of the situation.'' He took a sip from the bottle, lit a smoke, and laughed again. ''Fact is, we haven't got a prayer.''

Fact was, most everybody in Fleet nowadays was a rookie. Over sixty percent and rising. That meant six months of advanced training. Nine months tops in the military altogether.

Not much hope there.

Still, the equipment was marvelous and many were surprisingly good with it. He remembered his astonishment at discovering clearly apparent aptitude for, of all things, the battle armor. Most found the power suits almost impossibly alien in practice and couldn't bring themselves to react in a sufficiently normal fashion. But he, and a few others, had taken to them easily, readily utilizing their potential as the long-sought key to a machine as extension of man's own puny form.

How odd, he thought, that he should have such bizarre talents. He, of all people, had fit with Fleet's hopes. . . .

And from there his drunken thoughts slipped into the past like most drunken thoughts of terrified humans. He lay back on the template and blew smoke at the distant cranes. He sipped steadily from the bottle.

He feared.

The hours passed.

Lovers in niches surrounding the perimeter of the Bay took advantage of the sexually integrated warrior class. They rocked and moaned and grasped one another. It was a united, if unorganized, effort by each and all to push the tension-taut present far ahead into the horrors of the future. After a while they would rest from their labors, draining the last of the bottles and lighting the last of the cigarettes. And before thoughts turned inward each and all would notice the glow of the cigarette coal coming from the lone figure who lay on the center template strut in the middle of the vastness of Drop Bay One. They would wonder what the hell it was he was doing there.

Felix, alone and unaware of their curiosity, wondered the very same thing.

Drop was just under four hours away when Felix reached the chow line. The turnout was sparse this morning. Not surprising, considering the night before. He watched several people back out as the line advanced toward the food. As the smell grew stronger, their faces grew greener until at last they couldn't take it anymore. A broad-shouldered woman wearing a warrior patch and red eyes got so far as to actually have a plate of the heaping whatever placed in front of her before she vomited loudly onto the floor.

She looked around, wildly embarrassed, to apologize at all others in the line, but found only Felix left. Puzzled, she nodded to him and rushed out the door with her palm clamped firmly over her lips. Felix looked around and laughed. He was indeed alone in the chow line. The young woman had actually emptied the place out.

He wasn't surprised, but neither was he affected. He stepped over the grumbling clean-up crew and, to the cooks' amazement, ordered them to heap whatever it was onto his tray.

"I'm hungry," was the only response he would make to their pale faces.

Actually, he was just lucky. Two hours before the rest of the ship had reveille, he had been rudely awakened by the chief of Drop Bay One who had wanted to know just what the hell he was doing sleeping on the center strut. That early start had allowed him to miss the long lines at Medical for a little something for his stomach.

After he found an empty table a fellow from his squad bay, whose name might have been Dikk, appeared beside him.

"Felix, right?" the man asked.

Felix nodded without interrupting his eating. That foamy something the meditechs had given him made him ravenous.

"Well, I'd be careful with all that food if I were you," said Dikk as he sat down. "It's supposed to be real bad for you if you're wounded. Like in the stomach, you know?"

Felix nodded that he knew and continued eating. He didn't want to say that he thought the idea of not eating before this battle was incredibly naïve. As far as stomach wounds were concerned . . . Anything that could tear through battle armor would leave not a wound but a tunnel.

It wasn't that he didn't appreciate doctors. He did. He was impressed by their knowledge, dutifully in awe of their equipment. But doctors didn't make drops. Doctors didn't have to fight for days at a time without eating anything but what they could carry. Come to think of it, neither did he. Or at least he hadn't until today.

He looked over at Dikk's nervous face and at the hunched shoulders of the handful of others who sat about him in the mess.

None of us have had to fight yet, he thought. But maybe that part was not so bad. What was bad was that they weren't ready.

Something in his face must have made Dikk uneasy. He mumbled something and left the table. Felix realized he had never said a word to the guy. He had a sudden urge to get up and catch him, to ask him if his name really was Dikk after all. . . .

But he didn't. He sat where he was and finished the plate and lit a cigarette and watched the silken plumes rise and twist.

A few minutes later his thoughts rose to him out of the daze of smoke and fear. "We're not ready. We're not even close." Then he started, looking around to see if anyone was nearby. To see if anyone else had heard him. For he wasn't at all sure that he hadn't said it out loud.

Felix stared at the black scout suit with the unsurprised attitude of one whose emotional spectrum has retreated to just two colors: frustration and disgust. Fear at this point could no longer be thought of as an emotion. It had more the consistency of gravity.

He sat down on the bench across from the now-gaping maintenance chamber that served as long-term lockers. When sealed, an elaborate testing system would commence. An amazingly varied series of forces—from hydro-thermal to magnetically directed laser probing—would come into play. The testing would continue on a more or less constant basis until the chamber was reopened. Most of it was to find a leak. Which was silly for a scout suit, thought Felix. After all, plassteel doesn't leak. You could vaporize it, warp it, tear it even (if sufficient forces were applied just right). But it didn't leak. And scout suit outer armor was 100 percent plassteel.

He snorted. Scout suits. A damn scout?

"Shit," he said out loud. No one could hear him inside his cubicle, so no one could appreciate his display of disgust.

From under his arm he took a wad of crumpled writ he had taped there before drop inspection. They still held inspection, even though everybody already knew it was suicide to carry personal belongings inside the perfect fit of battle armor. They had shown that one to the troops over and over, always dwelling on the scenes of the surgical teams trying to remove religious medals crammed halfway through some idiot's rib cage. Of course one could wear jewelry on one's nose and such where there was some freedom of movement. And many did. But Felix's interest in a nose ring was the same as it was for a religious medal—none at all.

He produced five cigarettes from the writ and lit one and stared at the suit and thought about why he wasn't surprised he had drawn scout duty.

Training again, he decided, the source of many first clues. He recalled their excitement at his scores, at his times. They had made him run the tight course twice more before they were convinced.

"Sure got the reflexes for this . . . uh, Felix, is it?"

He had nodded. He should have caught on then.

And later, when that same officer had called him into his own quarters and talked to him about "natural leadership abilities." Cigarettes were offered him. And something cool to drink for the first time in many days. He had accepted both and refused everything else.

He was furious with himself for not having been more careful.

The officer kept trying, kept spouting garbage, but Felix wouldn't budge. He knew it wasn't for him. Though capable of giving orders and probably having them obeyed, he was, of late, an uninspiring man. Not at all what a leader, a real leader, should be.

He sighed and puffed on the cigarette. Looking around he had seen several such men and women, he supposed. But though admiring of their energy, he had little faith in their potential effectiveness. With such a bunch, that kind of leader could likely get chewed in a battle long before decoration time.

And Felix wanted to at least try to live. No blaze of glory. No blaze at all.

So of course they had gone and made him a lousy scout anyway!

He sighed, resting his face in his hands.

His world shrank toward him. He panicked, as he always had before. Sweat poured down his face. His lips trembled. It was completely, terribly, dark.

He keyed the master switch with a dry tongue. Air, heat, light . . . life began again. For a moment he paused as he always did and simply breathed and stared. It was a foolish fear, he knew. But it was very real to him. Each time he felt the suit close about him, felt the armor seal itself about him, he also felt a deep inner terror that no amount of training could prevent. For with the simple fright of claustrophobia came something else: he feared the suit.

It was a machine. It did not care. It would work if told to. It would not if not. It was no serpent. It would not crush him. It did not crave his flesh.

But still he feared. And later simply breathed and stared and felt relief. This time, as at other times, the suit had chosen to obey him.

He examined the holos on both sides of the faceplate. They seemed far away, deep and wide in their illusion of three dimensions. Thousands of bits of information could be displayed on them. Maps of terrain. Known enemy locations. Distances and probable routes to Retrieval points. Many, many facts. They were blank now.

He worked the keys on the inside of his forearm and the holos showed him where he was: Starship *Terra*, Deck AA12, Warrior Section, Armor Vault One. He ran through the Function series. He made exaggerated gestures with arms, legs, head. Everything worked.

He made Connection and watched the gauge swell as he and his suit drew from the very heart of the ship the thing that seemed in awesome abundance everywhere: Power. Power throughout the ship for thousands and thousands of different uses. And more Power in the combined form of Fleet. And even more from home. Power. Everywhere, sheer Power. Force. Might.

He thought of the tiny sparks that moved and thought and eased more sparks together to form and ease even more sparks, the strength of which would ease together still more, tinier, sparks which, in proper conjunction, made Power. The tiny sparks would then ease beside Power. And together, with awesome brute force and intricate silken precision, wonders could be created. Wonders like the Starship *Terra*, whose marvelous stature and beauty could serve as man's ultimate loving gesture to the darkness which surrounded him—We are good. We are hopeful. We have built this. See her, the Starship *Terra*, the jewel of our being

But jewels did not long shine when Power was still about. Not when any fool could reach it. Felix, deep within the jewel already, could rend and tear her. He could grind her workings to rubble, blight her glowing entrails. He could disembowel this jewel of Man.

For he had Power.

Inside these layers of plassteel armor even a fool such as he, a dumb broken sonuvabitch with no future and a past he refused, could stomp the idol to clay.

Such power had thrilled him at first. Later, he was appalled. Now . . . now, he didn't care.

Felix read a dial. It was time. He left.

The Briefing Room mirror created what was termed "Positive Psychological Feedback." It allowed a simple soldier to see what a monster he was in battle armor. Some psyches had felt it would have a negative effect on some warriors, particularly the females. It was a stupid notion, immediately overruled. All killers like to look the part.

They did. Two meters tall, they weighed six times their norm. Their armored powered hands could crush steel, stone, bone. Armored legs could propel the fastest around 100 kilometers per standard hour. The suit protected them as well, automatically and instantly distributing most concussions in an evenly expanding pattern from the point of impact to the entire surface of the armor. Standard warrior armor carried blaze-rifles on each sleeve. Hold the arm out, palm down,

drop the wrist: blazerfire. Even plassteel would boil before it.
The blaze-bombs clipped on racks on their backs provided not
only an explosion, but spherical delivery of blazerfire in a
single heartbeat.

And there were other gifts. They were, for example,
complete. They carried with them all air, food, etc. Deepest
ocean or vacuum. They needed no help from home for five
standard days. Three, with a major battle a day. Only one, if
always fighting.

The mirror helped. They were monsters, they could see
that.

Felix took the blaze-rifle, the blazer, from the slot in the
long row which had a number to match the one pulsing inside
his helmet. He checked it for charge, attached it to his back.
Scout suits, much smaller than standard issue, had no blazer
capacity built in. Scouts carried rifles used by open-air troops
for thirty years. Also, they had fewer blaze-bombs—only
nine as opposed to the two dozen the warriors carried. Scouts
must be fleet, must be able to realize their much greater
potential for speed and agility. And, where warrior suits bore
different colors for rank and group, all scouts were black.
Flat black. Dull, non-shiny, space black.

Death black, Felix thought as he watched the five other
scouts collect and attach their rifles. Then he followed them
out of the armory alcove into the Briefing Room proper. The
room held twenty-one warriors, group leaders representing
two thousand line warriors and one assault commander. Each
bore the broad colored stripings of rank and its attendant
responsibility. As scouts had no effective rank, they likewise
possessed no real niche in the line of command—Warrant
Officers technically, but with no command in standard
situations. Many enlisted personnel requested scout duty.
They sought the partial privileges of officer rank and the
chance for rapid advancement much heralded by the grapevine.
In truth, no scout advanced more than a step or two. Instead,
they died. Even Felix's paranoid fatalism had not considered
this. Though he had heard, as had all, that the scouts' survival rate was considerably less than line warriors'.

"A lousy scout," he mumbled disgustedly.

The Briefing Officer's helmeted head glanced up at the

muffled sound. He surveyed the ranks. There was no way to tell who had spoken. All were on Proximity Band. He returned to his briefing

Paying attention at last, Felix was surprised to hear that the man had not yet begun to discuss details of the assault. Instead, it was a pep talk. Felix realized this alarmed him.

It wasn't the pep talk itself which made him uneasy. It wasn't the Briefing Officer. It was something in that positive, no-nonsense tone of his. Something. . . .

He doesn't believe, thought Felix suddenly. *He doesn't believe in the plan. He doesn't believe in us. But he'll be damned if he'll let us carry that. So he's trying to make us believe instead of him.*

Felix admired the officer for his concern and for his effort. He also hated him for failing

The pep talk mercifully ended.

"All right," snarled the Briefing Officer in his best Drillmaster manner, "it's time to get down to it."

On the wall behind him a large screen warped into light with a holo display of the target area. Felix noted the code on the lower corner of the image and keyed it onto his own holos. The map showed a peninsula some forty kilometers long jutting due north into a vast expanse of ocean. The peninsula terminated in a formation the shape of a large, three-fingered, hand splayed flat over the surface of the water. A choice spot, thought Felix, on Earth or Golden or any other human planet. Loads of sunshine and beach. The ocean frontage would supply fresh sea air to sweep leisurely across sculptured terraces where happy vacationers would collapse contentedly after a long day of water sports and laughter. A choice spot.

Except it wasn't Earth and it wasn't Golden. It wasn't a human place at all.

It was A-9.

And the water wasn't water. It was poison. And the fresh sea air would kill an unsuited human in a second— more poison. And the sunlight did little human good in a place where the average temperature was -20° at high noon. And the breezes were a near-constant hurricane that drove the noxious atmosphere deep into the sandy soil, carving vast furrows into the land, forging riverbeds overnight, toppling mountainous formations in handfuls of years, and giving this nightmare place its name: Banshee.

Only the enemy thrived here. Still another reason, thought Felix, not to go.

"B-team," began the Briefing Officer, "will drop here on the western edge. They will drive northward in a clockwise manner to rendezvous with C-team, who will drive due south to meet them from the northernmost section, the tip.

"The B-team, C-team, rendezvous will take place here, four kilometers due north of the Knuckle." A tiny arrow appeared on the holo showing first the rendezvous point, then the Knuckle itself, a steep crag one thousand meters high in the exact center of the splayed hand.

"We expect only moderate resistance during this stage of the assault. The bulk of the enemy is concentrated around the Knuckle. Nevertheless, there is more here to cover on the western edge than the eastern. And for that reason both B and C teams will carry nine full groups and two scouts apiece."

A flood of hatred rose within Felix as the A-team insignia appeared on his ID screen. Simple arithmetic left only two groups for A-team. Only two hundred warriors for half the area.

"Now before you members of A-team get too excited—" too late in Felix's case—"we want you to know that there has been absolutely no evidence of enemy activity on the eastern side. None at all. Your job will be mostly sightseeing.

"So . . . you will be split up to cover the eastern half. One group, with scout, will drop here, on the far eastern edge. The other group, with scout, will drop here, ten kilometers south. The two groups will converge here, due east of the Knuckle, to await rendezvous with Assault Main, driving northward up the peninsula.

"Don't worry about the lack of back-up. As I have already stated, there is nothing there. You should spend a boring few hours simply waiting."

It was then, for Felix, it began. The hatred for the Briefing Officer had expanded to include his superiors, the Captain of the ship, the commanders of Fleet itself, and finally the thick-headed idiot humans who had undertaken something as asinine as interplanetary war in the first place. The hatred blazed brightly, then vanished. From somewhere inside came then a shock of all-consuming rage, the nova-like intensity of which startled even him. But then the rage was gone, too. It seemed to shoot away like a comet or a torch dropped flickering and shrinking into a bottomless well. What replaced the loathing and fury was something very different, something cold and distant and . . . only impersonally attentive. It was an odd being which rose from Felix and through him. It was, in fact, a remarkable creature. It was a wartime creature and a surviving creature. A killing creature.

From a distant place, the frightened Felix scanned himself. He recognized little. Still, what he saw was a comfort of sorts and he concentrated himself toward it, toward the coldness, the callous machine-like . . . *The engine,* he thought. *It's not me. It's my Engine. It will work when I cannot. It will examine and determine and choose and, at last, act. It will do all this while I cower inside.*

With furious concentration, that which kept him Felix gave itself as fuel to that which could keep him alive.

There was more to the briefing. More figures of time and distance, more numbers of men and probabilities of enemy. The Engine heard and made note. Felix, watching himself, fueling himself, psyching himself, felt disgust at all that was about to happen and all who had caused it. And once more felt the distance between himself and those about him. Again, as he briefly scanned their armored forms filling the chamber, he thought: They're all going to die.

It stood three meters tall and weighed, on average, four times more than a human being—damn near as much as a suited warrior. It had six limbs, two for walking upright and erect, four for work. The upper limbs, call them arms, were incredibly massive, hanging down one and a half meters from two titanic shoulder joints. The arms ended in huge, hulking, two-pronged claws twice the size of an armored human fist. The middle arms were smaller, approximately human size. Curved, two-pronged pincers here for delicate work. The legs were the size of tree trunks, ending with semicircular pads splayed flat to the ground. There were two knarled knobs on each. Each limb, upper, middle, and lower, had three joints.

The body had three sections: shoulder, abdomen, pelvis. Each was covered with coarse, hairlike fibers spaced widely apart

The head, half again larger than a warrior's helmet, bore a dull globular eye on each side. The mandible-mouth opened in three vertical sections of varying width and shape. Closed, it resembled nothing so much as a smooth-sheened, toothless, human skull. The skin was not skin at all, but bone. Ectoskeleton. The muscles were inside. It was awesomely powerful.

It was the Enemy.

It was an ant.

It was called something else, something long and technical and dreamed up out of range. But scientific jargon had nothing to do with what men had felt when they saw it move, saw it coming. It didn't matter that it had no antennae and walked upright and was too, too, damn big. From the beginning, men had called it an ant.

Felix saw no reason to change that. He stood watching the holo of the enemy in the wall of the passage leading from the Briefing Room. The others had long since filed past. They used their last minutes before drop as a time to be with friends or check equipment or fight panic or yield to it and vomit or to pray with undreamed-of piety.

Felix, alone, watched the ant.

The screen on the back wall of Drop Bay Four was purely representational. It served no actual purpose in the mechanics of Transit. It merely informed the dropping parties of the various stages. First it would glow white: Attention. Next would come yellow: Transit beginning. Then the yellow would be interspersed with flashing bands of red light: thirty seconds. As the ten second mark arrived, the red bands flashed the countdown. They would turn slowly inward across the surface of the wall until a square had formed. The square would shrink, coalesce, brightly pulsing all the while. If all was well, the red square would turn bright green at the two second mark and the drop party would step quickly forward toward it.

Actually, they were trained to all but throw themselves toward the green square. "Try to bust that wall!" the Drillmasters had demanded. And they would try, surging forward en masse. But they never actually touched the screen, never even left their drop squares. Instead, they would Transit. To the next room, to another Drop Bay, to another ship. To another world.

The presence of Banshee loomed uncomfortably as Felix entered Drop Bay Four and stepped through the others to the scout position at the very front of the formation. As he took his place, he appreciated at last the decision not to forewarn him of scout duty. One could do anything at all for a warrior's supposed sense of confidence—show him his high test scores, pat him on the back, tell him he was superhuman. None of it would affect in the slightest the growing sense of desperation that began the instant he realized he was going to be the very first of the bunch to touch down on alien soil. Given a few days' notice, the candidate would be, at the very least, hallucinating by drop time. Given a week, a basket case. Given two weeks—nobody would show up.

By springing the assignment on the morning of the drop, there was, presumably, too little time for such paranoia to develop.

Enough time for me, thought Felix sourly.

But only a small part of him thought anything at all. The rest of Felix thought nothing. The rest of Felix was psyching, psyching. Becoming the Engine.

For no amount of reassurance, no amount of technical data, or surveillance figures or probability curves or anything else—however thorough—had convinced him that he would not be slaughtered a split-second after Transit. And if they were to try for another year, the result would be just the same. Nothing they could say would make the slightest difference to him. For they, They, stayed put. They computed. They theorized. They were pleased at Their brilliance or stunned by Their failure. Perhaps even guilt-ridden at the result.

But from the ship.

Psyching . . . psyching. . . .

Dimly, he had been horrorstruck by his fellow warriors' attitudes. Some had actually complained at being left out of the "big show." None of them, it seemed, felt as he did. They stood about talking, gesturing, laughing. A slight hint of nervousness, of course, but that was damn well not enough.

Are they insane? he wondered. They actually have faith in fools who would throw us into armed combat—by the *thousands*—after less than a year of training? *Madness,* he thought. But, again, only a small bit of him thought anything at all.

Psyching . . . psyching. . . .

The wall, formerly a bland shade of confident blue, turned suddenly white. The hundred regulars assumed formation behind him.

"Attention," said the CO unnecessarily. His voice sounded deliberately bored.

Psyching . . . psyching. . . .

Yellow light appeared at the edges of the screen. It flowed smoothly toward the center in what the psychs had called "color comfort pattern."

"Look alive," said the CO. Someone coughed directly into his microphone. There were several nervous titters. "Shut up, there," said the CO.

Psyching . . . psyching. . . .

Red bands began their pulsing march across the screen.

"Good luck, ladies and gentlemen," purred the even-toned voice of the Transit Control Officer.

"Go get 'em!" urged someone else in the booth.

"Don't worry," assured a warrior, a fierce female voice.

"Shaddup!" growled the CO with a nervous edge to his tone.

Psyching   psyching

As the red squared formed and pulsed, Felix, against all orders and procedures, reached behind his back and disengaged his rifle. He held it in front of him at the ready, safety off. Someone cleared a throat to speak, possibly to object, to chew him out, to. . . .

But it was too late. The red square flashed to green and

all were moving forward and there was loud breathing from some and no breathing at all from most and stunned shock from the inhabitants of the Transit Control Booth when they saw that the lead man, the scout, had goddamn near hit the far wall and . . .

. . . and ANTS! ANTS EVERYWHERE!

Felix fired and fired, the blue beam slicing through the ectoskeleton like it was butter and long stiff tentacles slammed into his faceplate as he collided with their hurtling bodies and he tripped on one, still firing, and felt himself fall and, in a desperate lunge to remain upright, brought a plassteel leg forward with such brutal speed that the toe of his boot tore completely through the stumbling ant's midsection. Black fluid spouted but Felix was already gone. . . .

Slamming forward into them, firing wildly about, he had to get, to get out of them, had to, had-to . . . Mandibles flashing by him and at him, tree-trunk arms and legs and claws crossing in front of him. . . . Most didn't seem to know he was there and the few who saw and reacted were blazed down or passed by but still there were more to come and more still, rows and rows of them, he'd been dropped right *into* them and the overworked blazer was signaling frantically of overheating that he swore he felt right through the goddamned plassteel and still there were more—he must keep moving, he must and then—

Then he was through them and past them and in front of him was a long dune of that sand. Without conscious thought he leapt over it with a quick, powered, leap. The dune was perhaps three meters high. His leap carried him perhaps half that distance above it and he was down again, blazer ready, spinning around to cover all directions at once but. . . .

He was alone.

No ants here at all. He was in what looked like a dry river bottom and he was alone. He blinked, straightened up from his crouch, took an instinctive step back toward the way he had come.

And the ants appeared. First one, then three, then nine, a dozen, all clambering over the dune toward him. He blazed them all, severing limbs, melting giant skulls. More came and he blazed them, too, and then more and more from each end of the dune and he was having to swing the gun back and forth to cover them all and it was getting to where he could just barely get the ones at the far ends and then one vaulted at him from the center and he ducked and flashed blazerfire and the headless torso careened into him and he ran.

He stomped madly down the riverbed. The dune, he now saw, was a ridge of sand forming one wall of the bed. He looked for a break, thought of leaping again. But wouldn't that make him a target? Wait! Was he a target now? He twisted to look back over his shoulder.

Dozens of ants rushed toward him, jamming the narrow passage with their writhing flailing legs and heavy swinging arms and *huge* claws. . . . Globular eyes bore down on him. . . .

The Engine Felix skidded to an unexpected stop, took careful aim, and killed them.

There was no place for them to go, no cover to hide behind. They were all jammed together, all headlong urgency and targets doomed. Only when he had gotten them all— forty, eighty, two hundred twitching bodies?—only then did he think to notice that none of them, not a one, had been armed.

He stared at the remains for a moment. He had been told to expect blasters, heat rays that could, eventually, boil his suit on his back. There was nothing here. He ran on.

A gap in the ridge appeared. But it was on the wrong side, back toward the ants, and he thought he should just rush past or maybe sneak by or maybe leap over the opposite wall. Instead, in his indecision, he ran into the open without altering his stride.

It was terrible-terrible, awful-awful. . . . Ants still, more ants still in columns and rows and marching and they saw him and turned toward him, so many seeing and turning at once like they knew him personally and expected and as they burst through the gap he was past it with powered kick and stride. Coming for him—that was bad, very bad, but what was worse was that sight, that terrible-terrible, awful-awful sight, that split-second sight back along their horde to where he had been and where the others were still. The ants were swarming over the others, the dead and dying warriors, his fellows, his humans, being peeled open and apart by too many claws and pincers and mandibles snapping, plassteel shredding and no one getting a chance to fire enough to stop the peeling, shredding, swarming mandibles with globular eyes. . . .

They were all dead or all dying back there.

The riverbed turned, bent to the left and then the right and he came to another gap—on the wrong side again—and *ground* to a stop, staring-stunned-shocked. . . .

Six endless rows of ants poured up from out of a squat cubic structure sitting half-buried in th sand. Those are supposed to be supply dumps! They told us they were only supply dumps!

From behind him came more ants boiling around the bend and he blazed them at first but his blazer got immediately hot—Oh-oh, overload!—and he thought of running and he thought of leaping out of the riverbed and he thought of using a blaze-bomb and it was already in the air, a line drive straight into the crowd at the bend. He dropped and flattened himself and it blew.

They died, the ants. The ridge walls, narrow here, crumbled and closed the riverbed off. But the other gap! He turned and through the new gap they were coming—so *many*. He threw another blaze-bomb into the ranks and it blew as he crouched, ants flying everywhere but still more and more from the cube in the sand, globular eyes, and he aimed more carefully and missed—too much adrenalin—but the next bomb flew true with a slight arcing trajectory only meters above their heads and down into them and right into the mouth of the cube, right on the upward sloping ramp, and blew just right.

The sides of the entrance disappeared outward. The roof kicked high, lifting and opening and then falling and shattering and then the whole damn cube collapsed on itself.

Another blaze-bomb over his shoulder to the other ants already out and coming and he was off and running again. The riverbed veered to the left and left again and dropped downhill. He was accelerating, really moving now. And when he burst out into the open space beyond and accelerated even harder, harder, to the best he had, he knew he had lost them. They couldn't keep up and he was safe now, for now, but alone and the only one left and he concentrated *hard* on the vision of the collapsing cube and what he could do to them instead of that other vision, that terrible-awful sight of peeling plassteel and what they could do to him.

Alone on a hostile planet, Felix the scout, the soldier, the Engine, the killer, ran.

He ran and ran and ran.

Felix stood on the uppermost tip of a sand-blasted crag which rose three hundred meters above the desert floor. He stood with his black-helmeted head thrown back, his arms hanging limply at his sides, his legs braced far apart. His eyes peered intensely into the gray-yellow sky. Inside the helmet he worked frantically at the Emergency Recall key between his teeth.

After several moments he changed frequencies again, as he had done countless times before. And as before, there was no response.

Not on the Emergency Recall.

Not on the Command Channel.

Not on the ship's beacon.

Nothing. There was nothing

He lowered his head and gazed, unseeing, at the breathtaking drop millimeters away. He had to admit it. He was just what he appeared to be. Just what he had been every second since, from the first few moments after Transit to now, standing alone atop this majestic, totally alien, peak. Alone. He was completely and utterly alone.

He had hoped the altitude might make a difference to communications. He had hoped to climb above those blinding torrents of sand and any interference they might have caused him. But perhaps the sand had already done its job. Perhaps it had managed to infiltrate the suit and jam the relays. Or maybe it had that blaster-fire or the impact of those bludgeoning claws. He doubted the last. Despite it all, he was physically unharmed. The suit had held. It was probably the interference from . . . what? The sand? How?

Could be the magnetics, too. Something wrong with them here, they had said. Irregular, shifting, the polar interval was never where it was supposed to be. It was why missiles wouldn't track.

"Unless they've figured it out, too," he muttered at last, voicing it outright. Unless they, too, those masters of warfare at Fleet, had discovered what he had known for hours: they had no chance.

None at all.

"Not here," he said, gazing blankly at the western foothills. "Not on Banshee." For even in this supposedly deserted area, he had seen thousands upon thousands of ants

The blazer-rifle lay at his feet, useless. It's barrel was warped from the heat of overload. The stock looked worse, crumpled and split from having been used in a way its creators had never intended—as a club. The suit had also been changed. The left shoulder was now dark green instead of black where a full twenty-second burst of heat ray had ruptured the thin outer covering of the plassteel. Other parts of the suit bore gray-brown splotches of the sands which had clung to the black ant blood which had clung to the armor. The splotches were mostly thin, irregular streaks, except for those on his arms. There a dense unbroken coating of sand covered the plassteel completely, from biceps to fingers.

Many, many, ants.

Idly, he kicked at the remnant of his blazer and watched it for the long seconds it took to fall. He sighed. Incredibly, he had but 63 percent power remaining after a mere five hours on the planet.

Maybe they have figured it out, at that. And run away. I would.

He turned around and began the long difficult descent with the unhurried manner of a man with nowhere to go and nothing to do.

"I would," he said to the wind.

The warrior, a blonde woman, was dead. But the ant didn't seem to realize that—it kept killing her. Her body shimmered gruesomely beneath the blaster's effect, exposing a meter-long gash in the armor. Scattered randomly about her on the hard canyon floor were the remains of other warriors, some twenty-five in all.

A-team One, thought Felix from his hiding place at the far end of the enclosure. *Now it's just me. I'm A-team.*

He sighed. And then, Engine once more, he pulled his attention away from the carnage, away from the grotesque sight of his fellow humans, some halfway out of their armor, their swollen features fast-frozen in the thin alien air. He would not, could not, stare at them any longer.

Instead, he watched the ant. And waited. He had to. He needed power.

After only ten hours on Banshee, he was down to 24 percent of capacity. At that rate he had less than four left. Four hours until the Larvafern, deprived of laser-induced photosynthesis, would cease to emit oxygen. However, he needn't concern himself with that. He would be dead long before that. The ants would kill him first.

Two hours, perhaps. Two hours before the suit began to slow down. He would no longer be able to fight, no longer be able to dodge and duck. In two hours, he would no longer be able to run. They would have him. He would lie down somewhere. The weight of the armor would force him down. And in some canyon or gorge he would lie and wait, a helpless statue, for the ants. Shuffling slowly up to him and around him, gesturing to one another with heavy claws and snapping mandibles. They would prod him, poke at him, lean over and stare into his helmet, great gray globular eyes his last living sight.

And then, pulling together, they would split the plassteel like a ripe fruit and he would blow out dying, his scream falling about him like frozen ice crystals.

There was no question of hiding from it, no hope of a dignified sleep. Somehow they would find him as they always had before. Felix suspected they could detect armor by some natural process, given enough time. Never having any equipment—only a handful with blasters even—they must possess some inbred instinct. Whatever it was, it didn't matter. What counted was the fact that, so far, they had always, always, found him.

He needed power. He waited.

Three more ants, unarmed, appeared at the far end of the

canyon. They gestured. The ant with the blaster stopped killing the dead girl and joined them. They left.

Felix was out of the shadows in seconds. He inspected the corpses. Armor that had retained its integrity, he had been informed, also retained its energy supply. He found a charred warrior and lay down beside it to make hip-to-hip Connection. There was an instant's brief hesitation as the young man, recalling the constant fighting and fleeing of the past hours, screamed silently. Why?

Why continue? He was alone and lost and without hope. Why string it out?

The Engine ignored this, grasping the armored shoulders before him and muscling the corpse into the bizarrely sensual embrace of Connection. The Engine smiled as the power surged to 42 percent. The Engine refused to die.

A black warrior still carried twelve blaze-bombs. Felix removed nine, made Connection, and raised power to 60 percent.

A sergeant with a broken neck brought it to 71 percent.

The CO's command suit brought it to 87 percent.

Disgusted at gaining only 4 percent, he shoved the next corpse angrily away, refusing to recognize Dikk from the mess hall.

The last possible source was an Asian girl looking far too young to be there. Her legs were twisted under her back, forcing him to lie with his faceplate against hers. He gazed blankly at her delicate features, then made Connection. She screamed.

Felix vomited against his screens. Then he jerked as though electrocuted, throwing himself back and away. But Connection was made and her face stayed close to his, wide and screaming. He gagged and panted and, for just a moment, could not move.

Until at last he, too, screamed, a hoarse sound. "Shut up!"

She shut up. He paused, took a deep breath, and hit the stasis key. In seconds the helmet was, except for a fading odor, clean. He looked at the girl again, who was just then seeming to realize what he was.

"You . . . you're a man?" she asked timidly, like a small child.

"Yes," he replied, nodding.

"I thought you were. . . ."

"I know."

"You're a man," she repeated. "You're human."

"Yes."

"You're not the ants again."

"No."

"I thought you were . . ." she whispered and her eyes flared with growing hysteria.

"I'm Felix," he said quickly, trying to disrupt the momentum of her panic. "Scout, A-team Two."

Her calm firmed somewhat as she focused on this information.

"I'm Taira. Warrior. A-team. . . . You said A-team Two? You're A-team Two?"

"I am," he replied impassively.

"Oh, thank God, thank God! We thought. . . . I thought I was . . . alone! A-team One is . . . is. . . ."

"Hit your tranq key," he said quickly.

". . . they're all dead! All! The ants were . . . Oh, God!!"

He growled. "Hit your tranq!"

"Huh? What?"

"Key your tranq! Now!"

She blinked uncertainly, obeyed from instinct. From just above her elbow a tiny stream of compressed air shot against her skin, opening a pore and injecting the drug. Felix watched her pupils swell and contract as the tranq took effect. Taira blinked again, shook her head, blinked once more. Slowly, she pulled herself together.

"How many made it?" she wanted to know.

Felix ignored her. "Are you able to move?"

"No," she replied brusquely, businesslike at last. "My legs are broken."

Judging from her contorted posture, he could well believe it. "I suppose I could carry you," he mused aloud.

"How many are. . . . What's your name?"

"Felix. What's your power level?"

"Uh . . . 84 percent. Pretty low."

He laughed dryly, felt the disgust welling.

"Okay," he said. "Key your painers. It'll be a rough ride and. . . ."

"Felix," she said slowly, her voice now as cold as his. "You're alone, aren't you?"

He met her gaze. He nodded, She stared a moment, then closed her eyes. She sighed loudly.

"Two hundred and four people," she whispered to herself. She opened her eyes. "Two left."

He said nothing. His eyes were blank.

"And you'll carry me?" she asked with more than a trace of bitterness.

"I'll carry you," he replied in an even colder tone that told her she was right to think what she thought.

She grimaced, taken aback. Then she relaxed. "All right, Felix," she said wearily. "I'll be all right here. Just g. . . ."

"Freeze!" he barked suddenly.

"Oh, come now, Scout. I know what you think you . . ."

"Freeze!" he snapped again, looking past her down the canyon. "Ants!"

Just around the corner of her helmet, he could see the four ants coming back into the canyon. He was in a lousy position to see anything, but he was afraid to attract their attention by shifting. He settled for severing Connection, a slight movement.

"Don't move," he said. "They'll come right by us."

"I can't move," she replied softly. "Where are they now?"

"Shut up!" he ordered bluntly, watching them shuffle across the hard-packed sand. The one with the blaster was trailing behind, he noted.

"Are they close? Do they see us?"

"Shut up!" he snarled.

"*Tell* me!"

Her tone of fear—and pleading—got through. He looked at her. His eyes relaxed a bit. He looked back to the ants. "They're coming right past us. You'll probably see 'em when they go by. My view is bad. About twenty meters now. . . ."

'How many are . . . ?"

"Four. Quiet. About fifteen meters, ten. The last one's

back a ways. It's got a blaster. They're not looking at us. Five meters . . . There they go. See 'em?''

''No. No, your helmet is . . . Yes! Yes, I see one! Don't move! Don't . . . Okay. Okay, it's moved off. I only saw one . . . and it's gone past.''

''All right,'' said Felix in a dead voice. He took a deep breath. ''Sit tight.''

For several seconds their two pairs of eyes flickered about straining to see. They kept their bodies rock-still. Occasionally, they looked at one another. Once, Taira smiled. Felix looked away.

''All right,'' he said at last. ''There they go. On my side.'' He felt her relax. ''They're going away. It's okay.'' He found he had been holding his breath. He let it out in a rush. ''Okay . . . okay, there they go. The one with the blaster is first. Now . . . the second. Good. There's the third right behind him.'' He glanced quickly at her, his lips forming a pale smile.

Her eyes shot wide with terror.

He was already moving when the claws clamped down on his shoulders, moving back from her and up. He struck out with a boot, hitting something. He kicked again, felt the claws quiver against the plassteel. He kicked a third time, striking solidly. He spun about, sprung free, and slammed a forearm into the hairy abdomen.

The ant loomed over him. He took a step back, retreating, but the ant closed, grasping his waist with its smaller middle pincers. One of the claws slammed thunderously against the side of his helmet. He ducked the following blow from the other claw and lunged forward. He planted a boot, quite randomly, atop one of the ant's footpads, pinning it in place briefly. Then he drove upward, slamming his open armored palm against the flat chinlike space below the mandible.

The ant's head popped off.

Felix froze, staring unbelieving, as the gushing torrent of black blood erupted from the gaping spinal shaft. And then the ant fell backward. To his horror, he found himself being pulled along. The pincers still held him tightly to the ant. They landed brutally against the hard canyon floor. Felix twisted wildly, trying to break away. He stole a glance over his shoulder, saw the next one almost upon him.

He groaned. He wrenched back, got a knee against the abdomen, and lurched to his feet. One pincer tore loose from its grip. Another, still clamped to his waist, tore loose from its socket. Felix spun around, to meet the charge with at least. . . .

The second ant crashed into him like a tank, knocking both of them rolling across the headless stump of the first. Felix spun himself on top and clamped an armored hand viselike around the thorax. He shouldered aside a grasping claw and drove a powered fist through the center of the right eye all the way to the brain case. The creature shuddered violently, then became still.

Felix planted his boots on the midsection and leapt forward to meet the rush of the third ant. But he was all wrong, too straight in the air. He collided full-faced with the hurtling ant. Even through his suit, the concussion shook him. The ant seemed to feel nothing. The pincers clamped onto his sides firmly, holding him fast while the upper claws pinwheeled in unison, bashing his helmet from side to side with tremendous force.

Felix felt himself rising helplessly as the ant lifted him off the ground. He had no leverage, no place to run or dodge and the claws kept slamming into him and he reached out, groping for those hideous eyes. But they were too far away, he couldn't reach, and the blows kept coming and his vision blurred . . . and he was losing it, losing all sense of what to do or how, losing, about to die.

And then the two of them, man and ant, were suddenly enveloped in the crimson beam of blasterfire. It was incredible. The last ant was boiling them both to kill him. He felt the intensity increase as it rushed forward to finish it.

Felix, encased in plassteel, could take it a lot longer. The arcing claws became erratic as they, and the rest of the ant holding him, began to literally fry. One claw fell to its side, useless. The other swung, missed, missed again. The ant slumped, stumbled to one side. He felt one boot, then the other, touch the ground. He braced them firmly, grasped the simmering-oozing form before him by thorax and pelvic joint, and lifted it high into the air. The pincers at his waist stretched, disintegrated. Still holding the ant high, he threw his weight backwards, twisting around, and hurled the broiling monster directly into the source of the blaster-fire.

The heat ray ceased abruptly as the last ant staggered backward, clawing at the bubbling ectoplasm spattered about its skull and shoulders. Felix leapt forward and tore the blaster from a claw. He swung it mightily, in a long arc, and slammed it against a leg joint. Exoskeleton splintered loudly and the joint gave. But the ant flung itself forward anyway, against Felix, and the two of them banged to the ground atop one of the armored corpses.

The ant grabbed the blaster, triggering it into the sand below them. Holding the barrel away from him, Felix pounded his free forearm into the side of the thorax. The ant shuddered, stunned, but did nothing to evade another blow. Instead it tried to grasp control of the blaster, discharging it harmlessly all the while. On a sudden impulse, Felix moved the barrel within range of the other claw. The ant grasped it hungrily, both claws on it now, and still firing at nothing.

Felix reared back and slammed out with his forearm again to the completely exposed thorax. The ant shuddered again but kept both claws on the blaster. So Felix hit it again.

And again. And again. The creature slumped, sagged, as Felix pounded his target over and over with every bit of power at his command. After a while, the claws relaxed their grip, the gray eyes convulsed. The ant collapsed.

Felix clambered to his knees, dragged the blaster free from the lifeless claws . . . and froze.

For a long moment he didn't move. Then he gently lay the blaster on the ground beside him like in some somber ritual. He paused, then gripped the dead ant and dragged it to the side. He sat back on his heels and stared.

It had not been a corpse he had fallen upon. Not then. And the blaster-fire had not been, after all, harmless. Gently, carefully, he picked up Taira's armored arm and lay it across the gaping, smoldering, hole in the center of her faceplate.

"Damn," he said softly.

It took him six more hours to travel eight kilometers westward for the terrain rose treacherously and there were many ants. He had only 49 percent power remaining. There were no blaze-bombs left. Idly, he wondered why he didn't care.

He sat down in a sand drift and machinelike, Enginelike, went through a communication check. For diversion, he decided to try the ship's beacon first. Nothing. Next came the Emergency Frequency. Nothing. Last came the Command Channel. Unexpectant, unhopeful, and, frankly, bored by it all, he keyed it on.

As if in response, the ground suddenly rocked beneath him from a tremendous explosion less than five hundred meters away. Before the rumbling echo could die, he heard, clear as a bell, a man's bitter voice saying:

"I don't *care* about it, goddamnit! You hear me? I don't care! And I ain't fighting ants any goddamned more! Fuck Earth, anyway!"

Felix stood up. He looked in the direction of the explosion, at the distant and majestic spire. He smiled. He was no longer alone.

He began to run toward the west. Toward the Knuckle.

The bands were jammed with a hopeless overload of garbled voices. There were frantic exchanges between warriors, impatient officers' directives, sergeants' flat commands. Underlying each was a growing tone of panic. It had been a sporadic chord when Felix first detected it. Now he heard it everywhere—a faint coating.

War sounds were also constant, rumbling, thundering waves of noise occasionally punctuated by another of those heart-stopping blasts that had first told him where he was. After each of these, the chattering would cease for several seconds. And despite himself, Felix would each time envision all having been killed by it. Then, seconds later, the chattering would begin again, a little more desperately.

He was homed in on the center of the transmissions, a point just south of the Knuckle. He had to stop often to check his bearings, for the terrain had made anything resembling a straight approach impossible. A seemingly endless series of eroded gulleys and draws produced what amounted to a maze of narrow alleys between random groupings of walls five meters high. There was no pattern to either level or direction. And there were many dead ends

He had just completed another bearing check when he noticed he was no longer alone.

Two warriors stood shoulder to shoulder in a clearing a few meters in front of him. Felix stared at them, too delighted with their very existence to speak. By the time he had gathered his wits enough to call out, one of them was already speaking

"Don't try to stop us," said a man's nervous voice.

It was the last thing he would have expected to hear. He took an instinctive step toward them, then stopped. There was something wrong with these two. They seemed to edge away from him, like children, like schoolboys caught. . . . And then he had it: deserters.

"Don't try to stop us," said the nervous voice again.

"All right," replied Felix dully.

"We don't want to hurt you," said a second voice, equally as strident as the first.

"Then don't," answered Felix blandly.

The two exchanged glances, then stared at him some more. They were privates, he saw from their markings. They began to ease by him slowly, not trusting him.

"Don't try anything," warned the first.

"All right."

"We don't want to fight you," said the second.

"Fine."

"We're going now," said the first.

"Where?"

For just an instant, they hesitated and Felix thought he had gotten through to them. But then they were gone around a bend and out of sight.

"Where?" he asked again. "Where will you go? This is Banshee!"

There was no reply.

He keyed a dose of stimule into his system. He had had another less than an hour before, but suddenly he felt very weary.

* * *

The war sounds increased as he grew nearer. The great blasts had continued as well. The floors of the gulleys were being filled by the cascades of sand pouring down from atop the shaken walls. He must be getting very close. He leapt easily over a particularly large deposit and hurried down the widening passage beyond. And then he was surrounded by perhaps a dozen warriors stomping past him from the opposite direction. He held out a hand to stop them. A heavy warrior's glove slapped it away.

"Get out of the way, damn you," shouted someone. "Can't you see the beacon?" The group disappeared the way he had come without slowing.

Dismally, Felix considered the possibility that the entire assault force was now composed of deserters running away from this battle only to encounter, inevitably, more fighting. Each would, in turn, flee from the new battle, only to run into another and another. For where, on a hostile planet, can a warrior desert to?

He noticed the Transit Beacon for the first time. Beacon? Why, he wondered, would they run *away* from that? Transit was the only way home. He raced off toward the source, the way he had been headed all along.

He dashed around a corner of the maze and collided head-on with something coming the other way. It was another black suit.

"Come on! Get up!" cried the other scout, a woman. She grabbed his shoulders and tugged.

Felix leapt to his feet unaided. "Go on, if you want," he said disgustedly. "I won't tell anyone."

"Huh?" asked the other scout, genuinely puzzled. "Tell who? What?"

"Never mind," Felix answered, starting off again toward the beacon.

The scout stopped him with a gloved hand on his arm.

"Are you crazy?" she asked.

He shook his arm free. "Are you?" he retorted angrily.

A split-second before the shock hit them, he saw it coming.

And then he was flying sideways in the air against the side of one of the embankments which was already crumbling as he hit it. Great chunks of sand fell down upon him, covering him. He struck out wildly, shoving at the sand, trying desperately to keep from being buried, from disappearing beneath it forever, trapped and held by Banshee herself, for her children the ants and more sand fell on him and around him and the ground trembled with a terrible sense of fragility and then it was over.

He sat on the floor of the gulley, buried in sand to his waist. Directly in front of him, the other scout's helmet bobbed abruptly into view with a hissing rush of sand. Felix got to his feet and helped dig the rest of her out.

"What *was* that?" he asked.

"Another goddamn tank. What else?" she replied bitterly.

"A tank . . .? he repeated dully.

She looked at him closely. "Don't you know?" she asked. "Where've you . . . Uh-oh! Another beacon."

Felix saw it on his own holo. The beacon was quite near this time.

"Damn!" she exclaimed. "It's right on top of us! Come on!" She made a step in the direction she had been traveling before—away from the source.

Felix hesitated, bewildered.

"Move!" she commanded desperately and he found that he was already moving with her, blindly following.

They raced down several passages, careening wildly around corners, bouncing off walls, until they slammed together against the solid bank of a narrow cul-de-sac.

"Shit!" she spat bitterly. "Another dead-en. . . ."

This blast was closer. It was much worse. They thudded back and forth against the walls of the cul-de-sac like insects shaken in a bottle. The walls swayed, warped, bowed outward at them . . . but held. They were not buried.

It took him a moment to clear his head. He found her on hands and knees at the base of the wall across from him.

"What the hell *is* that?" he demanded.

She raised her helmet slowly to eye level and regarded him for a beat. Then: "You really don't know?" she asked in a quiet, thoughtful, tone. "Where have you . . .? Who are you?"

"Felix. A-team."

She sat up. "A-team? We thought they were all dead."

"They are."

"Huh? But you just . . . Oh. You're it, huh?"

"Yeah." He paused, seeing it all, briefly, once more. "Tell me about the tanks."

She straightened, rose slowly to her feet. "The ants get the Transit Beacon somehow. They home in on it. I don't know what this is they're using. Not like their mortars, obviously. Some kind of rocket, maybe. They don't have any exhaust, though. I've seen 'em. More like a streamer. . . .

"Anyway, we all run like hell when we see the beacon indicators 'cause we know what's about to happen. Now you do, too. The Hammer is about to fall."

Involuntarily, Felix glanced upward. Why don't you just tell the ship to stop Transit?"

"What ship is that?"

"Huh?" He turned and stared at her faceless helmet.

"The *Terra* was hit. We haven't heard from her in . . . not in a long while, anyway."

"But the Transit. . . ."

"Those are the jeep carriers. Automated. Robot pilots."

He stood there for a second or two before saying: "Damn,"

"Uh-huh," replied the scout. "Damn. Well. I have a place I'm supposed to be. We've a rendezvous of sorts." She read dials. "It's not far."

She led the way through the maze, stopping often to check her bearings. Twice he thought he heard her mumble to herself, but said nothing to prompt her. They saw no one else for several minutes.

Suddenly she stopped.

"They've figured it out," she said, half to herself. "They've stopped shelling."

Felix listened, nodded. "They'll be looking for us."

"Yeah. Then we fight again. And then we move again. Then we fight."

"You've moved before?"

"Twice. It delays things a little, not much."

She turned and faced him then, shoving out a gloved hand.

"I'm Forest," she said. "Third Scout, Forward Group One."

"Felix," he said, returning the handshake.

"You want to hear it all? The whole deal? We won't have time later. Or maybe you don't care?"

He found himself smiling. "Maybe not. But give it to me anyway."

"Right." said Forest, leading off again through the maze. "First of all, it was easy."

Ten thousand warriors had made simultaneous Drop on the "wrist." They drove due north toward the Knuckle, arriving at the edge of the maze well within estimated time limits. They quickly arranged themselves within the classic semicircular battlefield pattern and waited for A, B, and C Assault teams to arrive. They had excellent communication with the *Terra*, good morale and, at that point, nothing to report.

An hour later, the *Terra* stopped transmitting abruptly, in mid-sentence. All efforts to reopen communications were to no avail. No one was really worried though. The weather, someone suggested. Two hours later, however, and all were getting awfully nervous about being alone. The idea of losing contact had, frankly, never occurred to anyone.

Nervously, all eyes turned to the Knuckle.

And, on cue, it opened . . .

The ants came in waves that were perhaps half as wide as the Warrior emplacements. They came right at the center of the humans' strength. Because of clever positioning, the ants in the front ranks were clearly visible long before they reached the trenches. Also, only one or two in ten actually carried the blasters, which were of dubious value anyway considering the length of time they must remain centered on a single target.

So it was just what the human commanders could have wished for.

The first wave was literally obliterated without a single human life being lost. Likewise the second wave and the third.

The commanders could find no evidence that the ants were trying to flank them, so they drew in most of the forces from each end of the emplacement, leaving only scouts at the edges.

The fourth wave came and went the way of the others. Then the fifth died as well and the sixth and the seventh and by now everyone was having a helluva good time killing ants. It was easy. More, it was fun.

The ants stopped coming for a while and everyone cheered until they remembered that they still couldn't talk to the ship. Until B and C teams straggled in carrying bodies and missing many more.

The officers got together and gave the warriors make-work to keep them from thinking too much and it worked for a while until there simply wasn't anything else for them to do and they got a chance to sit down and look at what they had done.

"That's when I knew," said Forest. "That's when a lot of people saw it."

It was the bodies of the ants. There were thousands of them. Thousands and thousands and thousands. There were more than the entire loaded complement, not just of the *Terra*, but of the entire wing. There were too many. Too damn many.

The next wave was more than a wave. It was a solid mass. The first attacks had been only scouting missions, they realized, as they watched the choking, boiling rush swarm toward them. Just scouts.

They called it the first assault. During its half-hour length, two thousand warriors died. One out of every five humans.

"What's incredible," said Forest, "was that we held at all."

But they did hold. Against that assault and against the next and the next. But by then all was a mass of warfare and death and smoke and blistered ants and ruptured plassteel and some officer got smart and called for troops to move back and dig in at another spot.

About then the mortars started falling, coming from the Knuckle itself and it got so bad that they moved again almost immediately.

"We weren't just retreating. We were running. But then we found a real good spot and dug in a little better than ever before. We had the best of the best left, you know. And plenty of power left. And we blew big holes in 'em then. Big, big, holes.

"But, dammit, we were still getting chewed. We should

have just run like hell and I told 'em so. But they wouldn't listen to me. Those idiot officers . . . Felix, they still didn't know what was going on. Not even then. They hadn't seen the fighting from up front like the rest of us. They still thought the Knuckle was a goddamn mountain fort."

"Isn't it?" asked Felix, puzzled.

"Felix," she said slowly, stopping and looking at him. "That is no fort. It isn't even a mountain."

"Then what is it?"

"It's a hive."

The warriors hastily erecting the fortification couldn't have numbered much more than twenty-five hundred.

"Where are the rest?" asked Felix.

"I guess this is it. Except for some stragglers."

"This couldn't. . . . You mean you lost three-fourths of your entire force?" Felix couldn't believe it.

"Well, we had about twice this before the Transit idiocy. But the Hammer did a bad job on us. Hold on here, Felix. I'll see if I can find someone for you to report to."

She trotted off down the lines. Felix watched a squad of warriors demolishing large sections of the sandy ridges on either end of the barricade to inhibit encirclement. Another group was busy leveling the maze for about fifty meters straight out in front, to provide a flat killing area for the enemy to cross before reaching them. It looked, he thought, like they would be in a good spot in any normal encounter. But this was not normal. The ants were not. . . . He shook his head briefly to clear his mind of the image of those waves and waves. He wondered how it had affected those around him. He watched them go about their duties in what seemed to be a trancelike haze.

Forest reappeared. "Can't find anybody much. Colonel said you're with me for now. Right?"

"Sure."

She went to a stack of blazers surrounded by piles of assorted bits of equipment. She picked out two, handed him one.

"This blazer's almost empty."

"Yeah," she replied calmly. "I gave you the one with the

juice in it. Clubs, Felix. Welcome to the interstellar Stone Age.''

''I thought we had plenty of power.''

''Not for blazers they tell me. Okay—we're the backup team for this area.'' She waved an arm at an area behind the barricade perhaps twenty meters wide. ''The procedure is to let breakthroughs alone. The line warriors ignore them. We, that's you and me, are supposed to get them as they come through. Go for the head first. If you can't reach that, try for the thorax.''

''What about the eyes?''

''The eyes are good, too. Yeah, I guess you must have done this once or twice before just to get here. Well, try not to look too bored, huh? You'll spoil it for me.''

She laughed and started toward the barricade, waving for him to join her. ''Come on. We're scouting some.''

He wanted to say something that matched her bravado. He wanted to laugh with her while he could. Or just smile. But it was too far away from him already. Slowly, but with growing speed, he felt the Engine rise, felt it gather itself and surge forward to the front of his consciousness. And once again, he felt the rest of him begin to fade

They stepped across the barricade of packed sand and dropped the two meters to the floor of the killing area. He looked about at the scarred pattern of the pulverized dunes made by the planted explosives. The entire area held a gritty, gray-black coating that made an unpleasant crunching sound under his boots. He saw that certain areas of the sand had been shocked into something resembling glass.

''Key the command frequency,'' she said as they approached the maze walls. ''The CO wants to know what we see before everybody else does.''

He nodded to himself and made the connection.

She stopped when they reached the edge of the maze, gazing back and forth at the various possibilities. ''We need some height,'' she mumbled as if to herself. She picked a narrow gorge that rose steeply and began to climb. He followed silently.

They followed the passage through several turns, always rising. Around a sharp bend, they came to an abrupt dead end. She turned and looked back in the direction they had come as if she could see through the walls. "Okay. This is probably far enough. Up we go."

With that she bent quickly into a crouch, seesawed her arms for balance, and leaped to the top of the far wall. Felix gauged the height. He leaped after her. He misjudged his leap and banged a thigh against the lip, sending a spray of sand into the air. But he was up.

"The world's greatest athlete," she said when he had knelt down beside her.

"What?"

"That's what they'd say on Earth if I could have done that without a suit. Look at the jump we just made. Seven meters easily."

Felix glanced down, nodded.

"You from Earth?" she asked.

"No," he replied.

"I am," she said cheerily. "Born and bred. Ever been there?"

"Yes."

She looked at him at last. She had noticed the change in him. But she felt the need to talk and began to rattle on again. It was all about her childhood on Earth and about her decision to sign up some six years before. Some of it was about some man, either a lover or relative, Felix was not all sure.

He wanted to listen, wanted to help her out. He felt her need acutely and knew it would be much better for her if he could manage to respond. Perhaps it would even be better for him. She was, after all, Third Scout for the Forward Group, quite a high rank. Perhaps she knew better. Mostly, though, he just wanted to help.

But this was a distant want, coming from a distant place where all his human thoughts were thrust during what he had come to think of as the Enginetime. The rest of him, the Engine, was scouting.

Below them could clearly be seen the entire lengths of some two dozen passages in the maze. Bits and pieces of several dozen more were also in sight. It was a good spot for them.

Felix's eyes raked back and forth across the lines of curving passages, from left to right and back again. He would make two of these scans at a time. And then he would look upward at the most incredible sight he had ever seen.

He had no idea what the Knuckle was made out of. He supposed that it might very well be composed of the same sort of material used to make the ants themselves. He had read somewhere once about some forms of insect life that created their homes in this manner. He wondered if the same pattern would hold true for these ants, these three-meter-tall ants.

These monsters. . . .

"Forest?" asked a sharp commanding voice in his earphones.

"Forest, here," she replied.

"You in position?"

"Yessir."

"All right. Look, the Can is coming down your way pretty soon. You need to make Connection?"

"Yessir. I could use it."

"What about the other scout with you? Felix is it?"

Felix looked at her, nodded.

"Yessir. He needs it, too."

"Very well. One of you stays while the other comes back. Then rotate again. I want someone scanning the whole time. Got it?"

"Yessir. Will."

"Right. Out."

"Forest out. You want to go first?"

"It doesn't matter."

"I figured you'd say that. You sure turned into the quietest damn. . . . Oh, shit. See it?"

Felix followed her gaze. He saw it. An ant. Then another and another.

"Colonel, this is Forest again."

"Right, Forest. You got something?"

"Yessir."

"Right. How many do you see?"

"About twenty or. . . . No, make that forty or. . . ."

"It's probably just a scouting party. Sit tight while I. . . ."

"Eight, ninety . . . one hundred and fifty, seventy. . . ."

". . . mark the spot on the grid. Now, Forest. . . ."

"Yessir? One ninety, two twenty-five, two seventy-five. . . ."

"Forest, I want you two to stay put out of sight and wait until the main force arrives."

"Three hundred fifty, four hundred, call it five hundred. . . . did you say something sir?"

"Yes, I did. Forest, are you paying attention?"

"Six hundred, seven hundred . . . I'm a listening, Colonel. You were saying something about this being a scouting party."

"That's right. Just scouts, I'm 90 percent sure. . . ."

Felix watched some two thousand ants boiling throughout the maze almost underneath him and thought about idiot officers and running away.

"Colonel, this is Forest and I'm listening but I don't think you are. Three thousand, four thousand . . . You hear? Five thousand ants are in sight right now?"

"Now listen, Forest. You . . . How many did you say?"

"Never mind, Colonel, I'll tell you in person. We're coming back."

"Huh? Forest? What the. . . ."

"Forest out," said Forest simply and Felix heard her cut him off. Felix did the same. They turned together and slid off the edge together. They landed easily on the floor of the cul-de-sac and began running back down the passage with Felix in the lead. He could hear her panting along behind him on the Proximity band, could hear her mumbling something about that "dumb-fuck Colonel" and he thought about how much he would have laughed if it had been funny.

They crossed the killing area with only four powered strides apiece and over the barricade and the warriors behind it. As they leaped over the rows of helmets, Felix heard a Warrior's deep bass voice muttering: "Sure as hell found us fast. What's their blinking hurry?" and then he was past and down. He turned and faced the barricade, gripped the muzzle of the blazer and took several deep breaths

Forest was busy talking to the group leader and gesturing with her armored arms. The two seemed to reach an agreement. She laid a gloved hand on his shoulder and turned away toward Felix.

"We'll get the starfish first. They aren't really much. It would take two or three to match a blaze-bomb. But duck anyway. If one were to actually hit you as it detonated, it would split the plassteel.''

Felix nodded, took more deep breaths.

"We've got a bigger area than most to back-up because we're Scouts and can move so quickly. I'll take the left for now, I guess. You all right?''

He looked at her, said nothing.

"Right," she said and moved into position. "Don't forget the starfish.''

Felix was still wondering what starfish were when he saw them.

The air was suddenly filled with a cloud of what looked like six-spoke rimless wheels that arced gracefully against the sky from somewhere in the maze. Most landed short, in the killing area. There they had a harmless effect. But several did manage to get over the barricade and the sounds of the explosions were quite loud all of a sudden. There were some screams when it had stopped.

"Here they come,''

Felix lifted his helmet up. He saw the first wave.

It had to be waves at first. The tight passages of the maze allowed little room for a full maneuver. Instantly the warriors began to blaze away at the open mouths of the tunnels. The bodies of the ants began to pile up and for a fleeting instant, Felix thought that they would get them all by killing the handful that could squeeze through effectively.

Then a full wall collapsed in a rush of sand and dust. And then another and then there was a single line of scurrying, swarming ants coming at the barricade.

The bodies began to pile up on the killing area.

Different piles began to swell until it was all one long, wide pile. Then that pile began to swell and move and flow . . . closer and closer.

With astonishment, Felix counted five thousand bodies dead in his section alone. Thousands and thousands. . . .

The ants made no attempt to protect or shield themselves. Only one in five carried blasters and those were ineffective at that range. But still they were advancing. Closer and closer.

There were just too many targets.

Within moments, the mass had reached the barricade. And

from there it stretched straight back into the openings of the maze without a break. The human Felix was stunned, awed by the sheer immensity of such numbers. A tiny thread began to well up, the only sane reaction.

The Engine, unsane, ignored it all. Instead, it leaped forward and drove the muzzle of the blazer into the left eye of the first ant to break through. Without waiting for effect, he turned and slammed an armored forearm into the thorax of an ant that had lost a claw in its rush. And then there was another to the left. Two to the left. And then one to the right. He swung the blazer, slammed it against enemies. He drove plassteel fists into eyes, alongside great staring skulls. He killed, rupturing and splintering exoskeleton, bursting those globular eyes, ripping and tearing limbs from their sockets, he killed.

and again and again. . . . He killed.

He grappled a midsection, twisted about, and flung the ant back over the barricade. He turned to meet another and heard a click as the CO's override cut in:

"Down-everybody-down-bombs-now-repeat bombs-now . . ."

Felix ignored the ants around him and dropped full length into the sand as two hundred blaze-bombs flew high and deep and landed in the center of the killing area.

The explosion, even with automatic mufflers, was deafening

Felix started to rise. Someone shouted at him to hit it again. He hit it, just as the remaining warriors turned their fire inward toward him. The blazerfire scorched the air over his head, slicing the relative handful of ants around him that had gotten through. It lasted only a few seconds.

"All clear," said the CO's voice.

Slowly Felix rose, saw everyone had stopped firing. All seemed to be relaxing. He stood and stared, dumbfounded, past the barricade.

Dead ants, or rather pieces of dead ants, covered the entire killing area. Not a single living enemy was left. Instead, there was a twitching, squirming mass of crushed and burned ectoskeleton that stretched all the way to the mouths of the maze. The height of the stack brought it to just under the lip of the barricade itself.

Forest stepped up to him, gesturing over her shoulder at the carnage with a plassteel thumb.

"Ain't that something?" she said in a wry tone. She clapped him on the shoulder, turned away and looked out over the sight. He heard the beginnings of a dry chuckle.

And then, abruptly, she sat down. For a few seconds she didn't move. Then she looked up at him and gestured for him to sit beside her. On impulse, Felix obeyed. He peered hard at her face-shield, at the vague outlines of her face. He had expected her to speak again. Twice he thought she was about to. At last, he started to break the silence when he heard the sobbing.

She cried, and her great armored shoulders shook with the wretched agony of it. She cried and then cried some more. Then she simply lay down on the sand and shuddered.

Felix sat watching her framed against the broken alien bodies. He saw that her head was resting against the skull of an ant. He started to move it, then saw that he, too, was resting on the body of another. He looked around. The area was covered with the crushed parts of enemies, the sand drenched with their black spouting something. He shivered, stood up.

I can't lie on that, he thought. Dammit, I can't even lie down. . . .

It was some time before he noticed the tears in his eyes.

Because it was all going to happen again.

"It's a deathtrap," said the Colonel bitterly.

"It's all we have," replied Forest in a patient tone.

"There's no way down once we're up there. There's just that one set of steps. . . ."

". . . and only one place to defend."

"What if they decide to dig straight up through?"

"That will take awhile. Even for ants. Either way, we buy some time."

"I don't like it."

Forest snorted disgustedly, a harsh blast of white sound into Felix's earphones. "Dammit, I don't like it either," she retorted. "But there simply isn't any other place to go but the mesa. We ought to get started moving the casualties as soon as the able-bodies have made connection.''

''I don't like it. I don't like not having any avenue of retreat.''

The Colonel looked up at her then, startled. For perhaps five seconds the two stood there, commander and scout, and traded glances. At last the Colonel looked away. He sighed.

''It's a deathtrap,'' he said again.

''It's Banshee,'' said Forest, simply.

Felix turned away and walked down the rows of casualties toward the Can. He was down to 37 percent power. He found a long line of warriors lounging about on the sand. He asked the first, found out that this was indeed the line to make Connection. He sat and waited.

He wondered why Forest bothered to argue with the Colonel. ''Why waste your breath?'' he thought. There really isn't any choice. The Colonel had to see that. ''It's Banshee,'' Forest had said, as though that explained everything. Felix smiled slightly, bitterly, to himself. As far as he was concerned, it did explain it all.

They had moved three more times. Each time, after a short delay, the ants had found them and attacked. Each time, the attacks were the same. Walls of ants choking against the barricades, a seemingly endless supply. The lines would hold as long as they could. He and Forest and others would try to keep those that broke through from killing too many. Sometimes, not always, they did a good job. Certainly Felix was getting better. He had found that he no longer needed to think before acting. He only reacted, killing often two ants at once.

And if he had gotten quite good, Forest had become amazing. Never in all his life had Felix seen anything remotely resembling her reflexes. Many times she had managed to cover not only her own area, but his as well. She was absolutely phenomenal. A real-life killing machine.

He sighed. Not that it had been enough. Not that anything could have been enough.

For despite all their combined talents and all their combined resources, the ants were slaughtering them. Each attack was merely a holding action saved at the last minute by a hail of blaze-bombs which would temporarily demolish every ant in sight. But they were running out of blaze-bombs. Soon, very soon, there would be nothing to throw at the boiling mass and they would all be engulfed.

They must get everyone atop the mesa.

Felix and Forest had stumbled across it. It was a squat, ovular plateau of sand rising some twenty meters above the desert floor. It had walls that were almost perfectly sheer on all sides. Only a slanting drainage path, carved from erosion, provided a route to the top. If they could get everyone up there, the ants would be forced to bunch together to attack them. No more than two abreast could scale that little path at a time. *We could make it damned expensive for them*, he thought. *But of course, they can afford it. They have the bodies to spare no matter where we are.*

But did they have the time? That was the question. Surely there was someone up there doing something about getting them off the planet. Surely there was a rescue operation being implemented. And if they could just draw it out a little more, if they could stay alive just a little while longer. . . .

Or maybe not. Maybe there was nothing. No rescue, no reinforcements, no Fleet. Maybe they were all destroyed in space. Or maybe they all got smart and ran like hell.

Felix took a sip of water from a tube, spit it out into another tube. No. There had to be something. There had to be someone. Now that they had found the mesa, and some kind of chance. And not when they had gotten the break with the eclipse.

He looked up into the dark gray sky. The entire section of Banshee was currently in darkness. It was not full nighttime, more like dusk or dawn. Still, the effect was similar. It had become, even for Banshee, very, very, cold. It didn't bother warriors who could see in the dark with their suits and fight in absolute vacuum. But it, apparently, got to the ants. They had been obviously slowing down. Their movements, never graceful, were now almost ridiculous. They had become parodies of themselves with jerking, puppetlike gestures and slow-motion running. It helped a lot.

No. They had to be coming to get them. It couldn't all be going for nothing. Now now. Not with the mesa and the cold.

Someone tapped him on the shoulder. It was the warrior who had lined up behind him. Felix followed the pointing armored finger and saw that the line had moved along several meters while he was daydreaming. He got up and walked over to join the others.

As he sat down, he heard the warriors in front of him, all male, talking on Proximity band.

". . . not like real night at all, y'see? It's just the eclipse. The place has got four moons, you know, and it's. . . ."

"Whatyamean, it ain't night. Looks like it to me."

"Not to me. Not dark enough."

"Give it a little while. It'll get darker."

"No, it won't. It'll get lighter. It's just an eclipse, like I said."

"Well, that's just like this blasted planet."

"Earth has eclipses . . ."

"Got ants too, but I wouldn't rightly compare 'em!"

"Hey, look here. It's our scout," said the one closest to Felix. "You are the one, ain't ya? Been working our end of the barricade last coupla fights?"

Felix nodded.

"Gotta be him, Obel. There's only two scouts. This one and Forest. What's your name, Scout?

"Felix."

"Hello, Felix. I'm Bolov, that's Yin and Obel."

Felix nodded at each of them.

"Yin's the Colonel's aide. He was just telling us the latest."

"Yeah," said the one called Obel. "What's gonna happen now? Forget the rest of that eclipse crap."

"Well," began Yin. "Felix already knows. He and Forest found the place where we're moving to, the mesa."

"Ah, shit," said Obel. "We moving again?"

Felix nodded. "The Colonel agreed?"

Yin laughed harshly. "What choice did he have? Just after you left, he began to get down to it with the staff. Gonna be as soon as everybody hits the Can."

"What's this mesa?" asked Bolov.

"It's a big hill with only one way up. We're gonna hide up there and make the ants come and get us."

"What about the wounded? We got more than three hundred warriors that can't move on their own."

"We're gonna carry them up there."

Obel snorted. "What happens if the ants come in the middle of this?"

"That's what the Colonel was worried about. But his Flank figured a way. Seems there's two sets of . . . kinda steps . . . up to the top of the mesa. We're gonna move everybody halfway up first. Then we can take a little more time moving 'em the rest of the way up."

"What happens to the ones waiting on the steps?"

"It gets tricky there. Colonel's gonna ask for volunteers to defend the steps just below the landing while the rest of the moving is going on."

"Oh yeah?" began Obel. "Count me out."

"What's the matter, Obel?" asked Bolov sarcastically. "Don't you want to be a hero?"

"Fuck it. You volunteer."

"Like hell. This looks to me like the kinda deal where somebody always gets left behind. They got anybody yet, Yin?"

"Just Forest."

"She's volunteered for this? Hasn't she had enough?"

"She's had more than enough, if you ask me," replied Yin bitterly. "And she didn't volunteer. Colonel just put her in charge of getting volunteers."

"He volunteered her himself, huh."

"That's about it. She was mad as hell, too. She said, 'I didn't volunteer for anything, Colonel,' and then he started that same old shit about needing only the best warriors and how she's the best around and how she owes it to her fellow warriors and. . . ."

"That's enough," groaned Obel. "I know the rest."

"That's what Forest said, too. Said she didn't want to hear it. Walked away from the sonuvabitch."

"But she's gonna do it, isn't she?" asked Bolov in a tired voice.

Yin nodded. Equally tiredly, he replied, "Oh, yeah. She'll do it. She always does."

"Stupid woman," offered Bolov. "She's gonna let that Colonel kill her yet."

"Him or somebody else. Seems they always find a way to stick it to her," said Obel angrily.

"Every shit duty that comes along, they ask for Forest," added Yin.

"Why?" asked Felix, suddenly interested. "Why does she always get those duties?"

Bolov exchanged glances with the other two. He shrugged. "She came in second."

"Yeah," said Yin. "If she'd won, she'd be the one floating from star to star making demonstrations and meeting the rich and famous."

"Instead of Kent," added Obel.

The three men nodded in unison. It had meant nothing to Felix.

"What are you talking about? Second at what?"

"You kidding? the Armored Olympics. On Militar. . . ."

"She met Kent himself in the finals. . . ."

"Hell, she's famous. Or should be. . . ."

"At least she's famous to all the CO's in the Fleet."

"Fat lot of good it does her," said Bolov. "Second is just good enough that the CO's call on her in a pinch. But not good enough that anybody else cares. Felix, I bet you never knew that she was the same Forest who met Kent in the finals, did you?"

"No," began Felix. "In fact, I've never even. . . ."

"See what I mean?" interrupted Yin. "Only the CO's keep track of that sorta thing."

"Especially our CO," said Obel.

"Can you really blame him?" suggested Bolov. "She's the best around."

"She's the best there is," said Yin firmly.

"Well . . . Kent's the best there is, Yin," said Obel.

"Shit," said Yin with sudden anger. "Friend of mine was there for the whole thing. He told me all about it. She was robbed. She shoulda won it, but the brass wanted a three-time winner."

"I don't believe that," said Bolov.

"Me either," said Obel. "You can't beat Kent."

"My friend was there, I'm telling you."

"Oh, yeah," said Bolov. "Who is it? What's his name?"

Yin managed to look stubborn even through his face screen.

"She was robbed," he insisted.

"Well," said Bolov with a trace of bitterness, "that is the way her luck usually goes."

"Yeah. Can you imagine that?" said Obel, musing. "That she's stuck here getting the worst of the shit because of some cheat while Kent spends his time showing off?"

"That would be something," admitted Bolov. "If it were true."

"It is true," insisted Yin again.

"I don't know, Yin," replied Bolov. "She's awfully good. . . ."

"She's the best I've ever fought with, true. But to beat Ken . . . ?"

"Hell yes, she's better'n Kent ever was."

"Nobody's better'n Kent," said Obel firmly.

"Forest is," retorted Yin.

"Ah, Yin. You only say that because you know her," said Obel.

"Fuck that. She's the best," replied Yin. He looked at Felix. "What do you think, Felix? You've fought with her. Right with her. You think she can beat Kent, don't you?"

"Kent who?"

All three stared at him.

"Kent who . . . ?"

"Nathan Kent, who else . . . ?

"Three time Class One Armor Champion Nathan Kent."

"Never heard of him."

They stared again.

"You're kidding. You've never heard of Nathan Kent?" asked Bolov.

"Where've you been?" asked Obel.

"Out of touch, I suppose."

"Where you been posted? Were you a starprobe or something?" asked Yin with a laugh.

"No," replied Felix seriously. "Nothing like that."

"What were you?" asked Bolov, equally serious.

"A civilian."

There was a long silence while they stared again. In a hushed voice, Bolov finally broke the silence.

"Felix," he asked slowly, "how long have you been in the fleet?"

"Nine months."

"Nine months? You're a greener?" asked Yin, amazed.

"What's that?"

"He means," added Obel quickly, "is this your first Drop?" Felix nodded. "This is it."

"Holy shit," breathed a stunned Bolov. "On Banshee."

"But . . . but you're a scout. How could you be a scout?" Obel wanted to know.

"I just drew it."

"I don't believe it," said Obel with finality. "That sort of thing just doesn't happen."

"It might," suggested Bolov quietly. "They needed a lot of people fast. This is a full-scale war, after all."

"But scout duty?" wailed Obel. "For a man with less than a year? A greener?"

"How long have you guys been in?"

"Eight years," said Obel.

"Nine years," said Bolov.

"Five years," said Yin.

It was Felix's turn to be amazed. "You mean this is . . . your career?"

"Hell, yes," said Obel.

"So you've . . . done this before?"

"Fought before?" asked Yin. "Sure we have. Fought the Barrm on Silo."

"And the Zee's. Don't forget them," added Bolov.

"How could I," replied Yin dryly.

"Hell," blurted Obel, importantly. "My very first Drop was Ervis Three . . ."

"But you were back-up then . . ."

"Yeah, yeah," drawled Yin. "We know you've been around. We've all been around."

"Had to have. That's why we're alive and talking about it," said Obel. "You can't match experience."

"Felix has," replied Yin with a short laugh.

"So far," admitted Bolov, "it's incredible."

"Why is that?" asked Felix.

"Felix, you ask around. I bet you a month's credits that you're the only greener still alive."

"I'd bet more than that," muttered Obel. "And as a lousy scout, too. I still don't see how he got stuck with that."

"Maybe he volunteered," offered Yin.

"He's not that stupid," replied Obel.

"Maybe he wants to be a hero," returned Yin. "Some do. I bet he did volunteer."

"Bet he didn't," replied Obel.

"Which is it, Felix?" asked Bolov. "Are you stupid . . .?"

". . . Or just unlucky . . ."

Felix smiled slightly to himself. "I didn't volunteer for anything."

"You volunteered for the goddamn war, didn't you?" prompted Bolov.

"Yes."

"That was your first mistake," said Bolov.

"Maybe your last," added Obel. "Why'd you do it? You from Earth, huh?"

"Yeah," added Yin. "Your family in South America? You here to get revenge?"

Felix stared, taken back. "No," he said at last. "I'm not from Earth."

"Yeah?" asked Obel. "Then why did you sign up?"

Felix stared at him, hesitant. Bolov saved him.

"It doesn't matter now," he said. "He's here now. He's on Banshee, a scout, and fighting. Fighting damn good, too."

"A lousy scout," mused Obel. "A greener scout. Do you know where that puts you on the stat? at the very . . ."

"Cut that, Obel," growled Bolov. "That won't help anything."

"I figure he's got a right to know."

"Oh, is that what you figure? Shaddup."

"No," said Felix, resigned to it all. "May as well give it to me."

"It's the survival table, Felix," said Yin in a quiet voice.

"And . . .?"

"And . . .?" Bolov was hesitant. "Look, Felix, it's like

this: They have this scale that gives the odds for survival for any given warrior on any particular Drop. They change for each Drop. Like, for a greener warrior it's a four.''

"Four what . . ."

"Four for ten," offered Obel.

Bolov sighed. "It means that there are four chances out of ten that he'll make it. A statistical survival rate of 40 percent."

Felix couldn't believe his ears. "You mean to say that only 40 percent survive their first Drop?"

"If it's a major Drop," added Obel quickly. "You know, an assault Drop."

"Look, Felix," explained Bolov. "There are two kinds of Drops; Major, an assault Drop. That means you're one of the first to hit. Then there's the Minor, or backup. The scale I'm talking about depends on it being a major with a casualty rate of at least 10 percent, and with all that being so, a greener warrior would be four on the scale if it was first."

"Course, it changes with each Drop," offered Yin.

"Yeah," agreed Bolov. "It gets better. Second drop rates a six. Sixty percent chance. Third is seven. Fourth is as bad as the first, though. It's four, too."

"Overconfidence sets in," added Obel. "Know-it-alls that figure it can't happen to them just because it hasn't yet. Forget to duck."

"Yeah," said Bolov, continuing. "Anyway, it's . . . uh, four for the first, six for the second, seven for the third, back to four for the fourth back to seven for fifth. Sixth, seventh and eighth are the best. They're all eight. Then it starts down again. Ninth is seven. Tenth is only five. You get tired, you know? Anyway it stops at ten. Nobody's ever made more than ten major Drops."

"And most Drops aren't majors," Yin reminded him. "Most are just backups. Only one out of seven are majors because they rotate you that way. The odds are a lot better on backups. Nine for vets. Even greeners get eight."

"That's why greeners should always drop backups first," offered Bolov. "You get experience that way which helps you later on. It works out better, somehow. I don't really understand it all. But say you're like us and you do seven back-ups before your first major. The stat says you then get the same rating as if it were really your third major. You get a seven. See?"

"Vaguely," replied Felix, understanding a little. "How many Drops have you made, Bolov?"

"Me? Eighteen. But only three were rated as major and, really, only two of them were really bad. For the other fifteen, I was rotated to the rear where it's a hell of a lot safer. And there's lots more warriors around you, most times. Course, *none* of 'em were this Banshee shit."

"So your odds would be . . .?"

"I'm at eight, now. We all are. We've got experience, the know-how, plus we get lots of rest."

"The more rest you get, the less chance of battle fatigue," added Obel.

"Hmm," said Felix, thinking aloud. "Then I'm at four."

"Uh, no," replied Bolov, a trifle embarrassed. "You dropped a scout. That's different."

"That's worse," said Obel.

"A lot worse," added Yin.

"Scouts never get better than six, no matter what. And since you're also a greener . . ."

"So I'm a what?"

"You're a one."

"What?"

"One, Felix," Bolov said tiredly, sadly, as if pronouncing sentence. "That's one out of ten. A ten percent chance."

Felix stared at him, not speaking.

"You should never have been Dropped as a scout your first time," added Bolov hurriedly, consoling.

"Not as a greener," agreed Obel.

"You were robbed," insisted Yin.

Nobody said anything for awhile after that. Occasionally the other three would stare at Felix, awaiting some reaction. But Felix was long past reacting to any of it. Long past lots of things, he thought.

And then the line had brought them to the Can. There were only three spaces. Felix waited while the other three made Connection. And, just as he was about to step up, Forest appeared beside him.

"You're just now making Connection?" she asked, surprised

"It was a long line."

"You don't have to wait in line. You're a scout. You get

priority." She stepped in front of the warrior behind Felix and made Connection. "Being a scout is a lot different from being a warrior, my friend."

Felix sighed, made Connection beside her. "I've heard that," he said in a tired voice and watched his dials rise with the surge of power.

He found that he could no longer finish the stick of nutrite he had started chewing. He spit it into the tube. He rinsed his mouth out with water and spit that out too. Beside him, Forest was making noisy chewing sounds.

"I see you met our little trio," she said after a particularly loud swallow.

"Who?"

"Bolov, Yin and Obel," she said with a slight belch. "What did they tell you?"

"Odds."

"Aw, shit," she muttered. "What did they say?"

"They said I was a one for ten. Were they right?"

"Well, yeah," she replied reluctantly. "Did that get to you?"

"Probably."

"Well, I can see how it could. But Felix, that's just a probability scale, you know, not a death sentence. It doesn't have your name on it. For one thing, it assumes average ability, average reflexes. And you're a lot quicker than that. Besides, you've already beat worse odds than that just by being here."

"You think so?"

"I know so. So do you. Remember A Team? Two hundred and four Dropped, only you survived. As a scout, yet. Far as I know, that's a first. You're some kind of record."

"Some kind . . ." he said, distantly.

"Never mind that stuff. What else did they have to talk about?"

He turned and looked at her. "They talked about you, as a matter of fact. About your athletic career. The armored. . . ."

"Olympics," she prompted. "The Armored Olympic Trials."

"Yes. They seem to think you're pretty good."

"I am. Damn good. One of the best."

"They think you're the best they've ever seen."

"I probably am at that."

"They seem to think that you should have won that thing. One of them thought you'd been cheated. Were you cheated?"

"I was beaten. Badly. Cheated, huh?" She laughed softly, a pleasant sound. "What a lovely thought. Felix, I was never really in it. He slaughtered me."

"He?"

"Kent, Nathan Kent. You've probably heard of him."

"No, I haven't."

"Really? I'm surprised. He's quite famous. Not just on Earth, either. He's recognized on sight on about a dozen planets, and his name is well known on about two dozen more. People care about him that aren't even sports fans. Everybody's Hero, he's called."

"Everybody's Hero?"

A warrior with corporal's markings appeared beside them.

"What's all this about a hero?" asked a feminine voice. "Who's a hero?"

Forest laughed. "What for, Lohman? You volunteering?"

"Not a chance," replied Lohman. She sat down on the sand in front of them.

"Lohman, meet Felix."

"Howdy, Felix."

"How do you do?"

"So who's the hero?"

"We were talking about Kent," said Forest.

"Oh, yeah," responded Lohman dryly. "He's a hero, all right. Everybody's Hero."

Felix found himself drifting, wanting to be alone. But he was determined to stay and try.

"I suppose every war needs heroes," he offered.

"Especially this one," said Forest and Lohman, in unison. Then they looked at each other and laughed. Felix managed a small grin.

"Well, we better take care of him. Can't lose him now," he said.

Lohman laughed again at this, but her laughter had an edge

of bitterness to it. "Lose him? How? He'll never even see an ant."

Felix looked at her. "I beg your pardon?" he asked

"Can't lose him," said Lohman sarcastically. "Not the darling of good old Earth. Hell, if something happens to Kent, the people back home are liable to figure out that we aren't invincible like the politicians have been telling them. No. They'll be real careful with Kent. Treat him like a newborn baby, instead of a warrior."

"That's not fair, Lohman," said Forest quickly. "He's doing his part."

"Really? By staging more phony demonstrations while people are getting killed? He's not a warrior anymore. He's a joke."

"He could tear you in half with ten percent power," said Forest evenly.

"Sure he could," snapped Lohman, undismayed. "He could wipe me out. But *ants* are the enemy. What's he done to *them*? Where do you think he is right now? He's so far away, he couldn't see Banshee with a star-probe."

"I don't see why it should bother you," said Forest.

"Oh yeah?" retorted Lohman. Then, suddenly, her voice became gentle. "Well, what I'd like to know is why it doesn't bother you, Forest. You did pretty well yourself, but all it gets you is the dirty jobs. Doesn't it bother you? Don't you ever wonder why you're stuck here about to die when the warrior with the best odds for survival in the Fleet will never get a bruise? Just because somebody decided he was gonna be our symbol?"

"Somebody didn't decide, everybody decided. Or maybe he decided it. He is the best, you know."

"I know," snapped Lohman. "That's the point."

"Lohman," asked Forest patiently. "Do you really think he has any choice about where he's sent? Do you really think he's a coward?"

"No, of course not. But just the same, I'd like to see him make a Drop."

"Suppose he did. We could all say: Lookee there, he's just a regular warrior like the rest of us. Would you like that?"

"Yes."

"Would you? Would you really?"

"I said, yes," snapped Lohman.

"Fine," said Forest, sitting up straighter. Felix noticed that she had become quite animated all of a sudden. "So you'd be happy for a while. But what if he bought it? What then? That would be pretty bad, wouldn't it?"

"Of course it would be bad. I wouldn't want. . . ."

"You're goddamn right you wouldn't," retorted Forest with a growing fervor. Felix looked at her. "And you know why, too, Lohman. Because he's not like everyone else and you know it. He's not. He *is* a symbol. He's everybody's symbol. And more. It's like . . . he's the kind of thing that we all . . . that's all of us put together to. . . ."

" 'He's the best of us,' " said Felix, reciting. " 'The best of our best, the best that each of us will ever build or ever love. So pray for this Guardian of our growth and choose him well, for if he be not truly blessed, then our designs are surely frivolous and our future but a tragic waste of hope. Bless our best and adore for he doth bear our measure to the Cosmos.' "

"Hot damn," shouted Forest. "That's it. That's exactly it."

"Where did that come from, Felix?" asked Lohman, equally touched. "Is that a prayer?"

"Not precisely. It's part of a coronation ceremony."

"Coronation?" repeated Lohman. "You mean like royalty? Like a King?"

Felix wished he had kept his mouth shut, replied evenly. "A king in a way. The title is Guardian."

"It's beautiful," said Forest.

"Yeah," agreed Lohman. "But what's that part about choosing? You don't choose royalty. Don't people just have to okay it, no matter what?"

"No," said Felix. "They can refuse a potential Guardian before he assumes the title." He was lost, then, for an instant. In the past. "In his youth," he continued after a moment, fumbling somewhat.

The other two seemed to sense his unease.

"Sounds interesting," said Forest.

"Fascinating," echoed Lohman. "What planet did you say this was from?"

"I didn't," replied Felix curtly, deciding, suddenly, to end it.

There was a long pause while the other two exchanged glances. Finally, Lohman broke the silence.

"You're a strange one, Felix. What are you doing here anyway?"

Felix lifted his helmet and met her gaze as best he could through their two face screens.

"Fighting ants," he replied evenly.

"And what else," Lohman wanted to know.

"Fearing ants," he added.

"Hmm," said Lohman after a slight hesitation. "Well, I must be off. Nice meeting you, Felix."

And she was gone. Forest got up then too, mumbling something about some sort of duty.

Felix sat there alone and tried not to think but, of course, could not help it. He thought and he wondered and realized that he couldn't really conceive of what Forest had meant when she had spoken of Kent. He was totally unable to effectively associate what he was doing with symbols or inspiration or . . . love. For it was a form of love that he had seen in her voice. Perhaps, he thought, it's because I didn't start this with any of those things in mind. Or more likely, it's because none of those things have anything to do with me now. Maybe they never did.

He lay back prone on the sand and gazed up into the artificial twilight caused by the eclipse. In his mind he saw the names of Forest and Kent and Felix and tried to feel some sort of connection between the three of them, some common . . . something. A little while later he gave it up. And a little while after that, he decided that it didn't matter at all.

"I'm sorry, Felix," said Forest.

Felix said nothing. Instead he watched the retreating form of the Colonel, ambling up through the gorge past the jostling lines of warriors passing casualties head over head to the top. It was an awkward exercise. Battle armor was bulky and difficult to get a good grip on, even for similarly suited warriors. Those wounded who were awake helped as best they could, which was little enough. For some positions, though more convenient for the carriers, were quite painful for the cargo. The unconscious were worse, since suits were programmed to spread eagle when a warrior lost consciousness in order to keep the spine erect and avoid complicating possible fractures. This posture with arms and legs outstretched wide, made for a cumbersome package. Passing these people along, already a tricky piece of work, was further complicated by their potential delicacy.

Like dolls, thought Felix, as he watched the hurried loading. Mannequins, or cookies. That was it: cookies. Giant gingerbread men.

The Colonel, he noticed, had stopped on the lower section of the landing. He was busily directing the loading, or attempting to. His blue and white striped arms, symbols of his rank, made exaggerated gestures to punctuate his instructions. No one seemed to be paying any attention to his orders, or even acknowledging his presence. Felix turned away, wearied by the sight.

"I'm sorry, Felix," repeated Forest. "He shouldn't have ordered you. He should have waited for you to volunteer."

He looked at her, looked away, said nothing still.

Forest persisted. "It's not that he's got anything against you personally, Felix."

"He said that," Felix answered at last.

"It's just that you're a scout, with a scout's ability to maneuver."

"He said that," Felix replied.

"Felix," said Forest with some emotion, "try to look at it from his point of view. We've got all these casualties to worry about, and you're damned good at this, you've got to admit and. . . .'

"He said that, too. He said it all."

"Oh," replied Forest hesitantly. "Well, I can see how you must feel about it. He was wrong. He should have waited for you to step forward. He was wrong."

"No," said Felix in a tired voice, "he was right. I wouldn't have volunteered."

He turned then, and faced her squarely, closely, so that

their faces were dimly visible to one another. For several seconds, warrior faced warrior, pragmatist faced fatalist, silently, eloquently.

"Yes," said Forest at last, averting her eyes as she spoke, "he was right." She turned away and started up the hill behind the last of the casualty bearers. "Come on. I'll explain the procedure." Felix followed.

At the halfway mark of the gorge, a broad, smooth-faced chunk of tightly packed sand formed a two-tiered landing of sorts. Forest stepped from the gorge onto the first, lower, section and stopped. Six warriors, evidently the actual volunteers, stood in a row, waiting. Felix eyed them curiously.

"This is our station," Forest began. "I figure they can only get to us in two ways. From the gorge directly, or by using that ledge there." She pointed to an outcropping of sand which ran the lower length of the landing. "We'll try to hold them here first. If we can't, then we move up there to where they're loading. We only have one route to defend from there."

One of the warriors stepped forward. "Why not just start up there?" he asked in a high-pitched tenor.

Forest shrugged. "The CO wants us to try to stop them here, before they even get close to the helpless."

"Figures," muttered another, deeper voice

"Okay," said Forest calmly. "If it gets to be too much, we'll move in a hurry. Just remember to keep the escape route open. Don't let anything get behind you."

"Don't worry," said a third voice.

"Maybe we won't even have to worry about it," offered the tenor hopefully. "It's still pretty dark and it looks to me like they're moving 'em pretty fast."

"Hey, yeah," said someone else. "We might get lucky at that. Look at 'em up there."

"No," said Felix coldly. "Not up. Look down."

All turned to look in response to his statement. Below, the ants were steaming toward them from the edge of the maze.

"Okay," said Forest hurriedly. "You three get with Felix over there on the right side. Cover the ledge. And you three stay with me. We'll take the gorge. Get moving."

Felix stepped over into position. He stood stone still, and

waited. The others in his group were considerably more animated.

"Wish we had our blazers working. . . ."

"Lucky it's still dark. Look how slow they're moving. . . ."

"Fast enough for me. . . ."

"Damn, I haven't fought 'em hand-to-hand before. . . ."

"Just club 'em with your fist. Give 'em a taste of plassteel. . . ."

"I don't want to encourage anything. . . ."

There were several nervous giggles in response.

"Shut up," said the Engine firmly. And all were silent as they waited and watched.

The ants streamed steadily up the gorge, with only one in the lead. Forest, deciding apparently to take a chance, leaped down a few meters and clouted the lead ant on the side of the skull with the toe of her boot. The ant was caught off balance. It literally climbed upward into the blow. The right side of its skull caved in instantly. It slumped, twitching, into the path of the ants behind it.

"Hot damn," shouted one of the warriors beside Felix.

"See?" said Forest with a quick glance over her shoulder. "There's nothing to it. Get ready. Let's hurt 'em."

The warriors beside her took heart in her words and shuffled eagerly forward to help. They pounced on the ants as they appeared. One grabbed hold of a claw while another pounded awkwardly at the skull. That ant fell, and then another fell to Forest's forearm and then there was too much happening for Felix to continue to watch.

He met the first ant on the ledge with a wide swinging blow with the open palm of his glove against the left eye. The eyeball burst, streaming. Felix finished it off by simply shoving the creature backward off of the ledge with his foot. He grabbed an awkwardly groping claw from the second and dragged the creature forward into a thunderous forearm smash that shattered the thorax. Without waiting for the ant to fall, he turned to the next.

Beside him the other three plunged bravely forward. They slammed at the ants with their much more powerful warrior armor. They punched and kicked and gouged, missing often, sometimes way off balance. But in that limited area, the ants couldn't reach them en masse and their crude efforts were effective. Noting this, Felix elected to let the heavier, bulkier warriors match the initial brunt of the attack. He skipped back and forth between the three, lending a well timed blow to each individual struggle. The warriors had a tendency to become entangled with the grasping claws and pincers. But before the embrace could become lethal, Felix was able to step in and make the kill.

At first the warriors would verbally acknowledge his aide, but as the height of battle slowly grew, the acknowledgments were limited to grunts and then finally silence.

The battle continued in this manner for several moments. Despite the lack of skill of the other three, Felix found that they were managing to hold their own. The ant bodies were stacking up onto the ledge, making further attacks more difficult. And when the bodies were used as stepping stones to reach them, Felix stepped down onto the ledge itself and heaved a large, twittering stack over the side. That effort brought a rousing cheer from all three of his fellows, a sound that the engine was no more aware of than it had been of the earlier sounds of gratitude.

It got tougher after that. The ants became more numerous, more insistent in their rush. The time to retreat would obviously have to come soon. Still, it would be awhile. And time was what counted. All seemed to be going well.

And then the Hammer fell again.

Felix had managed to notice the transit beacon's flickering light a second before the concussion. He had thrown himself and one warrior to the ground and shouted for the others to do the same. But in the excitement of the struggle, the other two had merely looked in his direction, not really thinking about what he had said until it was too late.

The landing shook and rocked and skittered off to the side. A great cloud of sand splashed up the slope into the air around them. There were several horrible cries mixed in with the thunderous roar. Felix stood up as soon as the tier stopped shaking beneath him. Through the cloud of dust and sand he saw that Forest still had two warriors with her. He looked quickly around. His other two men were nowhere in sight.

"Back up to the others," shouted Forest. "Get up there."

"But where are the other two? They were right here—" blurted the one man left from Felix's group, the tenor.

For answer, Felix hauled him to his feet, and shoved him stumbling toward the upper section of the tier. At the steps, the tenor turned to protest. Felix ignored him, lifting him bodily onto the next step. Forest beside him, was similarly hurrying her charges.

"Move it," she urged in an icy tone. Then, "Oh, shit," as she turned back around to the edge.

The ants, only momentarily stunned by the blast, were now shuffling five abreast toward them across a recent break in the tier.

"Heads up, Felix," she said as she met the first ant.

Felix slammed a boot through the first ant, effectively stepping right through its severed midsection, and bashing the one beside it with a backhand blow to an eye. He spun around, freeing his foot, and jammed an armored elbow at a thorax. He took a step back, then leaned quickly forward and rammed his shoulder into another. He lifted the ant and flung it away from him into the paths of several others. He took another step back, then another.

The Hammer fell again.

The tier rocked mightily, ants and pieces of ants were catapulted through the air, some ramming him. He fell to the floor of the tier just as it broke loose from the face of the mesa itself. A crack appeared in its face. There was another quick jerk, the sound of more ripping sand, and Felix was flung into the crack.

Forest struck the wall beside him, tumbled sideways by the tilting sand. A half a dozen ants followed.

They grasped at him, scraping loudly against his face screen with their clattering pincers.

He shoved at them, grabbed at exoskeleton and twisted and heard the sound of it splintering. But there were so many and so little room and then he saw Forest was holding on to an ant that had fallen across his face and he took hold of it too and they both pulled and there was a snapping sound and the ant came apart. He struggled to his feet, felt the ground rumble beneath him. He held out a hand to Forest, saw that she was engulfed by claws and skulls. Again he grabbed one end and she grabbed the other and again there was that sound and again and again and then they were suddenly alone in the crack. Both on their feet now, Forest in front, as they tried to clamber out and once again, the Hammer fell. The tier they had vacated tilted wildly, shuddered and finally sheared loose completely, rolling and tumbling down the slope, crushing hundreds of bodies of the thousands of stunned ants that packed the gorge.

Together, they grasped the edge of the upper tier and heaved themselves up onto it. "Goddammit," shouted Forest breathlessly. She grabbed one of the able-bodied loaders who sat frozen, holding the floor of the tier for dear life.

"Move it, goddammit. Move these people."

The warrior looked up at her, unmoving. Forest cracked her open palm against the side of the trembling helmet. "Don't you hear me? Get moving. You too," she added to the other loaders, each of whom had been likewise occupied with panic. "Who's gonna move these casualties?" she shouted, sweeping an arm toward the more than a hundred who still occupied the tier.

With painful slowness, the warriors began to react to her stinging words. They rose and grabbed at the injured and resumed their jobs. Forest was unsatisfied.

"Where the hell's everybody else? Where are the other loaders?" she wanted to know.

Felix looked around, noticed there were only half a dozen warriors still remaining at the job. He didn't have to ask where they had gone. He knew. They had run away. Emotionless, he picked up the crumpled form of a warrior and, despite her loud and painful protests, heaved her up onto the mesa itself. He grabbed another, this one unconscious, and cartwheeled its frozen form behind the first.

"Felix, forget that shit. C'mere," shouted Forest. "Ants. . . ."

He turned just in time to see her deliver a hammer of her own, a crushing fist through the eye of the first of a half dozen ants that had appeared in the gorge beneath them.

Felix lived because he was shielded by the line of warriors between him and the edge.

He wasn't blinded because he happened to be looking away at the time. Still he saw the flash as though there had been nothing at all to obscure his view, and still he felt it, the worst pain he had ever experienced, as he was tossed far into the air, a helpless puppet. He flew perhaps twenty meters before touching the ground where he rolled and skidded and slid and when he finally came to rest he saw his power dials drop almost to zero.

He had time to lift an arm across his face to cover it from God's angry boiling gaze and then all was darkness.

The can was only a few meters in front of him, but the body was in the way. He knew he would never make it.

Still, he tried. He focused all his concentration on the muscles of his right thigh and, with incredible effort, managed to draw it forward underneath him. He was afraid to pull it too far, afraid he would overbalance and fall off his elbows. It had seemed to take hours to get them propped up beneath him. If he should fall now, he would never be able to get back up again.

He rested then, as much as he could with the weight of five hundred kilograms relentlessly trying to drive his body into the sand. The helmet was the worst part, he thought. Fifty kilos alone right there. I'd better not fall. If I do, the helmet will break my neck.

He took several deep breaths, then held the last one. He strained and heaved and tried to move his right elbow forward. The pain from his shoulders erupted again instantly, as he had known it would. But somehow he had forgotten how bad it was.

He screamed as bolts of agony lanced through his shoulders and down his back. For a moment his vision unfocused, his head swam wildly. Oh, God, don't fall . . . he thought desperately before he fainted.

Later, when he had awakened again, he decided that he was insane and that it was good. I have to be mad. I must be, to get this far. To make connection, I will have to be madder still.

He shut off his mind, then. He didn't want to carry these thoughts, or any others, further. I will stop thinking right here. At this spot, where I have reached resolve.

And so, not thinking of the pain he must certainly feel, not thinking of the damage he was doing to himself, not thinking of the mere twelve percent power remaining, not thinking of the ants who would surely return. . . .

Not thinking, he tried once more. This time the scream was shorter. He hadn't enough strength to do it properly.

When he awoke the next time, and tried again, his body refused. Amazed, he tried again, but his body would not respond. *This is absurd. I have strength, still, I'm thinking. I must have some energy left.* But he could make nothing move, no limb, no muscle.

He became angry. He strained and groaned, sweat streamed from his brow, mingling with tears and fogging the screen and at last something gave. But he was not truly moving, only shuddering with uncontrollable spasms. This made him even more angry. He threw himself against the inside of the armor, he rocked back and forth against it, he yelled at the top of his lungs. . . .

He fell.

He should have died. The fall should have crushed the life from him. But, in this at least, he and his body were united. Together, they refused to die. And then, still together, they slept.

Forest wanted to know where all the real Medics were.

"Dead," said the man monitoring Felix's physchart. Vaporized. Like most everyone else. He tapped Felix's helmet. "You'll live . . . for a while. But I'd hate to have your shoulders. What made you try to crawl in a daysuit? Most of the skin around your joints is scraped off. Are you crazy?"

Felix considered this. "Yes," he replied, and stood up.

The pain doubled him over.

"Whoo . . . Watch it there. Give the painers a chance. Go sit down somewhere for a few minutes. Better, lie down for as long as you can."

"I'll watch him," offered Forest as she stepped up to his side.

"You're in worse shape than he is. You'd best watch each other."

The suits made it impossible to lean on one another, but the feeling of mutual support was strong between them as they shuffled slowly past the rows of warriors collapsed around the medical area. Felix crossed toward a likely spot, but Forest said, "No. A little farther. I want to show you something." So they continued on past those that were wounded and past those that were dead and farther yet, past those who could no longer be distinguished as warriors.

Like a slag heap, thought Felix, glancing briefly at the fused hunks of plassteel strewn about the sand.

They reached the edge of the mesa, where the sand was glazed slick and black by an ugly film.

"Do you know," asked Forest as they gently lowered themselves, side by side, to the ground, "what thermonuclear means?"

Felix looked around him at the hellish landscape. "I do now," he said. Only then did he notice the shiny newness of Forest's suit. He looked down at himself. The black plassteel had been scoured clean by the same wall of sand that had flung him so far.

"You noticed that, have you?" asked Forest, following his gaze. She chuckled dryly. "Good as new."

He smiled slightly, briefly. "Why did they wait so long?"

"Who? The ants? They didn't do this. We did."

"Us? I didn't know anyone carried atomic weapons."

"Hell. We are atomic weapons." She swept an arm about her wearily. "A suit did this."

"How?"

"Overload. Somebody keyed every relay at once, and then tried to eject. Any warrior suit can do it."

"I didn't know."

"You aren't supposed to. No one is. It's a way to go that might be too dramatic to resist. Can you imagine what this would have done to the inside of a starship?"

"Hmn. But still, what about accidents?"

She shrugged, a bulky gesture. "Shouldn't be too likely. The odds against it happening randomly are enormous, or so I'm told. Makes sense. Some suit functions would be contradictory to others. Who would key every one of them at once and try to eject at the same time?"

"Somebody did."

"Martinez did."

He looked at her. She returned the look, glanced away.

"I found out about it at the Olympics. Sounds silly, I know. But there are lots more things a suit is required to do in competition. When I qualified, one of the wardens took me aside and warned me."

"And Martinez?"

"Martinez was there. As a yeoman. He must have found out somehow. Sounds like him, anyway. Crazy guy, Martinez. We got in a lot of trouble together. See we were bunked in the same tract, right across the quad from each other. . . ."

She stopped talking suddenly, then sat up and began to cough. It was a horrible, choking sound, the sound of something terribly, irrevocably, wrong.

Felix moved toward her as she slipped down again, still coughing. She tried to reach her panel, but failed as the spasm intensified.

"Painer . . key . . . painer," she managed to gasp.

He picked up her left forearm, found the panel. He fumbled with the keys from his opposite perspective before locating the switch and activating it. Slowly, too slowly, her coughing subsided. He leaned close to her and waited for her eyes to open. When they did, she smiled at him. It was not a smile he would have wanted, it was wistfully sad, heartbreakingly tragic.

"I don't blame Martinez," she said at last. "Being carried off by those bloody . . . I'd do it myself if a scout suit had the capacity." She noticed his position, still looming over her.

"Don't worry, Felix. It's not as bad as it sounds." He nodded, sat down beside her. They both knew she was lying.

For awhile there was no sound but the uneven rush of her tortured breath against her microphone. Then she rallied a bit, managed to speak.

"Poor, poor, Marty . . ." she began but choked it off quickly when she heard the break in her voice. Felix winced when he heard her stifling sobs, surprising himself. *Why be surprised?* he thought. *What's not to understand? No matter how brash she was before, this would have to terrify her now. Who wants to die?*

From somewhere deep within him, a tiny voice answered, "You did." He ignored it.

Her sobbing, now beyond control, turned to weeping. He looked away from her, gazing at the distant spire of the knuckle. It was getting light again, he noticed. Soon the ants would be back at full strength and. . . .

He noticed the slope, suddenly, for the first time actually seeing it and realizing what it meant. This entire end of the mesa had been collapsed by the explosion. Instead of a single narrow route to the top, the ants now had a smooth, black ramp that rose at an easy, convenient angle. My God, they could come up that a thousand abreast. And, of course, they will.

"What a silly choice for a symbol," said (blurted) Forest abruptly.

"Who?"

"Kent. Nathan Kent. Everybody's hero." She laughed softly, gently. Her voice had a dreamlike languor to its rhythm. "I remember the first night away from the compound. He had to buy a meal for all the final qualifiers. The people recognized him and rushed away from their food to surround him. They cheered and applauded and they all tried to touch him. And he looked at me in the middle of all this and . . . You know what?"

"What?"

"He was so bewildered. Completely lost. And later we talked and I knew he felt bad because he hadn't known what to do or say.

"Oh, he was charming enough. He couldn't help that. And funny, too. He made everyone laugh. But he wasn't . . . It's just that they wanted so much from him and . . . he wanted to do it for them, wanted to be a certain way for them. But . . . when he tried to be what he thought he should be, it came out as rudeness, like some sort of arrogant. . . ."

She moved, to change position, he thought. But he saw her key another painer.

"He was shy. So shy. And it was so tragic. Because he wanted to be the leader. But he was shy instead. And loving and gentle and he could be hurt so . . ."

She broke off. She sat up. She peered at him. "I told the

Colonel to order you. I used you because I didn't want to be alone on that landing and I knew you were too smart to volunteer. I lied. I blatantly used you to save my life."

"Yes," he replied with soft firmness.

That seemed to exhaust her. She lay back down. She was having trouble breathing.

"I loved Kent, Felix. I loved him so, I thought I would die. Did I ever tell you that?"

"Yes."

"I knew I must have," she said and died.

Felix couldn't believe his ears.

"That's ridiculous," he said.

The Major who had replaced the now dead Colonel as CO, looked up suddenly. "Is that what you think?" Was his surprisingly calm reply.

Felix noticed that the other members of the command staff were also watching him. He ignored them.

"I have no command experience," he said. "This is my first Drop"

"Your first Drop," repeated the Major idly, as if even then he couldn't believe it. "Yes, I had heard that. Remarkable."

Felix peered quizzically at the Major, at the others, wondering why he couldn't seem to get through.

"Get someone else," he said abruptly.

"There isn't someone else," said the Major. "All your officers are dead."

"Get a non-com then," persisted Felix. "A sergeant."

"No."

"Don't say no, just do. . . ."

"No," said the Major flatly, his voice now carrying an edge.

"Why not? Why can't you just?"

"Because you're the one they want," blurted the Major suddenly. The anger in his voice now bristled.

"What?" asked Felix, equally angry. "Who wants?"

"The warriors. Your warriors."

Felix was disgusted by this. "They don't even know who I am."

"Not your name, maybe. But they do know who you are. And they want the scout."

Felix stared at the Major, at the others.

"This is insane."

"Yes," replied the Major firmly.

"You're out of your mind."

The Major, finally, had had enough.

"I'm out of officers, Felix. That's what I'm out of. Now you just stand there and shut up while I give a couple of facts of war: One. Of the 642 survivors from your original assault force of ten thousand, only 285 are combat ready. Got that? Now. . . . Two. Of the twenty-three hundred *I* Dropped with, over six hundred died the first minute because of those goddamn ant missiles homed in on the Transit beacon. That so-called Hammer of yours. Of the remaining sixteen hundred or so, more than three hundred lost effective suit function or were killed outright when that maniac blew his suit. Three. Of the people that leaves me, only ninety percent are combat warriors. The rest are medical, supply, and maintenance types. Which leaves a grand total, if you can count, of less than fifteen hundred available combat personnel. Four. The *Terra* cannot pick us up for another eighteen standard hours. Five. This damned mesa can't be held with what we get for one hour, even at night. And last, but not least. . . . Six. The sun is coming out . . . now."

Involuntarily, Felix followed his gaze toward the lightening sky.

"And so, Felix—who thinks that this is insane and who is dead right about that, anyway—what the hell are we gonna do?"

We're going to die, Felix thought. But he couldn't say that. Or maybe, he thought again, he should. Why shouldn't he? He looked again at the Major standing there aggressively a few meters away and thought about the man's tone, about his fear. He said nothing, finally. He simply met the Major's piercing gaze.

After a few seconds of this, the Major broke the silence.

"Well, I'll tell you, Scout, what we're gonna do. In less than one standard hour, we will assault the Knuckle en masse"

"Assault . . .?" repeated Felix dully.

"Attack, Felix. In one hour, we attack."

Lt. Fowler, second-in-command, introduced him to the "volunteer." "His name is Bailey, I believe," said Fowler, pointing. "He's a veteran. Four years."

Felix only dimly heard her. He was looking at the mass of silicon plaster being hurriedly applied to Bailey's suit by three medics. He took a couple of steps toward the group and peered down into Bailey's screen. There was a lot of blood in there.

Felix stepped back, choking with a sudden desire to gag.

"I know," said Fowler. "But they say he should live just long enough to do the job."

"Does he . . . ?" Felix began, then found he had lost his voice.

"Does he know, you mean," asked Fowler.

Felix nodded.

"Yeah. He knows."

"And. . . ."

"And he'll do it. I told you. He's a veteran."

Felix looked at Fowler, looked away. "Is that what a veteran is?" he asked.

"Partly," said Fowler.

Felix, for no clear reason, nodded again.

"Come on," said Fowler brusquely, her voice returning to a businesslike tone. "It's time to show you the target."

Felix followed her back to the circle of officers that served as command center. They passed hundreds of warriors preparing to travel.

"Have a seat," offered Fowler. "And key your input relay. I'll show you the picture."

Felix sat, keyed the proper key. After a brief pause, his holos swelled and the three-dimensional topograchart of the Knuckle, appeared transmitted from Fowler.

The view was of the Knuckle's southern face. The side closest to their position, at a distance of perhaps 700 meters.

Fowler's disembodied voice began to narrate: "This is from about the center of the maze. Rather imposing is it not?"

Felix grunted in response. The viewpoint altered.

"This is from the nearest edge of the maze. Notice the sides still appear smooth."

Felix already had. Like a sculpture, he thought, gazing at the apparently sheer sides that seemed to have poured upward from the sandy soil. It was as if it had been molten ore at one time. How else could the smooth sloping texture be achieved?

The scene changed again. Now he could see the various sloping folds at the base. And something else: A black ovular hole less than 20 meters above the ground and partially obscured by a vertical ridge. He stared at the ridge—its edge looked sharp as a knife.

"That's your target, that black oval," offered Fowler. "There are others that you can't see from this angle. But the computers think that this one goes almost straight through to the core underneath." A thin dotted line appeared on the screen, running a twisting course from the sand to the hole. "That's your route," said Fowler. "Watch that ridge, it's as sharp as it looks."

"How?" asked Felix.

"I don't know," answered Fowler distantly. "But it doesn't matter. It will blow like everything else."

The scene changed again. Felix seemed to be in the air directly above the spikelike summit of the knuckle itself. The terrain at the base was clearly visible, as well as the beginning of the maze. Several small arrows appeared at various maze entrances.

"The cannon will be here," continued Fowler. "They won't actually damage the surface of the knuckle. But they should be able to clear a path for you people."

Another arrow appeared.

"This is your starting point. Key that."

Felix touched a switch. The arrow became a permanent part of his "map." He had done the same with the dotted line showing his route.

"Well, that's about it," said Fowler as she stopped the broadcast. "Have you got it all?"

Felix nodded, looked at her sitting on the ground beside him. "A lot of information. Why didn't the assault force have this?"

"They did. But they never had the right opportunity. Or," her voice became slightly hushed, "the right weapon."

"But we do," replied Felix with bitterness. "Bailey."

Fowler looked away. Her voice was a faint whisper: "Yes." Then she turned back toward him.

"About your command. You're entitled to added rank. Would you like to be a Lieutenant?"

"Why?"

Fowler seemed to hesitate before speaking.

"Then you don't care about that?"

Felix thought about it. "No," he said at last.

Fowler hesitated again, then slid closer toward him on the sand conspiratorially.

"Felix, don't worry about the command part of it. We've found a vet to organize your bunch. He'll take care of most things. Just tell him what you want and let him do the ordering."

"What's his name?"

"Bolov."

Felix almost laughed. "Anything else?"

"Not that I know of, unless you have questions."

He stared at the distant spire of his destination, almost completely obscured by a rolling cloud of sand.

"Just one question. . . ."

"Why you?" prompted Fowler.

"Yeah," said Felix, his voice cold. "Why us?"

She breathed a long sigh into her mike before replying. "Felix, who would you use? The rest of us just got here. . . ."

"You've made other Drops."

"But we've never touched an ant. None of us. And you, you and your people, are the three percent, the only survivors from an assault of 10,000 warriors."

"Maybe it's luck. Random chance."

"Not likely. Not in this business."

"Business? What business?"

"War."

"I don't believe that."

"Why? Is it too simple?"

Felix shook his head. "Too sloppy."

Several flashes lit the area. The light was joined by the hot, razor scream of Blazer cannon.

Felix stood up, watching as the beams arced through the air toward the knuckle. But the beams landed short, in the maze itself.

"Right on time," said Fowler, standing beside him. "We'd better get started."

"What's this for?" asked Felix.

"The maze. We haven't got time to negotiate it. So we're leveling it up to the leading edge of the knuckle."

Felix nodded vaguely, watching giant shards of sand vaulting wildly into the air. Soon the entire maze was obscured by an enormous dust cloud.

"Come on," said Fowler. "The Major wants to see you before we go."

"How much time do we have?"

"About . . ." She broke off quickly, listening, Felix assumed, to some message he couldn't hear. "None," she said at last. "None at all. The ants are coming out."

Together, they ran to the cannon.

The Major was two hundred meters east of the carnage standing off from the rest of his people watching the battle. Lines of warriors met the onslaught of the ants without the help of the barricade—at the mouth of the channel blown through the center of the maze. The ants, jammed together in the middle of the channel for some reason, were growing steadily toward them as rolling dead piles.

Felix was impressed. They were really holding. For now.

The Major had been standing with ponderous armored arms crossed over his chest. He loosened one and pointed past the battle to the foot of the Knuckle just visible over the dust.

"That's the last spot we can see to cover you, Scout. See it? Looks like a saddle. Or a bench."

"Yes."

The Major looked at him. "We'll use the last of the cannon-fire to cover your approach down the side of the little highway we've made. But we won't be able to help you in there. That ridge blocks our line of fire. But the people you're taking should be able to hold 'em off you long enough to . . . plant the charge.''

"Yes."

"Do it, Felix," said Fowler from beside them. Her voice held muffled urgency alongside cheerleading. "Do it. We're all counting on you to. . . ."

Felix regarded her blandly. "To what?"

Fowler shrugged uneasily. "To . . . to do the job. We're all counting on you."

"You mean you're all counting on me to throw Bailey down that hole, don't you?"

"Yes," she whispered.

"Shut up, Felix," snapped the Major. "That doesn't help. And we can't hold them much longer."

Felix looked again at the line of blazing warriors. He saw them, then, as the desperate people they were. He felt the proximity of their panic. They're not heroes, he thought, they're stuck.

And he knew that they would never hold for his retreat. Once they reached the Hive, they would be alone.

His group was forming up beside them. A dozen warriors. Bolov.

Fowler faced Bolov. "All set?"

"Yeah," said Bolov, nodding shortly.

"They all know what to do?" she persisted.

"Yeah."

"What about Bailey?" Felix asked.

Bolov shrugged, looked at the sand between them. "I think we'd better hurry."

Felix nodded. "Okay. Where is he?"

Bolov gestured toward the warriors. "Teare's got him."

"You do it."

Bolov nodded. "Okay."

Felix sighed. "Better get him."

Bolov nodded again, turned to obey.

Felix regarded the warriors shifting nervously, all eyes on the battle. Or on him. He turned away.

The lines were still holding, the rolling twittering exoskeleton still coming on. He felt something he couldn't pin down.

Not eagerness, of course. And not simple excitement. Anticipation?

Bolov appeared carrying Bailey over a shoulder.

"You ready?" Felix asked him.

Bolov laughed shortly. "Hell, no!"

Felix smiled distantly. Yes. Anticipation. One way or another, it was finally about to stop happening to them all.

"All right, let's get down to it." He nodded to Fowler. "Give the word."

Fowler nodded, said something only she and the cannon crews could hear. There was a brief pause and then, with a searing scream, the remaining cannon fired. The main thrust of ants pouring through the channel died almost instantly as they were simultaneously broiled, sliced, soldered, by the intersecting hourglass beams.

Felix turned to the ones to follow him, met their joint gaze, turned away, and began the rush down across the blackened sand. He didn't look back to see if they followed, but loped firmly ahead at a pace a laden Bolov could match. The cannon ceased abruptly as he reached and passed the holding lines. He began to accelerate as the sand flattened out before him. Ant remains smoldered in his path, thinly scattered here to the side of the reeling main body. He glanced at the jumbled mass of enemy as he passed quickly alongside their length. He was drawing no obvious surge.

He chanced a little more speed.

He was almost to the next section of maze—and cover, past the last lines of remains, before he looked back to the others. They were right behind Bolov in the lead, stumbling up the slope.

Felix kept running, deftly avoiding the smoking ant refuse. He wanted to reach the base of the knuckle, perhaps even the bench itself, before the ants coud reorganize their attack. The flashes of blazerfire from off to his right told him he had been too hopeful. The other holes, unseen from his position must already be emitting more ants.

Still, there was hope. The others were still firing, still standing fast against a certain powerful impulse to flee. And, if he couldn't see ants yet, they couldn't see him.

Or would that matter . . . Wouldn't they be able to detect his presence on the very walls of their hive? Would they actually have to see them?

With that thought, Felix leaped over the last rocky steps of the desert floor and pounded up the slopes of the Knuckle itself.

The footing was firm, the grainy surface perfect traction for his plassteel boots. He saw instantly that his proscribed route was unnecessarily cautious; he changed direction abruptly and climbed the slope to the bench in three giant powered strides. The others, he knew without looking, would follow his lead.

The bench was, for the time being, empty. The target hole loomed over him invitingly, only ten meters or so up the slope. The wall here was steeper than he had realized, but still easily navigable. Felix nodded to himself. It was going to work.

He turned and looked back, and the others were almost there. Bolov had dropped back a bit into the crowd to protect his irreplaceable cargo. Felix waved them exuberantly toward him, felt the rush of relief from those others who reached the bench and found it still empty. They turned too, and began to wave Bolov quickly forward. He heard their voices, exultant with unrestrained happiness, "We can do it. We're gonna make it."

And then Bolov was there on the bench itself and moving through the crowd, holding out Bailey toward him like some honored trophy, and then the nightmare began. There were screams and shouts and people pointing and firing their blazers at close range and the ants were everywhere, everywhere around them. Not from the saddleback, not from the multitudes, but from the target hole itself. Ten, twenty, fifty ants appeared in its mouth and slid, clawing and flailing, down the steep slope into them. Someone screamed again and Felix was knocked off balance as the ones closest to the attack tried to push back away. He fell to one knee, but dragged himself up quickly, yelling Bolov's name and trying to reach him through the panicking mob of warriors.

Dimly he heard Bolov respond and then he saw him through the jumbling mass. Bolov had dropped Bailey and was being pushed away from him by the crowd. Felix and

Bolov slammed toward one another, reaching Bailey simultaneously, lifting him, staggering, toward the slope and the hole. A blazer struck the slope beside them and Felix screamed for the warriors to stop firing before they killed one another or him.

He stumbled and drove himself against the crowd toward the slope, punching through at last and leaning against it, with Bolov beside him, holding Bailey's legs in one arm.

Pandemonium. Warriors screaming and firing and trying to run all at the same time. Beams of Blazerfire struck randomly everywhere and Felix motioned to Bolov that they must climb the slope, must do it now while the slightest chance still remained. Bolov seemed to nod or at least seemed to understand for they started up the slope together, slipping and sliding and being jarred by the jostling, teeming warriors and then a mass of ants was upon him and he lost Bailey; he was covered, engulfed by the ants that slid down into them.

He struck out blindly, wildly, smashing, ripping exoskeleton, struggling to get his feet underneath him. Twice he struck not exoskeleton but plassteel and the thought of it made him shudder, cringing. He was up then, and Bolov was beside him and had Bailey and they shouldered through the ants and started again up the slope and there was a horrible agonizing scream as a flash of blazerfire split the air between them, carving a deep, irreconcilable hole through Bailey's faceplate.

"Oh, my God, my God . . ." shouted Bolov and he saw that it was not just from the shock of losing their only weapon but from pain as well. For the stray bolt of blazerfire had cut not only through Bailey but through Bolov as well. A pulsing, red-hot bubble had appeared on the inside of Bolov's shoulder. Felix stared in morbid amazement as the bubble rose and expanded and threatened to burst as it surely must. Bolov screamed again and clutched at his shoulder with his free arm and shouted over and over that he was dying, dying. . . .

Felix had him then, dropping Bailey. He had his helmet clamped tightly to his side with his left arm as he launched them up the slope. His right arm stretched out high for some purchase, the fingers of his gloves clawing wildly at the grainy hive. He jerked and kicked and struggled and slid back some at every movement but somehow managed to get the two of them up the slope and away from the crowd.

They were several meters to the left of the hole itself, parallel to it and the ants couldn't reach them without slipping down. The few that managed to leap toward them he met with a resounding kick that shook them free of their grip on the wall and sent them sliding down into the roar of battle below.

Briefly, Felix noted the many who were already running away, with the ants hotly pursuing. And farther, he saw that the covering fire from the maze itself had long since halted. He was alone as he knew he would be.

He struggled and kicked out at another ant, sending it sliding and at the same time pushing himself and his cargo farther up the slope. Bolov was completely limp in his grasp, moaning loudly, unintelligibly. Felix grasped him with both hands and yanked him upward onto the slope beside him. He reached for Bolov's forearm and began to work the relays.

Bolov, seeing what he was doing, began to sob. He tried, feebly, to struggle out of Felix's grasp. But Felix held him firmly against the slope, slapping away his futilely waving arms. Grimly, he continued to work relays. He looked up once and saw that the mouth of the hole was less than three meters away and just beneath him. He was just in the right position, the ants couldn't reach him in time. If only they wouldn't know to toss Bolov away. . . .

The last relay controlled the interior light of Bolov's suit and then Felix saw the man's face clearly for the first time, saw that he was perhaps five years older. Saw that he badly needed a shave, saw that he was weeping openly. . . .

Felix placed the surface of his face screen against Bolov's.

"You know what to do?" he asked in a cold, distant, tone.

Bolov cursed him deliberately, soundlessly and Felix knew that he would do it. He nodded, almost to himself. He judged the distance to the hole, tensed his muscles. Bolov's voice stopped him cold.

"You, Felix," said Bolov calmly, hopelessly, "are a filthy human being." Felix saw the lips working, saw the tongue accentuate each syllable, and felt a weight upon him growing and growing.

But the Engine only nodded in agreement. And then it rolled over, holding Bolov with both hands, and flung him into the hive.

Felix was sliding, down into the mass of humans and ants and tearing himself away and through them and then he was sliding again down the slope of the saddleback and then he was running, running, across the blackened sand toward the maze. He leaped and turned and darted through the ants and the warriors. Some were alive, some were not. But he paid no attention either way.

He shouldered past several slower moving warriors and stomped wildly into the entrance of what remained of the maze. He passed more and more warriors as he reached the levelled area. But he didn't stop, didn't hesitate. The fear, and only the fear, controlled. The terror. . . .

Past the blackened sand and to the slopes of the mesa, traveling now as fast as he could travel. Arms waving, eyes flickering, tears welling up in his eyes, he ran. And ran and ran and then he was up the mesa and crossing it and he thought that it was too late now, that Bolov would never be able to do it by now. He must be dead already.

But still he ran, the terror ruling all.

He tripped at the edge of the mesa. He fell, at 100 kilometers an hour, he struck the sand and rolled. He carved deep ruts where elbows and knees dug into the sand. A great cloud erupted around him. He continued to slide across the last few meters and then he fell, completely out of control, down the long slope of the mesa.

As he struck bottom, Bolov ejected, and the battle, finally, ended.

He awoke, briefly to the sound of the Medic's impersonally soothing tones. He was told that Connection was being made. He was told not to move. He was told of his myriad injuries. He was told that Transit to the *Terra* was forthcoming. He was told that he had been found at the end of the last sweep for survivors, that he was, in fact, quite lucky.

But he heard none of it. Instead he only stared at the black sky above him. Night at last, he thought. And his eyes reluctantly closed.

The Doctor eyed the worst of the cyst-like bruises, the one that completely covered his right shoulder. "You can't wear a suit like that, no," he said.

Felix felt a surge of relief so overwhelming that the awful pain was momentarily eclipsed. He noted the Doctor's glowering, disgusted expression and felt his cheeks to see if they were red.

They debriefed him and fed him and were surprised to learn, from his recorder, that he was the one. They had surely thought the hero of the Knuckle suitable for martyrdom. They later became angry when he ignored their questions. They thought it was because he now thought himself to be too superior to respond. This belief intimidated one of the officers who marked his personal log with a negative entry. But Felix had been silent not from a sense of superiority, but from shame and suspicion.

They woke him up entering the bay. They laughed and joked and were nervous. Then they became hushed and reverent, when they found his lone sleeping figure at the end of the line of what they thought were empty berths. Quietly, they stowed their gear and crept out into the hall to talk. Out of respect for a Veteran.

The nightmare was odd, intangible even at the time. Some nameless formless fear was reaching out to him. It grew and swelled toward him until he admitted he was waking, that most of him had been awake for some time, and that the fear was not of some nebulous terror, but of his next Drop.

The rest of the bay was asleep. He pulled himself up out of his berth gingerly, wincing from the pain of the cysts. He padded back and forth between the rows of berths. He found he was repeating the doctor's words over and over again in his mind. It was reassuring, he found.

The lone head of a young man appeared over the edge of a berth. The two blue eyes followed his pacing. Felix stopped at last and stared back. But the young man was not embarrassed by this. Instead he spoke:

"What's it like?" he asked.

Felix told him to ask someone else.

"Who?" replied the young man. "You're the only survivor from this whole group. The first one I've even heard of."

"You're some kind of first." Forest had said.

How many firsts, he wondered, am I going to have to carry?

He left, just outside, away from the blue eyes. He wandered aimlessly about the corridors of the silent ship. After a while he realized he was naked and returned.

The blue eyes were closed, the boy asleep. Felix eased himself slowly into his berth. He slept almost immediately, the doctor's words his last conscious thoughts.

The console at the foot of the berth had called to Drop all "available combat personnel" from his squad, his group, his sector.

And his was the only name left.

He kept the horror out of his face when the replacements read this on their consoles. Trying to keep from running, he stepped quickly from the bay. Outside, in the corridor, he skipped toward the Infirmary.

This doctor was pleasant and understanding, refusing even to notice the tremor in his voice as he spoke of computer error. She only nodded and led him to the bed. "Those must really hurt," she said about the cysts. He nodded gratefully, managing a nervous smile.

The medics came soon and gave him salves and treatments and then a machine covered his body in an ultra-sheer, ultra-thin envelope, leaving gaps only at the necessary orifices.

At first he fought to hide his elation

Then he was embarrassed by his needless fear.

Then he was slightly ashamed at his attitude.

Later, when he realized that the envelope was designed to enable him to wear his suit despite his injuries, he was too numb to speak, too wobbly to stand.

In the cubicle, the Black Suit embraced him. Dully, he made Connection and watched the dials respond. Then he sat and wept openly.

Heedless, uncaring, Banshee awaits.

PART TWO

JACK CROW

I

The only other humans in the cell had already passed through the dispenser, which was good. I couldn't afford to deal with their notions of justice and rights of life and the rest. Not that I disagreed with them necessarily. But now I just couldn't afford them.

I got to the plate and stomped on it hard, holding my cone underneath the funnel. The puryn slopped obscenely out, filling my cone and spattering me with dozens of little gray flecks. The same gray as the dispenser itself, the walls, the floor. The same color as me, covered with weeks and weeks of unwashed Lynsalt dust and rotten puryn. I moved out of the line and sat down in a corner on my heels with my back to the wall.

Like I always did at "dinnertime." I scraped my hands clean as best I could with what was left of my fingernails. This time, like the last dozen or so times before, I knew it was useless. The layers were now too deep. The Lynsalt, the puryn, the stinking filth of the place were winning. Like all the other poor dumb bastards in there, my skin was giving it up to the gray.

But this time it was different. This time it was happening to me

I coughed. Or snorted. Maybe I snarled. Then I took a greasy lump of puryn out of the cone with thumb and fingers and wedged it through my beard into my mouth so I would at least appear normal.

The dwarf was next, shuffling along warily between two Lyndrill, almost hidden by their towering gauntness. Their great height—almost three meters—made him seem even shorter. Their featureless gray bony faces made his face—all fat nose and bobbing whiskers—seem even more animated.

He became frightened as he neared the plate. His head twisted from side to side to cover all movements. His eyes darted pitifully about in their gray, dust-caked lids. He was a bundle of nerves as his cone was filled, so ready to bolt that the sound of the muddy stream erupting from the funnel made him jump.

He should have been scared. In that netherworld of Lyndrill giants and other madmen, he was the easy meat. And in prison, easy meat quickly goes.

The dwarf's impossible attempts to see all sides at once increased after he had actually gotten the food. He stepped away from the plate and stood in the clear place beyond uncertainly, as if expecting an assault from everyone at once. But apparently no one wanted to go to the trouble. Today had been a full day and we were all too beat to care.

All but me. I still watched the dwarf.

I watched him gradually relax, begin to breathe again. And then I saw the greater weariness descend on him as he again remembered that he would have to go through it all once again in three more hours. With his customary shuffle, he moved around the corner to his usual niche to eat.

With a last glance at the others for any signs of pursuit, I stood up, went around the same corner, and killed him by driving my gray boot through his gray face and into the softer gray beyond. Red blood.

I gathered up his cone before much could spill out. I had saved most of my portion—only pretending to eat before—and I took them both together for the maximum effect.

Almost immediately, I felt stronger. Puryn will last three

hours and three hours only. But if you take more, say twice as much, you'll have six hours of strength for that time. Six hours of prison strength, that is. Which was still only half as strong as I should normally feel.

I shook my head. I had no time to enjoy. There was more to it.

From its hook on the underway I took the slabpike. Before I could never have lifted it. Even now it was heavy. Carrying it across my shoulders, I stalked away through the dust. Gii had caught his footpad in the belt that morning and would still be weak.

Weak, he was, but still no fool. He spotted the red glow to my eyes from the near-double portion of puryn the instant I appeared. He stuck a pawpad against the wall and reared up to his full Lyndrill height. Even in that dim chamber, his stature was awesome. Two steps closer and he recognized me. "You!!" he had time to shout before I swung the full weight of the slabpike down atop his archplate

Gii's eyecubes lost the glint of amused disgust they had held when first seeing an assault from a puny human. They became instantly opaque from the Lyndrill pain response. He screamed that terrible scream. He clawed frantically at his footpad, lost his balance, and fell against the wall.

I was already on him, scrambling along his length, lunging forward. His throat was open wide, gasping for air. I wedged the barbed end of the slabpike deep into the passage, felt it lodge tightly. I bounced to my feet and threw my entire weight against the free end of the pike.

The cartilage warped, split, then ripped. The screams peaked, ceased.

Even with what Gii had already eaten, there was still twice as much remaining as I was accustomed to. My eyes blazed crimson through the settling dust cloud.

Those who had come to watch faded quickly out of sight as the glow—and my strength—increased. Another puryn-rage is on, they thought, and nobody wanted to be next.

They were wrong. I was in no puryn fugue, to kill blindly and gorge myself until dead or ruptured inside. I was going out.

The saltbore clamps gave easily to my newfound strength.

But then I had trouble with the treads. Those few moments of futile fumbling drove me into such a rage that I finally grabbed up the saltbore itself, by drillbit and casing respectively, and threw it across the cell against the belt mechanism. I shoved the drillbit deep into the machinery, braced myself with feet and back, and keyed the power. Sparks flew, metal shrieked, grinding against itself. The belt drivers began to buckle as the saltbore tore into its center. The wall shuddered, then the floor. My back felt like it was breaking from the force of the saltbore torqueing against it. Something, probably my back, had to give. But I couldn't let go. I might never have another chance, another day . . . another life.

"My skin is turning gray!" I shouted at the top of my lungs, just as the belt drive—and the supporting wall—erupted.

The saltbore casing saved me, shielding me from the flying debris. I shoved my way through the wreckage, hot metal and fused Lynsalt, and I was out. The brightness of the sun, of any sun, was a searing blow. It blinded me, staggered me. I almost didn't see the lumbering guard.

Almost.

Guards were twice human size with shell-hides like rhinos' and looked just like what they were designed to be—invincible.

But they had stalks for their eyes. And I leaped up between those trunk-sized arms, planted my knees on his chest, and, grabbing a stalk in each grimy fist, yanked backward with all my might. They popped neatly out. The guard swayed, tripped, righted itself. Those arms clamped around my back like falling girders as the third stalk, undismayed by the streaming stumps on either side, swung toward me.

I bit it.

I *plunged* my teeth into it. I shook my head from side to side. I think I screamed. The eye ripped loose. The guard fell, fortunately, backward. I disengaged myself from underneath his heavy paws and ran.

And ran and ran, tears streaming with relief. I was not only out, I was free.

Ahead, at the port, the ship was there. It *was*, after all. The sounds I had heard from deep within the mine were not, as I had feared, only the product of desperate fantasies.

I had to stop once. The taste of that bile the guards used for blood made me heave and heave again. But I was up and running again before my stomach had emptied completely out. I was out! I was free! It *was* a ship!

It was Borglyn's ship.

II

At first I thought it was a standard Coyote. Bad for me. Though there weren't any Fleet warrants out on me, any Captain who was only half bright would know enough to order me held for questioning. Then the whole mess of extradition would begin. Different guards. Different cages.

But that looked pretty good at the time. Behind me the Lyndrill prison had come alive. Alarms, coded sound beacons, shouting . . . all could clearly be heard. They kicked up huge clouds of dirt as they ran. With a last quick glance over my shoulder, I stepped up onto the ramp of the Coyote and prepared to be arrested.

There were two crewmen on ramp duty. A big one with white-blond hair and walrus mustache—and a short one with dark shiny hair and dark shiny eyes. The little one was going to be the problem, as the little ones usually are. Apparently lost in conversation, they hadn't notice me. As soon as I was on their ramp, though, they perked up. The big one seemed appalled by my putrid coloring. The small one, on the other hand, displayed a grin of amused disgust.

"Good God, who the hell is that?" said the blond.

"You mean 'what the hell is that?' " replied the shrimp.

I figured groveling would do it.

"Kind sirs," I began plaintively, managing to both bow and scurry a few steps closer at the same time. "Help me, I beg you!"

The shrimp didn't buy it.

"Hold it there," he said.

"Who are you?" asked the blond.

I thought I caught a touch of sympathy in the blond's voice. I turned all my attention to him.

"I'm a man of Earth, same as you. I've been . . . kept here by these. . . ."

"He's a damned escapee, Thor," snapped the short one. "Look at him. He's covered with their salt. He's been in the prison mine."

Thor frowned. "They use a mine for a prison?"

"Of course, Idiot. This is Lyndrill! How'd you break out, 'earthman'?"

The sneer he gave to "earthman" was his first major mistake.

"There was an explosion in the mine. I found the way open. I simply ran without thinking. Then I saw your ship. Please sir," I wailed, managing a few more steps toward them, "you must take me aboard. You cannot leave me in this place."

"Like hell we can't. Move it, convict. You're stinking up our ship," snarled the shrimp, and took a menacing step down toward me. That was his second major mistake. Or the third, if you count his coming that step closer. For that last step gave me a much better view.

This was no Fleet Coyote. Not with a crewman as sloppy as this. His robe was dirty, unwashed. His hair needed a good shower. His tunic was frayed about the collar. No officer, any officer, would let such slovenliness get by. Which left only one answer: There weren't any officers around to object. Mutiny, most likely. That, or outright theft. Whichever, this was no ship of Fleet. This was a *pirate* ship!

That changed everything.

Thor eyed me for several moments in silence. Then: "I'm gonna call Borglyn, see if we can take him in."

The shrimp was furious. "Are you out of your mind? Why do you want to get involved in this . . .? Uh-oh. Look here. I knew we should have kicked him off."

Both men looked past me at something. I knew what it had to be, but I turned around anyway.

Reinforcements had arrived. An even dozen guards stood in a ragged semicircle at the base of the ramp. I shuddered. I had never seen that many of them altogether at one time. One was enough. Damn, they were big. Monsters.

They made no move for me up the ramp. They knew better. Awesome as they were to an unarmed prisoner, they were nothing against a starship. Almost anything aboard could be a monster eater. They simply stood there, waiting.

Thor took one look at them and stepped toward the interior of the hatch.

"I'm calling," he said.

"Don't be stupid," snapped the shrimp. "Borglyn doesn't want to be bothered with Lyndrill affairs."

Thor stopped, gestured at the line of guards. "They can't do anything to us," he said calmly.

"Yeah, what about the rest of the planet? Besides, this guy's not worth the effort."

"Well," said Thor slowly, turning back toward the hatch, "I'm not giving him to *them*."

"You're crazy, Thor. What are we gonna do with this gray scum, anyway?"

"Scum," in my present condition, was too true to be funny and his last major mistake. I took a couple of steps toward him and whispered so that Thor, just inside the hatch, couldn't hear.

"Listen to me, you slimy little pig," I croaked. "I know why you don't want me on board. You're sick of being the ship shrimp. You're sick of knowing there isn't a man on board who couldn't rip your balls off and shove 'em up your nose."

Thor may not have heard, but the shrimp sure did. His eyes all but bugged out, his face got red, his chest expanded. I thought he was going to explode right there.

But he didn't. He waited 'till he got his stinger out of its strap. Then he flew at me down the ramp.

The bastard was quick, very quick. Worse than that, he knew how to use a stinger. It may look like a club, but it's a whole lot more. Instant paralysis at best.

I had to jump sideways to avoid his first lunge. I teetered at the edge of the ramp a moment before regaining balance, and out of the corner of my eye I noticed the line of guards surge forward an eager step. I reminded myself that I'd be theirs on the ground. Not only did I have to win unarmed, but I had to do it only on the ramp.

His second lunge was wild but still too close. I felt the burning tingle as the stinger brushed past my cheek. I had to move. I feinted left, ducked another lunge, and slapped him twice on his left cheek. Slapping is better than fists and usually enrages enemies. The shrimp got so mad that his next swing of the stinger threw him off balance. I stepped in again as he fell to one knee. I blocked a hook at the wrist and slammed the butt of my palm under his chin. He squealed as his teeth cracked together. Then I backhanded him across the throat.

He was tough. Even as he fell he managed to graze my knee with a swipe from the stinger.

The pain seared up and down my thigh. I bellowed like some animal and lost it.

Maybe him personally, maybe the prison nightmare, maybe myself. Whatever it was, it was strong. I saw nothing, heard nothing, cared even less. Hate rode.

I broke his arm, the arm that held the stinger, twice. Once across my knee, once by just stomping on it. He may have screamed, then. He may have screamed all along, but I couldn't hear. I was too busy pulverizing his face and neck and chest and. . . .

And then it was over and he lay there, half on and half off the ramp, covered with blood and gray Lynsalt. I stood over him, breathing heavily, until WHAM, and I was face-down on the sun-scorched metal of the ramp.

Thor had driven his foot halfway through my spine.

I looked up at him, stunned, my head spinning, my back beginning to throb.

He was looking at what was left of the shrimp. His eyes were wide, aghast; his chest heaved.

"You filthy . . ." he blurted and kicked me again.

He caught me just right, just under my left ear. I spun backward—in midair—into a full somersault, and crashed onto the other edge.

Dimly, distantly, I saw the guards, now directly beneath me and reaching, up for me. . . .

I clawed, scrambled my way onto the ramp. I got a knee up onto the edge. I heaved.

Thor was waiting. I saw the black boot rear back, saw his weight shift, thought it finished.

"Hold it," shouted an incredibly deep and commanding voice.

Everyone froze. And I mean everyone. Thor, the guards, and me, still clinging to the ramp with two bleeding hands and a knee.

It took me a second to realize that there was no electronic speaker involved. It was simply the unamplified voice of Sar Borglyn, chief mutineer and pirate, commanding.

A few breaths later and all relaxed somewhat. And I, scared of everyone in sight but especially the guards, scrambled all the way onto the (safety) ramp. The guards paused a moment, then resumed their ragged formation at the foot of the ramp.

Borglyn found out what was what in a hurry, a way he had. I told him some smoke about being Benn Lawl, a missionary from the Church of Episcoblue to the heathen Lyndrill. Lawl had been a cellmate of mine, jailed, caged rather, for blasephemy, so I figured it was a pretty good story.

Borglyn didn't come near buying it. I thought he was going to toss me off right then. He would have, too, I think, but Thor saved me.

Thor didn't mean to. He meant just the opposite. Started sputtering furiously about poor little busted up Praun, the shrimp, lying there on the ramp. How I must have jumped him, how Praun was only trying to help and this "dirty scum jumped him."

Seeing the stinger already unstrapped and out as well as knowing Praun as he probably did, made it easy for Borglyn to see the lie in the ambush theory. Also, Borglyn was irritated at Thor for butting in unasked. He didn't listen long.

Then with a sharp "Shut up," that made everybody's mouth close, he walked down and looked at me.

Looking up from the position of a crumpled wretched heap was no way to meet Borglyn. To begin with, he was a real-life titan. Well over two meters tall, with long dark-brown hair and a dark-brown beard and a dark-brown star-tanned face, he had a bulk to him that was . . . well, ridiculous. He was damn near as big as a Lyndrill guard. In fact, everything about Borglyn was big. His body, his voice, his appetites, his plans.

There was something eerie about him too, his eyes. In the midst of that great flat face of that huge forehead and forest of beard were the two most exquisitely beautiful blue eyes I had ever seen on a human creature.

He was a handful.

He peered at me, bent over with massive hands on muscular thighs, and made a decision.

"Bring him," he said crisply.

Thor started to speak, thought about it, thought he would shut up and live instead—all in the one brief half-second glance he got from the boss.

But someone did object. A dry-hoarse croak erupted from below. It was the warden from the prison cage, on the scene at last.

It seemed that everyone else was there as well. All the various penal assistants to the warden, most of the major civic officials and quite a few spectators. The clearing at the foot of the ramp was a small field of long green robes fluttering in the breeze.

The warden was Lyndrill-eloquent. He began by welcoming Borglyn's "seeds" and promising prayers of virility.

Borglyn was silent.

Only momentarily nonplused, the warden continued. He spoke of the great gulf between stars, the greater gulf between beings. He talked about the further greatness of communication and said he knew that Borglyn would agree.

Borglyn was silent.

Now a little nervous, the warden went on about sovereignty,

about different cultures and customs being included therein. The warden implied possible disfavor—Lyndrillwise—concerning breaches of that authority.

He meant me, of course. When Borglyn was silent about *that*, the warden stepped back.

The—call him Major—of the city then stepped forward in his regal best. Gold trimmed his green robes. He carried a solid platinum hoop over a "shoulder."

The Major was Lyndrill-tough. He threatened Borglyn's ship. He threatened his men. He threatened his "seeds." Lastly, he threatened himself.

Borglyn stood there awhile in the ensuing tense silence, watching the Lyndrill. Then he took one step toward the throng and pointed a thick finger at the end of a thicker arm directly at the Major and said: "Go away."

And they went away. Every one of them. They didn't even have to think about it.

An hour later, in orbit, I stepped into the 'fresher. Two hours later, now out of orbit, I stepped out. Except for a couple of spots, I was no longer gray. I was pink, actually, like a pinched baby, but still better than gray.

Borglyn called me into the captain's stateroom after I had eaten. He was surprisingly courteous, asking me all about myself and commiserating about my prison time. I spent well over an hour inventing a past. It became a lot of fun and, toward the end, terribly convincing as I got into the role. Throughout, Borglyn said little, merely nodding and agreeing or even chuckling at some instant escapade from my youth.

And then, after all my lies and all my talk and all the work involved, he leaned back in his chair at last and said, with a sickening smile: "Well, Jack, I'm glad you got that off your chest. Now, do you want a job?"

So he had known—all along he had known—that I was Jack Crow.

III

When Borglyn first gave me the deal, I thought he had lost it. The fear, the constant pressure, has gotten to him, I thought. His thinking is out.

I was about half right.

There *was* a lot of pressure involved. And a hell of a lot of fear too, for a man with his imagination. Never mind the mass murder of the officers, actually stealing the Coyote afterwards meant mutiny, the all-time favorite crime of the military mind. They do special things to mutineers.

"Not that I won't actually be ordered in for a trial, of course. The lucky arresting officer—meaning the captain of whichever ship might nab me—is given quite specific instructions to bring me in to Militar."

He paused and lit a cigarette, looking like a photographic smear on a 3-D plate, little white dart.

"I'll never see Militar, though. On the way I'll have an accident. You want to hear about it? I know of one that took four days."

I told him I didn't want to hear about it.

"Just as well," he said, puffing. "Just as well."

He drifted off for a bit, staring and puffing. No doubt remembering details of the four-day goof. But he handled it well, I thought. Damn well. Not an inch of trembling. Long smooth deep breaths. In fact, he showed no sign at all of being aware of his position in about the deepest hole there was. It was impressive, the way he sat there smoking.

"So," he continued after a while, "to the problem." He swiveled around in his seat, leaned across the captain's desk and stared into my eyes. "The problem is fuel. We are just about out."

"Uh-oh," I said.

He stared harder at me, his eyebrows raised.

"Uh-oh? The man says 'Uh-oh'? I describe what is quite possibly the most tenuous situation in the galaxy and that is all he has to say? Well, I suppose the prospect of a particularly nasty death at the hands of some lucky crew is nothing to the great and famous Jack Crow. The fact that I am being actively sought by every ship in Fleet, most of which have forgotten the damned Antwar in their eagerness to slice me apart, should be of at least passing interest, even to a man who moves stars . . . how did you so cleverly put it? . . . 'Move stars hell outta the way.' Even to such a superman my situation should rate just a little goddamn more than uh-oh. Care to try again?"

I said nothing, wincing, in fact, at that quotation. I *had* said something like it at the time. But I was pretty well frayed at the edges and it infuriated me that that was the only thing I said that the Presswave people thought to broadcast. Show business.

"Nothing to add, eh?" continued Borglyn. "Very well. I suppose it was too much to ask to have you actually impressed with the gravity of the situation as it stands. So allow me, if you will, to try to bring it on home to you.

"I'm being hunted. I don't like it. I'm also running out of fuel and therefore running room. I don't like that. I *will* have fuel, Mr. Crow. I *will* obtain it. And, unless you wish me to rip you limb from limb and then stuff you bodily through an access tube, you *will* help me obtain it. Is that pretty clear so far?"

I nodded. It was clear all rght.

"How nice. We're communicating. Now, as to the 'how' of it; The only Cangren Power Cell available to one in my position is at some Fleet Scientific Colony which are, as you may know, completely self-sufficient fuelwise. My intention is to travel to one of these places, the remotest location available, for obvious reasons, and make Connection.

"Normally, of course, I could neither beg nor borrow such fuel for a mutinous craft. And the possibility that I could simply take what I want from a fully self-contained Project Complex is essentially nonexistent. As soon as I appeared overhead, they would simply button up the complex and that would be that. I doubt that even a fully loaded Coyote could pierce their defenses without totally annihilating the Can inside.

"So what to do? I will trick them, of course. Or, rather, you will trick them. You, Jack Crow, will make yourself known to the members of the Project. You will use your rather romantic notoriety to ingratiate yourself into the complex itself. And at the proper moment, you will render it defenseless from the inside. Is *that* clear, Mr. Crow? Are we still communicating?"

"Yeah."

"Wonderful. Now what, you might ask, is in it for you? What indeed, besides a grateful lack of excruciating pain, is your prize? Simple. I have an eight-man Sledcraft waiting for me in a safe place. If you do as I say, exactly as I say, you may have it. It will be yours, Mr. Crow, to wander about with as you will. There will also be an appropriate amount of credits logged into its banks directly from the treasury of this ship. I've checked the banks aboard, and it's quite a hefty sum. And if I can't make use of it, there's no reason why you should not.

"So, there is the proposition, famous and great Jack Crow. What shall it be?"

He was kidding, of course. Who really needs to choose between being rich and being dead? Between being anything and being dead?

"I've given your proposal considerable thought," I began.

"Good, good," he replied, nodding.

"And I've decided to join your little team."

"I'm *so* glad."

"Here's to the partnership," I said, lifting my brandy glass high.

"Oh, we can do better than that," he said with an uneasy smile.

More quickly than I would have thought possible, he was up out of his seat and around to my side of the desk. He held the flask in one hand. With an elaborate flourish he filled my glass to the brim. Then beckoning me to rise, he touched his glass to mine and gestured for me to toss it off in one gulp.

I took a deep breath, placed it to my lips and drank. It burned in my throat and in my mouth and after a few seconds, in my stomach as well. But I was determined to give as good as I got. I closed my eyes to cap the streaming tears and continued to swallow.

And then I couldn't anymore. I couldn't drink, couldn't swallow, couldn't breathe. My throat was clamped tight by a monstrous rock-hewn vise that deflated my windpipe in an instant. In the next instant I was rising slowly into the air where I simply hung. I opened bulging eyes and stared at the dead eyes of Borglyn.

He held me there at eye level to him with the grip of a single hand about my throat. A single hand. And there was no trembling, no effort involved that I could see. No hurry to put me down again. He simply stood there peering darkly into my eyes and hanging me with the force from a single limb. Hanging me

Years later, he let me slowly down. But he kept his paw about my windpipe.

"This is how easy it is for me to kill. It is this simple. Even for you. Remember this. Fear this."

He stared for a little while longer. Then he let go. A crewman appeared from somewhere and led me to my cabin. I didn't see him for three days. I was glad.

I stayed in my cabin as much as possible during the trip to Sanction. The crew made me nervous.

It's not that I really feared them. There was no obvious reason for that. They simply made me nervous.

They were scared, for one thing. Mutineers, after all, every one of them. No way to ever go home again. No future to speak of in the conventional sense. And totally dependent on Borglyn. And I got the definite impression that he hadn't let most of them in on his plans. As the days became weeks and on and on, the eagerness to know began to get to them.

What they did, of course, was to compete in their efforts to appear unconcerned. Gruff voices, too loud laughter, elaborate guises of disinterest, all eventually gave way to collective jeering at anyone showing the slightest trace of uneasiness. And then the jeering became rougher and the frustration now had an outlet: aggressive peer judgment.

They were getting ugly.

So I stayed in my cabin all the time except at meals. When I ate, I sat at the far end of the mess and appeared deaf to the too-boisterous horseplay and the accompaning sounds of battered bodies smacking face down onto the bulkheads. No matter what, I never took sides, never hinted awareness, even when the Amazon Drive tech bounced the little third-class sparks across the table and into the chair beside me

It had to happen though, eventually. I had known it would. I guess I had hoped Borglyn had put me off-limits. At last, somebody just had to know who the stranger was.

"Who *are* you, anyway?"

It was the Amazon. She was sitting at the far side of the mess quaffing down the daily liquor supply with her cronies and generally showing how untouched she was by the grimness of a bad situation which could only get worse.

I ignored her.

"Hey, you, at the end there. I'm talking to you."

What I wanted to do, was slide the plate into the chute right then and just walk out. But there was too much left to make it seem natural. And to appear to be running. . . . That would have been asking for it.

So I was stuck. Nothing to do but play it out slow, stalling all the way.

I ignored her again.

She stood up then, after a little mumbled urging from her mates, and came over to take it up personal. She sat down on the table less than an arm's length from my food.

"I'm talking to you."

I looked up at her. Drivetechs have to be big. During

combat fire control procedures, they have to be able to lift whole modular assemblies out of the grid and replace them the same way—all within seconds. This one was about a head taller than me, weighing probably a third again more. I counted that and I counted her mood and I counted the strong possibility that she would feel like she had to show off a little with the others watching. I even counted her looks. It came up: all bad.

I continued to meet her gaze with a blank look.

"Who are you?" she wanted to know.

I appeared to think about it, said, "Nobody," and went back to eating.

I had hoped to sound innocuous enough that it would stick. But the audience at the far end wasn't having any.

They laughed. Not at me, but, dammitall, *with* me. At her. I felt her tense uncomfortably beside me.

"Well, I can *see* that," she continued. "But what's your name. What are you doing here?"

I looked at her again, blankly as before. I shrugged. "Just along for the ride."

A loud guffaw from the far end. "I don't think he wants to tell you, Twala," somebody called. There was more laughter.

That did it. I stood up, faced her.

"Maybe you ought to talk to Borglyn," I suggested as calmly and reasonably as I could.

But she was having none of that. Bullies worry about their public posture too much.

"I'm asking you, not him," she replied harshly.

I looked deep into her eyes and saw nothing there but anticipation and I remembered something somebody had once told me a long time ago. "Bullies don't want to fight you. They don't want to fight at all. They simply want to beat you up."

"I can't hear you," she said when I hesitated. Then she took a long stout finger and prodded me in the right lung with it. "Speak up."

"All right. I'm Jack Crow. Now move your finger while you still can. Now."

She moved it, eyes wide at the sound of my name. There

was a long, heavy pause while they took that in. I dropped my plate into the chute and walked out. Whew.

I went to Borglyn.

"Yes," he said distantly, regarding the ash of his cigarette. "I did hear something about it."

"And?"

"And it seems there is considerable interest. Seems Twala and her crowd have some doubt as to your having leveled with them. They're afraid you didn't."

"And?"

"They wanted my comfirmation."

"Well, I hope you gave it to them."

"Why, no. As a matter of fact, I said nothing at all."

Dammit.

"Look, Borglyn, I'm not part of your crew. I'm not one of them and I want no part of them. Play your morale games with somebody else. Leave me out of it. Give me my meals in my room."

"Sorry," was all that he would say.

I slammed out there in a fury.

I don't like being used. I don't like having my name, no matter how ridiculous it may become, being used. I didn't like Borglyn, or his ship or his crew or his problems. And I had no desire to make it easier for him

But that's just what I was going to have to do. Not enough, for his purposes, to just confirm that it really was me. No. Much better to have to make me prove it, to make me do the Jack Crow Pirate bit, really drive the message home that Borglyn isn't just wandering aimlessly. That he has big plans using big people. Give the crew a little faith.

And give me a lot of shit.

There was no reason not to get it over with right way. I went straight to the mess and, on cue, Twala & Co. were there and waiting.

I went straight to the mess hamper and grabbed a plate.

"Well, there you are, aren't you 'Mr. Crow.' If that's who you really are."

I turned and faced her and wondered why this always sounds the same, always ends the same. Always is the same.

"What is it," I asked impatiently, belligerently.

She glanced briefly at her audience, then approached me in three quick steps.

"Why did you say you were Jack Crow before?"

"Why not?"

"Well, are you Jack Crow?"

"Am I?"

"Listen to me, you little skunk," she began, taking that last step into my airspace and towering over me, "I think you're a liar."

"So?"

"So I don't like liars."

And then, with infinite weariness, I delivered perhaps the dumbest, most worthless, line in all of human interaction: "So what are you going to do about it?"

When she kicked at me I smashed her instep. When she swung that massive arm, I broke it at the wrist and, for absolutely no good reason, at the bicep as well. And then because I was sick to death of it all, I picked out the biggest loudmouth in the crowd and beat the living hell out of him.

They all scattered then. It was left to me to take her to medical for the casts and Gropac connections. Then somehow she was all arms and legs and hair and thighs more than anything else. I tried because I felt I should try something. She moaned and strained to make it better than it was, feeling, at last, that it was something missing in her which it might very well have been. But, on the other hand, that's another part of the legend which is wrong.

So I held her for a while, or the other way around, nestled in those mammaries of surprising silkiness and warmth. Feeling bad. Feeling cheap. Feeling that I would get Borglyn back somehow.

The gong sounded for Sanction some hours later. We didn't move. She wasn't on and I knew we wouldn't land for hours. Then the claxon hit, general quarters and red lights pulsing in the passageways. Everybody moved at once. I ran for the bridge, buttoning up.

IV

The Fleet ship wouldn't *move*.

For three days standard, she simply hovered there in orbit. I was getting itchy. The crew was getting scared. So was Borglyn, though I doubted anyone but me could see it.

To save scanning power, we hid on the near moon, the one that, like Luna, has a perennially dark side. Borglyn thought he might as well take the opportunity to show me my prize. He was going to have to before I started moving anyway. So we glided down easily beside. I pulled on a suit and walked over to give it the eye.

It was a mystery, really. No evidence of a crash. In such a small ship, such a long, long, way from home, you would expect to see something dramatic. But the landing had been exceedingly clean. Everything was intact.

It was an Arcstar Model Four, the kind used to ferry the brass between starships for face-to-face meetings of top security, as if the ants could give a damn what we transmitted anyway. And for its designated task it was wildly overqualified in the best spend-military-spend tradition. I believe it sold, completely outfitted, for about C18,000,000 in the civilian world.

Throw in another four or five million for tactical blaze capacity. A sweet deal for me.

Inside I saw the reason for the clean landing. The pilot and or crew had abandoned it some time ago, leaving it on scanner recovery mode. There was no telling how long it had drifted before the scanners picked this moon to land on. I thought about it a second. They had started selling these to the military at the beginning of the war . . . It could have been drifting for over four years then. Probably had.

In the drop bay I found the suit. I had never seen one up close before, but anyone would know what it was. It was the black sheen worn by the guy in the Vidshow, the scout who never reported back. But unlike the show-business type, the scars and imperfections on this one were real. The poor bastard who wore this thing had been through it for a fact. The left shoulder was particularly discolored, suggesting a many-second exposure to an ant blast.

I felt myself shuddering. It might have been for the lot of the almost certainly dead owner. It might have been for the whole war.

Damn. Interstellar war. . . . Who'd have thought that we could be so stupid?

The speakers crackled next to my ears.

"Well, what do you think, Jack?" asked Borglyn from the Coyote.

"It's dead."

"Well, of course it is, dammit." He sounded exasperated. "What would you expect. Do you have any idea how far away we are from anything at all?"

"Activate the board."

"Like hell . . . I haven't got power to spare for that. I'll give you fuel when I get mine and not before."

"Activate it," I insisted. "This could be a null bank as far as I know. You could spare enough juice to let me see if it's capable."

He was silent, thinking. I could hear his heavy breathing from those huge lungs. "All right, just a minute," he said after a while.

There was a brief pause and then the panel flickered. It

flickered again, flashed on strong and glowed. I went through the check.

She was, as I had expected, fine. Except for power, she was ready to go. And for a brief instant, my frustration at not being able to lift then and there was so great as to be physically painful. What a ship . . . To be aloft and on my own and . . . well, aloft. There was so much left to do.

"While I'm at this business of showing good faith, I may as well go all the way. I heard him giving orders for a simultaneous relay transmission. Lo and behold, the treasury light beacon responded. I keyed the display and sat down on the pilot seat with a thud. C24,000,000 and change had just been transferred over.

Wow.

If I had been at least willing to go along with Borglyn before, now I was damn near eager. Hell, I was eager. To hell with mutinies and Fleet regs and the rest of it. With this ship and all those credits . . . Hell, I might become the great and famous Jack Crow I had read so much about.

I hadn't realized I was laughing out loud until I heard Borglyn sourly order me to cut it out and return. Without hesitation, I obeyed. On some impulse, I grabbed up the suit and carried it with me.

It was an offhand, thoughtless gesture. An icing deed to go along with my mood. And, incredibly, the singlemost important action I had ever undertaken.

But no one knew that then. Certainly not me. I was too busy planning and grinning, grinning and planning.

When I cycled back in, I heard the Fleet ship had driven away. We moved in immediately.

In the hours before landfall, Borglyn gave me what little he had on the project director. He read to me from the display.

"Hollis Ware, 31 standard, a list of the schools he went to. A long list. Hmmm. Seems the man is a genius."

"That would explain his youth."

Borglyn's eyebrows lifted. "What do you mean?"

"He's pretty young to be in charge of a Fleet Project."

"Hmm. Is that a big deal?"

"Pretty big. Essentially lord of all he surveys."

"Very interesting. Still, he's not the Fleet."

I lit a cigarette from the box on his desk. "Close enough. That Fleet ship could have been the last for a long time. That's why they have colonies like this. It saves money. You have to sign on for a three-year stretch. And during that time. . . ."

"The Director is all-powerful. Yes. I see. And he's a young man."

"A young genius," I corrected.

Borglyn nodded vaguely, lost in the possibilities. I changed the subject.

"What's the specialty?"

"The what?"

"The purpose of the project. What are they studying?"

"Oh. Says here he's a statistical historian. Never heard of it. Uh, let's see . . . 'projections of optimum conditions for specific permutations as regards to . . .' What the hell is all that supposed to mean?"

"Here," I offered, "let me."

I stood up and went around to the other side of the desk to check the screen for myself. Borglyn grumbled his irritation. He was already angered at the thought of losing any of the trappings of "Captain."

But I worked myself in there anyway, reading the display over his shoulder while he went through an elaborate ritual of lighting his cigarette, pretending not to be interested, and trying to keep up with the speed of the scan. All at the same time.

I read for several minutes, nodding to myself and occasionally muttering "I see" under my breath. Not because I really saw. Most of the stuff was as much beyond me as it was the mutineer. I only did it because I knew it would make him feel a little less invulnerable. I had not, would not, forget the incident with Twala.

At last I went back around to my seat and sat. I lit another cigarette and stared at the smoke as if immersed in the contemplation of all that wonderfully intricate data. The fact was that I had understood maybe one word in ten once it had gotten down to specifics. But I had learned a couple of things. One: it was a relatively new and fascinating field of study; and Two: Hollis Ware would have to be a genius to understand it, much less found it as the banks had said.

"Well," asked Borglyn irritably after he could no longer stand the suspense, a time span of perhaps twenty seconds. Before I answered, I filed the memory of his impatience in a safe place.

"Ware's working for Fleet."

"I know that much, goddammit," he snapped angrily.

"No. I mean the real Fleet. The fighting arms. He's involved with the Antwar."

"Really? How so?"

"From what I could understand, it seems he's trying to determine why our casualties have been so high."

Borglyn stared at me for a second, then burst into wild, deep uncontrollable laughter.

He laughed and laughed until his face got red and tears formed at the corners of his eyelids. At last he settled down into the occasional chuckle stage where he could talk. But even then he didn't speak, lost in his own thoughts and staring into space. Every few seconds his eyes would shine and the corners of his cavernous mouth would twist up, remembering.

I had time to take in the tone of all that. There was more than a little sadness in his hilarity. And an unsettling amount of bitterness. I wondered then, for the first time, what had happened to make him lead a mutiny. And why, despite the expected problems, the crew seemed more righteous about their previously violent actions than I would have thought possible. I thought about all of that and then I thought for the fiftieth or two hundredth time how glad I was that I had no part in the Antwar or the ants.

"All that money," he said at last. "All that money and time and all those people to boot. All to answer that question. To find out something any Grade Ten Under-Tech could have told him."

"What's that? Why *are* we having such terrible casualties?"

He looked at me with a sudden, heart-stopping sobriety. He looked right into my eyes, but he was seeing something I knew I would never see, never hear him tell.

"I'll tell you why, Jack. Because no one, I mean NO

ONE, at Fleet has the slightest idea of what they're doing. And every poor son-of-a-bitching one of us knew it."

I sat silently, taking in not just what he had said, but the . . . painful . . . way he said it.

"There's a little more to it than that, of course," he added after a moment.

"There always is," I replied, almost to myself.

He looked quickly at me, nodded slowly, almost suspiciously. "Yeah. There always is at that. But that's the meat of it, what I told you. That's . . ." And then he was gone again. "That's the meat."

We spoke little more after that. He went over my cover story a couple of times. We talked about communications and timetables. He gave me the name of my contact in the refugee village called "Sanction City."

I mentioned that I wanted to take the suit along.

"What suit?" he asked.

"The scout suit. Y'know, the black one I brought back from the sled."

"Oh," he said unhappily, "I ordered it spaced."

"What?" I cried, aghast. "You mean it's gone?"

"Gone or going. What difference does it make?"

"Call 'em. See if you can stop it. I want to take it with me."

Borglyn, clearly uneasy, nevertheless obeyed. He got on the horn and located the suit, a scant two minutes or so before it was to be ejected. On my insistence, he ordered it placed in the lifeship.

"What the hell do you want with that thing?" he growled after he had finished.

"It's an offering for Ware. Just the kind of thing an historian type would find interesting."

Borglyn frowned. "I doubt that."

"It's better than nothing," I countered. But I was puzzled. Why was he so cavalier with such an expensive—hell, irreplaceable—piece of equipment? I asked him.

The answer came in that dead-sober, grinding way he had when he talked about the war. "This ship is out of the war business. At least out of the Antwar business."

Then he made a gesture which clearly told me to change the subject. I did. We parted.

He had given me the only answer that interested him. If he could have gotten his bulk into that suit himself, he wouldn't have. It was the war, to him. It was the ants. This bloodthirsty criminal, so eager to kill when it suited him, so enamored of pseudo-sadism, was terrified of the ants

I filed that away too.

Twala, bless her endless thighs, was there at the lock to wish me off. Looking like an overgrown schoolgirl and acting worse. I had to stand on tiptoe to kiss her good-bye.

V

The lifeship dropped me onto the little delta just across the river from the Project. Semi-frantically I began to unload my gear before it lifted again. I had plenty of time, over two minutes, but the possibility of that ship darting for the stratosphere while I still had one leg in the door was particularly vivid to me. It had happened once. I straightened up from my small pile of goods and fished for a cigarette. That says a lot about you, I thought to myself. Too damn many stupid things like that have been significant. I sighed, began to light up, and stopped.

On the bridge, less than three hundred meters away, there was a riot going on.

Over four hundred people, I estimated, refugees obviously, were storming the bridge from the city side. I left my stuff where it was and hurried over.

Nearing the mob, I saw that they weren't actually trying to shove their way across. They were just screaming and cursing and waving their arms. Then I saw the reason why they had stopped where they were. A group of people wearing Project tunics and carrying side arms stood on the far side blocking their way. And in the midst of them stood a rather thin, rather short young man with spindly arms and long brown hair that he kept nervously pushing out of his eyes. The Director, obviously Hollis Ware.

About the time I reached the edge of the crowd, the good young Doctor tried to blow it.

"All right," he yelled suddenly, stridently, into the afternoon air. "If that's what you want. I don't need them to speak," he added, gesturing over his shoulder to the poised guards.

The mob crackled boisterously, and expectantly, at this. The group of guards sagged visibly. So did I. It was an incredibly stupid thing to do.

I moved into the edge of the crowd without being noticed and shuffled about halfway through while Ware was making the foolish mistake of stepping across the bridge alone. The members of the crowd closest to him moved backwards off the bridge to give him room. But not far enough. The way they were set up, they could snatch him if they decided to, before he could get back.

Everyone settled down to hear what was being said. I listened carefully as well, to find out what it was all about.

It was all about food. The City, it seemed, didn't have any. The Project had a lot, more than they needed. And so on.

". . . your lack of food is your doing. It is your responsibility, not ours." Ware was saying.

The crowd booed angrily at this. A barrel-chested fat man stepped forward. "Sure, sure, we talk about our kids starvin' and you give us *this* shit."

Loud angry agreement of this from the crowd. Fists waved, curses flew. But no surge forward. Not yet. The fat man, I noticed, had a bright red face from all the shouting and arm waving. He also had very little actual fat.

"How are a bunch of stupid words gonna help our kids," he added, as the angry cries peaked and dropped. The noise peaked again in responses. I noticed that he had actually turned to the people around him when he had said this. Under his red face, I saw, were two very calm, knowing eyes. . . . There was a lot more going on here.

Ware didn't see it. He swayed backwards on his heels with

every roar from the mob at his feet. He was blatantly nervous, close to fear, and had no apparent ability to hide it. But he hung in there. He wouldn't take that step back that his feet were itching for.

Another man stepped up to speak. Tall and thin, black hair shiny from lack of washing. He spoke in a nasal snarl.

"All I know is that I come a long damn way to get here and now all I see is the same damn Fleet tryin' to screw me again."

The crowd thundered their approval and, under their cheers, the thin man exchanged a glance with the fat man, who nodded imperceptibly.

That tore it. Ware was being set up by a couple of pros. He had no idea and no chance. I moved closer to the bridge through a forest of shifting feet and waving fists.

Ware tried to respond as best he could. But he was hopelessly hamstrung. First, he plainly feared the crowd in general and the fat man in particular. And he was disgusted by the crowd. The latter was probably doing more damage. When you're way, way, down and know it, you sure don't like to have it broadcasted by the sneers from somebody who is up. And Holly did broadcast his disgust, try as he might to hide it. He found them filthy, worthless and just generally beneath him and they could tell.

They really hated the little guy.

And so, abruptly, he made it worse.

He had had enough of that line about starving children. When the fat man used it again. Ware snapped back with: "Maybe you shouldn't be spending all that time distilling liquor then. If you're really so concerned about starving children, try staying sober for a while."

Oh, they didn't like that. The surge began. Ware was forced to step back a few feet so as not to be trampled. But the crowd stopped there, not yet incensed enough to do damage. Which meant that they weren't yet sure that everybody would do it at the same time seeing as how he had obviously hit some kind of target with the last bit.

But the fat man knew. He knew that mobs, like unions, have an answer to that eternal question of who deserves what. They just ignore it and grab.

The fat man got them mad enough to ignore it.

Talked about how easy it was for Ware to talk like that and how he would sing a different tune and how (surprise) he couldn't possibly understand because he had never known what it was like to live in Sanction City so (ta *dah*) he had no right to judge what he didn't understand.

It was the standard line, but even so, the fat man was a master of it. He went on and on about how tough it was for them and how it was easy for Ware a couple of more times proving, by repetition, that he was actually saying something significant. Then he made the move

He took a step up until he was actually standing on the bridge about a half step from Ware, intimidating the Director with his size, and asked the big question: "Just how long do you expect us to take this?"

And that was it, the big moment. The complete surge was coming. Mobwise, he had Ware in a hole. There was nothing he could say. And the next words from the fat man's mouth would start it all.

So I cut him off.

"You sure talk a lot," I began loudly, shouting over his next remark. I said it as belligerently as possible, moving the last step up to the pair as I did. The crowd turned to look.

"You sure talk a lot," I repeated, "about starving, for a man that's so fat." There were a couple of giggles from the fringes, quickly hushed. The fat man turned hard eyes at me.

"Maybe," I continued with deliberate leisure, "you're the reason the kids are hungry." I noticed then, that the unlit cigarette was still in my mouth. I lit it slowly and blew the smoke gently toward him. I felt the tall thin one move in over my shoulder. I had to do this now.

"Who the hell are you?" asked the fat man with red face and clenched teeth. He turned toward me raising his arms. He was furious. He had lost the peak of the mob. He had to do something about me in a hurry.

I smiled. "I'm Jack Crow."

Murmurs, eyes agape, shifting whispers drifted about. I loved it.

The fat man hated it. He had lost the initiative. But he was quick to reach for it again, starting with: "I don't care who you are, I. . . ."

I cut him off. "Make your move, tubby."

He blanched, stared, made it.

I ducked under it and drove a foot deep into the place where the sun never shines. He bent over with a whoosh of breath. He grabbed for me, still tough, and I decked him. Then I turned slowly around to look at the thin one.

"I believe you're next?" I asked pleasantly, expectantly.

The thin one stared at me, at the fat man. Back at me. He couldn't believe this was happening to him.

The guards saved him and, most likely me, by moving across the bridge at the first hint of violence.

"Clear the bridge," barked the leader. She turned to Ware, put a gloved hand on his shoulder. "Step back, Dr. Please." It was not a request. Ware stepped back, looking at me with the beginnings of a grin. I smiled back.

The rest of the guards formed a wedge on the bridge with blazers high and in view. "Back," shouted the leader. "Break it up and go home. Now."

The crowd, deflated, obeyed meekly. I felt a rough grasp and then a shove as I was encouraged to do likewise. I spun around to get into it with the guard who had shoved me, thought better of it, and turned to Ware.

"Wait," he said on cue. "This is Jac . . . This man is all right."

I smiled as warmly as I could. "So is this one," I said and offered my hand. As he took it I gave him the smooth lie: "That was pretty impressive, Dr. Ware."

His eyes widened. "You know my name?"

"Doesn't everybody?"

I was lucky. Lightning didn't strike me dead and Ware ate it up.

"Well, where did you. . . . How long have you been here?" I mean. . . ."

I sighed. He was like a goddamned eager puppy. I pointed down the riverbank to my stack of stuff. "I kinda hitchhiked in a couple of minutes ago."

"I didn't notice that," he said with wonder in his voice.

I shrugged, smiled. There was an uneasy silence. I coughed into it.

"Came to see you, in fact. Brought something you might like."

"Oh really?"

Now he really was like a puppy. He all but ran with me across the bridge to the other side. He had to keep restraining his legs from running as we neared my belongings. When we got to the pile I pointed but he had already seen.

"My God, an L-1625 Scout . . . I don't believe it."

He was all over it in a second, poking and prodding. He uttered another gasp.

"And it's still got the recording pod," he said breathlessly.

"Oh, you noticed that, did you?" I asked with a smile, looking over his shoulder to see what the hell he was talking about. Recording what?

He straightened up and looked at me. "And you brought this all this way for me?" he asked with genuine amazement.

"All for you."

His ecstasy was overflowing. He didn't know what to say. Embarrassed, he looked back and forth between me and the suit. "You're . . . you're really Jack Crow?"

I nodded.

He stuck out his hand to shake again. I shook. Now I was embarrassed.

"And you're Hollis Ware," I added lamely.

He hardly heard me. He was watching the distantly retreating crowd.

"Damn," he said with a boyish grin, "you sure do make things happen, don't you?"

He was already looking at the suit again. But I was watching the crowd now. Watching and wondering how badly what was coming would hurt this man. This nice man.

"Yes," I replied at last. "I do."

VI

He marched me across the bridge with his hand on my shoulder and into the complex. The guards followed with my belongings. He gave me a whirlwind tour of the place, pointing me out to people like a long lost relative. There was an incredibly fast tour of his private workshop complete with running dialogue on the problems of statistical history that was, quite frankly, beyond my grasp. I saw corridor after corridor of laboratories and computer banks. I saw recreation areas and living quarters and the room I was going to have. I saw secretaries and assistants and crew. I saw his fellow scholars and their growth charts and their equipment. I saw Lya, saw Karen, saw that they hated each other.

We ate. Twelve of us sat around a beautiful mahogany table and feasted on fresh vegetables and wine that I was told was home, Sanction, grown.

I enjoyed most of it, faked my way through the rest. I also learned a lot about Holly.

First: he was as smart as the Coyote readout had said he was. A for-real genius. The other members of the academic staff were all much older than he was, all rather stodgy, in fact. They faked it better than I did. For clearly, they could not follow the intricate workings of his brain. They spent a lot of time at the dinner table nodding sagely and sometimes in awe, sometimes in bewilderment.

But always hating the too-smart little bastard.

I also learned how to get along with Holly, as he insisted now that I call him.

He wanted to be *in* on things. Specifically, he wanted to be in on my things. I found that rolling my eyes at the stupidity of his fellows worked beautifully if I did it in such a way as to include Holly. When they asked the usual questions about me (anxious as hell to get away from Holly's theories) I would fake it in such a way as to say to Holly across the table: "You and I can talk about these things later, in private."

Holly sucked it in like it was his last breath.

After eating we went out on the terrace. I separated myself from the rest. I stood at the balcony, sipping and smoking. Sanction City glowed dully across the river. Waves of anger and hatred rose strongly into the sky.

Karen appeared at my elbow. She leaned against the railing, sort of uncoiling against it like a cat looking for a tummy rub. We stared at each other that way for a few seconds, my gaze blank.

"Did you really come here just to see Holly?" she asked at last in a husky tone.

"Really and truly."

"You've really heard of him?"

"Uh, huh."

"You know much about his work?"

"Not as much as I'd like."

She nodded vaguely at this, allowing her hair to slide lusciously across her cheek.

"How long will you be here?"

"That depends."

"On what, Jack?" She asked and rolled a smile across her shoulder.

There is a stench when somebody wants to fuck your name. It rolled across with the smile, on the way she had said "Jack."

I hated it, of course.

I wanted it, of course.

The way she had of sort of trembling with bursting sensuality . . .

"Are we fucking?" I asked bluntly. "Or just dancing? Or are we gonna dance now and fuck later? Nothing else will do, I'm a busy man."

She stood up straight and got red. Then white, reminding me, suddenly, of the fat man from the bridge.

"Make your move, Pudding," I added.

Her trembling was no longer the good trembling, but from fury against things women hate, like pointing out the obvious and laughing. She turned after a long hateful look, and stalked stiffly away. Her drink trailed liquid, unnoticed, on her white knuckles.

Across the terrace Holly stood red-faced himself, all but shouting at a crowd of younger scholar-types. Whatever it was that he was for, he was really for it.

The younger folk looked hesitant, but were smart enough not to buck the boss. The older folk had extended the nodding outside, mumbling echoes of his more vociferous remarks.

As I reached the edge of the crowd faces turned in my direction. Holly noticed this and followed suit. He looked embarrassed, suddenly, at his own intensity. He slipped out an arm to me as if for corroboration.

"Jack," he began, "Jack Crow. What do *you* think about fighting the Antwar?"

Uh-oh.

I froze. Holly did too along with everyone else.

"Not tonight," I blurted into the silence and added a punctuating burp.

Everyone laughed, hooting and hollering. I relaxed my suddenly taut shoulders and smiled. I had gotten away with it.

I dragged through the rest of the evening by drinking too much and, when absolutely necessary, relying on my store of meaningless but expected Jack Crowisms. Fortunately enough, the mood of this gathering was more inclined toward performance than most. No long silences while fat drunks awaited an exhibition of the "real, private" me.

Instead they took turns flashing their lore.

I learned from a biochemist the reason he and many others continued to prefer the old fashioned and acidic spirits over the physiologically harmless syntho. "Scotch and thuch . . . such, is—chemically, mind you—a better drunk," he assured me.

I learned from an ecological paleontologist the name—easily a meter long—of the local disease responsible for Sanction having fish, insects, and rodents but not reptiles, birds, or amphibians.

I learned from an apparent score of local ranchers the difficulties of breeding herds from embryos. The "immigrants" —meaning, of course, the newly arrived lowrent Cityfolk as opposed to the newly arrived high class Countryfolk—had so far managed to both steal and eat almost everything old enough to graze.

I learned from an assistant statistical historian, one of Holly's aides apparently, that not one person associated with the Project—from the scientists currently staffing it to the scientists who had initially authorized it—had managed to grasp the Director's theories. No one else was smart enough to really follow it.

But they were, all of them, smart enough to know that Hollis Ware was smart enough. Or something.

Then it was over and I was shown to my suite. I peeled out of everything, took aim at the bed, and somebody tap-tapped on my door.

Karen stood swaying, so blonde and precious I could taste her skin. She took a deep breath.

"All right," she whispered. "No dancing."

"You mean fucking?" I asked cruelly.

She bit her lip. Her eyes were shining. She nodded.

I pulled her in and *slammed* the door.

VII

I woke up hearing Karen bitching away at some servant type in the anteroom. Something about trying to show a little decorum around the place for a change and how she would not accept having to apologize to the great Jack Crow himself about the slovenly attitude on this dreary planet and so on and so on. . . .

The great Jack Crow, me, missed the rest of her tirade trying to find the edge of the bed. I had the great hangover.

A few minutes later, sitting up at last and drinking the morning-after goodie some gentle soul had left there for me, I heard the outer door close behind her. Immediately after came the sound of gentle laughter followed by the muttered grumblings of somebody who knew better than to take such incredible rudeness seriously. I smiled to myself, found something to wear, and stumbled into the next room to confront the victim.

It was a man. A rather nice looking guy, about forty or so. He was a couple of inches shorter than me with short blond hair and a beautifully cropped van dyke a couple of shades darker. He was wearing Crew garb. The name Cortez was stenciled over his left breast pocket. He was sitting on the arm of a chair, looking desultorily at his watch and tapping his foot with gentle impatience. I liked him right away.

I made some sort of noise and he all but leaped to his feet and stood staring at me apprehensively. I let him worry while I fished out a cigarette and lit it. Then I gestured through the smoke toward the door.

"She always such a bitch?" I asked

Cortez got stiffer, looking surprised. Then, abruptly, he relaxed. He smiled brightly and warm, a much better sight, and answered. "Always, Mr. Crow."

I nodded with understanding and took another drag. He gestured toward a chair. "Wouldn't you like to sit down?" he offered.

I waved him away. "I think I better just sort of stand here a bit," I said, gesturing toward my hungover head meaning- fully. I leaned against the door jamb as if for support, though in fact the morning-after goodie had already done most of its job.

Cortez laughed pleasantly.

"Why do you take it?" I asked.

He looked at me, shrugged. "Well, you *are* Jack Crow, after all."

I sneered. "The great and famous Jack Crow, huh?"

He smiled. "The very one."

"Hmm. We'll get into that later on. But you still haven't answered my question. You said she was always a bitch."

"Well," he offered sheepishly, "she was always the Chief Administrator too."

"Oh."

"Yessir: 'oh.' "

I sniffed the air. "Is that coffee?"

He stepped quickly over to the side table set against the far wall. "Yes. I just made it. Would you like some?"

"Please." I found that I was almost completely recovered. I sat down in one of the three armchairs surrounding a low coffee table. It was an awfully pretty room, I noticed, for a Fleet Project

Cortez noticed my gaze as he sat the mug before me.

"This is the VIP room," he offered helpfully. "Only the brass rate this. The rest of us live in dormitories."

I nodded and sipped. It was good. "So what's this about her being the boss? I thought Hol . . . Dr. Ware was top dog?"

"He is. He's Director of Project. But she handles everything that doesn't immediately concern the research. There's quite a lot to do, you know, what with over five hundred Crew and families and the like."

"Hmm. Do all of you work on the research?"

He laughed. "God no. Most of us don't ever even come in here. This is my first time inside the ship since we grounded practically. Most of us are the support team. We keep the scientists fat and thoughtful."

"A noble cause, no doubt."

"No doubt," he replied, then added with a smile: "And it pays damn well, too."

I smiled in return. "What's your real job?"

"I'm hydroponics. I spend most of my time in the greenhouse at the far end of the valley."

"Don't they farm this area in the usual way? Soil looks good enough."

"Oh, it is, I suppose. But we, that is, the greenhouse crew, don't trust it. Those agro folk are, by tradition, foulups. We keep the greenhouse going on earth soil for when something comes along and wipes out all their careful work. Then we'll save everybody's ass, if you'll pardon the expression."

I laughed. Interdepartmental rivalries were the same everywhere.

"Well, have you had to come to the rescue yet? Have they fouled-up?"

"Not yet," he replied, then added with a twinkle, "But the day is young."

I laughed again and waved him toward an armchair. "Have some coffee or something and sit down and tell me the rest of it."

He was quick to take advantage of my offer, seating himself gratefully across from me. He sipped from his mug.

"You mean you really want to know about why we are so wonderful? Or just why the agros are genetically inferior?"

I laughed and waved him off. "I do not. For the sake of argument, I will immediately concede the vast superiority, genetic and intellectual. . . ."

"Don't forget sexual," he offered with another twinkle.

"All right, dammit. For your sake alone, I hereby declare that you guys are bloody supermen compared to the farmers. Okay?"

He nodded. "The least you could do."

"No doubt," I growled. "Now tell me about the rest of it. You say that Holly, Dr. Ware, is the Director of Project. That means he runs the thinking. And Karen. . . . What's her last name, anyway?"

"Wagner."

"Okay. Karen runs everything else."

"Right."

"But who has the final say? Surely, Dr. Ware. . . ."

"Oh, he's the final boss. That is to say, he's over her as far as Fleet is concerned. Course then there's Lewis."

"Who's Lewis?"

Cortez smiled. "Damned if I know, exactly."

I groaned. "You aren't being very helpful."

Cortez continued to smile. "I know I'm not. I don't mean to be vague. It's just that . . . Well, Lewis is an interesting story."

"Why not start it by telling me what he does around here."

"Lewis? Nothing."

"Nothing? I don't get it? Then what's he doing here on this planet?"

Cortez grinned delightedly. "He owns it."

I stared. "I beg your pardon?"

Cortez shrugged. "Just that. Lewis owns the place. The whole planet."

"But I thought this was Fleet territory."

"It's Fleet *Space*," he corrected. "And the planet, Sanction, was Fleet charted. But by the time anybody actually set foot on it from Fleet, Lewis was already here. He's the one who named it Sanction. First Citizen and all that."

"I see."

Cortez grinned again. "Maybe you don't yet. You see, the Project only *leases* this valley. It doesn't own a thing here. So, technically, Lewis is the real authority."

"You seem awfully happy about it."

He laughed. "Oh, I am. Everybody is. That is, everybody who's Crew is. The brass don't like it much."

"Fleet likes control."

"They do. But what they got here is . . . well, what they got is the Cityfolk. You know, the refugee settlement across the river."

"Hmm," I mumbled. "I had wondered about that."

"Yeah, so have the brass. You see, Lewis won't let anybody touch them. He won't even restrict their immigration except medically. And they keep coming."

"You like that?"

Cortez looked surprised. "Of course. Hell, how many Fleet Projects get to have a frontier town next door? Hell, I've done three years on places with no place to have fun but mercury lakes. Having that wide-open place is like a dream."

"I thought they didn't like you guys, you Project people."

Cortez waved that aside. "Oh, it's just the brass that they don't like. They love having us come by."

I nodded to myself, wondering if Cortez really believed what he had said. Or maybe he just didn't know how deep the hatred was. What he probably saw as just being a regular guy was, and was certainly recognized by the refugees as, slumming."

"Just the same," I offered gently, "you'd best be careful when you go over there."

Cortez grinned mischievously. "Oh, we know they're all just a bunch of deserters and low-rents. But they're a lot of fun, just the same. And I don't think there's really a place for being a snob out here. I mean, we're all stuck out here just the same. We oughta try to get along. Besides, we aren't real Wild-West. No private blazers is Lewis's policy, so how much damage could two drunks do barehanded? Fall over is 'bout all."

I didn't say, just thought, about a lady I'd met once who, barehanded, blind drunk, pregnant and squatting to piss, could move so fast she could kill any two drunks, or four, "a half-second before they can die, by God!"

I lit another cigarette to hide a sudden desire to scream at him. But I knew it wouldn't have done any good. It would only frighten him, clam him up, and then I wouldn't be able to get any other information from him later on.

But, dammit! How could he be so blind? How could he miss the danger? How could he not feel it when he walked across the river? Maybe he had and just ignored it. Or maybe he was just too far apart from them. Too far apart from the *idea* of them and from the idea that being "stuck out here together" was a notion that didn't apply to the frightened desperate mass across the river who now and forever would think of this place, not as a backwater saloon to be used and forgotten, but as . . . Home.

I started to say something then, to somehow try to get a bit of it across. But there was a soft gong from somewhere and a light appeared glowing on the ceiling

Cortez set down his mug and keyed something on the underside of the table. There was a loud click, followed by the forming of a holo above the table surface. A man's head and shoulders appeared in the air.

"Who is . . . Oh, Cortez! Is he up yet?"

Cortez looked questioningly at me. Evidentally I was out of range. I nodded. Cortez looked at the display. "He's up."

"Good," replied the figure in the air. Could you tell him that Holly wants to see him. You know, Dr. Ware sends his compliments and all that sort of crap. And would he please come at his convenience?"

Cortez nodded, hiding his smile with a hand on his chin. "I know what to do. Where's he supposed to go?"

"The lab."

"Okay, I'll tell him."

"Thanks, Cortez. Out."

"Out," Cortez replied and keyed off. He looked at me. "When is it convenient?" he asked with a smile.

"Now," I said firmly.

"Oh," he said quickly, abashed. "I'll get your clothes together."

"Thanks," I said at his rapidly retreating back. I put out

the cigarette and leaned against the back of the chair with a sigh.

May as well get to it. Sooner I started, the sooner I could finish. And then, of course, the sooner I could start to forget what I had done.

VIII

The ship would never lift again. The Crew had made it a permanent fixture on Sanction by scattering windows here and there and brightening up the upper passageways with skylights. In order to maintain structural integrity in space, it would require the kind of tooling found only in Fleet Shipyards. I supposed it was no great loss. The ship had never had much control or power, requiring tractor steering the entire trip. Still it never failed to astonish me the way Fleet tossed about the taxpayers' money. And, of course, the changes were a definite improvement for its residents. It now seemed more like an office complex than a starship. More like part of the land than a tunnel that must be entered in order to get paid.

Cortez insisted on escorting me to Holly's workshop. It was lucky that I gave in. The place was *huge*. And despite the alterations, it still bore that twisting-turning efficiency of starships which is so confusing to newcomers. It took only a few minutes to make me confused. And not long after that I was practically light-headed trying to keep up with our gyrations. I stopped abruptly. I cannot stand to be lost.

"Show me where we are," I demanded.

"Sir?" he asked nervously.

I relaxed, smiled, explained the problem. He nodded and squatted down. He began to carve a rude map in the furrows of the carpeting with his finger. "See," he began, "we've come down four levels and over this way, past two of the bulkheads. We've been traveling east the whole way."

I shook my head. "Then why all the spiraling around?"

He grinned. "That's only the structural compression assembly. It's built into the lifts and into all the dropshafts and stairwells." He stood up. "It's a lot of bother, I know. And if you ask me, it's also a waste of good credits as long as we have the shield. But I will say one thing, when Fleet strands you in some God-knows-where for three years, they strand you safe."

I was still hearing the part about the shield. I asked what shield.

He looked surprised. "The defensive shield, of course. That's what I mean by compression assembly being a waste of credits. Nothing can get past that screen once it's in place. So we hardly need to be a fort to boot. And besides, I don't buy that structural compression idea anyhow. Conform doesn't bend. It cracks. I don't care how many knots you tie into it."

Cortez continued to complain as we resumed our previous pace. Trying to follow what he was saying was all the more difficult as he seemed to think I already knew what he was talking about. And after a while I decided that that was a very good way to leave it. For what I was getting seemed to be crucial to Borglyn's little scheme.

The main thing was the overall make-up of the Project Complex itself. It was a goddamned fortress. Heavy defensive screens were only the beginning of it (though I had never, in fact, counted on their being so powerful). After the screens came the shape of the dome itself, the structural compression assembly part. What SCA was, it turned out, was sort of a spring that ran connected throughout the outer bulkhead sealing in such a way as to allow the entire structure to compress when one side of it was attacked—like by heavy-bore artillery.

There was more. Eight blazer cannon where installed within the outer rim of the Complex, each controlled by the Master

Ground Control in the depths of the inner dome where the Auxiliary Control Network had been when the ship was aloft. There were other things as well, blaze-bomb catapults and a couple of dozen remote-controlled blazers as well. Evidently some were useless, since the dome had been wedged into the foot of a small hill on its eastern edge. But that still left quite a nut to crack.

I had to get busy in a hurry. I could think of at least four major perimeter systems alone that would have to be disengaged. Of course the dome would still be a fort. But I doubted that would be enough to comfort any stragglers.

At last we arrived in the passageway outside of Holly's chambers. "He sleeps and works here both," Cortez told me. "Sometimes he eats here too, they say." Then he keyed the outer door and we were inside.

The waiting area was crowded with scientist types mumbling argumentatively around a conference table over which was strewn a bewildering array of computer printout viewers and chart screens. They looked up and eyed me rather drearily as we entered. It wasn't especially rude. Only the kind of look any non-scientist (read: mere mortal) would have received. Cortez smiled in their direction and crossed the room to another door. He punched a key out and then muttered something into the grille I couldn't hear. I lit a cigarette and tried to look like a partisan. Or at least a fan. Cortez rejoined me and spoke too softly for anyone else to hear:

"They don't look very happy, do they?" he said, nodding toward the others.

"What are they doing here?"

"Waiting to see the doctor. Looks like they've been here a while."

So we stood there. I smoked and stared at the ceiling. Cortez sat down. The scientists continued to eye me uncomfortably. It was more, I knew, than just the fact that I was a stranger. It was my pirate's reputation that offended their scholarly dignity. How odd, I thought, that men and women whose very careers revolved around being open-minded were so often stodgy late-century moralists. Unless, of course, it came to their latest theory.

After a few minutes one of them came over to me and

began to speak rapidly in heavily accented standard about partial-waves and inertial development. It wasn't until several seconds after he had stopped that I realized he'd asked me a question and was waiting for my answer. I looked away, trying to be creatively vague and saw that Lya had just entered the room from the far side.

"Excuse me," I muttered to the man and stepped forward to meet her. She offered me her hand.

"Good morning, Mr. Crow," she said pleasantly.

I took her hand. It was firm and cool. "Call me Jack," I suggested.

She smiled. "How nice to have a choice. I'm afraid Lya is all I have to offer you. Trankien have only one name."

"How do you tell each other apart if you have the same name?"

"Oh, well, we each have a number as well."

"A number?" I frowned. "Not very romantic."

She dimpled. Delightful. "We make up for that in other ways," she replied.

Cortez grinned a knowing grin. "Well, I guess I can go now. See you later, Jac . . . Mr. Crow."

"Cortez," I acknowledged stiffly, annoyed at his leering.

Lya seemed not to notice. She turned to the scientist type still standing there and waiting for the answer to his question. "Dr. Angovitch, please allow me to take Mr. Crow from you."

Angovitch nodded the way people nod when they don't care what you are saying—they're just glad you stopped—and went right ahead with the amplification of his already too-technical questioning.

"Dr., please," she insisted with an arched eyebrow, "The Director is waiting."

At the mention of Holly's title, the man shut up as if he had been switched off. He nodded formally, if a trifle stiffly, to each of us and joined the crowd back at the conference table. Lya smiled at his retreating form the way an indulgent mother smiles at a trying, yet not unloved, child. Then she turned back to me, all brightness and hospitality again, and motioned us toward the inner door.

"Thanks," I said to her gratefully. "I really wasn't up to his conversational style."

She laughed. "It is a little early in the morning for shop-talk, I imagine." She glanced at me sideways. "Particularly after the night you just put in."

I searched her glance. Was she talking about the booze? Or the booze and Karen? Probably the latter. I didn't figure this one would miss something like that under her own roof.

"Well," I continued honestly, "it's never late enough for me as far as that stuff is concerned. He wanted to know a bunch of technical stuff about blaze-drive retrograde. Over my head."

She looked surprised. "But you developed the Blaze-Drive."

"I *stole* it," I corrected her. "Quan Tri developed it."

"Oh. I see."

"Do you?"

She smiled. It was a lovely smile. "No," she admitted and we both laughed again. "We have time for a quick tour before seeing Holly. That is, if you're interested in seeing our little shop. Are you?"

"Very," I answered which was true but dishonest.

A few minutes later she asked: "How technical would you like me to be?" and I answered: "As technical as you like," which was both untrue and dishonest.

So, of course, from that moment on I didn't understand a damn thing she was saying. Oh, I got the overall picture well enough, thanks to the briefing I had had back in the mutineer Borglyn's stateroom. And I suppose there was a thing or two about statistical history that I gathered up during those few moments among the computer banks. But essentially, the trip was only good for one thing—I discovered the seal into Master Ground Control. Trying to be subtle, I couldn't ask many questions about it, particularly since I had asked hardly any questions about anything else. I did find out, however, that there was another entrance and that it was direct to the outer dome. I logged that with stars beside it. I would have to learn how to get down there without going through all of the other seals. And, come to think of it, that would be a better way to bring Borglyn's people in as well. Maybe the whole thing could be over and done with before anyone had a chance to argue.

It was nice being with Lya, too. Well, not completely. For it made me wonder why it was that this sort of woman never wants a man like me. The great women, it seemed to me, wanted the gentle Hollys of the universe. And Holly's being a better outlet for maternal instincts didn't explain it either, I admitted grudgingly, when I noted the way she kissed him when we found him at last at a workbench. She kissed him in the unmistakable style of a woman who wanted him as a man. And maybe also in a way to make me aware of that fact, I thought, recalling Cortez's foolish behavior a few minutes earlier.

I noticed all of this while my stomach was dropping. Before him, on the workbench, Holly had the black suit laid out all disassembled and . . . disemboweled. Interface circuit sheets and piping and micronic lacing, each carefully tagged and colorcoded, seemed to have been blown, spewing, from the chest cavity. It looked like a corpse.

It wasn't a corpse and I knew that it wasn't, had known so since the first glance, however shaken I had felt, but still it looked . . . dead. Not inanimate. Not machinelike. Dead.

I shuddered.

Lya noticed my movement. She nodded without taking her eyes off of it. "I hate that thing," she offered firmly.

I nodded. So did I.

Holly, wearing a headset, had evidently not heard my approach. But when I nodded he must have caught the motion out of the corner of his eye. He turned to me and smiled and said, "Morning, Jack!" in that too-loud tone one has when feeling that irrational need to speak up over the level of earphones.

He waved a prodder key toward the suit. "Whadya think? Huh?" he asked cheerfully and, of course, loudly. I smiled dumbly. Lya moved toward him with an indulgent grimace, motioning at him to remove the headset. Holly hadn't yet noticed her approach. With a smile toward me, he playfully extended the prodder key until it contacted the edge of the unfolded micronic lacing. As it touched, the right hand jerked into an armored fist.

Lya gasped. We both jumped.

Holly, still smiling, looked back and forth between our two pale faces a couple of times before getting the message. "Oh, shit," he barked suddenly, as it dawned on him. He leaned back on his stool and un-keyed the power.

"Sorry if I startled you," he said, slipping off the earphones and extending his palm. We shook hands. He waved at the suit. "Damned impressive, huh?"

I nodded. "A little spooky, too."

Lya rubbed her arms briskly. "More than a little."

"So how's it going?" I asked. "Learn anything?"

He looked sheepish. "Having too much fun so far."

I laughed. "What about the recorder pod? Have you played the coil?"

He shook his head. "Something's wrong there. I'm having a lot of trouble with the display mode. I finally quit until I had a chance to fashion something with a more delicate touch than our standard gear. I'm afraid I might lose what little might be left otherwise."

"You think some of it's been lost?"

He shrugged. "It's years old, after all. Easy to lose your foundation charge in all that time. Passing through all those different fields."

I frowned. "Well, I'm sorry, Holly. I had no idea."

"Oh, no-no-no," he said hurriedly, appalled at the notion of my unease. "It's wonderful, Jack. Really. Even without the coil it would be. And I'm *sure* I can tease out something of value. It's just a matter of tuning the output patterns." He glanced guiltily at the cluttered workbench. "I should have been at it hours ago instead of . . . well."

"Instead of playing soldier," offered Lya dryly. But gently.

He grinned a shy grin, hid his hands in his pockets. Then, with a determined shrug, out they came once more. He faced the workbench with studied will.

"I'll get started right away. Soon as I do a little rearranging." He began to sort through the tangle.

"Holly," called Lya with quiet emphasis. "We didn't come here to make sure you were working, Dear."

He missed the signal. He nodded without turning. "Just take a second . . ."

Lya smiled her exasperation at me rather than hide it. "Holly," she tried again.

"Oh, there's no problem," he assured her in the same absent tone. "It's just a matter of constructing a baffled relay. . . ."

She sighed and gave up. She put a hand on his shoulder and turned him around. Her voice held the unmistakable shade of a cue; one damn well not to be ignored.

"Well, you don't have to do it right this instant. Besides, it's lunchtime and you've been wanting to talk to Jack since yesterday—you know you have, Holly—and I think it's a good time for the two of you to get acquainted."

Holly had turned red at her words. He looked sheepishly at me again. Like a little boy meeting the star of the vid instead of an all-universe brain. I smiled encouragingly in return while admonishing myself never to get the two personalities confused. He may be a kid. But he was the smartest one I had ever seen.

Lunch was awkward. Holly away from his lab was pure adolescent where I was concerned. He stumbled and started and in all ways looked the part of somebody with a million questions burning inside but afraid to ask them for fear of looking as awkward as he felt. It made me nervous.

I knew what he wanted, of course: Jack Crow Stories. But I wasn't really up to that, for some reason. I made do with the tails of tales and a little name dropping. Some of it was true.

As soon as I could, I tried to get the subject back onto Holly's work and my alleged fascination with it. Not to mention my eagerness to help.

"What made you so interested?" asked Lya in an innocent tone I couldn't quite be sure of.

I mumbled something in return, moving quickly to: "The thing is, Holly, I'm not sure if I can be of any help at all. This is all pretty technical to me." Which was a good way to avoid substance (and complicated lies) while sliding in a complimentary and admiring tone toward Holly.

Holly loved it, launching into a long and unconvincing diatribe about how he could always use what he referred to as "conceptual help" which meant, essentially, thinking up areas of research instead of concentrating on specific data as only a trained tech could do.

He was full of shit. But he meant well, I knew. And, clearly, he did seem to believe that having me around was going to be worth his while, if only so he could gawk at me.

His lack of specific conviction on the subject of my usefulness made everyone a little nervous. So we broke up the meal soon after that. He gave me a tape explaining the general areas in which he was currently involved. "Not too technical, really," he hoped more than meant. But I accepted the tape anyway and promised to get right at it.

"Fine," he said. "You think maybe we could talk at dinner? Not about shop," he added quickly. "Just in general. Sort of social."

"I'd love to," I said with sincerity and so we got through lunch without any of us having to break down and actually face the questions that counted. Such as: Just what the hell was I doing there? How did I get there? How long was I going to stay? What was going on? in other words.

I went through the motions because they suited my plans. Holly did because he loved having me around. Lya . . . well, she didn't buy it, I could tell. But she didn't seem particularly suspicious, either. Not yet.

But she'd want to know soon. Sooner than Holly. And probably a lot sooner than I wanted to tell her.

I dropped the tape off in my rooms without a glance. Then I headed outside, wandering lost only briefly, until I found the main scal. Security on the outer dome pointed me in the right direction. So I headed back across the bridge, toward the city and the refugees and, among them, my contact with Borglyn. Toward, in fact, exactly what in the hell I was doing there.

IX

I stopped on the near side of the bridge and lit a cigarette. Before me, due west, a storm was spilling over the top of the shale bluffs that formed the far perimeter of the valley. Thick blue mists trailing faint tendrils were beginning to darken the shade of the rock. A gentle glimmering moisture was gliding down the slope toward the City. I figured the storm would be on the bridge in less than an hour.

I blew out smoke and glanced around. It was the first opportunity I had had to get my bearings. Here it was still a pretty day. Here it was damn near Earth. Sloping flatlands. Blue sky. A clear blue river that sparkled cheerfully past the milk-white Complex dome. I shook my head in wonder. It wasn't Earth at all. But it could have been.

I had been to maybe two dozen planets like this. None of them had been Earth either. But they were man places just the same. It gave me the creeps.

Some thinker types claimed it was because Homo Sap was the perfect model for the universe. They cited things like bi-symmetry and opposing limbs and (ever since finding Ants) something called Adaptation By Individual to explain it. These weren't just made for man, they said. Man was made for them. Man was the model. I didn't buy it. I had drunk water and swatted flies on alien soil again and again and they had been man *places*. I had felt that with a subtle certainty. I still did.

Another idea used the model for the universe bit as well but extended it to mean that there were Homo Saps out there who had nothing to do with Earth at all. These other guys were supposed to have sprung full-blown from another place but be just like us. The thinkers who thought this thought something else. They thought we would run into them and soon. A statistical certainty, they claimed, that these other Saps would be along. I remember once seeing a vid on it with one guy claiming they would show up any minute and another guy boshing it with the question of how would we know if we ran into a new bunch or not, as spread out and weird as we already were. Maybe they were already here and we didn't know it, the guy had added and laughed.

The first guy hadn't laughed at all. He had just smiled politely. But the smile and the courtesy didn't stop the twinkle in his eyes from coming across. That had given me the creeps too. Man places.

I glanced back across the river toward the squalor of the City. Whoever these new folks were, I sure hoped they were neater. We're quite a bunch, I believe, but it's obscene what we do to our worlds.

It took me half an hour to reach the edge of the mess. The City's eastern boundary was marked by a second bridge that crossed what had once been a gently babbling brook. It was mostly sewer now. I stopped at the far end of the bridge, hesitant to go any farther. The rain was really coming down now. Clouds of it whipped up and down the narrow passages between the junkpile homes rusting everything that wasn't treated, driving everyone indoors and, of course, making more mud. I noted a couple of bootprints that looked knee deep and shuddered. I didn't want to go in there.

It wasn't just the mud. It wasn't just that this was another refugee camp, for I had seen those plenty of times. It was. . . . Even without the driving rain the City was dark. Dark and dreary and hopeless and clogged with despair. It was the

Antwar, maybe and the Fleet Project sneering downward at them. There was a texture of paranoia. A tragic uneasiness. Guilt.

It wasn't a happy place.

I took a deep breath and stepped calf-deep into the mud. It got a little better as I worked my way up from the creek bank toward the central "square," head bowed against the rain and my boots splashing against the minor torrents of runoff rain. Borglyn had said I would know which passage to take by a huge steeple constructed at the entrance to one of the paths. There was no sign of anything even faintly religious from where I stood, but that could simply have been the weather. It was now dark enough for sundown. I shrugged and picked the widest lane.

It shrunk so fast it made your heart ache, ending abruptly against a sheer wall of curved and warped plassteel three stories high. I backed out and turned around eagerly.

The next lane was worse. It narrowed at the first bend and then narrowed again at the second. There were two more sharp twists within the next few meters, making the passage tunnel-like beneath jutting scags of warped bulkhead plates. I paused in the darkness to wipe the rain from my eyes. From the shadows to my right came a long wheezing moan. I blinked, took a soggy, slippery step toward the sound. I heard the moan again and saw, tucked uneasily into what had once been an emergency recess panel, an old man. He was wrapped up poorly against the rain and growing cold with the sort of rags that this place would have created.

There was a faint click and a further movement of shadow that formed a little boy or a little girl wearing the same sort of rags and a determined look. A knife gleamed dully in a tiny but steady hand.

"You want something, Mr.?" asked a voice belonging to a trapped animal, which was just what he/she was.

"No," I replied, stepping back with my hands held out where they could be seen. I backed away a few more steps, then stopped. "I'm looking for the steeple," I called into the shadows. "You know where that is?"

There was no reply. I repeated my question and waited. Then I moved back up the path, again holding my hands where they could be seen. The recess was empty. No ragged old man, no desperate child. Both had disappeared into the maze of the place.

I knew better than to pursue that determined kid. I backed out around the corners and started up the next path. A few steps up there was piercing flash of lightning out of the east followed by a truly awful peal of thunder. Between shaking from one and jumping at the other I caught sight of what had once been the steeple. It lay over on one side blocking the passageway. It was black with soot from a recent fire. I stepped through the charred latticework of its universal elongated pyramid design. The spot where I braced myself was already worn smooth from the passage of many other muddy fingertips. The going got a little easier after that. Easier to see, anyway, for people were starting to turn their lights on inside their little cubicles or apartments or monk's cells or whatever you should call the junk around a refugee village. Apartments seems best, if you can imagine a giant like say, Thor, ripping spacecraft apart, just tearing cabins loose one by one like a child separating the petals on a flower, and then stacking what was left to make three-story nightmares. I couldn't imagine what made them huddle on top of one another like that. Sure, some of the ''buildings'' were made up of whole bulkhead seals on end and they usually came in threes. But most of the junk had just been wedged up there on purpose, as if they were shoved together by the timid members of some herd ready to accept anything, even smothering, to avoid the outer edges of the campfire where wolves could prowl and chase. It wouldn't matter to those folk that the wolves were inside with them. A new planet carries a primordial chill.

Anyway, mid-afternoon or not, the lights were beginning to come on. The rain had shrunk to little more than a sprinkling trickle. The thunder continued, but it was a distant rumble now accompanied by distant swellings of orange light rising unevenly from the edges of the craggy twisted skyline.

Borglyn had told me that once I had found the steeple I would be home free. He had said to stay on the main path with the steeple all the way to the end and I would be there. It was a lot easier trip the way he had told it. I was beginning to get an idea as to the size of this place. Within the next hundred meters or so I must have passed a dozen side paths—many of which were just as impressive as the one I was following. I trusted to direction for the most part, though even with this policy I ran the risk of getting lost. *Everything* twisted here. Every path, every alley, every bulkhead. I didn't even bother to try to ignore what that could've meant omen-wise; the way things were looking so far, I was already screwed anyway.

"It beats prison," I caught myself saying once out loud and wondered how often that had happened without my having noticed it before.

Just about then, it all got a little tighter.

I saw the bouncing, bobbing glow of their lamps first, coming around a corner of one of the side paths. Instinctively, I crouched back into a recess as they appeared.

There were five of them, all men it seemed in that light, stumbling hurriedly into the passage just ahead of me. Three of them carried lamps. Two of them carried—dragged someone between them. All had a knife or a club or some sort of weapon. They increased their pace when they got onto the passageway I had been following, looking back over their collective shoulders for pursuit. I held still where I was to give them a chance to put a little distance between us. I was now no longer sure whether or not I wanted to continue. Well, let's say I knew I didn't want to go up behind them. I had never wanted to go. But now I wasn't sure whether I should. I didn't want to get brained as one of the pursuers they obviously expected. But on the other hand. . . .

The pursuit showed up then, answering it for me. They came up from behind me, stomping rapidly past, about six, I guessed, without even seeing me in their determined chase. More knives and more clubs. I shuddered to think what would have happened if I had been standing in the middle of the path like the hapless fool I was when they had rounded the corner. Would they have stopped to see who I was? Or would they have simply splattered me first as a matter of course?

At any rate they were past and I was safe and the best thing to do was leave the way I came. But I followed with only slight hesitation.

It was tough keeping up with this bunch. They moved very quickly through the muck, without need for lights or whispered instructions. They seemed to know a lot more about their surroundings than the first group.

They lost me. Try as I might, I couldn't keep up with their stealthy, lethal gait. But I did get there in time for the fight.

I heard it before I saw it. Grunts and groans, boots stomping into mud and faces, the air-whirring of metal bludgeons swung wide and hard. I skidded to a halt in the mud at the first sound of anguish and crept around the last bend. It was impossible to tell which side was which. But I counted on the faster movers being the better fighters. From that reckoning, the chasers were beating the living hell out of the chased. The lamps were scattered about, sinking into the mud. From their dim ghostly glows I could just see a lone man through the moving forest of arms and legs up ahead of the struggle. He was crawling along somewhat frantically, dragging the limp form of another. The prisoner from before, obviously. He was trying to reach the entrance of a building which loomed like a cave-mouth before him. Belatedly I realized that this building was my destination as well, for it marked the end of this passageway.

Just then a figure burst loose from the struggle and leaped toward the one doing the dragging. He held a pipe in one muddy fist. The man on the ground released his burden and jumped to his feet to meet the charge. He showed a long ugly knife. The two sparred for a few moments, dodging and feinting with their respective weapons. Then they closed. There was a spark as they grappled, a sudden twisting urgency, then the man with the knife slid to the mud between the other's feet. The victor dropped his pipe in favor of the knife and moved over to the figure on the ground.

The rest of the fighting was over, the pursuers having finished the job on the pursued. The remaining five rushed over to join the man with the knife huddling over the now-liberated prisoner. Great effort was put into trying to inject a little life into the limp form. Someone lifted the head and gave the face a gentle slap. That was when I saw that it was a girl.

But the fighting wasn't over. The cave mouth was suddenly filled with more men carrying more clubs and pipes and knives. The girl was dropped gently back into the mud and the killing began again. More sparks and more groans. Someone died sinking to his knees and clutching the knife sunk into his chest to the hilt. Someone else died quicker, when a pipe connected with an awful crunching noise. It was very fast. And it was the same as before. Whoever she was, she was important to them. The rescuers fought so well for her that I thought the whole thing was over in a moment. And it would've been. But just as they went to pick her up and carry her away for once and for all a huge fat man loomed into view from the dead-end shadows carrying a blazer in his right fist. The blue arcing beam blinded me as it burst from the shadows. I heard screams and several men trying to run but by then it was too late, had been when he had appeared. In seconds each of the five lay dead, seared through by the latest of man's new clubs.

"Thank God, Wice!" gushed one of the fallen, surveying what was left of the rescue party about him. Wice, the fat man with the blazer and, I saw then, the fat man from the trouble on the bridge my first day, ignored the show of gratitude. Others appeared beside him from inside the building. One of them had been the dark skinny one on the bridge. Wice motioned him toward the girl, motioned the rest toward the casualties.

"Clean this up. Now!" he barked in that distinctive snarl. The others hurried to obey. I sighed. Wice was the name of my contact. Deeper and deeper.

In a few moments the area was almost clear. The dead had been dragged away. The wounded had been helped inside. Only Wice remained in the doorway, watching the skinny with the girl.

"Gettle!" whispered Wice impatiently to the skinny. "Is she awake?"

Gettle spoke without taking his eyes from her. "Well, I *thought* she was!"

Wice surveyed the area warily. "Well, never mind now.

Just bring her in. Come on!'' he ordered bluntly. With one last glance around, he slipped back into the shadows of the doorway. Gettle pushed a lock of black hair away from his face and bent to lift the girl. She lolled lifelessly in his arms. Then they too were gone.

I gave them maybe two seconds before I started my splashing sloshing way across the clearing toward the doorway. I stopped just outside the opening, listening. I knew what was coming, but that didn't mean I wanted to become a part of it.

I heard footsteps just inside the door on a rickety stairway that creaked and rustled rhythmically. I slipped inside and followed the sound. In the dim lamp shining down the stairwell I saw her make her move. He had had her in a fireman's carry to negotiate the narrow passage. She began by driving an elbow into the back of his neck . . . collapsed stunned to his knees, arms up to protect his face . . . her feet dribbled against his chest . . . a flat-handed *smack* against his forehead. . . .

Then she leaped easily over him and trotted down the stairs and froze stock-still before me. Her eyes shown wide and . . . and spectacular in the lamp. So deep! So green! Emeralds floating, glistening. . . .

I blocked her first forearm, sidestepped the kick and brought her shoulder out of position for the killing blow by pulling her roughly and unexpectedly to me. She gasped as her eyes, her incredible *eyes*, met mine. Was it recognition, astonishment at her effect on me? Was it a reciprocal delight? Maybe? Possibly? I blocked another forearm, slipped a flat-hand uppercut, twisted beside her kick and. . . . And did nothing. Nothing at all. I didn't fight back, had no thoughts of doing so. I just didn't want her to hurt me.

Or maybe, I thought suddenly, I just don't want her to leave.

And as I hesitated with that thought, she left, slipping past me and out into the black afternoon and mud. She was gone.

I closed my eyes. Hers floated clearly still before me. Such *eyes*!

Gettle was coming to. I wrestled him out of his impossible position on the stairs.

''C'mon, Gettle. We've got to get to Wice!'' I urged him.

"Huh? Wha. . . . Wice?" he mumbled, dazedly.

"Yeah, Wice! C'mon," I added conspiratorially. "We've got to tell him what really happened."

He sat up, holding his head. "What do you . . . Hey! The girl! Where's the girl?"

"That's it, Gettle! The girl's gone off! We've got to tell Wice. Hurry up, damn you!" I dragged him to his feet and shoved him a couple of steps up the stairs. He stopped, still hesitant. I shoved him again,

"Dammit, Gettle! You want him to find out from somebody else?"

That did it. Mumbling, "Yeah, yeah, yeah," he staggered ahead, semi-waving for me to follow.

I did. And so we passed through much of the labyrinth that made up Wice's lair. Gettle, weaving and stumbling and not quite running into things up ahead of me, led us down several faintly illuminated corridors and through several manned doorways. For the most part I ignored the scum standing guard. Occasionally, when one looked too alarmed at my presence, I would wink or shrug or smile and gesture obscenely at Gettle's lack of coordination. That got me up several flights of stairs and through many ugly possibilities.

Suddenly, Gettle stopped. He slumped down to the floor before a handful of steps jury-rigged to make easier the transition from one level to another that was, on second glance, a joint between plassteel bulkheads from two different ships. He held his head with both hands. He rocked forward on his buttocks, grimacing in pain. She, Eyes, had really belted him. I stifled a smile and leaned forward to help him up. He glanced up at me in bewilderment. "Who are you?" he asked before recognition descended.

"You!" he screeched in an uneven, harsh whisper before I clamped my right hand around his throat.

I didn't waste time with threats. I simply lifted him to his feet from there, gripping down on his throat as much as I figured he could take. Once on his feet I pressed the back of his head against the wall just beneath a lamp. His face looked green and scared. It had every reason to be.

"Wice!" I hissed meaningfully, flexing my fingers. "Wice!"

He didn't even have to think about it. He gestured with one

limp hand and off we went again. I removed my fingers from his throat but retained a firm grip on his left shoulder as we moved along—he knew what was what.

The only hazard was a guard standing before the most impressive door we had passed so far. It was made out of something that was either wood or could pass for it. It was wide and squat and had a huge door latch. It was obviously the boss's place. The guard eased forward from just off the side and raised a huge right arm in a gesture meant to slow us down for proper admittance procedure. I kicked him in the balls. We both stepped over him. Gettle worked the latch. I slammed him through the opening door and faced Wice, standing up angrily on the far side of his messy office.

"You! Crow," he shouted angrily and reached down for what I figured for the blazer.

I ignored him. I found what passed for an easy chair in that dump and plopped down in it across from the desk. Gettle was doubled over on the floor whimpering. I ignored him, too. Wice came around from behind the desk carrying the blazer. He stopped beside Gettle and glowered at the pair of us. He was mad.

"What's the idea, Crow? You still trying to show everybody how tough you are?" He looked down at Gettle again and shook his head. "I'm getting pretty sick of you," he added menacingly, tightening his grip on the blazer.

I lit a cigarette. "Does Borglyn know you're using his blazer to carve up locals?" I asked calmly.

"The blazer's mine," he retorted furiously. "What I do with it is my business—get that straight." He slammed the pistol from one hand to the other for emphasis and then pointed the butt at me. "And get this, too. You keep stomping around here playing big man with my men and I'm gonna show you just how lucky you were that first time!"

There was a loud banging on the stairs outside followed by five lackeys jamming themselves into the room. Gettle looked up at their approach and smiled sourly at me through bleeding lips. He stood up straight and joined them while they took turns staring back and forth between Wice and me and waiting for the order to "Sic 'im!"

Wice gestured meaningfully in their direction before

continuing. "You got it, Crow? We can get done what needs getting done or it can get tough. What's it gonna be?"

I had been watching this whole deal from a distance, without feeling or rhythm. It was a long-hated feeling, like being a step behind. It blundered me ahead badly.

"I'll tell you, Wice," I began, all thumbs. "I don't much care. We can work if you want." I tapped an ash to the floor. "But we don't have to and I'm not sure I like the idea anyway." And then I stood up, abruptly, anger roaring through me from out of nowhere. I slammed the cigarette to the floor, scattering sparks. "I'm tired of dealing with scum like this, with cowards and deserters and bullies. Your threats don't mean anything to me. I can still go either way." I pointed a shaking finger. "I pounded you once. I can pound you again. And I can crater this bunch at the same time!" I wheeled toward them "Who wants to be first?"

Gettle answered in a low, sinister tone: "Maybe everyone."

"That's fine, too," I retorted, now shaking all over.

Wice stared at me like I was crazy. Which, of course, I was. I don't know. That cloudy picture! Wice, Borglyn, me—we were all so bizarre!

Especially me.

Wice kept staring for several moments, then relaxed. He sighed, shook his head. Was that compassion I saw in his eyes? Or flat pity?

"Say the word," prompted Gettle, tensing.

"Shut up, Gettle!" barked Wice, suddenly angry again. "Shut up and get the hell out."

Gettle and company stared at him, unbelieving. But they left. Slowly for Gettle, hoping for a change of heart. It didn't happen. We were alone.

Wice nodded toward the closing door. "Him I oughta let you stomp again," he suggested, going back around to his desk.

"Didn't the first time," I offered, resuming my seat. "Some girl was doing that on my way in."

That froze him halfway into his chair. "What? Is she gone?"

I nodded. "We passed over his whimpers."

"Why didn't you stop her?"

"What for?" I asked, lighting another cigarette. "Far as I know, that's her job around here—to teach your punks what tough is."

He mumbled something angrily at me under his breath and left. I sat and smoked and listened to him growling orders to his people in the hallway. He came back in after a full minute of that and resumed his seat. He looked disgusted.

"If you saw the blazer, you saw the fight. You knew we wanted her."

"That's true, Wice," I agreed.

His fat face got very red. Was *that* it? Was it my always just hating fat men?

"You rotten son of a bitch!" he growled, accusing.

"What the hell do your little local feuds have to do with me? I've got nothing to do with that!"

He blinked. His anger disappeared. He looked genuinely surprised. "You mean you really don't know?"

"Huh?" I blurted, as stupidly as I felt. "Know what?"

But he just shook his head again. "Never mind," he said. He sat forward in his chair and reached for a cigar. His voice was businesslike. "What about the Project's defense screens? Can you get to them?"

"I can do it. When do you *need* it?"

"Don't know yet," he said, lighting his cigar. "We may want to wait awhile."

"How long?"

"Don't know yet," he repeated, eyeing me. "Maybe as long as a standard month. Can you handle that? What's your setup over there with those people?"

"Just let me know."

Wice puffed a couple of irritated puffs. "All right, Crow. Go ahead and play independent. But you may need me later on."

"Not likely," I replied coldly.

"Okay, dammit!" he retorted, stung. "Just tell me this much—what do they know about me?"

"You?" I echoed, surprised. "Nothing."

"Well, then, what do you plan to tell 'em when they find out you've been coming here? Or did you really think there were secrets in a place this small?"

I felt my cheeks heating up with embarrassment. I hadn't even considered the problem. Even worse, Wice could see that I hadn't.

But he let it slide.

"Tell 'em we met on Illyre," he pushed on. "During your piracy trial."

I sat up. "What do you know about that?"

"I know about it. Saw most of it. Cost me a half term's worth of credits for court tickets." He smiled then. "But I was there at the end."

Now what the hell was this? Admiration? *Damn* the bastard!

"Well sorry to disappoint you by getting off," I said sourly, which was damned idiotic for me to say. But why the hell not? I was *being* an idiot, wasn't I?

I stood up to leave before I got any worse. Between Wice's insulting me and admiring me and my own dazed, thumb-fingered lack of touch, I knew it couldn't get anything else but.

I stopped at the door and looked back. Wice was eyeing me without emotion through the cigar smoke. I had a sudden adolescent desire to shatter that.

"Tell me, Wice, how did you and Borglyn get together? Is there a regular meeting place for deserters?"

Wice frowned. He looked disappointed, as if . . . I had let him down.

"We met on Banshee," he answered evenly. "A year ago."

"A year ago? Wice, you're full of bull! Banshee was destroyed two years ago!"

He stared. And then instead of looking insulted, he looked amused. A smile began to form at the corners of his mouth. "Destroyed? Is *that* what they're saying?" The smile became a chuckle and then a laugh. "Destroyed, eh?"

"Well, all the Ants, anyway," I added lamely.

That only made him laugh all the harder. A bitter, knowing laugh.

"What's so goddamned funny, Wice?" I demanded desperately.

He looked at me and stopped laughing. But the smile, now

bitter throughout, remained. "Never mind, Jack," he said in a patronizing tone. "You wouldn't understand."

I jerked the door open angrily, stopped, barked acidly back: "Or care."

He only nodded. "Or care," he agreed reasonably.

I went hurriedly out, slamming the door behind me. I made too much noise stomping away to be able to hear it if he was laughing behind me.

So bizarre. . . .

X

Grumbling, I retraced my steps back through the maze. The rain was over for now. The last bit of sunlight slanted out over the western bluffs and sparkled, steaming, on the grimy rooftops. There were several people out, milling around and surveying storm damage. Some were already busy with repairs. Much of their work appeared to my untrained eye as little more than glueing seams back together. I saw no more dying old men, no more fierce children. I figured I still had a couple of hours before my dinnertime/showdown with Holly and Lya. I decided to get a drink.

The way back was harder. Clouds soon obscured the last of the sun making it even darker than before. Yellow pools of light spilled out at me from doorways and windows and hatches opened wide to combat the heavy humidity. I was left alternately blind and blinded.

I found the ''square'' with difficulty. It had become, with the rain, a broad reflecting pool. And without any lighting of its own, it was visible only by the gliding contrasts between long shadows cast, spreading and bobbing, across its surface by the ghostly forms tiptoeing around its outer perimeter. I stood at its edge for a few minutes staring idly at the glimmering patterns on the water. I was hoping some general direction would emerge from the eerie traffic. But none did. People sloshed in and out from all directions with no hint of common purpose. Heads down and peering determinedly before them into the gloom, they showed not the slightest interest in anything beyond their individual missions. There was no curiosity about me, no recognition with one another. No one spoke.

The only thing these people did together was huddle wall-to-wall. At least at night.

But surely they gathered to drink. Every settlement builds a saloon of sorts. Usually it's the first thing they build. I could have asked someone but I didn't want to question those shadows. And they didn't want me to, either.

Instead I picked a direction away from the pool and found it right away.

It was a long dull rectangular structure with a pair of cheap plastic facade windows hanging along one wall at a uniform slant from a single brad. The windows were significant in that they were the only attempt at decor that I could recall having seen in the city. Maybe because of that, or maybe because they were just so cheap, they made it worse instead of better. They had been designed to look like they belonged in any modern Terran city. But they didn't. They belonged here.

There was one good sign. A half dozen horses stood outside, "tethered" to a small boy sleeping on the stoop. If the local ranchers came here, it probably meant that this was the best place. Or maybe the only place, which was the same thing.

I stepped up out of the mud onto the stoop, which squeaked and shook with my weight just enough to rouse the boy from one dream to another without disturbing his tight, two-fisted grip on the reins. The door dragged open inwardly just as I reached for the catch and I had to step back into the mud to make way for a rancher who staggered out clutching a jug of syntho and giggling. He took a short sip from the jug. He took a deep breath and stretched, looking around. Then he hopped, flat-footed, into the mud, sprinkling a halo of flecks from each boot heel. This made him giggle harder.

He noticed me at last and nodded in my direction. He offered me a swig from the jug. His eyes were dancing as though I was in on the joke. It didn't matter that I wasn't. His bubbling giggle was plenty by itself, full of wicked mischief and infectious as hell. I was already grinning by the time I got the proffered jug to my lips, making for a sloppy swallow that increased his laughter all the more.

I had another drop and handed it back, grinning like a fool and thinking that this was exactly why I had come. The doorway filled suddenly with the other five horsemen who were laughing just as hard as the first, if not nearly so well. The first man could have been my age or half that or something in between. But the others were young men, younger even than Holly. And they treated the giggler as their leader, stomping loudly off of the stoop into the mud and arranging their young grins in a tight semicircle before him.

The middle kid started to speak but stuttered on his own laughter, causing a wave of conspiratorial guffaws from all present—including me. The kid tried again:

"Who *is* that guy?" he asked the leader, gesturing back over his shoulder toward the bar.

"No idea," replied the older man.

"What the hell did he want with you, anyway?" asked another of the five.

"He just wanted you to watch him propose?" asked another before there was a chance to answer.

"Looks like," suggested the leader with another swig.

"What for?" asked the first kid.

The leader smiled. "Dunno. Maybe he was just tired of getting turned down alone."

"Didn't look tired to *me*," offered still another kid. "Hell, he musta asked a dozen women in just the time we've been here."

"Must be in some hurry to get married," said the first one. "Did you see that last one? Ugh!"

"Serve him right if she'd said yes," said somebody. "Can you imagine being married to that?"

The older man smiled again and reached for the jug. "I dunno," he said, holding the jug to his lips, "let me try."

With that he took a long long swallow and then stood in a mock-parody of fierce concentration. His face relaxed suddenly. He shook his head. "Nope. Can't imagine it."

The kids, and I laughed, a willing audience.

"Take more drinkin' than that!" suggested the first kid.

"I've got time," replied the older man, swigging some more. He broke off his chugging with another laugh and seemed to remember me. He offered the jug again, saying: "What about you, Stranger? How's your imagination?"

I laughed, took the jug. "It needs a boost," I said, and tilted the jug back.

"Sounds like a bachelor," suggested the first kid as I drank.

"Drinks like a goddamned *couple*," growled the leader in mock irritation at my determined swallows.

That remark, for some reason, did me in. I exploded with laughter, spraying myself and everyone else with syntho. He made it even worse by adding, completely deadpan, that he "usually just swallowed it right on down" himself. But, he added while I convulsed with laughter, "I don't get out much and different people enjoy booze different ways."

I could *not* stop laughing. Maybe it was the liquor or maybe it was just my needing to laugh so bad. Or maybe it was just the man's infectious grin. Whatever it was, it was fun.

"Here, friends," he said, holding the jug high. "Here's to the Syntho Spraying Stranger!"

With that everybody drank to my toast and then applauded sloppily. I managed a small bow and was reaching for the jug to try again when the door to the saloon slammed open with a ragged crash. Everyone, even the suddenly awakened stableboy, turned toward the sound. In the doorway stood a huge beast of a man, drunk and swaying in the half-light. He peered down at us dazedly for a moment before focusing on the older horseman.

"Hey, you!" yelled the beast, pointing a finger. "Goddammit! Goddamn killed the whole damn deal for me!"

"Uh-oh, Lewis," said one of the kids, naming their leader.

The name seemed to ring a bell, but before I had a chance

to react, the beast was performing again. He launched himself down the steps toward us. Only he missed the first step and catapulted out into the darkness, landing face down and full-length in the mud.

Lewis took a step forward and, raising the jug again, offered another toast. "Gentlemen," he said formally, "I give you the groom."

The kids giggled, but their amusement had a somewhat dutiful tone to it. For whether Lewis seemed to have noticed it or not, the beast was clearly enraged. He picked himself up quickly out of the mud. Resting on his heels, he pointed a finger again. "Goddamn ranchin' crud," he said.

Lewis laughed delightedly, completely unoffended. The kids laughed too. They seemed more relaxed, as if it couldn't be serious as long as Lewis was not. I figured they were wrong, all of them. The beast was mad. Wildly drunk, perhaps. Barely focused, maybe. But still very. . . .

Without warning, the man lunged to his feet toward Lewis and swung a truly gigantic fist in his direction. Lewis stepped back smoothly out of range, still laughing and relaxed. Not anxious, not even taunting. Just . . . good-humored.

The light from the open doorway dimmed as a young and, well, not pretty so much as . . . solid woman appeared. She took in the situation in a glance and shouted at the beast in a hard strident voice.

"Foss! My God! Are you psycho?"

Foss, the beast, froze halfway through another backswing and turned toward her voice. "Leave me alone, Del," he muttered sourly. "Goddammit, you told me no once already." And he made ready another punch in Lewis's direction.

Del refused to be ignored. "Foss!!" she barked again, stomping her hefty foot on the stoop. "What are you doing?"

". . . kill me this rancher pig here . . ." mumbled Foss uncertainly.

"Who? Me?" asked Lewis with friendly innocence.

"Goddamn right, you," snarled Foss.

"Why?" asked Lewis, sounding genuinely hurt. "Hell, *I* didn't turn you down!"

Foss lunged at him again. Lewis stepped easily aside, still calm and happy, holding the jug by the neck high over his head to keep it out of range of the fat droplets of mud the Foss's scrambling threw into the air. Foss lunged twice more, once trying to punch him again, once trying to grab the smaller man in a bear hug. He failed miserably both times.

It was a charade. Foss stomped and missed and Lewis dodged and smiled and Del looked worried and the kids giggled. But it was a lot worse than it appeared. It was still serious as hell. Foss was *not* harmless. In fact, he wasn't even that bad. Lewis just moved so smoothly that it looked that way. That and the way Lewis kept smiling made the whole thing appear to be a joke. It was great.

I was grinning myself, unabashedly delighted with Lewis. He just would not get angry, no matter how close Foss came. He simply refused. It was a talent I could use a little of myself. More than a little.

"Stop this, Foss!" shouted Del after it seemed to be going on forever. She came running down the steps toward us, scattering the kids who were still watching eagerly, their mouths now sagging open at half mast between laughter and concern—and ready to go either way. "Stop this!" Del repeated.

"I'm for that," offered Lewis, taking a swig.

Del pushed between the two, her hands resting firmly against Foss's muddy chest. Foss ignored her, shouting past her to Lewis.

"Shaddup, you sumbitch! If it wadn't for you, I'd. . . ." He hesitated, glanced at Del, seemed to lose his resolve. "Well . . ." he trailed off.

"Well, what?" demanded Del. "What's this man done to you? I thought you just met him, for God's sake!"

"I knew him before this," he mumbled. Then louder, pointing his finger again: "I know about you, ranchershit! I know you!"

"What do you know, Foss?" asked Lewis pleasantly.

"I know . . ." Foss hesitated again, looked embarrassed. But that only made him, on reflection, more angry. "I know that you're queering it for me and for . . . hell, for everybody. Riding around on some big horse all the time like some big deal and looking down and makin' us look like nothin' to . . . to *her*!"

Then he stood there, red-faced, looking stupid and huge. And sad.

Del took a deep breath. She let it out. Her voice was gentle. "That's insane," she said.

"Maybe," agreed Lewis as Foss lunged at him yet again, "but it's sincere as hell!" Lewis sidestepped Foss's charge neatly and smoothly, as he had all the others. Foss tried to correct his momentum in mid-slide, lost his footing, and collapsed once more into the mud.

He lay there, snarling and cussing under his breath. He was panting with the effort. Idly, pitifully, he tried to snag Lewis with the toe of his boot without standing up.

"You ever gonna stand still?" moaned the beast.

"Of course," replied Lewis easily. "But not here. G'night!"

Gathering up his crew of kids with a wave, tossing a coin to the boy holding the reins, Lewis vaulted onto one of the horses and tried to make a clean exit.

But Foss was up as Lewis came past him. "I ain't finished with you yet!" he called, stumbling awkwardly onto the horses' path.

Lewis dodged a wild swing that had been aimed too low to do much damage anyway and pulled his reins out of range of Foss's groping. "I can always come back tomorrow, if you like," he offered over his shoulder as he slipped past toward the edges of the saloon door light. He reined up briefly and said cheerily, tilting the jug.

Foss looked suspicious. "You with him?" he toasted me briefly: "Here's to you Stranger. Take care," he said cheerily, tilting the jug.

Foss looked suspicious. "You with him?" he demanded sourly to me and, before I could think of a good answer, swung a fist at my chin.

I dodged that swing and another and then another while Del screamed, "Foss, you idiot!" But she did no good with my troubles either. Foss kept at me, lumbering with his arms open wide and better speed than I would have guessed he still had in him. I turned his arms away, slipped another punch, and . . . allowed him to trip over my ankle. But as he went down, his huge right arm lashed out, nearly snagging me. I felt fingers like plassteel tongs slip along my shinbone. Damn, but he was a strong one!

Instinctively, I positioned myself to finish it as he struggled to regain his footing. Instinct? Or was it just habit? Maybe it was preference. . . .

"You know what you need, Stranger?" I heard Lewis ask from just over my shoulder.

"What's that?" I asked without taking my eyes off of my muddy target.

"You need a nice little horseyback ride in the fresh air."

"Think so?" I replied in a dull voice just as the beast and I matched stares. I tensed slightly, shifting my weight . . .

"Come on," urged Lewis gently, sounding more than a little . . . What? Disappointed?

And that shook me out of it. *He* had messed with the man for half an hour without a blow being struck and here I was . . . Here I was going to hurt somebody again. Wanting to? So I turned away and took a couple of steps and vaulted onto the back of his horse behind him and the six of us rode away out of range of Foss and Del and the ugly inevitable.

Not because Lewis had cared. Because Lewis hadn't given a damn about Foss. And not because it was the "right thing." Not because it was right. Because it was . . . new?

I thought about that as we rode easily out of the City. I thought about it as I drank, bouncing and jiggling and unsanitarily from the jug. But not much. I had never liked thinking about that part of me much. Never.

We passed through the lake of the square, scattering a couple of kids playing with something at the edge of the water. The horses made a lot of noise on the wooden slats that crossed the sewer/stream. Lewis spurred us into a canter across the next hundred meters and then pulled up sharply as we approached the main bridge across the river. He slid off in front of me. He tossed me the reins.

"Here you go, Stra . . . Hey, what is your name, anyway?" he asked.

One of the kids, pulling up beside us in a spray of muddy water, broke in:

"I know you. Aren't you . . . Yeah! You're Jack Crow!" he exclaimed. The other kids loudly echoed this. "Don't you recognize him, Lewis?"

Lewis peered up at me. "Nope."

The kid looked embarrassed. "Well, he's heard of you though," he said quickly to me. "You've heard of him, haven't you?"

Lewis thought a minute. He shrugged. "Maybe," he allowed with a slow nod.

I'd have bet a hundred credits on the spot, a hundred credits I didn't have, that he hadn't.

"Why are we stopping here, anyway?" someone wanted to know.

Lewis brightened. "I thought I'd give you boys a chance to count sailboats while I take a small piss on the nice fish." He trotted around the buttresses as he spoke, opening up his fly. His voice faded as he descended to the river's edge. "Here, fish! Here, nice-little-fishies-that-won't-take-my-hook! Here, you contrary little bastards! Come and gettt ittt!" From over the railings came the sound of him pissing merrily, the way he laughed, into the water. The kids and I sat there on the backs of the horses sipping from the jug and watching the swiftly passing current. The one who recognized me began a halting and involved question about some exploit or another he had heard that I'd done. He seemed embarrassed to be asking it. I let him be, thus avoiding the need to give a civil reply.

Lewis returned shortly. He hopped up onto the railing and motioned for the jug. I tossed it to him. He drank, frowned at the amount that was left, drank again.

"C'mon, Lewis," complained someone, "let's go."

Lewis shook his head sadly. "Ah, youth! What's the hurry? Didn't I promise you that puberty would come? Trust me."

Several of them laughed. So did I. But the impatient one was insistent. "How long are we gonna be here?"

Lewis shrugged. "Dunno. You in a hurry, Jack?"

"I've got an hour or so."

"Splendid. I'll see you young bucks later on."

In a few seconds they were all gone, even the ones in no hurry. It had been a dismissal.

"Take a load off, Jack," he said to me when we were alone, "and let me explain to you the real reason why I never catch any of these little fishies."

I slid off the horse and joined him on the railing. He handed me the jug. "Tell me everything about it," I urged.

He feigned shock. "Everything? You mean everything? Where oh where shall I begin?"

"How about the beginning," I suggested, burping softly. The syntho was getting to me.

"Nope. Not the beginning. I've been there already. It was worse then than it is now and I want to tell you, Jack, right now is a dark, dark time."

"What seems to be the problem?" I asked, all sympathy.

"The real problem, Jack? Or," he struck a tragic pose, "the REAL problem?"

I pretended to give it some thought. "The REAL problem," I said at last in a hushed whisper.

He eyed me narrowly, as if judging my trustworthiness. Then he glanced around us to be sure he wasn't overheard, just as if we weren't really half a kilometer from anyone. "The real problem with these fishies and me is: personality conflict."

I laughed.

"That's it," he said, "laugh. But I will bet you that I can prove to you right here and now, using logic, insight, and . . . syntho, that what I'm saying is true."

And damned if he didn't do just that. His way, anyhow. The man was an absolute marvel. Talked for over an hour the most convoluted, contrived and contradictory horseshit I had ever heard. I could follow maybe half of it and I can't remember any of it. But I do remember having a hell of a good time listening to it all. He never hesitated once during the entire lunatic harangue, never lost his place, never stopped grinning.

Or drinking. He pulled a fresh jug out of his saddle case and went to work on it like it was his first in a standard month.

He closed with what he referred to as "critical advice" on how to catch the local fish, which he never, or rarely, seemed to do himself. The finale consisted of a rousing demonstration of what songs to sing (and, vastly more important to him) or not to sing, while fishing. Had a *rotten* singing voice. Knew it. Didn't care. But I cared. It hurt to listen to him.

He said I wasn't a true fisherman. True fishermen, it seemed, didn't care about such frivolous details as musical notes. Not a bit. True fishermen care about volume. True fishermen "sang loud." Then he threw his head back to show me, cocking that awful noise muscle of his . . . and fell backwards into the river.

I was afraid he would drown, drunk as he was. And drunk as *I* was, I raced down around to the bank to help. He was okay by the time I got there. He was kneeling on the bank with his back to the water looking over his shoulder at the rushing current. On his face was a comic-opera expression of suspicion.

"Did you see who it was?" he asked, not taking his eyes off the water.

"What?"

"Did you see which one did it?" he insisted.

"Did what?"

"Pulled me into the water," he said gravely, looking at me at last. "Which fish."

A marvel. By the time he dropped me off at the dome I was semi-sober and thoroughly cheered. We had already said our good-byes and I was halfway up the ramp when his name finally sank in. Lewis! He was. . . .

I turned around and searched the landscape for him. I heard him before I saw him, galloping lazily out of sight over the gentle grassy slope that rose away from the river and the city, and loudly practicing what he had referred to as "scream-singing." This was supposed to be the guy that owned Sanction?

Nooo . . . Couldn't be. There had to be another Lewis. Surely. . . .

But, of course, there wasn't. He was it, that lightweight drunk. He was the owner, ruler, master, of everything in sight.

I laughed on my way up the rest of the ramp. And then I stopped laughing. Because it wasn't really funny. I suddenly appreciated Borglyn more than ever. For this place had been a perfect choice. It was just what he needed. Distant, alone, and utterly helpless.

No. It really wasn't funny at all.

XI

It was, I knew, incredibly stupid of me to feel as I did after that dinner with Holly and Lya. After all, it had gone very well for me. Perfectly well, in fact. Not only had their suspicions been relieved, they had ended up practically encouraging my little machinations. Hell, they *had* encouraged me! Without having any idea what I was up to! By the time that dinner was over they had opened up completely to me, given me free rein, unchecked and unhindered.

And why? Why did they welcome the wolf into their midst? Why did they succumb to such insanity?

Simple. They trusted me.

Madness.

But that wasn't what made me feel as rotten as I did. What really bothered me was not simply their trust. It was their faith. The two of them looked at me with it shining from their eyes. They looked at me like, well. . . .

Like I knew what I was doing. Madness!

On a distant planet all but lost on the outskirts of the spread of Man, a man who is both highly disreputable and a total stranger suddenly appears and crowds you for company. He provides no explanations for his actions and no clue to his motives. He is at best a rogue, at worst a psychotic, and in any case a known powderkeg. Yet you not only accept his good intentions, you trust his *aim*! From this gypsy you expect . . . control.

Why? Why, from such as he, do you assume accuracy? From where do you sense this precision, anyway, the *fable*?

Can no one imagine an incompetent Legend?

It started off predictably enough. The three of us sat eating and chatting alone in the main dining room. We smiled fiercely at one another while nervously pursuing a hundred avenues of small talk and in all ways avoiding until the last minute the point.

We talked about the food and how good it was and we talked about the food we missed, our favorite foods and our favorite places to eat our favorite foods. We talked about the rotten weather that had been about recently and about the good weather they had had before that and about the good weather we hoped we would get in the future. We talked about Sanction, me mentioning that I thought I had met Lewis, the owner, if it was the same guy. And they said oh yes it was in fact the owner I had met and oh yes he did drink a great deal, always had. Lya mentioned some gossip she had heard about Lewis's having been sent here by a wealthy and influential earth family who had been embarrassed by the scandal of having what was, face it, an alcoholic son. And we all agreed as to how that made some sense or it was a good story anyhow, ha ha and then Holly told me about the strange thing that happened when they got an uncontrolled mutation once and had to shut down the syntho vats completely. Seemed that Lewis had simply stopped drinking until the syntho was ready again, refusing to accept their offer of real liquor from the Project stores and thereby forcing himself to go over two standard months without a drink. And we all agreed that that was certainly unusual behavior for an alcoholic, yes it certainly was, by golly and then we sat there staring at one another and still smiling like crazy.

Then Holly spoke up at last. Speaking of Sanction, he began, and then talked about what a nice place it was, how Earthlike and so on. Lots of planets like that, Lya added and then we played the game of naming all the other places like that we could think of. How convenient for us, somebody said and we all laughed. I mentioned something about it bothering me, all those man places, how I thought it was a little spooky and we all laughed again, ha ha, stringing it out as long as we could to avoid that damned silence but still ending up staring and smiling for several seconds until Holly cleared his throat and talked about an interesting item he had read off the Fleet Beam on that very subject and I said, oh what was that? And he said it was very interesting, really, that it seemed there was some sort of religious cult that believed that all these planets had been designed just for us. Oh really? That *is* interesting—Yes, isn't it, these people think there is a trail of these planets and if we follow it to the galactic core we will find and meet the builders, meet God himself, I guess they meant ha ha ha! How about that?

Yes, how about that? Uh, huh. . . .

I could see how nervous they were. More, I could see how embarrassed they were. And I could see that they wanted me to start it all off, had seen that in their eyes from the beginning. And I wanted to. I wanted to lead into it myself so that I would seem more upfront while at the same time controlling the discussion somewhat.

Only I couldn't think of anything to say. Not a thing. It was inexcusable. What I needed, and quickly, was an extremely plausible and not too elaborate lie or set of lies and why, for God's sake, didn't I have it ready? Why hadn't I taken the time to think of something instead of wasting my day with two different kinds of idiots, fighting idiots and drinking idiots, the way I had? Damn!

I *had* thought, initially, of trying to get Holly off alone to pull it off. I knew I would have a much easier time with him alone. He would have been even more nervous by himself. He would have been eager to glide past those anxious moments, perfectly willing to buy my non-answers. Anything to avoid turmoil. And damn *near* anything to keep palling about with the Great & Exciting & Romantic (and just a wee bit Notorious—for spice) Jack Crow.

But Lya would have squashed it all if we had left her out. Not that he couldn't have ignored his own doubts without help. It's just that he could never stand up to her actual opposition. If she wasn't satisfied, he couldn't be. Sooner or later—make that simply soon—we would be sitting there again with Holly reluctant to demand more and me reluctant to give it but both of us having to. By the strength of her will alone, she could force us to both do the one thing we dreaded most: get to the Point. Just what *was* I up to?

It wasn't that she didn't like me. She did. I liked her, too. But it was a bigger decision than that. I was an unknown, potentially destructive element in a situation already far too sloppy. And something else: the decision was *her* decision. For, if Holly was their focus, Lya was the Couple.

I sat there watching the two of them together, thinking about that and thinking about how, well, sweet they looked together. He was young and warm and brilliant. She was young and strong and wise. And, of course, lovely. They fit.

And all I could think of was the truth that would get me hung. Truth, a real burden against people who fit, especially for someone like me who hardly fit myself . . .

I had it then. If the truth was all I had, then that was all I could share. So share it I would. Generously, equitably. . . .

I'd give 'em half of it.

I cleared my throat. Firmly. They saw the cue, sat up a little straighter, just managed to avoid the impulse to trade a brief glance. "Holly, you've been most kind and very patient. Both of you have," I added with a quick smile for Lya. She responded in mechanical kind without blinking a lash or easing back one bit. "But I know you want to know: just what does someone like me—interstellar pirate—want here?"

They smiled a little at the pirate part. Not enough.

"Well, the fact is, Holly," I continued and then stopped, took an obvious breath, shined what I hoped was a conspiratorial smile, and said, ". . . I can't tell you."

I saw them, felt them freeze, counted a single beat, then jumped in to thaw them out.

Of course, I *wanted* to tell them and of course there was something in the works, but then I was sure they had suspected that, knowing me as they did (sigh). I followed that crap with more crap just like it on the principle that lots and lots of nothing can sound like something. And then on to the obligatory truth part about how I wouldn't want to do anything to damage their situation and how I didn't *expect* that I would but that (also obligatory) I would certainly understand if that was unacceptable to them, I certainly would, and if they wanted me to stay out of their way and move to the City all they had to do was say the word and out I'd go, yes sir!

I had to go through it all again before they had a chance to really consider it, more lots and lots of nothing, while never missing an opportunity to look shy and a little embarrassed by the need for secrecy and, most importantly, intimate. Intimate in the sense of acting like they understood what it was like to be me since they were so exciting and knowing themselves.

Stringing that out, layer upon layer, until the rhythm was right for my secret, personal confession that I really hated to burden them with—it wasn't their problem, after all.

Holly jumped to assure me that I could speak freely, snatching at his cue. Lya echoed his assurance, snatching at hers. Only the bolt of lightning, which should have torn through the ceiling of the dome and splattered my lying teeth on the dining-room table, but didn't, missed its cue.

". . . the other reason I want to stay with . . . with you . . . is that, well, I hate the City, Holly. I hate those people. I've spent too much of my life with people like that and with you it's. . . . It's nice. And I'm just so tired of pounding the fools who are always out trying to test themselves against Jack Crow."

I gave them a minute to enjoy the compliment and have fun pretending to feel an understanding sorrow before:

"And I *am* interested in your work, Holly. And I do want to hear whatever you will take the time to explain to me, though I know there's nothing more boring than trying to explain things to a layman. . . ."

"On the contrary, Jack," he said quickly. "I. . . ."

"C'mon, Holly," I said with a wave, "you don't have to pretend with me. I know the last thing you want is an audience," knowing damn well he wanted nothing more in the whole wide universe.

"On the contrary, Jack," he repeated, "I'm terribly flattered by your interest. I just hope I won't bore *you*."

"Not a chance, Holly. I'm the sponge type."

"I do think we have a few projects of interest in the works. And, without getting too technical. . ." he began, before becoming too technical almost at once.

It didn't matter. I was only half-listening. The other half was waiting. For Lya.

Because it wasn't over until she said it was. So I sweated. Holly had already bought it all, luxuriating in the brotherhood of anything even faintly man-to-man.

I had thrown in the part about wanting to stay with them for her, mostly, figuring she would demand, in lieu of facts, something personal at least, before being satisfied. But was she? I could damn near feel her probing gaze, which had strayed not one inch from my eyes the whole time. She's not buying, I thought at last, mustering more sugarcloud to float toward her, when suddenly she relaxed.

And I knew I was in.

I could turn and look at her then, and smile. She smiled back. It was a sweet smile, a warm smile, and, incredibly, an "I'm-sure-you'll-do-the-right-thing" smile.

Madness!

But I don't know what I'm doing! I shouted from my mind to hers. How can you? you stupid bitch! Your faith in me is insane!

But her gaze didn't even darken. She had decided. And that was that.

I shuddered, passing a hand over my eyes. It was so stupid to feel this way! What was I upset about, anyway? *Winning*, for crissakes? What the *hell*? Guilt for deceiving her? For being *able* to? Dammit! Forget it! Go on, go on! It's a done thing. A completed task. Go on!

"As regards the armor?" I blurted blindly, interrupting Holly in mid-esoterica.

"Why, yes," he said, surprised. "I was just coming to that. You do follow this, don't you?"

I didn't hit him. I just clamped down and tried to slide into his voice, into the sense of what he was saying. Long slow deep breaths.

I bolted suddenly upright as, out of the blue, I realized what it was he was suggesting.

"But Holly, the one thing that anybody, that everybody knows about battle armor is that no one but the owner can wear it. You'd be crushed!"

Holly smiled, completely unconcerned. "Oh, of course I would, Jack," he replied happily. "I know that. I'm not planning to wear the suit. Not even the helmet. But, Jack," he added, looking excitedly at me and leaning forward across the table eagerly, "what if I could use routing feeds to another helmet!"

I stared at him. "Why?" I asked.

He looked surprised. "The record, Jack! The record is there!"

"Then why not just play the coil?"

"Because it's not on the coil, like I've been saying . . ."

Oh.

". . . electro-magnetic scattering of some time caused it to bleed off."

"Holly, I still don't understand you," interrupted Lya thankfully. "You say it's there and then you say it's been, what? bled off? Bled off where?"

"Bled off into the pod itself, Dear. It's on the inner surface of the pod shielding plate. But it's still intact. It's still there."

She frowned. "Then how can you get it off?"

He smiled indulgently at our inability to keep up with his racing brain. I imagined he had had much practice in his short but brilliant life. "But don't you see? That's what makes it such a fascinating problem! To draw it out of such an irregular surface while still maintaining its cohesive interval requires an ability to adjust to millions of split-second alterations of power level. We're talking about a tiny, tiny bit of charge here. And the smallest change in resistance factor—an imperfect allow on the shield plates, a drop of paint, even the fact that the surface is curved can make a difference. You see, if you draw it too quickly, the chain breaks and the electrons lose their cohesion. If you draw it too slowly, then the field halts for the microsecond required for it to produce its *own* field and . . . bingo! It's gone!"

"You mean you'd lose the record?" I prompted. "It would go blank?"

"Well, not blank. It would become a regularly interspersed

pattern of dots and dashes which, for our purposes, is the same thing."

"Just like that?" asked Lya.

He nodded. "Just like that. Listen, I've seen six hours—that's six computer hours, mind you—turn static, coalesce, and pop across to a lab assistant's belt buckle. All before the computer—much less us—knew there was a problem. No matter how good your hardware, or how large your storage capacity given current limits, there are still too many bits with too many problems to allow for."

"I don't get it," I said and I didn't. "Then you're saying it can't be done?"

"No, no, no, no, Jack! I'm saying no *computer* can do it?"

"Then what can?" asked Lya, sounding as confused as I was.

Holly's face broke into a wide grin. His right index finger stabbed the air. "The brain!" he said triumphantly.

Lya looked at him. I looked at him. She and I looked at each other.

"That's absurd," she said at last. "No man can think as fast as your smallest relays; you told me that yourself."

"I said process," he replied with a tolerant but firm smile, "not think. Computers don't think. They simply sort."

"What's the difference?" Lya wanted to know.

"Four or five billion bits of data, for one thing."

"For the computer . . . ." I interjected.

"No. For the brain!" he retorted. "We don't focus as well, true enough. And our data priority system is horridly uncontrolled. But whether you call it panicking or 'going blank' or just stuttering, those are generally breakdowns in the delivery system, not the storage. The answer, and about two million others per second, is there."

"So the computers are more effective, Holly, which is the same thing!" demanded Lya.

"Yes, yes. But it is we who do the programming for the effect we want. Computers are, in limited areas, much better devices. But we are vastly superior *machines*."

I took a deep breath. "Let me get this straight. You're saying that in order to suck this record out of that pod, it takes a zillion decisions every second which then require an equivalent zillion alterations in the . . . strength of the pull, right?''

''Right.''

''And you say that no computer is fast enough and big enough at the same time . . .''

''Right now none are. Maybe later, they do marvelous things with fluidics these days . . .''

I waved that off. ''Don't confuse me. And the only thing that can make those instantaneous decisions and the like is a human brain?''

''Right again. You see . . .''

''Just hold it a minute, Holly,'' I blurted, more bluntly than I meant. ''I still don't get it. You're talking about all this . . . computing being done on an unconscious level?''

''Yes.''

Lya looked unhappy. ''But nobody could . . . How could you direct the focus of your unconscious mind to do this for you?''

Holly smiled again. It was infuriating. ''Ah, there's the part where the computer can help. It's not so much a matter of concentration in the conventional sense. It's more a matter of frequency. It's just a problem of getting the two brain-wave patterns close enough so that they begin to work in harmony and . . .''

He stopped when he saw the shocked look on our faces. But he continued anyway, like a schoolboy trying to get in the rest of his excuse before being punished too severely.

''You see, if your drawing field, your brain wave in this case, is on a compatible interval pattern, then all those adjustments would be made automatically. I admit there can't be a complete match-up,'' he added sheepishly, ''since no two people have exactly the same frequency. Both sides would have to give a little. . . .''

''Give a little,'' Lya shouted with outrage. ''You're talking about allowing a machine to alter your brain-wave pattern to fit someone else's??''

''Only briefly,'' he insisted lamely. ''And not very much. And it wouldn't *really* fit. I mean, you wouldn't be able to read his thoughts or. . . .''

"My God, Holly . . ." I began.

"You're insane!" Lya finished. "It would drive you crazy."

There was a pause before we all laughed at the absurdity of her remark. It lowered the tension level somewhat. But the issue, with all of its implied horrors, still hung before us.

"It might very well, you know," I said seriously. "It could cause all sorts of psychological damage. It might simply burn your ego away."

Holly sat up straighter in his chair. He looked offended. "I believe I have made allowances for such a problem. Special entry and exit procedures, for example."

"It's madness," muttered Lya bitterly. "It's . . . wrong."

"You're being emotional, Lya. And only because you can't think of any rational objections."

"All right, Holly," I said, rising to the challenge, "here's one: What if you're him in there?"

"I beg your pardon?"

"What if you became him? At least thought you were, anyway, as long as you were in there. You would be reliving— for the first time—and then forgetting afterwards."

He regarded me quizzically. "Complete submersion? Hardly likely, Jack. The brain *is* self, after all. You would conflict first."

"There's still some 'ouch' in that," I pointed out.

"Yes, but if you consider the. . . ."

"That's just what you're not doing, Holly Ware!" blurted Lya angrily. She had become quite upset. I saw tears in the corners of her eyes. She was terrified by this. I didn't blame her. "When did you come up with this insane notion, anyway?"

He met her gaze without blinking. "Just now," he said in the absolutely unmistakable fashion of one who knows what he is and what he is doing and who also knows that he and he alone is qualified for it.

An interesting thing happened then: Lya backed down.

It caught me by surprise, left me wondering if, in my own stereotypical haste, I had misjudged the young mad scientist. But then I had it. She was *not* giving in to his machismo. She was retreating before his expertise.

Holly was, after all, the genius.

"Well," she said after she had calmed a bit," I don't want

to talk about this anymore today. I need a little time to get my feet back on the ground. And I shall certainly dream about this tonight.'' The last came with a tiny self-deprecating smile, a gesture which made the sculptured lines of her mouth seem even more delicate and frail than before. It was especially endearing, even for her.

Holly and I agreed with matching smiles of relief. We all went through the straightening and adjusting needed after too long at the table. We stretched, yawned, grinned. At the door I turned to shake hands with Holly and found that I was doing it with a man I had not yet met. It was a man who seemed to me to be, at that time, the very best of Holly Ware. His grip was firm, his eyes bright, he looked more confident than I had ever before seen him. And more, he looked excited, hopeful, eagerly intrigued. Lya, despite her own buoyancy having apparently returned, seemed a faded shadow before the warmth of his creative glow. The image of those two at that moment struck something in me. It stayed with me, hanging before me, as I went through the seal and down the passage to my own suite. I couldn't stop thinking about the way her face had looked, set with gentle firmness, eyes lifted to him, half-turned to him, half-eclipsed as his moon.

And I couldn't stop thinking about something else, that there was little wonder that such women preferred the Hollys to me. The only time I ever looked that alive, I was probably killing.

Damn.

The lounge was dark. There was no sign of Cortez anywhere. I thought for a moment that I had stumbled into the wrong suite. Then I saw the light filtering through underneath the door to my bedroom and I froze, stock still, in my tracks.

I could feel her.

I wanted a cigarette, but reaching for it seemed a noisy affair. Not loud enough for anyone to hear me from the bedroom—I wasn't worried about that. I didn't want to make, well, *any* sound. Absolutely still. Dead still, rock still. Bolted to the floor and long empty tubes for my arms . . . Long enough like that and it would all go away or better, much, much, better they, They? THEY? would come for me and take me out, lift me up and away and say everything is all right, of course you failed but you were only. . . .

I shrugged mightily, violently, forcing my boots to make that horrible, rasping, barely audible shuffle across the carpet as I stepped up to the door and eased it open with my wet hand.

Upper lamp on lowest gain glowing down to white sheets and yellow hair and golden skin—so *much* gold for so little skin—and all of it, the gently rising flat tummy, the wide eyes closed or shielded or hidden, the positively dreamlike sweep of lines from throat to forehead and back again to the partial view of more yellow hair, but tufted, promising more hair and more gold . . . all of it glowing back up into the lamp, shaming it. Shaming me.

I could feel her. From the doorway, I could feel her.

And she was real! Karen was real, had been all along. This other thing, this vague dream, this fantasy, only now half-remembered of a ship of my own without cares or destination or, face it, purpose, this sloppy goal, was never as real as the vision of her exquisite promise in my bed.

I stumbled out the door, easing my wet hand trembling from the plastic door. I sat, then lay on the couch my tubes and trembling neck. Why didn't I?

Why didn't I? A *worthless* sacrifice, a horrible choice. Even if it was real. Even if it did hurt. Or especially. Or not.

I slept, my face feeling sunburned somehow. Blasted.

XII

I had horrible dreams that night that lasted years. Not true nightmares, really, not at first. But very odd, in a macabre, intriguing sort of way. There were many distorted figures lodged and packed into a room that was at the same time a-geographic. They and I stumbled around with staccato gaits, first windsome, then fierce, getting faster and faster until the whole thing resembled some sort of spastic frenzy. By then I knew it was a dream, but that didn't help. It was a commentary on me, the daytime me, the message seemed to be. It was about the recent me. The lately irrational, emotion-taut me. Other me's too, I supposed, but in any case, too damn many me's.

It would only get worse. I would stretch to the frenzy. I would warp. So I woke up, fast as I could.

Cortez was sitting beside my bed. He smiled when I opened my eyes, the lids of which felt puffy, ponderous. It seemed I had been out two days with a raging fever. The muscular spasms had stopped hours before, now even.

The local bug, in other words, had struck.

"Welcome to Sanction," said Cortez with a wide grin, adding, "Didn't you feel it coming on?"

I ignored him. I hadn't, of course. But, God knows, I should have. Idiot.

It took me eight days, a full local week, to get over it. Mostly, I slept. Peacefully, for the most part. I did meet a couple of doctors. Or maybe just one as the only things I remember about either of them were youth, athletic postures, and greatly affected, pretend-deep, bedside voices.

Lya came often, cheerfully unconcerned for my welfare. "Everybody gets it," she reported gleefully. Holly came twice, ever-friendly but vague about progress with the armor. Cortez left only once, when Karen came.

She hated being there, hated looking at me as I was. She was gone in minutes, again replaced by Cortez who entered looking like the gossip I supposed he was. I ignored him, rolling over into my pillow for my hourly nap. I drifted off wondering if I had not, in fact, learned more about her in those few anxious moments than in all of our previous hours. I thought I knew at last what she wanted from me.

It was nice to be able to just sleep instead.

I was sitting up smoking a cigarette on the morning of the eighth day when Lya came in and told me about the picnic. I didn't answer at first. I was still trying to get used to her appearance. I hadn't seen her in the past couple of days. She looked rotten. There were dark circles under her usually china-pure eyes. She was somewhat pale as well. And her movements seemed a bit shaky, hesitant, and uncoordinated.

Worry. And only one thing could make that one worry. I was anxious to ask her about him but I couldn't seem to get through her let's-be-cheerful-if-it-kills-us-me-him. It was all for her sake, of course, though I doubted she was aware of it and, to be sure, I got all the fussing over. Lya had a great time directing the expedition to the out of doors, insisting I be carried on a springsheet by two attendants—one quite short, one quite tall—and laughing delightedly at the bouncing their mismatched gait gave me.

It was, thankfully, a short trek, just three hundred or so meters along the riverbank to a grove of very Earthlike trees. If it had been much farther, I'd have gotten out of the springer and walked. I was still pretty weak, but I figured anything to be better than that bouncing seesaw.

It was a beautiful warm day. Bright sun and blue skies, the rains now long gone. It was a nice spot, too, beside a rancher's grazing stretching down from a low hill all the way to the edge of clear sparkling water. Damn, but it looked a lot like home.

I was still looking for a chance to ask about Holly, remembering that it had been quite a while since we had spoken. But before I got an opening there was the milling about spreading groundcloths and unpacking utensils and getting me propped. The attendants left then, only to be replaced by Cortez, face glistening with sunscreen. He was helped by Karen, of all people, with the carrying of the food and liquor. She smiled pleasantly at me, said hello and the rest. She even went to the trouble to feel my forehead, a more token gesture than could be believed. Then she picked a spot a couple of trees away, cuddling up with a glass of wine and a shaded bookscreen and looking, well, perfect.

Others from the Project wandered by, snatching bites of chicken and sips of wine, a long procession which was apparently planned, since there were ample stores for the long afternoon. At one point there were a good three dozen people gathered around us, chattering, gossiping, giggling. I was left pretty much alone, either in deference to my health or my notoriety or, most probably, both. Just the same, I missed nothing, however juicy or dull. Lya, sitting beside me, was the favorite of all. Everyone stopped to chat with her. She charmed each of them individually and thoroughly and made it look easy. She seemed to know everyone by name, for one thing, which was damned impressive. Particularly since most of those in attendance were Crew, rather than the scientist-types she was usually around.

Occasionally I would break off from admiring the performance of Lya's social flair to check on Karen. Infinitely more beautiful than anyone else—and growing more so as the afternoon sun blazed multicolored in her hair—she was nevertheless left alone. It may have been her position that discouraged approaches. She was Boss to most of those people, after all. Or, for all I knew, she had the reputation of a loner or a bore or even a bitch. But I didn't think so.

It was her beauty. Curled up on the grass reading, a glass

of wine in her hand, she was more painting than real. Her face, in classic profile, was unusually calm and serene and framed with casual perfection by a few golden strands which had slipped free from the lucious whole flowing across her shoulders and halfway down her back. She was wearing a spotlessly white Crew jumpsuit. It provided the fundamental thread linking the necessary contrasts of blue sky/eyes, blonde hair/skin, green grass/trees.

The view was a painting. Angel descended among mortals. I was frankly grateful to be there at that instant. For all those who were not, however well or long they had known her or would, had missed it. I could not imagine she would ever, in her strident life, manage to repeat that breathtaking image.

It was her beauty that kept them away. It was intimidating! No woman could stand the comparison that side-by-side conversation would inevitably illuminate. And the men—how does one approach and disturb the angel in repose? Even should he wish to crack the crystal? Look. Touch not.

And everyone, to be sure, looked. The gathering about Lya stirred constantly with the oft-repeated turning of heads. The women snatched, or rather sneaked, glances. Brief, probing, envious. Some of the men followed suit, not wishing to be obvious, but many didn't care. They simply arranged themselves so that she was in easy view and thereafter rattled conversationally along with people they never saw.

I leaned against my pillowed throne and did some serious staring of my own. Unmistakably Karen, but still so unlike her. It was her. It just wasn't her life.

If you could see this from my eyes, I wondered at her, the admiring hosts, the idyllic setting . . . If you could see you as I see you now, would it help? Would it reinforce your faith? Would it revive sinking dreams and hope? Or do you hate the beauty that has helped make your life just so?

I never could decide. No way to tell, of course, but I'd expect some of each. It would have cheered her, even thrilled her, to have seen herself then. It would have had to. It was simply too lovely.

But afterwards, with time and doubt leaning so heavily on the memory and with that placidly desperate struggle of her vs. her . . . And some hate did exist, I felt certain, for the beauty. For the brand of having it.

I shook my head, shook it again. I found that I was no longer even looking at her, hadn't been in a while. The sun was no longer framing and she had moved position a little. Christ! I thought, has it come to this now? Too much wine and bug-eating drugs and afternoon sun and . . . Guilt was still about too, still leading me away from the point. I shook my head a third time.

Most of the party had wandered off. Two hours or so of sunlight remained. It was still pleasantly warm. Lya was encouraging, gently, the departure of her final moth, a stoutly muscular Asian woman seeking inside influence for a transfer back to her old position in the Project Dome Galley.

"The Agritechs know nothing about food," she complained in a shrill whine that had been installed, no doubt by mistake, in that massive chest. "They hate everything I fix."

From the way she strove to suppress a giggle, Lya was hardly surprised at this piece of news. Clearly, she found both the issue and the woman hilarious. But somehow she maintained her composure until at last free of the cook, sending her marching robotlike down the bank, short thick arms held firmly immobile at her sides.

Lya collapsed into helpless laughter before the cook had gone twenty meters. She jammed her peals of laughter against the corner of one of my pillows to muffle the noise. It was a compassionate gesture, and more than a little comical in itself. When she had resumed some semblance of control, she turned to me. I beat her to it.

"Let me guess," I said. "You're the one who had her moved out of the Dome in the first place."

She looked surprised, but nodded. A pixie's grin curled up. "Worst cook in the world," she said. And then the laughter bubbled out again. "She cooks like she looks!" she added before collapsing once more into hysterics, now unmuffled and bell-like.

Lya laughed so long and so hard she cried. I found that I was laughing as well after a few seconds, so joyous was the sound. Cortez, asleep for hours, broke off his gentle snoring abruptly. He sat up, rubbed his eyes. "What's so funny?" he asked sleepily. Then, without waiting for an answer to that question—a wise move since it had only started Lya off again—Cortez asked another: "Anything left to eat? I'm starved." He followed this by immediately rummaging through the stores, opening and closing food seals. Still half asleep, he was spilling everything. I lifted my leg to avoid a stream of some sort of purple fruit juice.

Lya, now relatively calmed, sighed, half-smiling at his childlike grogginess. I groaned audibly, having little of her tolerance and even less of her tact. After some four hours of garden-party gobbling, I had yet to have my private moment with Lya and I refused to cater to this sloppy sleepyhead on top of that.

"Cortez," I said as calmly as I could, "there's no food. No more wine either. Why don't you run fetch some?"

He frowned, scratched his head. "Now? I'd have to go all the way down to Storage. I don't know why. . . ?"

I cleared my throat. "Let me rephrase that: Cortez, you will run and fetch the wine. Dig?"

"Huh?"

"Understand?" I quickly amended.

He stared at me, at Lya, who was suppressing yet another giggle, and nodded. "Uh, yeah," he said. "I'll be right back."

"Take your time," I added quickly. "Don't run."

Lya smiled at his retreating form. She sat up, stretching her arms over her head and yawning. She looked around.

"Is that about everyone?" she asked.

I pointed to Karen, still absorbed with her reading. "Must be some story," I offered. "She do that a lot?"

Lya shrugged. "I've no idea," she replied coolly, thus establishing, for my future reference, her lack of any connection with the other woman.

"Hmm. I see," I replied, no less editorially.

But Lya didn't bite. The subject had already been dropped. Fine with me. I was plenty ready to get on with something else.

"Now," I began, "what's wrong with Holly?" She sobered visibly, her shoulders stiffening. "Is it the suit experiment?"

The look of concern on her face managed to both age her and compliment her at the same time. It reminded me of her depth and her value.

"Jack, he doesn't know what he's doing!" she blurted.

"Pretty bright chap, you know," I countered easily. "He's an expert at this sort of thing."

"Nonsense," she replied firmly. "No one's an expert at this. This is *theory*, Jack. And new theory, at that. It's never even been thought about seriously before, much less attempted."

"You've tried to get him to stop, have you?"

She glanced at me briefly, then away. She nodded.

"And he wouldn't budge, would he?" She met my eyes. I smiled. "Only on this," I added.

She smiled reluctantly in return. "How did you know that?"

I shrugged. "Well, I knew you ran the rest of it."

She made a face, looking embarrassed. And of course, damned proud.

I sighed and leaned back against the pillows. I fished a cigarette out and took my time about lighting it. She watched and waited.

Finally: "I'll try it if you want, Lya. I'll talk to him."

"Would you?" she asked, just as if she were really surprised at the offer.

"Of course I will. Only . . . I wouldn't count on much."

"But he thinks a lot of your opinion, Jack," she assured me.

I blew a smoke ring. "Funny. If I were as smart as him, I'd never give me a thought."

She smiled broadly, placating. "Well, Holly *is* that smart and he listens to you. You know he does."

I nodded. "I do. But I don't know why! He doesn't know anything about me."

"Of course he does!"

I shook my head. "Jack Crow stories don't count. We're talking about me."

She tilted her head to one side, as though she couldn't believe her ears. But her voice remained amused. "Well, now. What happened to the smooth talker? Is this a confession or what?"

I laughed. "Well, I've been sick," I replied pitifully and we both laughed. "Okay," I said at last. "I'll go see him before we eat. He's been working at it all this time?"

She nodded. "Ever since the night you got sick he's worked on nothing else. He doesn't even go over the departmental reports."

"You know, Lya," I offered, "that's really a good sign. Probably means he's discovered something."

"Or thinks he has," she retorted bitterly.

I laughed. "Where's *your* composure, all of a sudden?"

She was not amused. "Where is *his*, Jack? What's the hurry?"

I shrugged. "He's on the scent."

She shook her head, stared at the grass. "Too, too fast."

"Too fast for us, maybe, but. . . ."

"Too fast for anyone, Jack. I don't care who it is."

I took her shoulders in my hands and turned her toward me. I looked into her eyes. "Who it is, Lya," I said firmly, "is Hollis Ware. A genuine genius. An upper mind."

"Unhand that woman, you drunk!"

We spun around together to find the real drunk, the screaming-singing fisherman Lewis, standing in the grass a few steps away from the water's edge holding a fishing pole in one hand and the inevitable jug of syntho in the other. He was soaking wet. Lya and I looked at him, then at each other, and burst into laughter. All the tension was forgotten with the sight of that idiot standing there dripping water. And the hat he wore! I couldn't imagine where he had gotten it. I wondered idly if it was made of real straw.

He ignored our laughter, stomping up to us in a shower of droplets and peering down with mock-theatrical disapproval. "While the cat's away, huh?" he accused.

I noticed I still had my hands on Lya's shoulders. I dropped them quickly.

"Too late, Crow!" He snarled, pointing a finger. "I have already seen enough. You!" He yelled at Lya, making her jump. "You scarlet woman, you!"

Lya tried to look penitent but couldn't keep a straight face. Lewis shook his head in disgust. "That's it, laugh, you hussy. And you!'' I jumped on cue. ''You know what Holly Ware's gonna do to you when I tell him what I've seen?''

''Uh, no sir,'' I replied meekly.

''He's gonna take you into some corner somewhere and . . .'' He broke off, thought a moment. ''And think you to a bloody pulp.'' He straightened up, tilting his hat back on his head. He noticed Karen. *''Now* what have you done? My God, this girl has died reading.''

I followed his gaze, saw that Karen had fallen asleep in front of her little screen. Something landed on my lap. I looked down. A wet fishing pole. Lewis plopped to the ground behind it. He eyed me narrowly. He was very drunk.

''Didn't catch fish one,'' he reported miserably. ''Fell in the river to boot.''

''Maybe you're not drinking enough,'' I suggested blandly.

''Yeah. Like you.''

''Me? I protest that.'' I held up my glass of wine. ''What do you call this?''

Lewis snorted, unconvinced. ''A smokescreen is what I call it. Or propaganda. Nope, just make that prop. That, Mr. Crow, is a stage prop. I'd take a phony beard more seriously.''

I sighed. ''Okay. I give. Get to your point, O Great Fisherman without fish.''

He took a deep breath and, taking great care to pronounce each word clearly, said: ''Point is, Crow, that you're not—among the many things you're not—a serious drinker. You are a pretender.'' He broke off, relaxing, and nudged Lya with his shoulder. ''Didja notice how well I 'nunciated that?''

''Lovely,'' replied Lya gravely.

He seemed delighted. ''You really think so?''

''Absolutely, Lewis.''

He smiled broadly. ''Wanna hear it again?''

That reminded me. ''Lewis! You *are* Lewis, aren't you?''

''Course I am. Whadja think?''

''I mean, you're the same Lewis that runs this place?''

He shrugged. ''Nobody runs this place that I know of.'' He paused, took a sip from his jug. ''I do, however, own this rock. Have for a long time.'' He turned again to Lya. ''Raised it from a pup. Boulder, to you. Yep,'' he continued, patting the turf fondly beside his leg, ''boulder first, then he became, uh . . .''

''Bigger?'' Lya offered.

''Right,'' he nodded. He eyed her with scrutiny. ''Hey, you know an awful lot about this sort of thing for a hussy. So where was I? Oh, yeah. Boulder. Then a bigger boulder—all easy so far. But next comes the toughie when he got to be an asteroid.'' He shook his head. ''Ugly, ugly, stage in life, let me tell you, is that adolescent asteroid period. No respect at all. No values.''

''But with a will of iron,'' broke in Lya, ''and the determination of a god. . . .''

Lewis looked delighted. ''Golly, that's pretty! Oh, yeah. With iron will and the determination of a god, I . . .'' he paused, right index finger poised, ''I did it.''

Lya clapped her hands. ''Hooray! At last.''

''The suspense was wrecking me,'' I remarked.

''Smartass!'' sneered Lewis without rancor. ''Smartass pretender-drinker!''

I turned to Lya. ''Do I feel a challenge in the air?''

She smiled. ''Could be.''

''Take your hands off my air,'' growled Lewis, ''and accept, dammit.''

''What do I get when I win?''

He frowned. ''That's 'if' you win, I b'lieve.''

''Whatever. What do I get?''

Lewis reached for my cigarettes, lit one. ''Why, the fish, of course! What the hell else?''

I shook my head as if to clear it. ''I think I'm having a relapse.''

''No excuse.''

''Then what have fish got to do with . . . We *are* talking about a drinking contest, aren't we?''

''We are when you can keep up.''

''Then what have fish got to do with that?''

He exhaled a long stream of smoke. ''Everything, Dummy. That's how you tell who won.''

''How.''

''We don't just drink, Crow,'' he said impatiently. ''We drink and fish.''

"At the same time?" Lya asked.

"Hell, yes. Drink *till* you catch one."

"You've been doing that without Jack," Lya pointed out.

"True," Lewis admitted. "But not fish-drinking. That was celebration-drinking."

"What were you celebrating?" she asked.

"My last fish."

"How long ago was that?"

He sneered at her. "Hussy."

He stood up abruptly, swaying. He seemed confused. "What's wrong?" asked Lya, concerned.

He scratched his head. "Can't remember. . . . What was I about to do a bit ago?"

"How many guesses?" I asked.

Lewis shook his head. "No, really."

"Uh, challenge Jack?" offered Lya.

"Did that."

"Tell about raising the planet?" I suggested.

"Did that."

Lya winked at me. "How about stagger around dripping water?"

"*Doing* that," said he and I in unison and the three of us laughed.

Lewis cut short his laughter ahead of us with: "Aha!"

"Aha, what?" prompted Lya.

He grinned, pointed in the direction of Karen. "Aha'm gonna see what read this girl to the grave." And he stepped awkwardly over me toward her.

I turned to Lya, getting to my feet. "Bout ready to go in?" She nodded. I started to gather up the mess around us. Her hand on my arm stopped me. I looked at her and saw that the tightness had returned to her features. I was amazed at how temporary an effect all the laughter had had on her capacity to worry. I squatted down beside her.

"Jack . . ." she began.

I cut her off. "Lya, would you stop fretting?"

"But you will talk to him."

"I said I would. And I will. Relax. Holly's a big boy."

"But Jack," she said, her eyes pleading, "he's taking such a terrible risk!"

I sighed, patted her arm. "Well, he hasn't taken it yet."

But he had. We heard Cortez's screams a second after that. He was bounding toward us across the meadow, slipping and sliding, falling once, waving his arms. We rushed to meet him. Through his panting and hysteria he managed to get out that Holly had been discovered lying unconscious on the laboratory floor, babbling incoherently. He was clutching some sort of plastic skullcap or something with all sorts of tubes and wires running out of it. Nobody had been able to pry his fingers loose from it. A seizure, the doctors had said. Catatonic.

Lya was already running back to the Dome before hearing all that Cortez had to spout. Karen, now wide awake, sprinted athletically after her. I gave it up after about a hundred meters. Damned bug still had a piece of me. I had to slow up to wait for Sanction to stop spinning.

Lewis appeared beside me, looking benignly helpful. "Here you go, Jack," he said and offered a shoulder. He was a good crutch, in considerably better shape than most drunks I had seen. But even with his help, it seemed to take forever to cross the field, enter the Dome, and work our way down into the lab. All the time the thought kept streaking through my mind that Holly, with his genius fried, would now be nothing more than the timid lad he had at first seemed to be.

As we stepped through the seal, I heard Holly's voice. He was sitting up on the workbench, surrounded by nervous faces. I broke loose from Lewis and rushed ahead to see him. Hot damn! He was alive, anyway. . . .

". . . no, really, really," he was saying to them. "I'm fine. A little weak, but. . . ." He noticed my stumbling approach. "I'm okay, Jack," he assured me with a smile that contained equal parts of shyness and pride.

I was still worried. "I can see that. You *look* great, but. . . ." How to put the next question?

He anticipated me. "It's still me, Jack." He turned to Lya, putting a weary arm around her shoulders. "Really. It's still me. I'm fine. Just a little tired."

The doctor was reading a gauge off a medigrip attached to Holly's other arm. "You're considerably more tired than that, Dr. You're near physical exhaustion." He pulled one of

Holly's eyelids up with a thumb and scanned the pupil underneath. "And emotionally drained as well, I'd say."

Holly nodded vaguely. "Well, maybe a. . . ." he began before pitching forward into Lya's arms, out cold.

The doctor was quickly reassuring. "He's all right," he said to Lya.

She looked about to faint herself. "Are you sure?"

The doctor nodded, gestured toward his gauges. "I'm sure. Just worn out, like I said. He'll be all right with plenty of rest and care."

"He'll get that," asserted Cortez importantly. "I'll see to it."

Lya smiled at him. "Thank you, Cortez. That's very sweet of you. Why don't you start right now." She nodded at Holly's still form, still crumpled between her and the tabletop. Cortez stepped to her side and the bunch of them managed him into a prone position. Lya stepped back. "Thank you, everybody," she said to us, "for showing such. . . ." She froze at the sight of something over my shoulder.

We all turned around. Lewis was still standing at the entrance of the seal. His face was hard as stone, his muscles drum tight. He was staring at the black scout suit which had been propped into a sitting position in a chair beside the workbench, wires and tubes streaming outward.

Lya took a step toward Lewis. "Lewis? Are you all right?"

He turned slowly at the sound of her voice. He raised a trembling arm and pointed at the suit. "What . . . is . . . that??"

"That's a scout suit, Lewis. Holly's been using. . . ."

"That, that's . . . WAR SHIT!" he shouted, livid with rage. *"What's it doing here?"*

"But Lewis," protested Lya meekly, clearly unnerved by the incredible transformation of personality, "you knew this was a Fleet Proj. . . ."

"I knew you were *in* Fleet! I didn't know you *were* Fleet, godammit!"

He turned and stared at us, fury and disgust rippling his features into a fist. Then he walked out.

Nobody moved for several seconds. Then came the collective sighs and all was activity again. Lya hovered over Holly mumbling rapid-fire questions the doctor gamely answered. Karen strode to the intercom and ordered a springer team to the lab and intensive hook-ups for Holly's sleeping quarters. Cortez and a couple of techs began clearing a path through the electronics for the springers to better reach the bench. I sat down heavily in a chair and lit a cigarette and pondered.

I took the opportunity moments later to add my superfluous assurances to those Lya had already heard while Holly was being loaded. Then I managed to evade questions put to me by the curious and morbid stopping by out of rumor. When Holly and most of the rest had gone, I stayed and talked briefly with the doctor, learning nothing new. Then, when he was gone, I helped the techs guess what should and should not be keyed off in the lab during Holly's absence.

When they left, I was alone. And so, with Holly safe in his bed and surrounded by professional concern and laymen's good intentions, I found the chance to betray him. In all the confusion I was sure to have several minutes alone with the security systems. It was a rotten act, to take advantage of him that way, but perhaps no worse than the act of sabotage itself which took a surprisingly short time.

A half hour later, only I knew how helpless Holly really was. . . .

More still. She was waiting in my suite when I got back, flushed still with the excitement and the running and . . . the point of being there.

"How dare you leave me in there the other night . . ." she began, clutching my arm furiously.

Mad, guilty, upset too much, I clamped my fist around her upper arm to jerk her away, clamped too hard, and she moaned with the sudden pain and our eyes met and her lips parted and I knew what our point really was. As I had known for some time.

This was it. Strength on her. The clamping fist, anger and muscles together. Brute, from me. And she screamed when I threw her down and was upon her, ripping at the spotlessly white Crewjumpsuit and she struggled and kicked but writhed too. She surged into it. Maybe I did too. But both of us fell toward it, scratching and clutching and it got very, very, rough. Perfectly awful/awfully perfect . . .

And then laid flat out, pinned and twisting. Blood seeping from her nose and a shiner coming on and screaming at me for . . . begging me to make her beg and please/oh/please—YES, YES, tell her over and over what she really was! She loved to hear me tell her what she really was.

And I did. But damned if I really knew. Either of us.

It was spectacular and all-encompassing and it racked through me, shocking, stunning bolts of pleasure and pain. Both of us beating on her, abusing her, degrading the angel's exquisite form and yes, the angel herself and, of course, whatever was left of both of us and always, always, so damn *rich* with rippling ecstasy. So damn *good*, somehow. So damn *rich*.

So horrible.

Eventually, mercifully, we slept.

In the nick of time.

XIII

"He had no *faith*!"

Holly said it like he still couldn't believe it was true. He looked at me with all the wide-eyed incredulity of a child learning for the first time that "fair" has nothing to do with the real world. Shocked, hurt, more than a little frightened. Angry, too, and morally indignant. Demanding an explanation.

I had none. None, anyway, that would do any good to him right then. So I changed the subject: "I thought you said you couldn't read the guy's mind?"

"I couldn't. Not really. I mean, I couldn't tell when he was going to move until he moved or what he was going to say until he said it. But I . . . felt it when it happened. It was so close. So *intimate*."

"You mean emotions?" I persisted. "You could read those?"

"Not read them," he replied carefully. "Feel them. Or rather, feel him feeling them."

I glanced across the bed to Lya for some reaction. No luck. She sat as she had for the entire hour I had been there: hunched forward in her chair with her elbow propped on a

199

knee, her chin propped in her palm, and her eyes staring dead blank at the floor. The only signs of animation came when she put out one cigarette in order to light another. But she was listening. Her face was drawn so tightly across her cheeks it looked like it should hurt.

I shifted back to Holly, looking skinny and out of place against the vast expanse of linen. Even his bedclothes dwarfed him, ignoring all but his broadest gestures. He was constantly having to drag his huge collar around to match the motions of his neck. And there was a lot of motion there. His eyes darted constantly about the room. From the ceiling to the walls to Lya to me and back again, pausing only when he had trouble choosing the right words. Then he would stare at the palms of both hands held plaintively before his face like twin viewscreens and his eyes would glaze and he would be back there, in the suit. In the War.

It was particularly eerie.

He wasn't away long this time. He dropped his hands on his lap. "He had no faith!" he said again, the same way as before.

I nodded, exactly as if I had any notion whatsoever. "Well, I've got to run," I lied, standing up. "See you . . . tomorrow, Holly. Lya."

Something in my uneasiness must have leaked through. Holly looked up at me, at *me* this time for the first time.

"No, Jack. Uh . . ." He glanced at Lya. "Tonight. Can you come back tonight?"

I noticed Lya watching me too. I nodded. "Tonight it is," I said and scooted too quickly out the door.

I hurried through the seals outside where the sun was shining and the sky was Earthblue and lovely, where there were horses and cattle-things on the meadows surrounding the western edge of the Dome. The guards on the bridge smiled at me and waved and said something unintelligible but nice. I took all of this in and relished it, filled my lungs with it. Got all the way across the bridge, sat down at the far end of it and got my cigarette lit before I let myself think.

On the other hand, I told myself furiously, Holly *could* be simply stunned. Instead of the vegetable he appeared to be.

Or, maybe he was just stark raving mad, an improvement over being a carrot anyway.

Shit.

Or maybe it was just my usual guilt funk dripping those pitiful images. I made a command decision. I decided to forget about it. Holly was just tired out and a little disillusioned, that was all, by the reality of war vs. the flag waving. OK? OK. Besides, I was busy with traitor business. I had to see Wice.

I walked across the sewer bridge into the City. It was its usual teeming desperate self. People stomped or strolled or wandered about looking for spots to hide what little bits of their past lives they had dragged through the staggering jolt of getting this far. The maze was dry now, but miserably pock-marked with hundreds of hard and dusty footprint-craters. I limped and tripped alongside everybody else on my way to Wice's passage. I was about halfway up the gradually ascending length of it in about a tenth of the time it had taken me before in the rain and darkness and despair. It was more than just the physical conditions which made this day different, however. There seemed to be a new touch of something in the air, crisp and clean and . . . hopeful, maybe, the way the people clamored about. Like the rain had washed something away and what was left was good and purposeful and. . . .

And so feeling poetic and the like, I got a little careless.

A guy came suddenly hopping out of a narrow side tunnel moaning in pain and fluttering his right hand in the air. *"Damn-damn-damn-damn . . . damn!"* he said to himself and then, apparently seeing that he wasn't alone, to me. Then he stopped his hopping long enough to hold his left thumb up and examine it critically. It was purple and, I assumed—yes, *assumed*—it was swelling.

"Can you believe it?" he asked. "This is the fourth damn time?"

I smiled, partly because of the way I was feeling and partly because of the way the guy was. Nice-looking man. Big, broad-shouldered with long black hair that was maned, squared-off around his forehead. He was oriental, Earth-orient, that is. He had an easy, powerful voice.

"Seems like a lot," I agreed pleasantly.

"My dumb-ass helper," he added with a shrug in the direction from which he had appeared. "Idiot has no grip whatsoever." He shook his head and sucked briefly on the purple digit. He grimaced slightly.

I shrugged consolingly, made a step past him.

"Hey!" he said, brightening. "Can you give me a hand? It'll just take a second. Just help Idiot hold it in place long enough so that I can. . . ."

And blah blah blah with me following him around the corner and, sure enough, there was a corner of one of the local throw-togethers exposed with this huge piece of what looked like plassteel heat shielding resting beside it that looked to have been carved out to fit the hole. Up above on the second "story" was this little guy with red hair, the Idiot, no doubt, leaning out of what had once been an escape hatch back during the time when this erector set used to be a star ship. And it *looked* all right. The redhead was in a good position to hold the piece of plassteel, if he leaned out the hatch, while the oriental on the ground could brad it in tight.

So I nodded and stepped forward and the oriental picked up one side and I reached for the other and the redhead stretched both arms down to get it and then I noticed that it really wasn't plassteel at all. It was that plastoform crap that was so popular because it was cheap and *looked* like plassteel and I thought: *Well, hell, he oughta be able to just hold this with one hand*. . . .

And that's when the oriental hit me.

He was a big guy and it was a damn good blow, a forearm to the side of my head. I went down flat.

Then rolling away into position for the next shot and then there was red hair flying through the air onto me out that hatch and he hit me as hard as the local gravity allowed for his fall—which was plenty—and before I got a good grip on him or the oriental who loomed over me or anything else, the sun was blotted out by many others crowding in for a piece.

The crowd worked well together, each getting a good grip on me and lifting me up off the ground making me helpless and, worse, making me know it. They hustled me around a corner and then around a couple others, the passage getting narrower and narrower until we stopped in this tight square claustrophobic little area surrounded on three sides by three stories of maze, crooked and ugly and seeming to lean in on us.

They had me. Absolutely goddamn *had* me. No one broke his concentration or loosened his grip or looked like he was going to. Two on each leg, two on each arm. One held the back of my head against his chest with two huge hands, the thumb of the left one painted purple.

Shit.

Shit because they had me, really *had* me and I hated, loathed, was repulsed . . . *sickened* by having hands on me without my consent. And double shit because I had been so utterly fooled and, come to think of it, triple shit.

Because not only did this group know how to handle itself against an enemy, they knew how to handle themselves against me. This wasn't a shake-down or a robbery or any other sort of thug-mugging gang. This was the execution of a plan dreamed up by someone who used well-trained, or at least well-drilled, disciplined people who knew just how good I was and who weren't taking any chances.

"Bring him here," said somebody I couldn't see. And they did, all eighteen legs of them spiraled around so that I might face the man who had spoken. He stood on a jutting piece of webform a couple of meters over our heads. He looked about fifty, which meant nothing, of course. Still, I had the impression that his appearance was "natural," non-cosmetic. Which would have made him a couple of decades younger than me.

But I only noticed those details in passing, the way I noticed his well-worn tunic and his beard and the unusually long thin fingers on the hands hanging clasped before him. For beside him, stood Eyes. Clean now and, amongst her folk, safe. Long brown hair tucked into something functional. Legging-things on the legs of her pants. Simple tunic like her father's . . . was it her father who stood at her side? I never found out.

She looked strong and capable and lovely and well worth the fighting that had gone on for her sake. Still Eyes, too. Hers shone in the sun.

"You must forgive us," began their leader, opening his hands in an expression of regret, "for having treated you in this fashion. But your somewhat lethal reputation has preceded you."

"Is that supposed to be an apology?" I snarled.

"It is."

"That the best you can do?"

He stiffened. So, in fact, did a couple of the ones holding me. Eyes, I noticed, showed no reaction at all. She was still waiting.

"I assume," he began again, "that your statement implies release." He paused, wiped his brow clear of a lock of sandy-gray hair with one of those long fingers. "Quite understandable, of course," he resumed. "Even reasonable, under normal circumstances." Those hands clasped together again and he peered forcefully into my eyes. "You, sir, are hardly normal circumstances, even for us. If I were to have you set free, how many of your captors would be killed or maimed or otherwise handicapped before they could get free?"

I grinned, shrugged. "Three."

He nodded. "At least three, Mr. Crow. At least." His hands separated again, palms upward. "So you see how my hands are tied."

I laughed. I had to. So, apparently, did everyone else. At the absurdity of the situation. And at our own, each and everyone of us. So bizarre . . . So *often!* Eyes, sparkling, laughed herself beautiful. I forced my thoughts and my feelings and . . . and *me*, away from the idea of that.

The leader had resumed. ". . . do hope you won't be too uncomfortable while I say what little I have to say. In any case, I. . . ."

"Get on with it," I snapped, hating buddy-buddy while being held.

That cooled 'em off instantly. We all got a lot more tense. The muscles on the hands that held me grew more taut. Good. This was not fun, dammit.

"Very well, Mr. Crow," said the leader stiffly. "I shall indeed get on with it. First let me tell you a little bit about who we are." He spread his hands wide to indicate, not just the immediate throng, but the City itself.

And then he gave a speech. It was a pretty good one. And

he didn't ease up much, either. He really did tell me who they were. And what.

They were crewmen and -women from the starships or couples with girls and boys of draft age or merchants fleeing the growing restrictions of wartime. They were Societies Against the Loss of Something or Other. They were people who had pushed off into the unknown one step ahead of Fleet expansion or two steps ahead of prison. They fled the loss of freedom, the courts, their wives or husbands, their past.

Most simply fled the Antwar. Quite a few were deserters. Each had, or had *been*, deserted.

So they crashed their shuttlecraft in the gorge or entire ships along the flatlands under the shale bluffs. Sometimes they left their empty ships in orbit. Sometimes the same orbit. The rare nightflashes of colliding bulkheads were the sources of much amusement as well as a small monthly lottery.

Many, many died.

Many had lived though, and those folk hung together. Raw and bleeding and desperate, they tacked the tortured metal together and hammered at the bulkheads and welded and strained and fought and lived. Outer hulls became outer walls. Airlocks became doors. First one battered ship became two battered ships. And then three and then four. Beside it another equally ugly configuration began to grow the same way. And then another and another. The first clearing opened into another outer one and so on until there was formed the maze, the Maze! The Maze, of dirty heat-blasted metal and plassteel through which trod an ever-growing horde. The streets were almost always muddy. So, usually, were the people.

Primitive hydroponics kept them alive. Then came other things. And though they were never fully organized in any formal sense, bosses had appeared to make the attempt. The tough guys didn't last long. They rose up and seized control for awhile until stabbed or blazed or beaten to death by one-time clerical assistants or pharmacists or third-class drive-techs who had come a long way to be rid of such men and would damn well not accept them now.

There were major setbacks and major villains, but each and all were vanquished, trod into the mud of the maze by a deeper, mightier vitality that came from desperation and the will to live. Soon it was just a naked force bigger than the sum of its parts. Bigger and stronger and, somehow, more mature. Ready, at last, to evolve into something else: a City.

"And then," I said, interrupting, "came Wice."

The leader broke off his rhetoric and eyed me narrowly. After a moment he nodded. "Yes," he said. "Wice. And his band of animals. And now the whole process has begun all over again."

I snorted. "The people seemed behind him on the bridge a few weeks back. Against the Project Director, no less."

"The people don't understand him. They don't know what he is. They don't see. . . ."

"What you want them to see?"

There was a murmur of anger through the bunch holding me. A couple of them increased the intensity of their grips. Even the leader was affected. His poise busted at last.

"Wice and his crew are a band of cutthroats and hoodlums who would do anything to take control and hold it. *Anything!*" He stared angrily at me for several seconds before resuming. "We know that you know Wice, that you have dealings with him. But we had hoped that from what we had heard about you in the past and from . . ." he glanced briefly at Eyes. ". . . And from other sources, that you were not the type of man to be helping such a brigand. Not if we could make you see what he was. If you only knew . . ."

"If I only *knew*?" I shouted, appalled. "If I only *cared*, you mean!"

That froze him. He started to speak, stopped. He looked suddenly unsure, uprooted. He stared at me. "But if . . . What do you . . ."

"Finish this!" I barked. "One way or the other."

He continued to stare at me a long time. No one else. The rest couldn't look. They looked away. But the leader seemed welded to me.

Dammit, I knew what he was about. It made sense. Borglyn gave me a ship; Wice would hardly throw in for free. But who the hell was I to cut out his piece? I didn't blame this man. I didn't blame him or Eyes or his people. I wouldn't have stood for it either. They were right to oppose this sort of bullying. But, goddammit, that didn't mean they were Right!

He broke the gaze at last. He looked at his feet. The long fingers intertwined, writhing incestuously. He looked pale and pitiful and . . . *damn* him!

"Let him go," he said.

They did. Reluctantly, then warily, then carefully. I made no moves when they set me down. I even gave them a chance to back away before standing. The leader hadn't moved. I looked at Eyes, saw she had gone. They were just eyes now.

But when she saw me looking at her, They returned. In anger and disgust, her eyes became Eyes once more. And I knew why they had affected me so. I saw the dreams in them then. The Right-ness. And, more importantly, the conviction. The willingness about the necessary risks. Her life on the line.

But I had already made all of those decisions, dammit. I wanted my ship.

Gradually I became aware of movement all around me. I turned my head to see that everyone was leaving. The leader had already gone. Soon there were only the two of us left there, staring at one another. And soon after that, only me. But not soon enough.

For before she left, she said, in a way I refuse to recall, "So *you're* Jack Crow." Then she spat. Then she left.

I wanted to kill her. I just stood there.

It took me half an hour to find out that the passage I had chosen to lead me out was a dead end. I kicked the web of Thermoflex blocking my path with a vengeance. I *could* have killed her then. I sighed, suddenly exhausted by my own anger, by the burdensome weight of it. "A perfect day," I muttered and turned back around. It took me another half an hour to reach the square once more. Only then could I think about finding Wice's lair.

His office had been straightened up somewhat, but he was the same old charmer. "What did you tell them?" he asked without preamble as I stepped through the door.

"Fuck off," I replied evenly.

"Is that a direct quote?" asked an unmistakably powerful

voice from behind me. "Or simply more evidence of your sparkling personality."

I spun on my heel and faced Borglyn, momentarily stunned once more by the sheer enormity of him. A for-real giant.

"Both," I snapped, gathering together quickly, as I always seemed to do in a pinch, my worst side.

Borglyn ignored my response, as he could well afford to. He motioned me to a chair and stood over me and talked strategy. And when the question came about the Dome defense screens . . . I could have lied, said that it couldn't be done. I could have simply turned the question aside, as I had before with Wice. But I didn't.

"It's done," I replied. "They're helpless."

Borglyn didn't stay much longer after that, just long enough to "thank" me for what I had done so far and to reiterate what Wice had said before about the uncertain timetable. He thought a couple of more weeks but he couldn't be any more definite than that. Then he left.

And why not? There was no need to stick around. He had what he wanted. He had gotten my assurance about the screens. And I had gotten the point of his being there, which was the knowledge that he *could* be there any time.

On the way back to the Project, I thought about what it had been like to have been hung in the air by those fat fingers of his. And I bristled, both at the remembered feeling of frustration and at the knowledge that it was just what Borglyn would want me to think about.

XIV

Holly wasted no time getting down to it. When I rang the secured seal to his lab he opened it himself with the manual key and then personally escorted me into his little briefing cubicle. There were several screens attached along the length of the conference table, each glimmering with rhythmically esoteric data. Lya was next door in an adjoining cubicle with a couple of screens of her own. She waved at me through the connecting window and flashed what I'm sure she thought was a cheerful and carefree smile. Her appearance was a considerable improvement over that morning. But the strain could not be hidden.

Idly, I wondered why she should even try to hide it.

"First of all," began Holly after we had sat down, "I want to apologize for being so uncommunicative this morning. I didn't mean to be so obscure. It's just that I didn't know how to express what I was feeling. And I . . . well, I'm sorry about it."

I grinned. "And what about scaring the shit out of me after the picnic? Not that I could care less if you burned out your brains, but the least you could do is try not to spring it on me."

Jack Crow Crap, but just the kind of compliment that Holly adored. He flushed a little and grinned shyly and glanced down at his hands folded on the table before him.

But all the boyishness was gone in the next instant as he continued.

"Secondly," he resumed, "I want to assure you that I'm fine. I was not harmed by the experience, however bad it may have seemed at the time. Neither physically nor mentally." He sat forward, made a steeple out of his fingers, and peered intently into my eyes. "I want to stress this, Jack. Every medico in the Project has been over my numbers and there's nothing wrong."

"Nothing that they can find, anyway," I amended.

He looked pained. He nodded reluctantly. "Yes. Technically, yes. However, I can think of no intelligent reason why one should simply assume damage without evidence, do you?"

I shook my head in response, amazed at the stern tone his voice had briefly assumed. A real Director of Project tone, that.

Holly seemed not to notice. "Thirdly, I want to report that the experiment was a success. Not only was it a success, but it worked better than I had hoped."

I frowned. "Well, that's one way of looking at it. There is a little matter of the catatonia."

He looked pained again. He started to speak, stopped, re-thought. Then: "I'm getting to that, Jack. But let me take it step-by-step, please."

"Of course," I said pleasantly. Inside I was thinking that there is nothing spookier than having someone "stress" to you how sane they are after having had a fitlike seizure a few days before.

What Holly did next was go over ground I knew already. Talked about how it was the magnetic drainage of the Record pulses off the coil which had caused the problem in the first place. Reminded me why this prevented a screen from being used to view it. Next he re-outlined how he had hoped that, using his own little helmet and his own mind, a commonality to the two separate brain-wave patterns could be artificially and temporarily induced. He had worried that it was either an impossible scenario to attempt the commonality at all, or that too much strain would result from the two different patterns conflicting in unison. But instead, a third thing had happened: A third field had been created "between" his pattern and the other. It had been this third field which had provided the channel of reception. And this was a real boon. For not only did it allow him to "see" what was going on, but it had also allowed him to retain perspective over the process.

"That's what you meant when you said you could feel him feeling his emotions?" I prompted.

He nodded vigorously. "Exactly. It gave me the immersion I wanted, but it also kept me a step back. Prevented the possibility of psychological conflict."

"*Some*thing conflicted," I pointed out.

He smiled wanly. "Well, yes. There was a conflict of sorts. But not the kind that you—and Lya—had feared. It was not a conflict of psyche."

"Then of what?"

"Of intensity." He leaned back in his chair and sighed, spreading his hands on the tabletop. "It was simply too strong. Even with the sense of detachment. Not that I felt I was being . . . sucked in or anything," he was quick to add. "It's just that the emanations were simply too powerful. They caused an overload."

I thought a minute. "Couldn't you simply turn it down?"

He frowned, shook his head. "We're on the lowest gain now. The trouble is, my helmet requires a certain minimum charge to function."

I nodded. "I see the problem."

He nodded in return, but rather unhappily. "There is one more possibility, however. . . ."

"And that is?"

He looked reluctant. "Well, it could be that the intensity of reception is not due to the charge needed to power the suit. It could be that, well. . . ."

"It could be," finished Lya from the doorway, "the fact that we are dealing with a very unusual man. A very unusual, highly dynamic man." She walked over and sat down in the seat next to me. In her hand was a coiltape. "Battlefield conditions produce inordinate stress in anyone, but in Felix. . . ."

"You know what his name is?"

"Was, yes. It was Felix," Holly amended.

"Was?" I asked, surprised. "You mean he died?" Well, no *wonder*. . . !

"No," said Holly quickly. "He didn't die on me."

"But you think he will," I persisted.

Holly's smile was grim. He nodded. "I think so. In fact," he added, looking sad and very, very far away, "I can't conceive of any other possibility."

It was very quiet while we thought about that. Something in how Holly had said it, something about the . . . hopeless finality of it. Eerie. I caught myself staring out the window overlooking the main lab to the black suit propped into a sitting position alongside the main console. A menacing sight, sitting there just so. Menacing and sinister and. . . .

I tore my gaze away, shoving such thoughts roughly back into the shadows where they belonged. I cleared my throat.

"Well, I can see why you're stuck, Hol . . ."

"Oh, we're not stuck!" he jumped to add.

"But if you don't have any way to turn down the gain . . . ."

"We don't need to turn it down. There's another way to reduce the intensity." He glanced quickly at Lya, who met his gaze briefly, then looked away. "A way to halve it, in fact."

"What's that?" I asked, stepping into it.

They exchanged glances again. Holly made a determined effort to sit up straight and look me in the eye. "By adding another helmet and another . . . experimentor."

My mouth fell open. I closed it. So *that* was it!

I was too stunned to do much more than nod through the following offer. That and stare back and forth between their two intent faces while they fell all over one another in their efforts to assure me that there was no reason to suspect that there would be any danger involved. Hah!

There was more of the assurances. And then came the part about the great strides that could be made with such an experiment, reminding me that I had expressed interest in helping and how this would certainly be of more help than anything else I could do. Oh, yes: there was a mention of payment from the extensive Fleet funding.

So, could I think about it tonight and then let's talk again in the morning?

I said I would think about it.

Holly couldn't let it be. He talked about how he thought he had hit on something terribly important, something he couldn't explain altogether but something I would certainly understand when, that is . . . if, I decided to take part. And how he would especially like to have me and only me in on this, how he'd like to keep this experiment just among the three of us rather than involve others from the Project. Then more assurances.

I said I would think about it.

Lya insisted on walking me to the seal. Still more assurances, to start. Then honey-bull. The tone of voice with its quiet intensity, its brave conviction, and that look of Oh-I-know-I-can-trust-you-Jack-you're-so-strong-where-else-can-we-turn complete with the soft pressure of her hand on the crook of my arm and, incredibly, batting eyelashes. It was exactly the same crap she had used so effectively on me the day of the picnic, except. . . .

Except then she had believed it. She had known what she was doing was right, had known her concern for Holly was justified, had known my warmth for him was genuine and appropriate to call upon. She had known she was doing the right thing. Further, she had known what she was urging me to do was equally right.

This time she knew no such thing. She was lying with each and every well-chosen word.

Why me? I kept thinking. Maybe it was the Jack Crow Bit. Maybe she thought that I could just dive through the wiring feeds running between us and snatch Holly by the scruff of the cerebellum and haul him out of a tight spot. Or maybe she just didn't want the other Project people involved on Sanction to know what a Mad Hatter her man had become.

I said I would think about it.

And I did, in a way. Once I calmed down a little with a brisk walk through the seals to my suite. Once I had gotten over the urge to slap Lya's sanctimonious holier-than-lesser sacrifice all-for-my-man face. How dare that bitch! Screw up my head?

I had experimented with the hallucinogens years—decades—before alongside the rest of my once contemporaries. Luckier than most on account of not really ever believing that this mental masturbation was the Way, or the Path or whatever else they were calling it at the time. Seeing it, knowing instinctively that it was a brain teaser and nothing more. A trip for people who couldn't afford to travel. But even with that to back me up, there had been a time or two. . . .

So I knew better. Life was tough enough. Climbing down into that hole with Holly and his tubes wasn't the same as the rushing chemical thrill. And maybe—well, probably, if Holly felt so—there was something of great scientific value to be found. But it was that same hole, no matter how I got there, the hole where the creature lives, the monster, the fiend who comes terrifyingly quick, slipping up at you out of the muck, grinding his teeth, popping his jaws eagerly, clawing at your clean flesh with gnarled hands sporting gritty black talons and . . . using your face to know where it hurts the most.

Bullshit! And for somebody else to boot. A risk for another means sacrifice for another. And even if I wanted to—which I sure did *not*—where was I gonna fit it in? Too many risks already, wedged tight. And the jamming of it all still coming up.

Madness!

Cortez was nowhere in sight when I reached the suite. By now I knew what that meant. From the bedroom I could hear the faint hum of the 'fresher. Her clothing, Crew jumpsuit, boots and things, were piled in the corner of one of four chairs surrounding a small table. On the table itself sat her viewscreen. I wandered over to it, idly wondering what she read. A bit fretful, too, of finding something else I might have to live up to. The screen was off but the tab was on, the reference sequence glowing softly and efficiently in red.

I cringed. Fleet ID's are fifteen-digit numbers. And I had only seen this one once before . . . I hesitated, then pushed restart, and found myself staring at the official Fleet dossier of one John Jacob (Jack) Crow. I blinked, stared, stood there trembling. I felt . . . invaded.

I hadn't heard the humming of the 'fresher stop. Her voice from the bathroom door whirled me around.

"I had to know," she said in a small apologetic voice. She leaned against the sealjam as if for support, idly wiping at the remaining flakes with a towel.

"Had to know what?" I growled, my voice hoarse.

"I had to be sure!" she whispered intently. Pleading.

"Sure of what!"

"That you . . . that you'd go through with it."

"Through with wha . . ." I began and then, of course I knew what she meant as I remembered what we both remembered. I knew as I saw the tear swell and sink and slide down that horrible purple bruise beneath her eye.

I ordered food for two to be delivered to the outer room. We waited in silence until we heard it arrive. I went out to fetch it, blazing down Cortez's questioning look with a glance. I brought it back into the bedroom, wheeling the trolley up to the edge of the bed where she sat still wrapped in the towel. I pulled up a chair for me.

And we ate. For close to three hours, we ate. Usually there was far too much food brought to me. But not that night. I stuffed myself; Karen stuffed herself. We stopped. I smoked. She drank wine or simply toyed with the stem of the goblet. Then we ate some more. Ravenously. Almost desperately. Until we could not take another bite. Then we stopped until we could.

And always in silence. "Music?" she asked once and I nodded, stood up, and keyed something neutral. It was the only word spoken between us the entire time. The music was a good idea. It gave us something to almost do while we sat between feasts.

Sometimes we looked at each other. Not often.

Over two and one half hours later, it was gone. Choked and still hungry; drunk and still thirsty. I stood up slowly, my head reeling with the wine, and went into the bathroom. There was nothing else to do. The feast was over.

I stayed in there a long time. Too long, really, to be healthy. I felt skinned when I came out. But that wasn't so bad either.

I didn't know if she would still be there or not. Didn't know what it meant either way.

She was there, under the covers. Her hair was spread like

dawn across the pillows. I noticed the music was gone and the lights were dim. My cigarettes had been placed on the bedside console. I got in beside her. She slid toward me, tucking in.

After a while, perplexed by my inability to feel where my skin left off and hers began, I became a louse. Said something idiotic and provocative about seeing her dossier. Her answer was to lift her head and rest her chin on my chest and peer at me until I was forced to meet her gaze.

Then she said: "I'll tell you anything you want to know."

It was *not* a qualification. It was not defensive or evasive or in any way devious. I knew that. I *knew* it. But. . . .

"All right, goddammit, tell me about it," I dared, lighting a cigarette.

And so she did tell me about it. All about it. I lay looking at the ceiling and seeing the pictures formed by her words and by the way the small of her back shuddered beneath my palm. Her voice was invariably gentle. Timid sometimes. Sometimes matter of fact. There was bitterness too, of course. And sadness and regret and wicked touches of irony. But never laughter. Not once that . . . a rich kid, happy little girl wearing pinks and blues and whites because those were the favorite colors of her Daddy. She wore black for the first time at twelve, at his funeral.

. . . the vacuum time. No brothers or sisters. Only Mother, who cried and drank in rooms with the lights out.

. . . hope and a stepfather at thirteen. Raped at fourteen. No trial. Divorce instead. They moved. Moved again. A short remarriage. A long second divorce. . . . spectacularly beautiful at sixteen. A first fiancé. Another. Two more. At seventeen and one half, a husband. "Mentally unbalanced" an exceptionally generous description. Long separation burdened by guilt but tinged throughout as well by brief flashes of genuine terror. Divorce, at last, followed on cue and as advertised, by the tragedy, sick and loathsome and out of her hands but still . . . His funeral left to her by his family who begged and pleaded and then used her symbolic resumption of the role as an excuse to blame and accuse.

. . . finishing school near the top of her class—never any

trouble there at any time for she is bright and curious and somehow inherently hopeful.

. . . joining Fleet a month later. A month after that, still in boot camp, raped a second time. Trial serves to both exonerate him and brand her as angel-haired slut, a blatant lie but a common fantasy in the courtroom.

. . . powerful military types crossing wires to get her transferred their way. When the last string is pulled, the last favor cashed, she finds herself on Capital Earth where she is promoted, pampered, and eventually raped again. There is no second trial. More promotions instead. And a transfer to Militar, itself, hub of Fleet. Corridors of power.

. . . picking and choosing, now. Not rape. Not love. Not enough.

. . . her second military rapist, the general who spouted promotions, has died in the Antwar. He dies rich. Dies guilty too, his will mentioning her a Fleet scandal. Karen laughs at hushed whispers and gestures just out of the corners of her eyes—she had planned to kill him some day but this does nicely. Tense negotiations in conference room surrounded by leather-bound precedents. The children sitting on either side of their bewildered, wooden mother, their eyes blazing hatred and envy for the lustre of her blonde hair and for what they assume to be the comparative richness of Karen's relationship with their cold, calculating, career-minded Father. They want to kill her but they sit still (as per lawyer's orders) for the money.

. . . another transfer. More promotions, often due to her considerable merits. She rises always. Higher and higher. Feeling like two people but the promotions are *something* after all, aren't they.

. . . tries a couple of times and nothing. Never knowing which of the two cared or could care. And if she doesn't know, the poor men . . . Transfers away from it twice, once too soon, once far too late. But, either way, gone from it.

. . . a year before trying again. Too little to matter. Another promotion, though. Rising Is.

. . . to her mother's deathbed. Terminal prognosis she is told. "No hope for me," says Mother, adding macabrely that she had been "born again." She urges baby to repent.

218 / John Steakley

. . . but this sanctimonious bastard Padre, who never misses a chance to touch her, however chastely, during her devotions makes her ill. And she tells him so. Stung, he informs Mother that Baby's penance is as insincere as the scarlet paint of the harlot she is.

. . . dies Mother, slowly and badly, refusing to admit her sinful daughter to the end, on the advice of her priest.

. . . over a year later, pinched with the hardness of despair, she tries again and it . . . almost . . . works!

His name was Leslie and he was a lovely man who loved her dearly. In return she felt a genuine . . . affection. She felt a true . . . warmth. And safe. She felt safe. At the crucial moment, she told Leslie all.

He ached with the jolt of her life. He wept.

Also, he questioned, over and over. Then he accused. Then he raged, then denounced, then beat her. Then he went.

Soon after came another, most important, promotion. Along with it came an offer to be number two on a Fleet Project. A three-year stretch on an unknown but earthlike place. Dr. Hollis Ware. The offer is an honor at her age, but no less than she deserved, one way or another. Still, she didn't want to go, to strand herself three years where she could not rise. She put off the decision for weeks, caught between the allure of being, for once, legit and with the tantalizing momentum of Rising Is. Without being aware of it, she dreamt of another choice.

Then Leslie returned, providing just that. He was tearful and contrite and ashamed, but filled with protestations of hope. She knew his love for her, his heartbreaking devotion to her, was genuine.

The next day, in secret, she signed with Holly. The next month, without warning, she went aloft to Sanction. It was, she felt, doing the best thing for the lovely man. He was so sensitive, so easily hurt.

He had brought his parents along with him, to meet her.

She slept at last on my soaked shoulder. I smoked. Sometime in the middle of it she had said: "I know it was all my fault. I guess I'm just no good, like Mother said."

I smoked and heard that still, still expecting to bleed to

death from the grinding rasp of those words. I felt numbed by the Vice.

And then she did an amazing thing. She stirred in her sleep and laughed. Giggled, really, like a little girl. A sweet safe beautiful little girl who knew only the blue of the sky and green grasses and party dresses of pink and blue and white. I reached over carefully and keyed off the last of the light. I doused my cigarette. I lay there. For hours, it seemed, I lay there, my eyes burning in the dark.

The next morning, bright and early, I went down and saw Holly and did the one thing I had been so certain I would never do: I volunteered me.

So bizarre. . . .

XV

Holly and I sat facing one another on twin loungers. Lya sat at a console between our feet. The suit sat propped at the other. Feeding circuits sprouted everywhere, linking the suit to a couple of other consoles which were keyed through a massive coiltape, Lya's board, and us. Today was the day.

"A couple of things," began Holly, all businesslike. "Firstly, the raw data." He reached over behind him and keyed something. A small screen lit up with light green letters against a dark green background. "Name: Felix, G. Age: 26. Current assignment and rank: Warrior Scout aboard the starship *Terra* in deep elliptical around A-9."

A-9? A distant bell rang somewhere. Something I'd seen on the vid? Lya helped me out with: "Banshee."

Oh. Yeah.

Holly cleared his throat. "More. This takes place—or rather, took place—almost exactly four standard years ago. Earthdate: July 4, 2077."

That *did* ring a bell. Holly noticed my expression and nodded. "Yes. This is the Independence Day Drop, the very first invasion of Ant soil. Quite literally, mankind's first step into the Antwar."

Holly continued in that efficient way he had, briefly recapping the events surrounding that day. It was hardly necessary. True, I had gone to some trouble in past years to avoid having news of that insanity intruding into my life. But I knew about that day!

I remembered it clearly, remembered sitting fixated before the vid like probably every other human in the known worlds. There had been something so spectacular about the events of those first weeks. About the idea of it. Interstellar war! Ants eight feet tall! Of course it was madness. But in a race where most children grew up playing war—breathtaking fun. It was a good two to three months before I stopped beginning each day by tuning in news of the Antwar. And it wasn't until the end of that first year, that horrible first year which saw over two million people wasted, that I turned away, refusing to even listen to Antwar conversation.

That had been four years before. The Antwar raged still.

I snapped back just in time to hear Holly's historical windup. He ended with a short explanation about why we . . . about why *they*, Fleet, had been unable to guide missiles in the Banshee atmosphere of poison and inscrutable magnetic fields. It was stuff I knew. Along with the fact that it, Operation Knuckle, the part involving our scout, was considered a brilliant military victory. Next came a brief recap of stuff I had missed in the few minutes Holly had already played from the record. Then he gave me the same predrop briefing Felix had received. Word for word.

When he saw my puzzled expression over his perfect recall, he merely shrugged his shoulders and said: "You'll understand in a minute."

I clamped down hard on a sudden impulse to shudder.

"Now," said Holly, "how do I know all this? The name G. Felix I got from Fleet records using his Fleet ID number. The number itself I got by reading it off the inside of his helmet. It's inscribed right between his twin holos. You'll see it."

That scared me. "I'll be able to see through his eyes?" I demanded, appalled.

"Not at first," said Holly quickly. "Never, really." He looked uncomfortable. His eyes stared past me at something within. He frowned, resumed. "The data is neither recorded nor delivered that way. It's not even vaguely photographic, Jack. But, after a few minutes . . . I can't explain exactly." He shrugged again. "You'll see."

I would *see*? Through the eyes, or whatever, of a dead man? This time I did shudder.

Lya shifted forward in her chair, moving quickly on. "There are a couple of anomalies. First, in the Fleet records. According to them, G. Felix wasn't even there at the time of this battle. Wasn't even moved to the forward zone until well over three months later."

I didn't get it. I said so.

Lya smiled. "Frankly, neither do we. Confirmation codes didn't exactly clear it up. They did, Fleet Center on Militar, I mean, come back with something about incomplete records on G. Felix and some sort of trouble with them, but that wasn't until months later, as near as we can determine. There was reference to a security code needed for further data. A rather high code, in fact."

"Too high?" I asked.

Holly smiled indulgently. "No. I have it. But I decided not to use it." He looked at the floor, smiled nervously. "Why bother, if I was about to get the truth for myself?"

Hm. Why indeed, Holly? Unless you didn't really want to know. Or maybe he didn't want to call attention to himself by invoking a high security clearance? Or unless he had no faith in getting the truth from Fleet at all . . .

"No faith," Holly had said that morning. "He had no faith!"

I searched his uneasily averted gaze. Was he, superpatriot Fleet scientist, beginning to have doubts? *Some*thing was making him all a-flutter. I shuddered again. That something would be plain soon enough.

"What's the other anomaly?" I wanted to know.

Lya shifted in her seat again. I really hated it when she did that. "Well, I'm not entirely certain there is one. It's just that . . ." She gestured to the coilreel recorder beside her board. "I was able to get a coil of Holly's experience. Some of it anyway. His vital signs—respiration, heart rate, acid level—were recorded along with Felix's. Using what I knew about Holly's history, I was able to filter the two apart. So we know how Felix's body was reacting as well. Nothing unusual there. But," she hesitated, "we also have both sets of Alpha Series brain tracks." She hesitated again. "Felix's were a little odd."

"How?" I asked bluntly, not bothering to hide my rapidly growing suspicions.

"Well, the Alpha resembles, on first glance, classic textbook symptoms of schizophrenia. . . ."

"Great," I snarled angrily. "We're going into the brain of a raving. . . ."

Lya held up a hand. "On first glance, I said. The pattern, after careful study, misses at several key points."

"Then he's not mad?" I prompted. "Or getting there?"

She looked very uncomfortable. But she managed a little something definite in her tone. "I don't *think* he is." She looked at me, her face impassive. "I can't be sure. But I don't think so."

"Then why *tell* me, goddammit?"

She looked genuinely surprised. "I thought you wanted to know everything?"

"Well, I don't!" I snapped. Then to soften it, I tried a small grin. It seemed to help; she relaxed somewhat.

And then, abruptly, it was time. One last check to be sure Lya's monitoring systems were properly keyed in. Another check to see that our deadman switches—to jerk us out in an instant—were functioning. The helmets were lowered over our heads, over our eyes.

My last glimpse was of the suit, sitting darkly beside us. It was an impulse I couldn't seem to resist. And then . . .

I went . . .

to hell . . .

PART THREE

PUPPY IN A WELL

I sat slumped on the lounger watching Lya escort the medicos to the seal. She was questioning them urgently under her breath, trying to make sure they had meant it when they had said Holly and I were fine. I looked over at Holly sitting across from me (slumped too) scratching at the residue of paste left on his upper arm from the medigrip. He looked terrible. He was pale and beat and still wet from the sweat. He looked like I felt.

But we were fine, I knew. No matter what the doctors said or thought or anything else. We were fine. I guessed.

The food on the tray they had wheeled in between us was getting cold or hot or whatever was supposed to happen when we hadn't touched it. Funny. We had been starving when we'd asked for it. The water was long gone though. First thing we had done was drain a pitcher apiece. I pulled out a cigarette. It shook violently along with my hand, either from sheer exhaustion or from the weight of . . . I dropped it on the tray, unlit.

Holly made some effort to sit straighter. Tried a smile, too. I wondered why he made the effort.

"Well," he began energetically enough, "that was some 'brilliant victory'! And Felix was certainly there, despite the official record." He paused, seeming to run out of steam. He smiled again, this time a little embarrassed. "Well . . . I guess we can worry about the rest of it next time."

Our eyes met, held. I nodded. Not in agreement, but at what our mutual gaze had shared: there would be no "next time." No way.

I stood up slowly but steadily enough. "Tired," I said and headed for the seal. There was a clock on the wall above it. It said only a little over two standard hours had passed. I stopped, looked back at Holly.

He nodded. "It's right. It *seems* like it's long regular time. But it's fed to us pretty fast."

I thought about it. From the ship to . . . to being alone to the Knuckle and . . . all that happened there . . . Two hours! "That's incredible!" I whispered and continued my old man's shuffle to the seal.

Behind me, Holly agreed that it was incredible.

Never felt less in tune with my surroundings. I usually hated that. But this time I was too tired to care. I marched numbly through the seals to my suite, idly counting the number of people I passed in the corridors. I caught myself doing it, stopped it, caught myself at it again. So I gave it up. If that's what my mind wanted to do . . . Passed twenty-three people altogether.

I went inside and fell into bed, exhausted. I had been up a little over three hours.

Woke up when the screen showed night outside. I lit a cigarette and sat up in bed. But I had to put it out before it was half-finished. I slept again.

Woke up to Karen getting in bed with me. She saw that I was awake and kissed me on the forehead, banging me gently on the tip of my nose with a nipple. Then she snuggled up with her bottom against mine and slept. Like a puppy. Me, too. More hours.

*   *   *

The curved railing around the Dome balcony was made out of something cheap that made a shoddy raucous clang when I gripped it with every ounce of strength in my hands, shook it, shook it, gripped it, gripped it hard! but I didn't scream. I did not scream for anyone else to hear. I just shook and strained and gripped until I could do nothing but collapse back on my heels and tremble.

Then fell back in a heap and stared through the railings toward the City. I didn't cry either. I wouldn't. But. . . .

I took a long deep breath and let it out. I shook my head, held it still. I sighed. I looked up at the stars. They couldn't help me either.

Dammit, *I* had always been the toughest man I knew!

Always. No matter how bad it got or hard or wrong or . . . stupid, sometimes. No matter how bizarre.

I had always *known* that. So the universe was a swallowing bottomless bitch—I was the toughest *man*! Not strongest or quickest or smartest or, God knew, best. But toughest? Goddamn yes!

I sat up, leaning against the railing. I put my face in my hands and tried getting down to it.

Could I have done that? Maybe. Maybe I had already; there'd been a lot up to now. But . . . could I have done it the way Felix had? Which meant: could I have done it while *knowing* what was going on? While knowing *exactly*?

I wrenched my hands together in and out. I pounded my fists across the tops of my thighs.

I didn't think so.

For energy I went to hate. In fear I went animal, to be the Fiend myself, instead of fighting it. Most times I needed nothing but the situation, true. But when it had gotten tight and taut and stayed that way . . . In the furnace, I had had to pick and duel with each flame. I was never able to face the fire roar. It didn't make any difference that it was the same fight. It didn't matter that the end was the same. But the *knowing* how bad it was and how bad it could be and, dammit!, what I was going to have to do over and over to get out . . . I had never faced that.

Still, I had always been the toughest man I knew.

Now this Felix faced it all flat as hell, head on and . . .

and *knowing*, all along, how dark. He was detached, sure, and serious and separate from the knowing. But all through there was the terror and, most of all, the *reason* for the terror clear in him.

Facing where he was *and* fighting too, like some kind of damned engine. . . .

It would have ripped me apart.

It should have ripped Felix apart.

It hadn't.

I moaned, gathered my knees into my chest. Damn you! I wanted to shout. It's not fair! This is all I have!

Because it *was* getting to him. I could feel it in him. The fear was just as real as it should be. The sense of . . . hopeless despair, *poured* from the poor bastard! He *knew*! He knew how bad it was! And *still* he kept at it!

God*damn* him!

I sat there awhile until a little calmer. Holly had been right, of course. This man had died. There was no other way. There was no help for him because there was no faith in him and . . . no hope for him. And I felt bad about that. About the loss of somebody who was maybe . . . better.

But I shoved that all away—I had to—and concentrated hard on what I had to do. I *had* to do it.

I had to see more. Felix was going to die. He had to. But before he did, he was going to crack. And I was going to see it.

You see, I had always been the toughest man I knew.

Lya hated Felix's Alpha series.

"It's too great a separation between Motive and Emotional," she said, shaking her head at a screen glowing before her. She keyed away, shifting graphs and comparison charts and the like with impatience. She had seen it all before, of course. Had studied little else. Maybe she thought looking at it fast enough would help it make sense. At last she keyed the relay off with an irritated gesture. She shook her head again. "Too extreme," she said.

Holly and I looked at one another and smiled. She didn't know what "extreme" was. Yet. But she was about to. She had announced that next morning her intention to use the spare helmet. She'd be there "in person" next trip. Something about not being able, professionally, to accept the data before her. Not even with Holly's corroboration. It reminded me that she was more to the Project than Holly's better half. She was a full-grade Psyche-tech in her own right.

And maybe some of it was her "professional" skepticism. But I figured a lot of it to be the fact that Holly and I had survived it. On top of that she was feeling more than a little left out.

She could see it had done something to us. But she couldn't tell what. And we couldn't explain it. Holly couldn't, anyway. I had been quiet as I could get away with. I didn't want to think about it, much less talk about it and maybe have everybody know how I . . . hated.

Holly went to a lot of trouble to act like he wasn't feeling the pressure stamped so brutally across his face. He ignored his fatigue. He ignored his sudden lapses of concentration. He ignored his nervous fidgeting. Well, I could if he could.

But I wondered at his lack of reaction when Lya had announced her intention to join us. Not that I blamed him. Certainly I felt relief at spreading it a little more. No qualms from me. But Lya wasn't mine.

Is that why you fake it? I wondered, watching him brief her. Do you pretend it's nothing so you won't feel bad about sinking her in it, too?

I glanced over at the black suit, still propped into a sitting position beside the main console. What are you doing to us?

". . . the *personnel* data confirmed Felix being there. I should have checked that first. But usually the medical records are better kept. The trouble is," and he paused and scratched his chin. It was already red where he had done it so many times before. "The trouble is that, after the Knuckle, there's no more data on G. Felix. Destroyed, they say."

He looked up at us. To see if we wanted to snort. maybe.

"Anyway," he went on, "a lot of other stuff did check out." He studied a screen recessed at his elbow. "I confirmed Forest, for example. She did exist. She did die." He paused, then looked up and smiled. "She did place runner-up to Kent at the Olympics, too."

Lya sat forward. "And you say Felix had never heard of Kent?" We both nodded, though the question wasn't really meant to be answered. She looked at me. "Jack, you've heard of Nathan Kent, haven't you?"

I nodded. "Of course."

She looked back at the screen. "Odd that Felix had not." She touched a key. "Maybe," she said, almost to herself, "he was lying."

Holly and I exchanged a small smile. "It was the truth, Lya," he said.

"But how do you know?"

I couldn't resist it. "You'll see," I said with a look of . . . well, an ugly look.

Lya caught the words and the look. She ruffled nervously. "Yes," she replied in a low voice. "I suppose I will."

Holly got upset when Lya asked him what further information he had gotten from Fleet about the battle of the Knuckle.

"Nothing more," he said shortly.

"Huh?" I asked.

He shrugged his shoulders. "That high a security clearance I don't have."

I laughed. I couldn't help it.

Holly smiled wryly. "Incredible, Jack. They expect me to come up with a solution to this morass they've created. But they lie to me about how they got there. Incredible!"

I laughed again. "Governmental," I amended.

This time his grin was a bit more convincing. He checked the clock, looked questioningly about at us. "Any last comments, Jack? Questions, Lya?"

Lya had one. She wanted to know about that recitation Felix had given. "That title you mentioned. 'Guardian,' was it?" Holly nodded. "That sounds vaguely familiar. If you could remember what all Felix said, maybe I could have it scanned."

"I'll give it to you," I said.

She seemed surprised. Probably because I had offered little else. "Okay, Jack," she said, keying a coil. "Can you remember it all?"

Was she kidding? Word for word. I wanted to know about this . . . that man.

In a few minutes, with Holly and now Lya, beside me, I went to Hell again. The next day, after Lya had gotten over her first-Immersion need for sleep, I went again. And again and again.

But Felix wouldn't die.

We, the three of us, slept and ate and rested and smoked and, rarely, chatted—all in perfect comfort. But once, and later twice, a day, we would put on these silly little helmets that looked like skullcaps and live and breathe and fear and despair within the very skin of a man rushing through a forest of gigantic mandibles and huge globular eyes, tearing through this forest, shedding and spraying its black blood, carving through it with blaze-bombs when he could or a blazer rifle while it lasted or, much more often, with bare armored hands that ripped and tore.

But he wouldn't die.

The absolutely incalculable pressure of Banshee and the killing and the . . . total alien nature of his new world . . . it grew and grew in him. We felt it, each of us. We felt him separate and fight. We knew his dipassionate talent for carnage. We knew his inner terror and revulsion. We knew them as different and as the same. We knew they were separating, these two people, from themselves. We knew they were getting farther and farther apart. And we knew there was no room for this.

But still he wouldn't die.

Fleet didn't seem to know that Felix was only a human being. Maybe they didn't know this because he wouldn't act like one. Maybe they didn't know this because his ID was stuck firm inside a computer glitch. Or maybe they didn't know because he never spoke when he wasn't dropping—we wondered a lot about what his life was like aboard ship. Or maybe they didn't know because . . . they didn't care. Because they sure as hell did not care; they just kept dropping him again and again and again and. . . .

But he wouldn't die.

God, how I hated him.

And so, of course, did Holly and Lya. But I didn't know that then. Because I was too ashamed maybe, of my own hatred. Or maybe because I didn't care about them anymore.

So more drops and more horror and more hate and Felix wouldn't, *wouldn't*, die.

Holly tripped on one of the suit's boots, splayed out in the passage between two of the three loungers. He spun about, furious, to see what it was that had interfered with him. When he saw it was the suit, he paused, thought far too long for spontaneity, then kicked the suit as hard as he could in the chest. The field wasn't on so there was some flex there, but it still hurt his foot a lot to kick plassteel. He groaned and hopped up and down for a few seconds. He didn't say anything when he noticed I was watching. He didn't have to. I knew it had been worth the pain to him.

The suit was, of course, unmoved by the blow.

Lya's hatred was pseudoscientific as long as she could string it out. Talked about how the graphs and charts of Alpha series readings and the like just didn't fit. It was, she said, getting to be a "sore point" with her. Nobody laughed when she said this. Or paid much attention.

But one day, I did. When she was stalking back and forth on our break and mumbling to herself about this and that and I thought I heard the word "breakdown."

I asked her if she thought that's what Felix was going to have and she said: "Oh, he'll have a breakdown all right. At the rate he's going, he can't miss." Her voice was bitter, bitter, when she said this. But still I held my hand in front of my face so that no one would see the eager vicious look her words had sparked.

Another time, at the end of the "day" . . .

She slammed her fist angrily against one of her screens. We, Holly and I, looked up. She noticed our notice and got red in the face. "It's just," she began by way of apology, "that it's the most spectacular survival mechanism I've ever seen! And it's killing him!"

We didn't say anything. We just sat there watching her. No quarter.

So she went on with: "He's too sane, you know, to split completely. Too firm a grasp on reality. And the situation isn't real!"

Holly probably meant to be compassionate. But it came out bitter with: "It sure seems real enough to me." And a small smile.

"Oh does it?" she demanded, the hurt in her tone too plain. "This constant ant horror, the killing the dying—and never getting a break from Fleet, his own, *our* own people?" She stopped abruptly. Her chin quivered. "Who'd ever believe. . . ."

And she sobbed.

The sound of that burned through Holly and me and we were silent and as unmoving as statues while she hurriedly, thankfully, regained control.

"I'm sorry," she said in a moment or two. "It won't happen again."

Not where we could see it, she meant.

It kept getting worse. Not as bad as that first time, not as bad as the Knuckle, not then. But the pressure was accumulating. It was building up in us. Because we knew it was in him.

We got weirder. We moved through the days like Zombies. Or like K Dick wireheads. But worse because we weren't even happy hooked up.

And because Felix wouldn't die.

Everybody else did, though. Or had or would. And that was one of the most disquieting and . . . disorienting . . . things. It was really so goddamned dreamlike. There were all new faces around him all the time and always dying. Slowly or quickly or quietly or screeching.

New players each time but always the same game.

And once through the mists of our shoddy little obsession, I remember thinking: Four *years* of this so far!

Goddamn us.

And Felix wouldn't die.

I awoke crying. In Karen's arms.

She was real good about it. She held me until the sobs stopped. Until I could stop shivering. She may even have rocked me a time or two. But it disgusted her. And as soon as I seemed to be okay, she got up out of bed, dressed, and left.

I didn't much care. No waking moments, however pleasant with her or barren without, could make up for the nightmares themselves.

I sat up and lit a cigarette. I couldn't remember what I had been dreaming exactly. But I had a damned good idea. It was always a bad night on those days when Felix had been seriously injured. And the day before had been one of the worst. Lya, with her medical background, had estimated that he had been hurt badly enough to be in intensive care at least three times. Or four, counting today.

But he wouldn't die.

I was the first one down that morning, furious with Lya because today was the day she had insisted we discuss the science of what was happening to him. I was furious at this waste of time. For a sense of imminence had begun to be felt by each of us. Any day now. Any drop.

Any ant.

But she would not continue, she said, until all the psychological and physiological and other ramifications starting with P were discussed. She wanted answers to this mystery.

It made me mad. Time was wasting. And it was so obvious anyway.

Looking impatiently around the lab I noticed a calendar. I sat up straight in my chair, astonished to see that over three weeks had passed since this had begun. Idly I wondered how many rendezvous I had missed with Wice. I thought two, but I couldn't be sure.

Holly came walking briskly in, hiding his anger better than I did. In fact, Holly had hidden his reaction to the whole experience pretty well. He had always been quiet, of course. Now he was quiet and surly, a small difference really. And cold, of course. But we had all become that. Even Lya, as much as she could. He sat down beside me and pushed a tape into the slot.

"Look at this," he said as he keyed it on. I did but I didn't follow the jargon of the local computer. I said so.

"It's about Lya's request for information on that recitation

Felix gave on that first day. You gave it to her. Remember?"
I nodded. He pointed to a row of abbreviations. "All this
means is the extent of the scan. This machine didn't have any
reference. So it asked the Fleet Beam. Nothing there, either.
Had to go all the way to Earth, to the Biblioterre' in Geneva."

"Holly," I sighed, not bothering to hide my lack of interest,
"where did it *come* from."

He looked at me. "Oh. Uh, Golden."

"Golden?" I cried, surprised.

"Yes. It's part of the coronation ceremony for Guardian.
But not just *any* Guardian—you know they have about twenty—
but for the First Guardian. The "Guardian of Gold," it says
here."

"The Boss, you mean."

Holly laughed. "Boss is *a* way of describing the most
powerful monarch of the richest and most influential planet in
manned space. The First Guardian *is* Golden." He smiled,
shook his head at me. "Boss indeed!"

I shrugged. "Anything else?"

"Yes, as a matter of fact. It's a secret."

"But it was in the computer."

Holly frowned. "In a way, it was. You see, we asked what
it meant. If we had asked what it *was*, we'd have gotten
nothing."

I didn't get it. "Then why have it in there at all?"

"History. The Biblioterre' is where everything is kept from
all the planets that they want to last forever." He grinned
wryly. "Once this colonizing 'phase' has exhausted itself."

I was wondering how much I liked this new sarcastic Holly
when Lya breezed briskly into the room, her arms full of
coils. She sat down across the table from us and began
inserting various coils into various slots. She made the panel
appear at that end and, with it, several screens rise into
position. She looked very determined today. Not as if she had
solved anything yet. But as if she was damn well going to
before anybody took another step.

I lit a cigarette and waited for her to finish her preparations.
Holly went to some trouble to appear calmly attentive, but he
was just as impatient as I was.

At last, she was done. She came around to our side,

transferred control to the other panel before her, and began to lecture.

Holly winced a little when he heard that tone in her voice. He glanced at me, his face expressionless but his meaning clear: Uh, oh, the cold dispassionate scientist is back. I kept my face equally blank, but I was wincing, too. Not so much at his coldness, but at the price of it. In fact, the price of the whole scene was getting awfully high.

No more Young Genius worshipping the Great Jack Crow, which was no loss. But no more sweet Holly melding warmly with his exquisite Lya either. And that was going to be missed.

I glanced at the suit, back to the two of them, already debating.

"Notice first these three frequencies representing stress," said Lya, pointing to the largest screen. "The figure for stress is found by correlating . . ."

"Yes, yes, I see it," Holly didn't quite snap. "It's a three. Low."

"Particularly since this was recorded during battle."

Holly blinked. "Huh? It can't be."

She shrugged, turned the panel toward him to have him see for himself. He did. He checked *her* figures in *her* specialty. If she was angry, she didn't show it. Holly sat back when he was done, "Your equipment must be faulty." Lya's eyebrows lifted. *Her* equipment indeed. But all she did was key another screen and say; "Not necessarily. This is the Alpha series for the same period."

Holly's eyes widened. "Whew! A nine! I knew he was scared."

"So we have an apparent paradox."

And an argument. Or what would pass for one during this zombietime. In general, they were trying to figure out about Felix's split personality. Why was he splitting? How was he splitting? How come it worked? Specifically, how come his mind was terrified but his body was not? Sort of.

"Felix's fear is as strong as anyone's," said Lya. "We know that."

"Or stronger," said Holly.

"Or stronger," she agreed. "But it would seem to be limited to certain parts of his brain."

"How?"

"Perhaps it's his overall sense of defeatism and despair."

"Then how does that correlate with his incredible battle energy?" Holly wondered aloud. "It couldn't be the instinctive will to survive."

"Not in the usual sense," she agreed. "For then the dispair would go. The brain would discard it in order to save the psyche."

Holly sighed. "Perhaps it is equipment failure. Since there is no apparent motivational pattern."

"But there is *a* pattern. The readings are consistent."

"Consistent but illogical. Psybernetically false. Because there must be overall motivational factors. There must be something to give it all a push."

Lya mused: "A terrified man, whose brain manages to compartmentalize the terror so that he is able to function smoothly. Yet the whole process is overlaid with total fatalism, a clearly discernible condition that, by electrical necessity, should negate *any* positive motivation . . . Hollis, no one exists like this. . . ."

I laughed. "He did. And damn well."

Lya was not amused. "We know that, Jack. We just don't know how."

"You keep saying that. I don't see what the problem is."

Holly tried a patient smile. "The trouble is, Jack, that there are a couple of blatant contradictions here. You see, in a high-stress situation like this one, requiring physical response to physical peril, usually one of two things happens: The emotional reaction, the fear, becomes predominant, thereby paralyzing the body. Or, conversely, the body takes control, forgetting, for the time being, the fear."

"You mean the guy either panics and freezes, or becomes a hero first and panics later."

"Essentially, yes."

"But Felix didn't do either one," I pointed out.

"Precisely," said Holly nodding. "But he should have."

"Why?"

Lya blinked. "Because he's a human being."

"But everybody isn't like everybody else."

"True, Jack," agreed Holly slowly. "And clearly Felix is an exceptional man. But there are limits even here. Particularly when you consider the rather obvious fact of his fatalism. A man as, well, as resigned as he is to death just shouldn't be able to keep going. . . ."

"He doesn't believe, Jack," interrupted Lya. "And without belief there is no positive motivational factor."

I sat up in my chair. "You keep saying that, too. 'Positive motivations.' "

Holly lifted an eyebrow. "Yes. . . ?"

I shrugged. "But there's nothing positive about Felix."

Holly stared at me quizzically for a few moments. Then his face brightened and his eyes lit up. "Of *course*!" he shouted. "It's not positive at all. It's negative!"

Lya loooked skeptical. "A negative motivation?"

"Sure," he said happily, turning to her. "It all fits. But you've got to take the factors in order of priority. First comes the fear. The defeatism comes next—Felix has *no faith* that he will live. But it's that very lack of hope which allows him to avoid, temporarily, the burden of the fear. For without suspense, the major effects of fear are sidetracked."

"And so, too," added Lya," are most motivational factors."

"Only the positive ones."

She looked at him oddly. "You mean . . . he *wants* to die?"

"Of course not," retorted Holly. "He merely expects to."

"Then the negative push?"

I jumped in. "He refuses to."

She looked at me. "I beg your pardon?"

Holly laughed. "Don't you see, Lya. He believes he will eventually be killed. Yet each time a danger *threatens*, he repels it. He doesn't repel all danger—he doesn't believe he could—but. . . ."

". . . but he does take issue with specific threats!" she finished for him, seeing it at last. She sat back in her chair, delighted with her revelation. "That's marvelous," she said, mostly to herself.

Holly sounded a little awed himself. "Oh, he's a marvel, all right. Imagine living like that! Here is a human being with absolutely no sense of optimism, no faith in his own future. No hope.

"Yet he manages to survive—not through an inherent craving for life—but through a stubborn refusal of death."

"No wonder he's splitting apart," breathed Lya and the two of them laughed.

I smiled.

After a few moments, Lya added: "But the ants will get him."

"Oh, hell," I snarled, angry at her. I held up my hands, indicating hordes in the unseen distance. "The ants will get him, sure. But," I stabbed the air before me, indicating an individual among the hosts, "not *this* one. And not the one behind him either, goddammit!" I looked at her beseechingly, willing her to understand. "Don't you see, Lya? The ants scare him. But he can fight the individuals because . . ."

"Because why, Jack?" she prompted.

"Because they piss him off!"

Holly had to perform a Fleet Citizenry Certification on a newborn baby girl so we got no chance to Immerse that day. It was our first break in weeks. Holly didn't like it any better than I did. At first.

"I don't know why I have to handle this personally," he said to Lya.

She explained to him, and me, that the father of the child, one Neil Phillips, was not part of Fleet at all. "He's an independent subcontractor, building some of the installations that aren't prefabs. Technically he's not under our direct authority. But he is a citizen, so he has a right to demand witnessing from the head of the nearest Fleet installation. That means you, Dear."

Holly nodded, looking at the request on the screen in front of him. "Wants to be certain his daughter can claim North American Humanity Privilege. . . ."

Lya looked confused. "That's the part *I* don't understand," she said. "He says he wants to be sure she's a Texan."

I laughed. "Sugar, Texas is in North America."

"It is? I thought it was a planet!" She shook her head. "The way he talks about it. . . ."

So we went. Reluctantly at first, and then with more enthusiasm. This Phillips dude understood how to throw a party. There were substances there even I, in all my years of debauchery, had never tried. I suspected that Phillips had made some of it himself, a charge to which he never responded unless you count a devious grin, which I did not. Still, he was nice enough to take me aside and suggest, kindly respectfully, what I shouldn't try that night for the first time. I took him up on his advice.

Holly took him up on more than that. Seemed neither he nor Lya had ever seen anyone that chewed tobacco before. Lya was understandably appalled by the notion, but Holly was delighted and anxious to try it. He was particularly curious as to how Phillips managed the spitting and a clean beard at the same time. Phillips, complete with devious grin, was pleased to provide instruction.

Holly swallowed a lot of it. But Phillips was instantly at his side, commiserating and bearing some obscure green stuff to "get that taste out of your mouth, Director." By the time of the ceremony, Holly was just barely audible. But he managed well enough.

". . . certify that Natalie Anne Phillips, daughter of Neil and Cindy Phillips, weighing five pounds and thirteen ounces on this fourteenth day of March, year 2081, Standard, is hereby and forevermore a full citizen of the North American Commonwealth."

And once the ceremony was over, there didn't seem to any of the three of us any pressing reason to leave. At least half of the Project was there for the occasion of the birth of the first earthchild on Sanction, all happy and excited and full of homesickness and booze. It was a lot of fun.

I didn't see much of either Holly or Lya for several hours. I think Lya spent most of her time with the proud mother. And Holly spent at least an hour talking with Phillips' first child, handsome blond ten-year-old named Nathan. I just sort of mingled randomly, the feeling of frustration about not Immersing temporarily offset by the joy of the people around me.

Toward the end of the evening, I had a chance to stand outside the nursery viewer and actually see the little baby girl for the first time. She was beautiful, exquisitely formed, pixielike in her soft little fisty sleep.

I suppose I stood there too long, long enough to think about all such things that never seem to have anything to do with me. Things like children, of course. But especially Things, like the birth of beautiful baby girls. She had sandy hair, I remember. It looked very soft.

Talking about him that day had gotten to me. I resisted sleep. I don't know that I was really afraid of nightmares. I doubt it. Nothing was that clear to me on purpose.

Back to the curved railing of the dome's balcony, staring at the city. I lit a cigarette and somebody close by gasped. It was Lya, standing a few paces away in the shadows. I started to say something but I turned around instead at the sound of a foot scraping behind me. It was Holly.

He looked as surprised as Lya and I did. I wondered how long the three of us had been there without knowing about the others. I had often caught the other two like that, in the lab or the dining room. Sitting and staring. Usually I just moved on. But tonight, either because of the party earlier or because of the things that had been said—if they weren't really the same—I spoke up.

"Can I buy somebody a drink?" I asked.

My voice seemed to boom across the dome. We all jumped a little. But then we relaxed and Holly smiled and said he had had plenty to drink already and Lya laughed at that, volunteering that she might never drink again and we all laughed at that. Lya said she was hungry, however.

So the three of us headed down into the dome, weaving slightly, in search of food. The surly galley-tech was like every other cook since the dawn of dawning. It may have been Holly's Project, but the kitchen was his. With great reluctance and muttered bitching about the hour, he managed to lay out a cold snack for three. Then he stood around waiting for us to eat it.

"Out!" said Holly when he had had enough editorializing. He pointed his finger toward the door imperiously. It scared the hell out of the cook and made us all laugh at Holly's new Command Voice.

We laughed a lot. We needed it. We needed a drink too and something, syntho, was found. So we drank and picked at the food and became, inevitably, talkative. It was an eerie couple of hours in the half-light of that immense Galley. Not just because we talked, but because of what we talked about. And something else: the way we talked.

We were fiercely cheerful.

And oddly enough, we didn't avoid talking about it. Rather macabre black humor as a matter of fact.

About how we had each of us been drinking a hell of a lot lately, not just tonight because even a hangover was better than some of the dreams we were having, ha ha ha. Maybe Lewis was right after all, ha ha. Probably have to stick to syntho ourselves once we got the habit. Ha.

Holly wondered aloud what it was that Lewis was scared to dream about and Lya said it was fish. I agreed. "He thinks they're plotting against him."

Holly laughed: "Paranoia is its own reward—who said that?"

I laughed: "Are there any fish in that river?"

Lya laughed: "Over sixty species catalogued so far. But that won't do Lewis any good."

Holly and I laughed; "Why not?"

And Lya laughed back: "Because most of the big ones are in on it."

And we laughed back at her and the three of us laughed at the three of us laughing.

Ha ha ha ha.

Later on a grain or two of truth from me. True Jack Crow. About how come I really didn't get the residuals from the Blaze-drive because I had discovered the Aiyeel in a stolen ship and how it came out at the piracy trial that Quan Tri couldn't really press charges against me for stealing the ship as he had stolen it from the Dalchek Mining Combine. And since Dalchek was already long-dead by that time without heirs or a will—and especially on account of the Blaze-drive being the single most valuable tool in history—Fleet had ended up with the whole thing. Or public Domain had, but at the time that was about the same thing.

They laughed at that story and at the part about me admitting being lost when I discovered the Aiyeel in the first place. It seemed to help.

So I told them the truth about how come the Darj regarded me as a God. Lost again and frantic again and then there I was with them spacesick and seasick and full of time lag and planet lag and throwing up the traditional feast prepared in my honor all over the Touch Mother who regarded, by doctrine-dogma, all aspects of regurgitation as holy. Meaning only sacred chow was good enough for me.

"I threw that up too," I added and they laughed. "But the Touch Mother didn't know because I was deep in the Inner Fold which was this very damp cellar, essentially, where gods hung out and I was alone and before anybody could find out, I was already on my way back."

Holly said he bet I was in an awful hurry to get out of there before they found out and I said yes, that too. "But mostly I was starving to death." Holly and I laughed at that and Lya, too, a little. But she was starting to drift.

Holly tried taking over, telling something I don't remember about being a young Progidy. He tried to make it funny and, of course, failed. But I egged him on just the same, laughing hard and trying to get Lya to.

But she wouldn't or couldn't and eventually, inevitably, it got very quiet in that huge dark place. Holly couldn't stand it.

"You tell one, Honey," he said at last.

And she did. But she didn't just tell it. She carved it, carved it deep in the deepest place for it, our shame. It didn't start out as a story. It started out as a confession. As The Confession. The tears were already welling when she began to speak.

"I haven't been honest with you two," she said, starting the thick beads rolling. "I know I've been cold and distant and," bitterly, "oh so scientific! But the truth is, Holly, Jack . . . The truth is that I feel so . . . so small and mean and. . . ."

She drifted off. Holly sat beside her like a statue. He could not move. And I knew what he felt, for I, too, wanted to shout: "DON'T! Don't crack us open!" But I didn't. I was a statue, too. And worse, I didn't even help.

She wiped her eyes and positioned herself more firmly on her stool. She stretched her hands out flat on the chopping board in front of her. She examined the knuckles. Then she curled her fingers securely together.

"It's like . . . it's like once on Trankia, when I was little and my brother had a dog. You know, a puppy." She looked at us to see if we knew. We nodded like the statues we were. "A puppy my uncle had brought him. From Earth, I think, or somewhere.

"Anyway, my brother, Gay, loved this dog. This puppy. He really did. I mean he did everything for him. Fed him and petted him all the time." She took a deep breath. "And all that. And I used to kid him about it. Not really much. Really! But some, I guess. Because he was younger than me and I was full of being the oldest and wise. You know, becoming a woman." She stopped, thought. "I think I was ten."

"Anyway, Gay was younger, like I said. And one day he had to go into town. Into the settlement. Cholesterol implants, maybe—he was about the right age. And Mom and Daddy were going to be away." She took another deep breath, a longer one this time. I begged her to stop. But she couldn't hear what I couldn't say.

"I was to look after the house. And after the dog. The puppy. Gay was so worried! He was sure I didn't like the puppy because I had kidded him so. And I laughed and acted really bored by his concern. 'Of course I can take care of one measely animal,' I told him. And eventually he left, left the puppy with me. Only because Mom told him to stop being silly." She paused. "Just before she left she took me aside and told me to please be sure and I got mad that she had so little faith in me. But I didn't show it then. I waited until they were gone and then I let the puppy out by itself."

The tears were really rolling by then. She made a half-hearted attempt to wipe them away.

"The puppy never went out alone. Just never! We had sunk a geotherm close to the house but, I don't know, we'd struck the water table or something and anyway there was this deep, deep, well. About ten meters and it was jagged on the side without plastiform and some water at the bottom.

"I was at the kitchen window and I could see him bouncing around and I knew that anybody could watch him that way—Gay didn't have to be a baby about hovering over him all the time and, well, I looked up once. . . ." She sighed like a death rattle. "And he was gone.

"I ran outside right then, of course. And I knew . . . instantly . . . I knew what I should have known all along. That I had known it was going to happen. I mean, I *knew* he was going to fall. I knew it. Why else had I let him out?"

And she sobbed.

"He was still alive but his little haunches—his hips, you know—were broken. The fall had smashed them. And the water was too deep for him so he was paddling with just his two front little paws to keep up. To keep alive.

"He paddled all the way around in a little circle until he saw this little ledge kind of rock sticking out next to the wall and he paddled over, his little paws just churning, until he got there and then he just dug and clawed and scrambled up there, all the way on top of it where he could rest a little. And where I could see his little hips all crushed."

She shook her head to clear it, gritting her teeth. She began to talk more quickly, anxious to get it over with.

"But the rock he was on was too small, even for him and he was so . . . *tiny!* It was wet, too, from the water and . . . and from the blood and slippery. He fell back in, when he twisted around to try and lick away the pain.

"But instead of getting right back up there he seemed to be lost and he paddled around some more until I yelled down to him to get back on the rock and . . . when he heard my voice . . . he looked up at me, right into my eyes, and whimpered for help."

She stopped abruptly. She buried her face in her hands. When she looked back up, she was a ghost.

"He whimpered all the time from then on. Everytime he paddled he'd let out this pitiful little yelp. And everytime he got back up on the rock where he could catch his breath he would howl up to me to come get him and save him. There was no way to do that. Just no way. It was too deep and I didn't have a ladder or a rope and even if I'd had one, it was too far for me to climb. So all I could do was sit there and listen and watch him paddle and dig and scramble his way back up onto that rock and then, in just a second or two, slide back into the water. Pretty soon the water was red.

"And he was such a tiny puppy—he couldn't lose that much blood and live. But he did. He was like a . . . I don't know. Like a little motor. Paddling around and around like he could always do it."

She looked at us as if pleading. Back and forth into our dead frozen eyes. "But he *couldn't*. He couldn't. He wasn't a motor. He wasn't a machine. He was a puppy! I could hear how it hurt him. He was in agony!

"But he just kept on, paddling and climbing up and slipping back down into that red water and blood, sometimes his little head would just disappear for a few seconds. But he'd always come right back up again.

"At first I admired him so! Oh, I thought he was the bravest, most noble little thing I had ever seen, to keep at it like that. But . . . after a whlile. After the first *hour* . . . I mean, there was just no . . .

"I just hated him. I hated him. Because he wouldn't die. He was putting me through it, too. And I couldn't stand it! I couldn't stand it! I mean, there was just no way. And . . ."

Her voice cracked, broke. There was no way to stop it. But she told the rest of it through her aching.

"I went to the garden, the rock garden Mom was making and I got the biggest rocks I could carry and I took them back to the well and I sat there at the edge and I threw them at him until he was dead. I . . . I crushed his head with them."

She collapsed into fitful, racking sobs. Holly, tears plainly visible on his own cheeks, rushed to her and wrapped her in his arms. She clung to him, letting herself have it for some seconds. Then her head began shaking violently against his chest. "No!" she blurted and tore herself away. Holly tried to cradle her again but she propped her palms against his chest, holding him off and looking him in the eye so he would really know . . .

"No! No, Holly. No, my darling you don't understand! It's . . . it's . . . I hate Felix, too, Holly. I hate him the very same way I did that puppy and I hate us for watching and for not being able to stop watching and I hate him for making us see how brave he can be and . . . But mostly. . . .''

She shrugged out of his grasp, stood up from the stool. Her voice was low and resigned and clotted with her shame. ''Mostly I hate me, Holly. Because I would do it again. Yes, I would. I would. If I could do it again, I'd kill Felix now. I'd kill him. *Anything* to stop the awful whimpering. Anything!

''Don't you see, Holly? Don't you see? You can't love me! Look! Look how hateful I am!''

And then she fell against him, surrendering at last to his care. And his judgment. But there was no judgment there. For Holly felt the same way. He told her so as he held her. And as he told her he, too, began to cry and shake with the pain and shame and self-hate.

I tried to reach them. God, how I wanted to! But I couldn't. I couldn't move. I couldn't speak. I knew what to say. I knew what to do. I needed the release so badly, more than they did, more, worse, than they could *ever* know.

But I was blocked. Stuck tight to the rim of me, to the meat of my fear and loathing and hiding out behind and from the legend I had bled for so long.

I remember trying to stand up . . .

I woke up on the cot in Lya's small office. Holly was nowhere in sight. Lya sat on a chair watching me. She stood up and moved to the edge of the cot. I looked up at her and . . . and all of it came rushing back. I felt the blood exploding through my veins. I opened my mouth—I couldn't talk. Realized my eyes had closed—hell, *slammed* shut. I couldn't see. I couldn't cry. I couldn't. . . .

And then I felt her arms circling my shoulders and I all but dove against her, clinging to her. My tears broke through at last, soaking her blouse. My sobs, unbid, rattled me. I babbled a lot. Most of it was confused and lost, except for saying, for *admitting* that I hated Him too.

And something else. I looked up after awhile, feeling and sounding like a child. Pleading. ''I want to be Jack Crow again!''

She smiled warmly. Glowing protective and sure. ''You will.''

"But Felix! He's . . ."

"Felix is dead."

"How can you be sure?" I insisted, my voice shaking. "Maybe he never died! Maybe he never will!"

Her face became startled-frightened-horrified in an instant. But then all was flung away with a toss of her hair and she pressed my head back between her breasts, cutting off my fears with her firm grasp and monotonous maternal coos.

She rocked me to sleep, I guess.

No. I'm sure she did. She did.

The clock said three hours until dawn when I awoke again. I was alone, thank God. I sat up on the cot. I fished and found a cigarette. The door to the lab was open. I stood up and used it, crossing the vast shadowy chamber hurriedly to the main seal and the bright corridor beyond. There was no one around, no sound of scurrying techs or late partygoers. Quiet. Fresh air seemed like a good idea. I began the long climb to the outer seal.

Halfway there I stopped and noticed something: I was okay.

I shouldn't have been. I should have felt embarrassed and ashamed and humiliated and . . . But I didn't. I felt fine. Relieved, in fact. Like a boil finally lanced. I smiled. Maybe so.

Outside was lovely, brightly starlit. Even the view of the City seemed pristine. I stepped to the bottom of the ramp and sat down to enjoy it. Somebody giggled.

". . . what else would you expect?" More giggles.

"Maybe he's going for some kinda record." Single giggle.

"Well, he's got my vote for stupid." More giggles still.

I stood up and followed the sounds. Not really defensive. But perhaps a little.

On the Project side of the main bridge stood three Security, the gigglers, in a tight little circle. My approaching tread broke the pattern in a hurry. They gasped together, whipped around together, reached for blazers together. A single voice, however, did the hailing.

"Identify," she ordered in a strong contralto.

I answered her, ignoring the momentary feeling of daring, with: "Crow."

They relaxed, peering at me through the darkness. A couple of hooded heads nodded. "Good morning, Mr. Crow," responded the contralto respectfully. I smiled at my own relief. It still worked.

"Good morning, yourself. What's so funny?"

Two of them exchanged a nervous glance. But the boss, the contralto, remained cool enough.

"Nothing much, Mr. Crow. Nothing you'd find interesting."

"Then why did I ask you?"

"Beg pardon, Sir?"

"Why did I ask if I wasn't already interested?"

"Huh? Well sir, I guess. . . ."

"Don't guess."

"Yessir. It was . . . well, it was that Lewis guy."

"That Lewis guy? You mean the Lewis who owns this planet? *That* Lewis guy?"

"Uh, yessir. Mr. Lewis."

"What about Mr. Lewis. . . ?"

"Well, it's just that . . ."

A sudden burst of staccato explosions had me already dropping to my feet before my conscious mind had recognized the long-unheard sound of automatic rifle fire. I looked around to see the three Security still standing. Bent over somewhat, startled even, but still standing.

"Nothing to worry about, Mr. Crow. Those came from the City," said the contralto, pointing a gloved hand across the river.

I stood up slowly, my gaze following her lead. "The City? They have guns there?"

"Yessir."

"I thought all weapons were forbidden them."

"That's the law, yessir. One of the only one's Lew . . . Mr. Lewis has. But somebody isn't listening. We've been hearing gunfire almost every night for the past couple of weeks."

"Hmm. What about blazers?"

"Oh, no. No beams. Just bullets."

Another burst followed the first. Random shots sounded

next, continuing intermittently for several seconds. Gradually it faded away to only a shot or two every minute or so. I thought about Wice and Eyes and their little bands of merry men running through that muddy maze playing shoot-'em-up. Maybe missing the past couple of rendezvous had been a pretty good move after all. We stood there for a while as we were, ears keenly attuned, staring out into that dim distant glow listening to unseen strangers fighting unknown, unexplained battles. Once we saw a muzzle flash. Another time I heard a sound that could have been a cry of pain. It could have also been the wind, or the river, or an animal. Or a cry of pain.

"You see what I mean, sir," said the contralto when the last shots seemed to have come and gone, "they got nothing to do with us. Just local trouble."

"Luck for them," said the youngest of the three from beside her. He gripped the butt of his blazer menacingly.

The contralto eyed him with amused disgust. "Meinhoff, you ever see what a little bitty piece of lead does to people with complexions like yours?"

He looked embarassed. But not enough. "No, Ma'am."

"Don't laugh at rifles. Up to five hundred meters they're every bit as good as blazers."

"Yes, Ma'am."

"And you?" she prompted the third Security, another woman. The other woman jumped to attentiveness.

"Yes, ma'am," she said. She thought a moment. "Only. . . ."

The contralto sighed. "Only what Bader?"

"Well, ma'am, you don't really think we need to take a bunch of potshotting deserters seriously, do you?"

"Bader, if those folks are all deserters, then who's doing the shooting?"

The other woman opened her mouth to speak, closed it.

"What about Lewis?" I reminded them.

"Oh. Well, it's just that . . ." She pointed the gloved hand again, this time toward a small copse of trees beside the river's edge. "He's right over there if you want to see for yourself."

"You mean he's here now?" I asked, surprised.

"Yessir. Comes down to the river to fish every night. Stays all night, too. He doesn't leave until morning when he . . ."

"When he what?"

"When he sleeps it off, sir."

"I see." I thought a minute. "Thanks," I said over my shoulder and headed down to the bank. She mumbled something back. I stopped after I had gone several steps and called back to her. "How long has this been going on?"

"A couple of weeks, Mr. Crow," was shouted back.

"Since the shooting started?"

There was a brief pause. Then, "Why, yessir."

"Good night," I shouted before actual conversation threatened. I headed toward the trees. The footing was horrible, I noticed. The grass was damp with dew this close to the water's edge. Not the best time to fish, when any spot you might pick to sit on was wet. But then, what did fishing ever really have to do with Lewis?

He slept peacefully, quietly. Except for his breathing, which was slight, he was as still as a corpse. He was on his back with his face to the stars. His feet were splayed out at a 45-degree angle from each other. His arms were twisted around with his elbows sticking out at his sides. His hands were underneath his back for some reason. Perhaps to keep warm. He looked like a cookie.

A drunk cookie, of course. Even from a couple of steps away, I could smell the syntho. There were a couple of jugs beside him, one tipped over on its side and both clearly empty. The fishing gear had been neatly stacked a step away. The line was still dry on the reel.

I sat down on his tackle box and lit a cigarette. I vaguely recalled someone—Karen, perhaps—saying no one had seen him around in quite a while. Well, this was where he'd been. Since the trouble in the City. And, of course, since the day of the picnic when he'd seen the suit. I vividly remembered the look on his face the moment he had seen it. The revulsion. The panic.

I sighed, tossed the cigarette at the river. It hissed momentarily. I reached for his shoulder, damp from the dew like the rest of him, with some indefinite idea of taking him inside to get warm. But when my hand touched him. . . .

I drew my hand back quickly, as if to avoid contamination. The disgust welled up in me. I think I snarled. I took a few steps away, glanced out across the river, then back to the . . . the cookie. I shook my head. I shuddered.

He had named Sanction well. That had been just what it was for a rich punk with too much money and not enough character. And he'd been awfully happy for awhile. He had the Project people there, to supply sanity and straight lines. And syntho. And then along had come a pack of gypsy refugees to provide just the right touch of slumming spice. The perfect cocktail party.

But sooner or later, usually sooner, the next morning shows up full of energy and sunlight and memories of the real world. It kicks most people up off their asses. But Lewis. . . . Without anybody to drink with, he drank alone. At night. In the dew. Away.

He began to snore. I wanted to kick him. The *idea* of his just running away, with the City heating up and the Project finally getting down to work—hell, *because* of those things—he ran away.

"You poor dumb drunken jerk," I said to him and turned away for good.

The funny thing about it, I thought as I walked back up the slope, or rather the unfunny thing about it, was that it sort of fitted. Lewis was, after all, the last piece this mess really needed. He had performed his function. If everything is to foul up, one must have a place for it. And Sanction was just the place.

"Everything all right, Mr. Crow?" asked the contralto as I passed the bridge. "Is Mr. Lewis okay?"

"Fine," I answered without turning, "if you like the type."

I kept walking to the ramp and up it and into the dome. I was surprised that I felt, suddenly, better. Not good yet. Not yet, and maybe not for a while to come. But . . . better. Bad as it was, and bad as it was going to get—bad as *I* was gonna get, I was no Lewis.

And even better, maybe I was still Crow.

*   *   *

Karen was in my bed. She flipped on the light as I entered the bedroom, brushed her hair out of her eyes, and smiled.

I started to say something but stopped myself just in time. Thank God; it was a no-speak moment.

I got out of everything and slid under the sheets from the other side. We lay there, parallel but separated, and looked at one another. Her smile had gone. It stayed gone for the several seconds we lay there.

"Good night," I said at last, scrunching my pillow meaningfully.

She looked at me coolly. Then, with equal cool, nodded.

"Good night," she said as well and turned off the light.

It was still a couple of seconds, then . . .

She was there and soft and pliant and demanding and everything about the touch of her was what it should have been after the look of it. She broke off and away an inch or two and said: "Well, where else was I going to go, Lewis?"

I laughed and drove my smile across her lips and my hands onto her breasts and my hips onto hers. Hot damn.

In the dream the Suit had somehow gotten loose.

It pursued us, rushed at us across the suddenly vast expanse of the shiny-smooth lab floor. Ripped and torn electrical feeds trailed behind it as it swelled toward us. They hadn't been strong enough to hold it.

"Run, everybody! Run!" screamed Lya at the throng of over a hundred who had for some reason become trapped down there with us. She shooed them like cattle toward the seal and safety but in their panic they were jamming themselves tight.

Holly was at some immense upright panel, the mad scientist, yelling: "Don't panic! Don't panic! I'll think of something!" and working frantically at the keys. I tried to pull him away to safety but he wouldn't budge. His grip was surprisingly strong with conviction. In disgust I reached down and jerked loose the panel's power feeds but still Holly wouldn't run, wouldn't come. Lya screamed . . .

The Suit was upon us, sweeping horribly at us soundlessly,

reaching its murderous armored hands toward us, black plassteel talons forming . . .

And Lewis was there by my side and he held out a jug of syntho and said: "Here. Just . . . *here*!" like that was all it was going to take and without thinking, I grabbed him and shoved him across the path of the Suit, to—I don't know—distract it maybe so that I could. . . .

Black arms struck out like serpents' tongues, snatching Lewis in mid-slide, grabbing him to its chest in a crumpled heap and the slick black face of it, the evil-smooth sheen of it, opened, revealing a wide black mouth of razor-sharp lips and the head tilted back and then darted abruptly forward and down across Lewis's throat, slicing and ripping out huge chunks of flesh and bone and cartilage and muscle and the blood spurted horribly. . . .

And then we were alone, the three of us. Lewis dead at its feet and it straightened up, blood streaming from its face and those thin razor lips twisting into an evil plassteel smile.

". . . Jack! Wake up! It's all right! It's all right!" Karen said, her arms managing to both shake me awake and comfort me all at once.

I found myself. I started to sit up, then relaxed into her. There was no sound for several moments but our breathing as it slowed, slowed, became steady.

"Well, at least you're getting better at this," I offered, for something to say.

She didn't laugh. But neither did she leave.

It was going to be a big day. I could feel it.

It was barely mid-morning and I had already been at the lab for hours. Amazingly, I was filled with a fiercely vibrant energy. It was innervating, exciting, rich. I couldn't wait to get to it.

Something was going to happen today. Something . . . conclusive. Something definite and explanatory and maybe . . . maybe good, I thought.

I was a fool.

The up-to-date list of Felix's drops was on the screen in front of me. I had already gone over it a dozen times. I keyed up a summary: elapsed time approximately six months standard, just under two of that under direct medical supervision. Eighteen drops, twelve of them majors. Four trips to ICU, nine medicals. We figured around a dozen broken bones, at least that many separations or tearings of tendons and muscles and major joint groups. Three head injuries, none requiring surgery. We couldn't be sure, of course. We only felt what we thought he felt as a broken bone or whatever.

In addition, Felix had been picked up on the last sweep for survivors on three separate occasions. Twice he had been the only survivor.

"You were really something," I said, half-aloud.

"Talking to ourselves, are we now?" asked Lya brightly as she swept into the room. "It's come to this, has it?"

I returned her smile. She had the same look as I did, I noted. I rubbed my hands together. It was going to be a big day.

"Look at this, Jack," said Holly from the doorway to his office. Then, seeing Lya, "look at this, Honey."

The warmth in his voice was plain. The returning glow of her quick acknowledgment was equally clear. Maybe not as perfect as before, but the Couple was again a fact.

Holly had that look, too. Bright eyes, eager anticipation. We were all fools.

He held a high-security coil up before us and shook it. "You know what this is? A priority beam from the Court of Nobles on—are you ready?—Golden."

"You're kidding," said Lya.

Holly shook his head. "Not a bit."

"What do they want?" I asked.

He smiled, shook his head in wonder. "They want to know—and this is practically a quote—what the reason was for our inquiry at the Biblioterre . . ."

"How did they find out?" exclaimed Lya.

"When you're dealing with Golden, you're dealing Big Time," I offered.

Holly nodded. "Quite true. I'm not surprised, really. They really are the . . . Oh! I didn't tell you the rest. They also asked if the reason we are asking is because we have knowledge of . . ." He shook his head. "This is incredible."

"Well, come *on*, Holly!" snapped Lya impatiently.

He smiled. "They want to know if we know where their Guardian is."

We stared at him, Lya and I. We stared at each other. We stared at him again. We stared at the coil in his hand. I rose slowly to my feet. Holly was right; it *was* incredible.

"You mean . . ." stuttered Lya, her eyes wide and unbelieving, "you mean to tell me that they've . . . *lost* . . . their *sovereign*???"

I was staring out the window of the conference room, the one that overlooked the lab and the loungers and the console. And the suit.

"Until now," I said.

So strapped in and ready to go, the three of us exchanging confident last smiles and pressings of hands, the least of our agreements. For we had decided to Immerse three times today. In one day. For the first time. My arm still tingled from the injection of vitamins and time-release stimules.

We were all so incredibly, wildly, maddeningly, *eager*. Something was going to happen. We knew it. We just knew it. Of course we were still apprehensive. Still frightened down in there somewhere. And the feelings of guilt were in there too, alongside the powerful inadequacy hue. But we had been through so much already and come through. We had strained and sweated and ached with this and come out of it. It had wrenched us about, turned us this way and that way and we had done even worse in our tortured acceptance. We had been . . . well, through Hell. What couldn't we handle now?

Fools!

We didn't know what Hell was.

PART FOUR

EVERYBODY'S HERO

Felix knew it wasn't going to work.

He stood up slowly and stepped again to the crest of the ridge and peeked out. A quarter of a kilometer or so below him, the hourglass shape of the Transit Cone faded luminescently in and out of sight with the shifting gusts of Banshee sand. It was an oddly dreamlike scene. He had never seen its like before. Usually the Cone was invisible to the unaided eye. But today the sun had been just right, the texture and composition of the sands just right, so that the outline became intermittently visible. He admired the sweep of lines that narrowed so tightly ten meters above the ground before swelling outward to form the skirt of the Cone. A sudden gust, stronger than any so far and bearing more sand, caused, for just a moment, almost the entire shape to form. It was very pretty.

Felix turned his head to see if any of the others had seen it. But they were busy at the bottom of the dune. Resting or moaning or simply sitting there where they had collapsed, waiting for painers to take effect and staring straight ahead and fearing.

Or dying, Felix amended to himself. At least two of the six are busy with that.

He sighed, turned back around. The gust had receded. Only the lowest part of the skirt was visible. And even that was partially obscured by the semicircle of ants standing protectively around it and waiting.

Waiting for us, he thought.

"How do they know?" said a voice on proximity band from close by.

Felix turned to see Michalk had crawled up beside him. The warrior looked terrible. The sand covered his entire suit save for the small area of the face plate. It was the blood, of course. Felix knew that. The black ant blood. It got on the plassteel and stayed there, cloying, to be covered over by layers of alien soil that would normally have slid off. And it didn't mean anything. It didn't affect a suit's performance in any way. Felix knew that, too. But it was ugly. A particularly gruesome badge of battle. A ghoulish reminder of what had just happened and what was about to happen and . . . Felix hated the sight of Michalk because he knew his own black scout suit must look the same.

"How do they know?" Michalk repeated. "How did they learn to stand there and wait for us?"

Felix shrugged. "How do they know we're here, as far as that goes?"

Michalk nodded, a brutal gesture in his huge warrior suit. "But they always seem to, don't they?"

"They have since I've been here."

Michalk regarded him for some seconds. "How long is that, Felix? How long have you been here?"

Felix looked at him. The warrior's anxious eyes could just be made out behind the faceplate.

"It's just," Michalk added uneasily, "that some of us were wondering."

Felix nodded. "What's the date?"

"Huh? Oh. Uh, it's December standard."

Felix thought a moment. "Six months."

Michalk stared. "Six . . . six months? But . . . Felix? You've been here six months? You mean six months on Active? As a warrior?"

"As a scout."

Michalk opened his mouth to speak, closed it. He was silent for several beats. Then: "How many drops?" he asked, in a soft whisper.

"Nineteen," said Felix. "This is nineteen."

Michalk continued to stare. Maybe he doesn't believe me, Felix thought. Maybe he shouldn't. I know I don't believe it.

"How many majors?" Michalk persisted.

Felix sighed. He had no idea. Further, he had no interest whatsoever in dredging back to find out. He shrugged, said: "Some."

"Some?" parroted Michalk. "Most?"

Felix nodded. "Most," he agreed woodenly.

"Shit," whispered Michalk to himself. "I wonder where *that* puts you on the stat?"

Felix eyed him uneasily. There had been someone else, a long time ago it seemed, who had talked about stats. "You're a one, Felix," he had said. Now who was that? He shook his head. It didn't matter. He nudged Michalk.

"How's Gao?"

"Huh? Oh. He died a minute ago."

Felix nodded. Down to five. "And Li?"

Michalk looked away, into the distance. "She's going. Too tough for her own good."

"Yes," Felix persisted, trying to keep a patient tone. "But how long?"

Michalk looked at him. "Soon," he said coldly.

Felix knew he wouldn't get any more. He slid down the dune to the others. He hesitated when he saw Goermann, the captain, sitting hunched over against the wall of the gulley which had been eroded at the bottom of the dune. Felix was certain the man had been sitting in the exact same position several moments before when they had last spoken. Was he dead? Or just gone.

A harsh scream-groan of anguished remorse blared quickly in his earphones and receded. Felix turned toward the other end of the gulley where a medico, his blue warrior suit long covered by the same blood and sand as the rest, knelt over the frozen, spread-eagled form of a warrior whose suit had gone into Traction Mode. Felix remembered the spinal injury that had triggered the Mode. He had dismembered—in passing—the ant that had been holding Li pinned down against a rock while another ant raked hulking mandibles across her back.

The Medico, Patriche, swayed slightly on his knees. Muffled rumbles of partially controlled grief slowly faded from hearing. With a last fond pat of a huge armored arm on the statuelike chest, the Medico stood and turned away.

So, Felix thought, down to four. Time to do it. He turned again toward the still immobile captain. Time to do it, he thought again. Even though he knew it wasn't going to work.

He knelt down before him. Goermann lifted his head and regarded him in silence.

Felix cleared his throat. "Li and Gao are dead, sir," he said gently.

The captain continued to stare in silence.

"Captain?" persisted Felix. "It's time to. . . ."

"Of course, uh . . . Felix. Of course," spoke up Goermann suddenly. "Of course. I was just . . . trying to think of an alternative . . . plan." His armored right hand raised up and settled comradely on Felix's equally insulated shoulder. "Always good to have an alternative route, you know, in case something goes wrong."

Felix nodded. "Yes, sir," he said, willing to accept the other's pitiful stab at leadership, or anything else, to finish this.

"Haven't been able to think of a thing, though, uh . . . Felix. You seem to have grasped the situation precisely."

Felix nodded, rose to his feet. It was true enough. He had grasped that they weren't going to get through. The Captain rose as well, and called the other two over to run it through one last time.

"Now don't waste time and energy," the Captain reminded the other two, "trying to use your blazers in a pinch. We're out of blazer capacity, you both know that. But get it strong in your mind now. I don't want somebody trying to fire an empty gun at a crucial moment."

The other two nodded.

"Felix will pick the spot. Don't try to out-guess him."

The other two nodded.

"And for God's sake, don't hold back on him. The only

chance we have is to slam in behind him all together." The captain regarded them. "Is that clear?"

The other two nodded. They said it was clear.

Felix wanted to laugh. He knew—they all knew—that the other three, including the Captain, were going to hesitate at the last second and leave him alone with the ants. It wasn't simply the fear and revulsion they felt at ramming into a wall of two dozen monsters. It was . . . maybe Felix could do it all before they got there and they wouldn't have to . . . be engulfed.

"Shit."

"Felix? Did you say something?"

Felix looked up, saw that he had walked away from the others. Saw them looking at him. He hadn't realized he had said it out loud.

"Did you?" the captain repeated.

"Nothing," Felix replied. *Maybe good-bye,* he thought. He headed for his spot on the far left edge of the ridge. He looked back. The others were spreading out twenty meters apart. He was perhaps twice that distance away from the nearest of them, Patriche, to give him time to reach the greater speed of a scout. He sat down.

Maybe it wouldn't happen this time. Maybe the Engine wouldn't come.

He wasn't at all sure how he felt about that thought. He wasn't at all sure what frightened him more, being alone with no protection at all from the fear and from the ants, or that horrible sense of dropping away, that terrible vertigo that seemed to make him feel as if he but hung at the edges of himself, watching himself, his Engineself, perform. Watching it kill.

But when he thought of what he was about to do. When he pictured himself streaking down the dune toward the wall of ants waiting at the Cone, guarding his only route to safety . . . When his mind's eye pictured the massing and gathering and lumbering together of those huge stalking zombies, their grotesque mandibles groping for him, globular eyes rotating obscenely in dry sockets as big as his head . . .

And when he saw himself dart suddenly toward them, as he must do, and accelerate right at them, as he must do, and plow into them, as he must do. . . . And when he knew it wasn't going to work. When he knew they weren't going to get through. . . .

The sudden nauseating spasm doubled him forward onto his knees, his chin plate struck his chest with a grunt. He thought his stomach would pull him in half. My God! My God! You'd think it would get easier! But every time it's even more wrenching than before.

His head swam, the vertigo shifting him randomly in eddies of its own. He closed his eyes, gripped his sides with his elbows. He gasped.

"Felix?" sounded the captain's frightened tones. "Felix! Is there something wrong?"

He stood up, his muscles still taut but released. "Fine," replied the Engine.

"Very well," said the captain. Felix saw him raise an arm, saw the others acknowledge the preparatory gesture. A second later he saw the arm drop and he was up and over the ridge and flying down its side, his piston-driving boots tearing angrily precise gashes in the sand.

Bolov, thought Felix suddenly, in a last plaintive desperate attempt at irrelevance. It was Bolov who had said he was a one. Bolov!

The man I threw away.

And then he had receded with his fear and guilt, had slipped back into his cowering. The Engine was on the move.

Below, the ants reacted en masse, jerking to ghoulish attention. There were maybe thirty of them lined up side by side and they shifted and bulged toward the direction of his approach, massing for the collision. The bulge flattened abruptly, however, as the other three were sighted as well. The ants scrambled uncertainly for a moment before flattening out their line once more into a semicircle. Every approach was guarded, covered. Thus thinned out, the barrier they formed looked deceptively vulnerable, as if it were only a line of men and not exoskeleton horrors.

He brought himself to the right with a slight lean and an added burst of acceleration. He must go faster! Faster! And his legs flashed beneath him.

To his right the other three had already, prematurely,

begun to veer in his direction. The captain was watching Felix so carefully he stumbled and almost fell. Patriche, he noticed, had already begun to slow up. Damn!

Only Michalk at the far end of their sweep, followed the plan. Head forward like a bull, he sprinted determinedly down the hill straight toward the ants.

Distantly, Felix wondered if it might work after all.

The Engine, uncaring and unexpectant, chose that moment to dart viciously to the right in front of the others. He picked a spot to strike the mass, saw the ants swell in anticipation, acclerated harder, gritted his teeth, considered a fake back to the left, discarded the thought along with its image of tripping and sprawling into the nightmare at one hundred kilometers an hour, out of control and flailing as they leapt to absorb him, pouncing. . . .

The last fifty-meter stretch of slope gave away abruptly to the flatlands, jolting his stomach but adding immensely to his speed. He strained even harder. Faster, faster, he must *slam* into them! *Slam* into them, tear them back and. . . .

And, at 120 kph, the Engine did just that. At the last second he leapt forward, wrapping his limbs into a lethal torpedo, and hurtled into the first ant. It seemed to simply disappear before his faceplate, crushed flat. Behind the first were two others leaning toward him. Not bracing or preparing, but just ants, dumb stupid mortal things that simply reached for him, the thing they were here to want and *Wham!* he was through their splintering bodies, exoskeleton disintegrating in the alien air and he was tumbling to his left and his legs were rolling up over his head out of control and the next ants rushed before him and he struck them faceplate-first, the concussion so staggering that for just an instant he saw nothing but lights and patterns on his retinas and Wham!—Wham!—Wham! he crashed into the last, decelerating massively in a single second until silence and stillness for a precious half a moment.

But as he jerked himself to his feet they were already reaching for him, crowding around him, groping, their mandibles clacking and clattering against the plassteel, huge globular eyes blocking out the ugly gray sunlight with ugly black menace. He bashed the flat of his armored hand through the thorax of one, slashed sideways with his elbow against a midsection, felt the splintering, twisted away underneath a massive looming mandible, gripped and jerked and tore loose a pincer wedged clinging into the waist seam, spun again out of still more grips, felt them close up behind him, all around him now.

Where the hell were they!! He was still five meters from the edge of the Cone! If they didn't back him up now . . . ! They must come now! Now!

The most jolting collision yet was Michalk slamming into him from behind. Thank God—Thank God! ''Michalk . . .'' he mumbled to him or to himself, twisting again to his feet and vaulting forward through the two in front of him, straining forward, only a few meters away, they could make it, they could *make* it! He butted to his left, driving the side of his helmet into an eye, grasped the midsection before him, ignoring the pincers and claws slamming viselike against his sides, and lifted and pushed and shoved and strained a step, then two, then three.

Behind him he could hear Michalk grunting, and slamming forward, gasping and stomping and straining, straining to follow. There were no signs or sounds from the others.

He slogged forward, ignoring the brutal blows that rained against his sides, his head, ignoring the clutching clasping pincers, ignoring the looming globular spheres rolling monstrously before his eyes. Another step. Another. He strained and heaved and struck out and butted again and stomped sideways against a trunklike hooflike leg thrust upward at him, drawing him off-balance. Another step.

''Felix!!! Feeeeliiixxxx!'' screamed . . . who? Patriche? The captain? ''Feelixx!!!'' sounded again, very close, and then cut off muffled by ants and fear and, lastly, horribly, by that most horrible Whumph! of air escaping a bursting, peeling, armored suit.

He twisted again, stomped again, strained some more and some more and whipped about breaking grips another step, clouting at last the pincer scraping his faceplate, growling and thrashing forward. The air filled suddenly with dust, a gusting blast of poisonous bile whipping the sand about him and. . . .

The Cone was there. A step away at most. It shimmered briefly through the tangled, clutching, exoskeleton jungle. It was there. There! He could spin some more or, wait! he could spin all the way around and drive backward with the leverage—there were only these three holding him, the other ants reaching awkwardly and without purchase in their haste.

He spun completely about, ripping loose at least two grips. He dug his heels into the sand.

He screamed.

Michalk . . . pieces of Michalk were strewn, stretched, entangled in the ants that had torn his suit open, ripped it open to their mandibles and pincers. They had blown him open into them. His eyes had exploded outward through his faceplate. His skin had fast-frozen like burned tar.

Screaming again, Felix vaulted backward into the Transit Cone, dragging two ants with him.

Blinding Transit light. Then darkness, then the patterned heaving, but a shaking, shimmering, too, a shuddering as though his suit wanted to explode and. . . .

The colt bright lights of the drop bay appeared overhead. He started to reach out for. . . .

And slammed again to the metal floor. The ants! The ants were still on him! They had stayed on him and they were *they were crazy!* The beam, the ship, the Transit, something had driven them wild. They shook in mad, impossibly rapid convulsions, palpitating, vibrating into a blur. They were dead. They had to be. But they still held him! They were still clamped to him with pincers and claws and as they churned and convulsed, they slammed him against them and between them and up and down against the floor.

The pain seared through him as his body rocked between them. He felt muscles tear, felt his shoulder socket quake and throb and burst loose, felt his leg being twisted . . . *thrown*, snapping, against his shoulder blades.

His suit relented at last, popping outward into Traction Mode. But still the ants held and still they shook him in their spastic frenzy and still the pain grew and he was frozen into the mode, unable to fight back or crawl away.

White-faced techs appeared over him. "Get them, god-dammit!" he screamed. "*Get* them!" And one of them held out a tentative gloved hand toward one of the ants to pull it away but the massive corpse vibrated so it was impossible to grasp. The pain was swelling, breaking over his eyes, rushing to the top of his head, slamming into his forebrain. "Get them *off*!" he screamed again.

And then, as one, the ants stopped. Turned off. Run dry. Still. Dead. He was no longer churning.

He opened his eyes, not remembering when he had closed them. The tech was leaning over him, hands braced on knees and saying something about the medicos and the ants being dead and not to worry, just lie there.

He closed his eyes again, the pain thrusting him down into cool darkness. He fainted, his teeth still gritted tight, his last thought: Never again.

Never, ever, again.

He awoke and remembered. It hadn't worked. Michalk. . . .

Michalk.

No one else had gotten through. No one else had gotten close.

But I got through. I got through. I always get through.

Damn me.

Never again.

He slept.

Felix remained an extra day in Intensive Medical because his nervous system had developed immunity to the standard formula propaderm. An alternative was found and administered, allowing time for the rebuilt musculature of his left thigh to set. When he suggested to a confused meditech that his several past exposures to the vitro may have caused the immunity, she merely laughed.

"You have any idea how many exposures that would take, Soldier? At least eight. Maybe ten."

She laughed, patted him on a cheek, and bounced jauntily away, missing his reply that it had taken, in fact, twelve.

There were no troubles with his broken bones. There never were.

*　　　*　　　*

He rode to debriefing in the Barrel, newly installed aboard the *Terra*. It was his first trip down the tubes. He hated it. It was not that he didn't appreciate the idea behind it. It did cut down the traffic of stretchers in the corridors. But when they strapped him into his conveyer pod, it reminded him of the worst of the nightmares about the suit.

The meditech awaiting him at Intelligence Station had been feuding with the steno before he got there. Felix provided more fuel.

"This is just what I've been saying, dammit!" said the meditech, his hands jammed angrily onto his hips. "This man should be given a lot more rest before having to submit to your . . . whatever it is you do that you think is so damned important that you can't even take the time to. . . ."

"Ngaio, please!" the steno replied, arching her eyebrows in Felix's direction. "Can't we finish this at some other time?"

"Oh, sure!" snapped the meditech disgustedly, shoving the stretcher against her with a slap of his palm. "Excuse me for living!" he added and stomped away.

Felix, still strapped in, could only refuse to excuse him for now.

The steno was apologetic, profusely, off-handedly. Then she became businesslike, running through the Sole Survivor Questionnaire like a pro. Felix's replies were equally businesslike; he was something of an expert at this particular routine.

Noting the time it had taken to get through it, the steno smiled at Felix and said: "You're pretty good at this." She patted Felix on the shoulder and added jokingly: "You must have done this before."

"Twice before," Felix replied, a response that would have astonished the steno had she heard it. But then came the angry return of the Meditech, complaining that he simply could not, "in the best interests of the patient," allow this grilling to continue. The meditech plucked the cigarette out of Felix's mouth and refastened the straps. Then he wheeled the stretcher to the access plate and stood there, grumbling to himself.

"Ngaio?" came whispered at them from just around the bulkhead. "If you could just give me a second to explain . . ."

It took an hour. Felix stayed strapped, out of earshot, out of mind. Out of giving a damn where he was. He slept, awaking in the Barrel.

When Felix told them he wasn't dropping again, they sent for a fresh-faced, rather handsome, young psychotech who managed to destroy his own credibility with a single, breathtaking observation. "Whew! I had no idea these Starships were so *big*! I damn near got lost getting here."

Next he plopped down next to Felix's bed, patted him on his recently dislocated shoulder, and produced a cigarette. "Mind if I have one?" he asked.

Felix not only didn't mind, he offered to install it.

The psychotech's glamorous features registered his startled surprise for only an instant before sliding quickly and easily—like slime—into the humor-him smile reserved for only the maddest hatters. His first series of questions fitted well with the smile. Felix, stone-faced and trembling, refused at first to answer. But he eventually relented. He found the man incredibly patronizing, even for an idiot. But the veteran's need for easy trivial conversation welled up in him strongly. Clinically.

The Psychotech left after half an hour, assuring Felix he would return the next day. On his way out of the ward, he managed to catch the eye of a meditech and request Felix's records. The meditech seemed astonished that the shrink hadn't had them all along.

The Psychotech clapped her on the shoulder and said that he never looked at the records first. "I look at the man," he added. "He *is* an individual, not simply a number."

Felix couldn't stop laughing for several minutes. Later that night, he awoke and laughed some more.

Three days later, the Psychotech returned to tell Felix ("It *is* Felix, isn't it?") that he had given his case a great deal of thought and had decided to have him transferred to a soft duty for the time being. Soft Banshee duty. "Like falling off a horse, you know. Got to get right back on."

* * *

That night Felix was told to return to his squad bay. He was told that the change meant nothing other than a shortage of beds for non-restrained psyches. Felix accepted the lie for what it was.

The next morning, his screen beeped him awake from the foot of his bed to inform him that he had been transferred to auxiliary duty as part of a squad due to drop the next day with Admiralty Staff. He was further informed that failure to report would result in charges being preferred against him for dereliction of something or other.

Felix slept the rest of that day and most of the next night. He awoke only once. He lay in his bed, staring at the overhead and smoking for almost two hours. He spoke once, just before rolling over and going back to sleep.

"And do what?" he said to the shadows on all sides.

The psychotech was just outside the lockers to wish him off. He brandished a coil before Felix's face. Felix recognized his service ID number on the casing.

"I'm going back right now and go over every word of this. We'll talk when you get back." He leaned forward next, almost whispering. "Don't worry, Felix. A lot of people doubt themselves in the beginning. It's only natural."

Felix tried not to hate him as he tried not to hate individual ants. But, as with the ants, he failed.

In the drop bay, surrounded by aides, staff, and, to his astonishment, members of the press corps, Felix met Nathan Kent. It was to be his first drop. Kent asked Felix if he had dropped before.

Felix said that he had.

It was morning on Banshee.

The sun sat low on the horizon, shimmering sickly green through the foul atmosphere making long shadows and heat for the ant coming up the dune to kill him.

Felix stood alone atop the dune, a bluntly jagged mass of coarse and crusting sand, and regarded the lumbering monster. It was clumsy, even for an ant. Clumsy and slow and ridiculous. It was, of course, the cold. He turned and glanced toward the hated sun. It would be ant weather in a very short while. Less than an hour, perhaps. He returned his attention to the ant, slogging determinedly. His examination was born of an oddly surreal detachment macabrely imbued with great attention to detail.

Such as. . . . How far away, at that instant, was the ant from being close enough to kill him? He figured thirty meters. Now twenty-nine. Twenty-eight.

How fast was it coming to kill him? Not very. The cold, still. Twenty-five.

How soon would it be there to kill him? Soon. A minute, maybe. Still twenty-five meters, he noted, as the ant stumbled against the slope.

How much difference was that morning sunshine making? An interesting question there, Felix decided. The staggering sluggish ghoul it was now could only kill him slowly. The skittering lunging ghoul it would become, on the other hand, could kill him . . . less slowly. He figured the ant would still be cold and slow by the time it arrived. There were only twenty or so meters left.

And how, while he was at it, would the ant go about killing him? Another interesting question. Fascinating. Would it, for example, simply stomp to the crest of the dune and hammer him to death by, say, bashing his faceplate into his forehead? Probably, Felix thought, at eighteen meters.

Or maybe it would just reach up and clamp onto his knees and drag him down where it could crush him to death by wedging the razor-sharp edges of its pincers into the seams of his suit. Might do that. Might do both. Hammer now and tongs later.

Ten meters. The ant had reached the last and steepest section and begun to heave ponderously up the pockmarked slope. It tripped. Both globular eyes rolled upward, the spinal shaft arched stiffly, the great skull-head tilted forward, and it fell. It fell straight back, in slow motion, like a huge tree. It slammed back-first with a dull thud, sending a great sheet of sand splashing into the air.

As it hit, the ant began twirling its claws for balance.

Felix shook his head. "Dumb jerk," he muttered. "Now you've got twenty-five meters to go again." He smiled, for some reason, caught himself at it, stopped it. He sighed deeply. He knew what was wrong.

He didn't believe.

Still. After six months and twenty drops. After uncounted injuries and countless horrors. After all the killing—of the ants before him and the people around him. After all the pain, all the terror. Still, he could not fully believe it.

He looked away from the ant and scanned the horizon. Endless dunes. Some were smooth, but most were stiffly crusted, with jagged edges and harsh crumbling bluffs, victims and creations of the searing erosive winds that could pack and jam even the largest of them together in a single day before blasting them flat in the span of another. Felix never recognized any place on Banshee, however often he might be dropped in a given area. There were always new dunes, new ridges, new mesas to be found. Even the damned sand could change. The geotechs had catalogued something like two thousand different grain patterns. And with the different colors and textures and formations of each, nothing ever seemed truly familiar.

So he never knew what footing to expect. Once, fleeing wildly and alone, he had leapt from atop one firm ridge and sunk out of sight into the next. It had taken him a long time to dig his way out. They had almost had him that time. Another time—fleeing again, alone again—he had come upon a wall of sand as smooth and strong as plastiform. His powered armored fingers had only just barely managed to carve the toeholds he needed to scale it. They had almost had him that time, too.

A kilometer to the west was a sea glowing a rich innocent blue between two towering ridges. The beauty of it offended him. For it held no water as man knew it. It wouldn't even freeze. Too much acid. Even the ants avoided it, the reason for dropping here.

Felix glanced down to see the ant managing, at last, to stand erect once more. It began, without hesitation, to clamber toward him once again. He watched it take a few lumbering steps. He couldn't be sure—it might be only his imagination—but it *seemed* more agile than before. The sun had barely moved; it couldn't be warm enough yet.

Still, it could happen very quickly and there was never any warning. More than once he had been surprised by sleepwalking ants which began needing thirty seconds to take as many steps but were suddenly, two seconds later, ten steps closer and *on* him and raking at his faceplate.

But this one, he decided after a moment, wasn't ready for that yet. Not quite done. What he ought to do, he knew, was change dunes. Pick one with a shaded approach that would keep the ant cool while it climbed. The ant wouldn't notice. Or care. It would simply come at him, directly at him, through sun or shadows or blazer fire. So Felix should move.

But he didn't. He just stood there where he was and watched the ant.

It was this sight, this creature, that he found hardest to believe. So damn big—half again as tall as a suited man. And incredibly strong, incredibly resolute, incredibly hard to kill. And it must be killed. There was no other way to stop it. It didn't care about fear. It didn't care about pain. It didn't care about death. It didn't care about anything but killing people.

But you really care about that, don't you? Felix thought. *You love that.*

Below him, the ant tripped again, this time on its own foot pad. It fell forward against the slope, driving its claws into the sand almost to the shoulder joints. It struggled a bit, trying to pull itself out but only shoved the mandibles deeper. For a moment it paused, staring at the holes it had made. It didn't seem to know what to do. Then it began to rock violently back and forth.

Felix snorted disgustedly. It was about the worst thing it could have tried. "But it'll work anyway. Won't it, Ant?" he asked. "Because you're so fucking strong." Felix smiled bitterly, without pleasure. "Too dumb to get out of the shade, but oh-so-strong! And so eager to get me somehow."

Anyhow. That was another thing about them. Ants didn't care what it took to kill people. Bashing them to death, burning them with blasters, peeling them piece by frozen piece from their armor—they didn't care how. Ants would kill other ants to kill people. They would kill themselves to do it.

And they didn't care how long it took, either. This ant

would climb this slope as long as Felix stood atop it. It would climb and slide down and climb and fall down and climb and on and on, trying, trying, through this day and the next and the next. Until it had climbed the dune, or had dragged it down around it grain by grain or starved to death trying. A robot.

Less than a robot. Much less. Mindless. A wind-up toy.

And yet. . . .

Ants had tools. Elaborate, sophisticated tools. They made them, knew how to use them. And they had their hives and they had their blasters and . . .

"Hell!" Felix cried aloud, "you've got space travel! Star travel, in fact. You attacked earth." He stared at it, shaking his head. *"Damn* you, anyway!" he groaned, impulsively kicking the sand at his feet. A small shower cascaded about the ant. A small patch struck one of the eyes and stuck there.

The ant had managed to work free one of its claws. It used the curved edge to scrape the sand from its eyeball. It made a harsh rasping sound. Felix shuddered and turned away.

Command Frequency sputtered. "Felix?" asked a voice he recognized as Colonel . . . what? Shoen?

"This is Felix," he replied.

"Felix, this is Shoen. Have you still got that ant?"

"Killing him now," he replied with relief, reaching for his rifle at last.

"No, no, no! Don't kill it!" cried the colonel. "I told you not to!"

Felix sighed, keyed the safety back on. "So you did, colonel. But I thought that, since you're. . . ."

"Don't think, Felix. I'll tell you when."

Felix counted to ten.

"Felix?"

"Yes, Colonel?"

"You didn't kill it, did you?"

"No, Colonel."

"Still got it, then?"

"Colonel, there's no third way."

"Uh, yes. Of course. All right, Felix. I have you on my holos now. We'll be there shortly." There was a pause. "Felix, I want that ant."

"I want you to have it, Colonel," he replied flatly, keying off the frequency with a vicious snap of his chin and turning to. . . .

The ant struck him so hard it unhinged his senses. He was unaware of the blazer flying from his grasp, unaware of spinning through the air, unaware of falling. Only when he slammed to the hard floor of the gulley behind the dune, some fifteen meters below his perch, did he react—in agony. He put a gloved hand to the back of his neck. He had landed there, a concussion that would have killed an unsuited man instantly and which should have broken his neck, but hadn't.

Why am I still alive? he had time to wonder before the shadow loomed over him and there was no time for anything but the struggle and maybe no time even for that for all was cloudy and indistinct, the ant hazy before him, but moving so quickly, hammering at him, smashing at his chest and face-plate but he couldn't seem to move so quickly as he should, as if he were in a thick mist that held him but freed the ant to rake and pummel him from side to side. My God! My God!

And then, suddenly, his eyes snapped into focus upon the coarse fibers of the ant's midsection swinging before him and the claws smacking down viselike onto his upper arms and the pincers . . . the pincers!

One of the pincers was already into the waist seam, it's curved, scimitar-sharp edge slipping into the narrow slot and sawing machinelike back and forth within it. The image froze him. The image, this image, of death—of Death, dammit!—seconds, moments away. The seam wedged through and splitting and him, Felix, all of him, his thoughts and memories and bones and intestines spewing out the tiny hole, pulsing crushed stone-frozen blood jutting. . . .

"No! NO!" he shouted in a disgusted furious refusal. "NO!"

And he erupted. He had no purchase, no leverage, no position—the ant had all of those, leaning over and down upon him, claws and pincers wedging and tearing. But he had fear. He had that. Felix erupted with that. He shook and warped back and forth. He vibrated and wrenched. Up and down and back and forth, none of it enough by itself, but none of it alone. He dragged one leg loose, got a knee up, got an armored boot planted firmly. He lifted up off the sand, bringing the ant with him, and slammed back down against it.

The concussion tore one of the claws free of its grip. It tore the pincer clutching his waist seam off at the joint. Felix used his free arm to hammer at the ant's skull again and again and again and again and. . . .

And then he was free from it and backing away, chest heaving. The ant stood erect, too, coming at him again. But free now and ready, he stepped inside of the arc of the sideswiping claws and pounded upward into the thorax with three rocketing forearms in a row. The ant staggered straight back and fell full-length into the sand.

All right! Felix thought, stepping forward to drive his boot into the brain case with a single, hurtling. . . .

"Felix!" shouted Shoen from the far end of the gulley. "What the hell do you think you're doing?"

He spun around toward her furiously, his chest still heaving. "What the hell does it look like?" he demanded.

There were two warriors with her as well as someone wearing one of those all-size p-suits. One of the warriors, he noticed, was holding his blaze-rifle.

"I told you not to kill that ant," she said angrily.

He pointed a shaking finger at the creature struggling to rise. "You shoulda told him," he snapped back.

"Felix, I told you I wanted it alive."

"He's all yours, Colonel," he replied stepping aside as it rose to its pads and lumbered toward them.

"Huh? Oh. Ling! Kill it."

One of the warriors raised an arm and blazed its head neatly off. It collapsed as if exhausted into a heap. Felix stared, unable to speak.

"All right, people, get to work," added Shoen. The others hurried past Felix toward the body. One of the warriors handed him his blazer.

"Here you go, Scout," he said pleasantly.

Felix nodded dumbly. He snapped the rifle into place on his back. He stared at the three busying themselves with the carcass. He stared at Shoen, walking easily toward him. He shook his head as if to clear it.

Shoen, looking at him, laughed suddenly, all trace of anger

gone. She patted him on the shoulder heavily. "Easy there, Felix," she began. "I know it must seem a little. . . ."

He shoved her arm angrily away.

She laughed again, turned to the others. "Is it all right? What you need?"

The tech wearing the p-suit looked up from her work. "Fine."

"No damage?" insisted Shoen.

The p-suit shrugged. "Nothing important. Missing a pincer."

Shoen regarded Felix once more. She seemed to be holding back more laughter with great effort. "What happened to its pincer, Felix?"

Felix forced his voice to stay calm and flat. "My guess would be birth defect, Colonel."

Shoen laughed again, a pleasant, breathy sound. "I see," she replied, reaching forward and pulling the pincer loose from his waist. "And what do you suppose this is?"

Felix glanced down. "Lodge pin," he said.

Shoen laughed again. She tossed the pincer away.

"Got it, Colonel!" cried the p-suit, holding something in the air for them to see. Felix stared. The tech held a length of ant spine between her gloved hands. It twisted and turned in her grip like a beheaded serpent.

"Great," replied Shoen. "You three hurry up and get that back to the Bunker."

"Have they dropped it yet?" asked one of the warriors, Ling, the one who had blazed the ant.

"They will have by the time you get back." The Colonel looked at Felix again. "You oughta come, too, Felix. Should be quite a sight."

Felix only stared at her. She laughed again.

"Colonel?" called the tech. "Aren't you coming?"

"No. You three go ahead. I'll stay here with our scout." She waved them off. "Felix, you really don't know what's going on here, do you?"

"No."

"You usually sleep during Briefings, do you?" Felix took a deep breath.

"What Briefings are those, Colonel?"

"Don't tell me you haven't been Briefed, Felix. . . ."

"Very well."

"Must've been ten Briefings on this drop. There were two on the bunker alone."

"Imagine that."

She looked at him. "Felix, they wouldn't have dropped you without a Briefing."

"Of course not."

"That would be insane."

"True."

"They'd never do it."

"Never."

Now she stared at him. "Are you telling me . . . ? But, why? Why would they do that?"

He shrugged. "Why not?"

She wanted more. Under her repeated urging, Felix gave it to her. He told her, wtihout detail, of how he had been both assigned and dropped within twenty-four hours. No briefing. No explanation. No option.

Shoen found it incredible.

Felix shrugged again. "Welcome to Banshee."

Shoen stared at him. "But, Felix, I've never heard of such a . . . Hold it a second," she said suddenly, cocking her head. For the next few moments she was silent, conversing, no doubt, on a frequency he didn't receive with brass he didn't know. She broke off at last. "C'mon, Felix. I've got to get back to the Bunker. They've got another snip for us."

"Snip?"

"Spinal section. C'mon. Uh . . ." She hesitated.

Felix pointed across the dunes. "That way."

"Of course," she muttered.

They set off for the original Transit Area with Felix in the lead. It took longer than it should have for Shoen kept stopping and looking around her. Felix studied her carefully each time she did this, furiously hoping for some sign of purpose. For any sign of any kind that would tell him that she was not what she appeared to be: a tourist.

After several stops and much rubbernecking he gave up. She was Lt. Colonel Shoen, his boss, and a rookie. She had never been on Banshee before. The realization chilled him.

Halfway there she stopped abruptly, said "Dammit!"

He stopped beside her and waited, not at all sure he wanted to know.

She looked at him and shook her head. "Dammit," she said again. "They've dropped it already."

He took a chance. "Dropped what?"

"The bunker, of course."

Felix sighed. "Of course."

"You don't know about that either?"

"No."

She stared at him, gloved hands on armored hips. "Felix, what are you doing on this drop? Why are you here?"

"Therapy," he said, remembering the psychotech.

"Come again?"

"I don't know, Colonel. I really don't. Tell me about the bunker."

They started walking again, side by side, up the long sloping edge of a dune. When they reached the top, Shoen pointed a heavy armored arm and said: "That's the bunker. Quite a sight, isn't it?"

Less than a quarter of a kilometer away, on the broad flat beach beside the poison sea where he had first dropped, where before there had been nothing but flat sand and nervous warriors, was a building.

Felix stopped dead still when he saw it. It was indeed quite a sight. Felix shook his head. A building. A man-made building, on Banshee.

"It's huge," he breathed, half to himself.

Beside him, Shoen laughed. "Ten meters high, twenty meters deep, twenty meters wide. It's got walls three meters deep and three stories. It could house our mere two hundred and fifty warriors and scouts . . ."

"House? What do you mean, house?"

She laughed again. "It's got pressure integrity, Felix. You can go inside that thing and take off your suit and grab a meal and a shower. What do you think?"

Felix looked at her. He decided not to say what he thought. Instead, he asked: "Why?"

Something in the measure of his appalled disgust leaked through to her. She studied him for a moment uncertainly.

Then she told him what he should have been told before, what the drop was all about.

"Felix, we're here to count ants." When he said nothing to this, she added quickly: "Of course, there's more to it than that."

But there wasn't, he saw after awhile. There wasn't. She only thought there was. She and Fleet and . . . the rest of the fools running the war.

Surprisingly, he had already had a few clues. They had dropped him along with three other scouts and some thirty other warriors that morning at dawn with instructions to head due east and look for what had come to be called a Dorm. Felix had known about Dorms. He had known about them for a long time now, ever since they had thought of them as supply dumps for the ants. And when he had, with the others, stepped over that last dune and seen that low squat structure sitting innocently in the sand, the full measure of that nightmare, that first nightmare, had come back to him. Of dropping that very first time in those rows and rows of scurrying, jamming ants and firing blindly in terror at everything and anything until his blazer had overheated and his mind had over-amped.

When it had all been over, in seconds, he alone had survived.

I am A-team, he had said to himself. There had been no one else to say it to.

And that had been only the beginning. After that had come the Knuckle and Forest and Bolov and other things that Dorms, the mere sight or thought of them, always brought back to him. And he had reached for his blaze-bombs as always, not wanting to remember or consider or anything else, just wanting to destroy this one as he had destroyed all others he had seen since. To destroy it quickly and move on and . . . and nothing else. Just *not* remember.

But the Captain that morning had stopped him. "We don't want it blown," he had said to Felix and to everyone else there. "Is that clear? We want it intact."

Felix had looked at the Captain as he had looked at Shoen and asked: "Why?"

And now he was finding out. Or at least he was getting an answer of sorts: to count ants.

Specifically, to count the ants in a Dorm. Fleet had learned that ants came in two packages, Hives and Dorms. Hives were the main outposts, the main threats, of course. It was from the Hives that the ants directed their assaults on the humans, both on Banshee herself and in space. The Hives were the main targets. But the Dorms were important, too. They did, in fact, serve as supply dumps of sorts. Supply dumps of ants. Thousands and thousands of ant eggs or larvae or whatever was used were stored in these Dorms throughout Banshee. They operated as support for Hives or, rarely, alone.

What Fleet wanted to know now, was their capacity for support. Their exact capacity. How many ants could be built before the supply would run out? That was the reason for the Bunker.

"There are no other ant outposts in this area," explained Shoen as they worked their way toward the activity. "Our job is to sit tight and wait for the ants to attack the bunker. Then we kill them and count them."

"They'll keep coming."

"Of course they will. And we'll get that bunch too. And the next and the next. But how long can they keep coming alone? There's nothing around here to help them. Sooner or later they are bound to start feeling the pressure, either in numbers, or in quality."

Felix nodded, seeing it. "That's why you want samples of the spinal cord."

"Exactly, Felix. Very good. We know the normal standards. When shoddy work starts showing up, we'll have a good idea how much they can take. So it's not just to count ants. It's to find out how they build them so damn quickly."

They had reached the last of the dunes. They started across the edge of the beach, circling toward the sea to avoid the construction. A huge machine surrounded by a dozen workers wearing bright orange p-suits was being set up along the perimeter.

"Watch this," said Shoen with some satisfaction.

Felix obeyed, stopping beside her. Ready to accept anything by now.

The machine started up with a horrendous roar and a huge

cloud of sand. Almost at once, the cloud began to settle. From atop the machine, which was now rolling slowly forward on huge treads, a nozzle had appeared. It was spraying some clear substance into the atmosphere that seemed to cause the dust to coalesce. Soon the cloud of sand was all but gone.

"Siliconite 18," Shoen explained, "a sand clotter. It keeps the dust out of the air and makes certain the foundation of the bunker is firm enough to hold it."

Felix nodded, barely listening, entranced by the incredible sight before him. From the back of the machine, a wall was appearing. It was like some bizarre magician's trick, an optical illusion. The front of the machine sucked in the sand. The back of it emitted that same sand in the form of a five-meter-tall, perfectly smooth wall.

Shoen chuckled beside him. Can't have a fort without a wall, can you?"

Felix looked at her. She pointed an armored arm. "The wall will go all the way around the fort in a square, protecting all three sides not covered by the sea. We'll have blazer cannon mounted on top with crossfire covering a killing area of a million square meters. Something, huh?"

But what he was thinking, what he had been thinking all along, through all of her explanations and enthusiasm, was that none of this had really answered his question. None of it really told him: Why?

He shook himself suddenly, angrily. Why should it, dammit? Why this time instead of any other time? What was the matter with him? The why of it made no more difference than the insanity. This was Banshee! He shook himself again. Banshee! Remember it!

"Felix? Is there something wrong?"

He looked at her. "No."

She wasn't satisfied. "Something on your mind?"

"What do you mean?"

"Is there something about all of this you don't like? If there is, tell me. I really want to hear your opinion."

"Why?"

She turned away from him. She seemed embarrassed. "I saw what you did with that Ant." She turned back to him quickly. "Oh, just the last part of it. You were free before we had a chance to do anything. Really!"

He shrugged. "I believe you."

"Do you really?"

He stared at her. "Of course."

"Good. I'm glad. Because, well. . . ."

He didn't want to hear this. He didn't want to hear any of it. He said something about her being expected inside.

"Oh," she said, rebuffed. "Right." And the two of them continued on to the bunker in silence.

Felix was grateful for the silence. It was not that he feared her confessing no combat experience, for he knew that already and knew what to say upon hearing it. And if she went further, if she told him she was nervous and uncertain, he would know what to say. Even if she went so far as to tell him, outright, how scared she was, he could handle it. He had heard it before, from many others. He knew the noncommittal mouthings that were required from him in reply and he could give them to her as easily as he had given them to everyone else. But if she went further still, if she took that next step, he was lost. If she asked him to help her . . .

He hated it when they asked him that. He hated it because he always said he would—what else could he tell them? What else was there to do but say, Yes, I'll help you? What else was there to do but lie?

For this was Banshee and the ants were coming for them as they always came and there would be too many as there always were and they would come so quickly—too quickly, it would all happen too damn fast for anyone to help anyone else or even think of anything but the horror of it and the desperate all-consuming need to escape it. And even if someone wanted to help her, wanted her safety so much that he would turn his back on the rampaging slaughter, would open himself to it for her sake . . . Even if someone cared *that much*, even if *he* cared *that much*, even if he *did* . . .

The Engine did not.

Shoen stopped just before they reached the crowd and stuck out her hand. "My name's Canada, by the way. Since we're going to be spending a lot of time together, we might as well introduce ourselves. Canada Shoen.''

He took her armored hand in his. "Felix."

"Just Felix?" she asked. "No other name?"

Not anymore, he thought, but said only: "Just Felix."

"Oh," she said, still gripping his hand as though she wanted to say something else but didn't know what. "Oh," she said again, dropping his hand a moment later.

Felix said nothing either, though he knew what he wanted to say, knew damned well.

"I can't help you," he wanted to say. But he didn't. He never did.

Everyone seemed to know Shoen, many by her first name. Dozens of voices called out to her when they arrived in front of the bunker. Several of the people wearing the bright orange p-suits—engineers, it turned out—dropped what they were doing and rushed over to her, blurting out progress reports and enthusiam. It didn't seem to Felix that they felt the need to inform her so much as they seemed to need someone to share their excitement.

Shoen was eager to do that, recognizing each and every one of them on sight, and, more importantly, understanding the significance of each breathless announcement. She tried, at first, to keep him up with it all. He was introduced to far too many strangers in the first several seconds. He had little hope of recalling even a third of their names, and no hope whatsoever of understanding their individual functions. After a few moments, he gave up, turning away from Shoen & Co. and simply staring at the bewildering chaos of construction. Shoen barely noticed his absence, becoming caught up in the momentum almost at once. Within seconds, Felix noted absently, no trace of her earlier uncertainty remained.

But he paid little attention to her group. The sheer spectacle of the rising fort enthralled him. There were at least three other wall-builders that he could see from where he stood, all in use. The corners of the walls had already been erected in place and atop them, more orange suits swarmed about installing what Felix recognized as blazer cannon. Another team of engineers were working on the walls themselves. Half of them worked their way along the top of the wall behind the machine, carving an indented walkway. The other half worked along the bottom of the walls, running power leads for the cannon and what appeared to be a huge command platform erected entirely of plastiform just behind the midpoint of the main wall. The platform had room for fifty people, bulky warrior suits and all, with three separate stairways to get them up there and a broad thick open-air roof to shelter them.

Another platform, this one only a meter tall, had been built in the center of the compound. It was circular, perhaps five meters in diameter, and bisected in the middle by a small wall of its own. Two separate Transit Cones shimmered faintly on either side of the wall, from which figures were being constantly dropped and retrieved, respectively. Also in the compound proper were several plastiform cubes, geometrically alligned, in which were placed a wide variety of equipment. Felix recognized a great deal of it, the Cangren Cells, the emergency allsize p-size, the extra blaze rifles, the spare parts for the cannon, some tools. But that left a vast array of paraphernalia Felix had never seen before. He couldn't even guess their purposes.

Felix glanced at the dial of his drop timer glowing faintly beneath his holos. He was surprised to see he was less than two hours into the drop. Less than two hours since he and the other members of the forward group had touched down at dawn. During that time he had managed to find the Dorm, chart much of the maze of dunes protecting it, scout for, find, and fight an ant, and return, with Shoen at his side. A busy enough morning, to be sure.

But nothing, he thought, next to this. He watched as the engineers connected a cannon-bearing corner from each side with simultaneous arrivals of twin wall-makers. Amazing. Less than two hours ago there had been nothing here at all and now a walled fort was all but finished—would be finished, in fact, in moments, before his very eyes.

All told, there were at least a thousand figures present. And, except for the group of some two hundred warriors formed up to one side, all were busily working engineers. They were like parts of a single elaborate machine, he thought, gazing at the teeming orange multitudes. "Or ants," he muttered, "building a hive."

The excited babble of engineers surrounding Shoen had been replaced by an excited babble of brass, their warrior suits boldly displaying the marks and colorings of their exalted ranks. Felix counted two full colonels and a major in the pack before Shoen turned to him and spoke.

"How long," she wanted to know, "before that Ant warmed up enough to fight, would you say?"

Felix considered a moment. "Three to four minutes after sighting."

The row of brass nodded at this, in unison.

Shoen continued, "Any idea how long it had been above ground?"

Felix shook his head. "None."

The row nodded at this as well. One of the colonels spoke up. "That's about right, isn't it? That checks?"

"Right," said the others, more or less in synch.

Shoen turned back to them. "It looks good to me, Ali. I think you should talk to the Old Man. Tell him you want to try it."

Ali, the colonel who had spoken before, nodded. "Won't hurt to ask him I shouldn't think. And I do think it's a good opportunity."

"Of course it is," Shoen assured him.

"Absolutely," assured someone else. Perhaps the other Colonel.

"It certainly should be suggested, in any event," said a third voice Felix couldn't place with a suit.

Colonel Ali hesitated one last moment, then nodded firmly. "Very well. I'll see him now."

"Good," declared Shoen. "Let me know what he says. I've got to get inside with my team."

With that, the group divided, the brass toward the command platform, Shoen and Felix toward the front of the bunker.

"That was Colonel Khuddar," Shoen offered in explanation. "He's senior staff officer and he's come up with something I'd like you to . . ."

She was interrupted by another engineer, this one bearing the same rank as her own, Lt. Colonel.

"Mind sharing the lock, Canada?" he asked brightly, gesturing toward the entrance to the bunker.

"Blackfoot!" she replied happily. She waved an arm toward the constructive frenzy. "It's beautiful, just like we planned it. You're a genius."

Blackfoot grumbled something almost inaudible in reply about everything going wrong that could and how she could only be so optimistic because she didn't know what she was talking about.

"But you're getting it done, aren't you? And on time?"

"Oh, yes," he replied distractedly, as though nothing could be less important.

The two of them continued to discuss the engineer's problems while they waited for the seal to open for them. Felix understood almost nothing that was said. When the seal parted, the three of them stepped inside the lock, a square featureless chamber with room for a dozen warriors seated and standing. The seal closed behind them. Sensors on the wall of the lock and inside each of their suits told them it was cycling.

Felix felt oddly uneasy. Though he had known about pressure locks and seals since Basic, knew, in fact, how to repair them in case of emergency, he had never been in one before. On Banshee, he had never thought he would.

Beside him, Shoen laughed, drawing his attention back to their conversation.

"But that's why you used Siliconite in the first place, isn't it? You wanted the sand more cohesive."

"Yeah," the engineer agreed sourly. "But now I'm cut off underneath."

Shoen shook her head. "What difference does it make, Blackfoot? You've already got your soundings. You got them up front."

"Well, sure, but. . . ."

"And they were positive, were they not?" she insisted.

"Well, yeah, but . . ."

"But nothing. Blackfoot, you're a hopeless worrier like every other engineer. If soundings showed a firm foundation *before* the siliconite, what makes you think it'd be any different now? My God, the stuff can only make it firmer and you know it." She laughed again. "Only you would sound now, anyway."

He laughed. "Maybe you're right. Still, I wish I hadn't used the eighteen. Maybe fifteen. Then I'd still be able to get at least an echo reading of the formations. But this damn eighteen cuts off everything we . . ."

The opening of the inner seal interrupted the engineer. The three of them stepped through the gap into the bunker itself. Blackfoot left them at once on his own errands, with an over-the-shoulder wave meant for them both. Felix managed a small wave in return before hurrying to catch up with Shoen, already heading off in the opposite direction past a long line of people waiting to get out. Shoen turned around only once, to see that Felix was in step behind her.

"Stay close," she cautioned. "You could get lost in here."

Felix believed her. Though clearly marked, the sheer number of passages was disconcerting. He figured it would take most of a Banshee day to see every nook and cranny, even if someone wanted to stay in there that long, which Felix most certainly did not. He hated the place, had hated it from almost the first moment. He hated it because it was a lie.

He and Shoen moved to the side of the corridor to make room for a man coming down the other way. Felix knew it was a man because he wore nothing more than a jumpsuit. Just that.

No armor.

No p-suit.

Nothing.

And really, there was no need to. The bunker was pressurized. It had air. It had heat. It had walls three meters thick built into it, not to mention the one surrounding it on the outside, with its half dozen blazer cannon and two hundred warriors to man them. Inside such protection, why shouldn't a man feel protected? Why shouldn't he feel . . . safe?

Just because this is Banshee, he told himself angrily, is not enough. The bunker exists, after all. It's here and strong and there is nothing careless about using it. There is no reason at all to feel that something will happen the instant the suit pops open. Popping it open is no signal. It will not bring ants. I will not die. Just because this is Banshee is not enough.

But, of course, it was. For him, for Felix, it was. Each new sight of an unsuited person chilled something deep within him. And he couldn't avoid the sense of the lie, nearby and malevolent and poised. He searched his mind for a specific cause for the fear but found none. Yet the dread remained, a swirling caress of paranoia and suspicion. He felt . . . lured.

Shoen led them, at last, to their destination, a door without a handle marked simply, "Ant Lab" at the end of a short hallway. Past this was a small alcove bearing jumpsuits and armor brackets on opposite walls. Without hesitation, she picked a set of brackets between two p-suits and backed snugly into it. Felix paused long and hard before picking brackets of his own and stepping between them. As he lifted his arms from his sides and slipped into place he discovered that he was panting like a small panicked animal. For just a moment, he didn't think he would be able to do it. He took a deep breath. He made one more irrational sweep of the tiny chamber for danger. He decided to go ahead and do it.

And suddenly, he had. He stood naked in front of the suit, wild-eyed and taut and expectant.

Nothing happened. Nothing at all. Except for Shoen, shrugging into a jumpsuit beside him and his suit hanging on the wall behind him, he was alone. No ants.

"Are you all right," Shoen asked.

"Fine," he replied shortly, grabbing a jumpsuit and putting it on. "Fine."

The lab was huge, several times larger than necessary. Only one corner was lit, giving the impression of a vast cavern. There were three techs in the corner of light, two of them bent over the single table, the third examining a row of dials on the wall. They turned at the sound of approach.

"Welcome to our little store, Felix," said Shoen. "Let me introduce you to everybody. First, there's . . ."

"Is this him?" blurted the nearest one suddenly, a thin young man with bright red hair. He stepped up to Felix and offered his hand. "You're Felix? Nice job! My name's Gavin and I sure want you to know I think a lot of what you do."

"Okay," replied Felix uncertainly while the young tech pumped his hand.

"I'm sorry," said another tech, a bald black woman as young as the first. She looked to Shoen nervously. "I'm sorry," she said again. "I told them what we saw, him fighting the ant like that."

"It seems your exploits precede you, Felix," commented Shoen with a grin.

Felix said nothing. He shook hands with the woman, who called herself something Geronis. The third tech, equally young, stepped forward last, shaking Felix's hand with slow deliberation while gravely insisting that nothing he could ever accomplish in a lab would mean as much as what Felix did with every drop. Felix didn't catch his name.

The introductions completed, the questions began at once.

"I bet you've seen a lot of combat, huh?" asked Geronis. "What's it like?"

"Have you?" Gavin wanted to know. "Have you seen a lot of combat?"

Felix shrugged. "Some."

"Tell us about it," blurted at least two of them in ragged unison.

"Yeah. What's it like?" "Is it scary?" "Are you scared?" "Is it hard to kill an ant?" "What does it feel like to kill one?" "What was it like the first time?"

Felix stared, unbelieving, at their faces, eager, excited, admiring. Those faces had nothing to do with Banshee and nothing to do with him and he could . . . not . . . imagine . . . why they didn't know it immediately. Were they blind? Retarded?

Felix's expression dawned, belatedly, on Shoen. She hurried to rescue him. "Enough," she barked, clapping her hands for silence. "He's here to see the lab, damnit. Shut up and show it to him. We're on a tight schedule."

Meekly, they obeyed. There wasn't much to see. Four pressurized vats, tools and trays for dissection, some specimen jars. The explanation for each was lost completely, in the style of the questions, in the sound of three voices at once. Shoen was quicker to the rescue the second time. She gave him, in seconds, the only two pieces of information he actually needed to have.

"When you blaze the spine, make sure you get a section as long as your forearm," she said. "And when you bring it back, put it in there," she added, pointing to a slot on the largest vat.

"Is that it?" he asked.

"That's it," she assured him and led him outside to safety. The techs were still wishing them luck as they hit the door.

"They've given the team a pretty good place to rest," she said as they once again entered the main passage. "I'll show it to you and then I've got some people I've got to see."

He nodded without answering. His mind was elsewhere—on his newly discovered delight at being out of the suit. It really did feel marvelous, however frightening it had seemed at first. He flexed his toes in his sandals happily.

Shoen stopped abruptly in front of him, turning to speak. He stopped and waited. She, in turn, waited for a small group of people in jumpsuits to pass before speaking.

"Look, Felix," she began hesitantly, "I'm sorry about those kids in the lab. I know they seemed a little . . . Well, you must understand that for them this is all very. . . ."

"Canada!" sounded from behind them enthusiastically.

As they turned toward the voice they were surrounded by half a dozen fresh-faced young officer-types wearing jumpsuits too immaculate to be anything other than custom tailored. They looked like they belonged on the vid, he thought. Like actors cast as the Fleet's finest. Or, he added wryly, like students dressed up for a party with an Antwar motif. He shrugged uneasily, failed once more to catch most of the names Shoen threw at him. He was ignored for the most part. Canada and her exploits were the center of their attentions. And when they found out she'd seen "action"!

"Well, it was really my scout here, Felix," she added somewhat patronizingly.

"Tell us about it," urged a pretty captain with a thick Slavic accent.

Felix looked at her uncertainly. He had no idea what to say

to her. He knew there must be a connection between doing it
and talking about it later—it just seemed beyond his reach.

Others chimed in with their own urgings, interrupting one
another in their excitement. The only response Felix was able
to effectively offer was a nod to the oft-repeated question:
"Seen much combat?"

Everyone of the group seemed to feel the need to ask that
particular question. Everyone of them got the same nod. And,
though few noticed, the same helplessly blank stare.

Mercifully, they tired of him. And Shoen had things to do.
Soon they were alone. She didn't try to apologize this time.
She only smiled nervously.

He met the other members of Shoen's team in the overly
large quarters assigned to them for off-duty use—a huge
rectangular squad bay holding seven bunks in a space meant
for thirty. Ling he had met earlier—she had been the one who
had actually killed the ant. The other warrior was a huge man
named Morleone. "I gave you back your rifle, remember?"
he asked as he shook Felix's hand.

Felix remembered, nodded.

Shoen looked around. "Where's Dominguez? Where's the
sergeant?"

Ling shrugged. "Said something about needing more gear.
He left as soon as we got here."

Shoen frowned at that. She ordered Felix shown the rest of
the area—which meant nothing more than Morleone pointing
to the door holding the head.

"Got everything you need in there," Morleone offered.
"Heads and showers." He shrugged his shoulders and vast
muscles rippled. "Not like any drop I ever heard of."

Shoen spoke up sharply, almost defensively. "Well, okay.
Wait here until Dominguez shows up. Then get back into
your gear." She glanced at a clock on the wall. "We'll be
seeing it all happen pretty quick. Sun's been up over two
hours now."

"Howdy, Colonel," said a cheerful voice. Standing in the
doorway was another huge man. He seemed, on first glance,
to be fat. But, Felix quickly decided, it was only because of
his enormous barrel chest. "You must be Felix," the man

said, dropping a packing case heavily onto one of the bunks. He stuck out a hand. "I'm Dominguez."

Felix shook the hand while Shoen inspected the packing case.

"What have you got there, Sergeant?" she wanted to know.

Dominguez smiled broadly. "Cigarettes, mostly." He reached inside and selected one of the tubes at random. He looked at Felix. "You smoke?"

Felix nodded eagerly, catching the tube thrown to him. "Me too," echoed the two warriors simultaneously. Dominguez waved them toward the case.

Shoen looked unhappy. "Is that what you've been up to, Dominguez? I thought I told you to check out your quarters."

Dominguez smiled easily, unrepentant. "Oh, I did, Colonel. I did." He looked around at the room. "And they're just beautiful!"

Ling and Morleone grinned. Shoen tried not to, failed. Even Felix smiled. There was something lovable about the sergeant that was undeniable. Felix found himself liking the other man immediately, and then surprising himself by realizing it.

Dominguez stepped over to Felix, lit his cigarette for him, said: "So you're the bully?"

Felix stared quizzically, wondering what the man meant and, more importantly, why he was grinning again.

"What's the idea of picking on the Colonel's ant like that this morning?"

Felix laughed, shrugged, amazed by it all.

Dominguez continued. "I know your type, Felix. Always starting something."

Felix tried explaining how he got taken by surprise . . .

"Oh really?" interrupted Dominguez with loud skepticism. "You trying to tell us that an ant eight foot tall weighing a thousand or so pounds just kinda sneaked up on you when you weren't looking?"

Felix laughed again with the others.

"What'd it do, Scout, tiptoe?" demanded Dominguez, spreading his arms into the air and hunching over. His face screwed up, his eyes bugging out, he pranced several steps around the room in a hilarious imitation of a tiptoeing ant. Ling, Morleone—even Shoen—were soon roaring with laughter.

Incredibly, Felix found he was laughing right along with them. And for those brief moments, he simply luxuriated in the sensation. Gratefully, blindly . . . It made no sense. But it had been so long.

And then it was over and he and Shoen were heading back through the corridors to the lab and their armor. Once more they were assaulted by a gang of young fresh faces loudly greeting Shoen as the old friend she apparently was. And once more they turned to him, besieging him with questions about the ant, about all ants, about fighting them.

About killing them.

He endured it, nodding, nodding. The contrast, between these Up and Coming and Dominguez was inexplicably striking. He wasn't sure exactly why, but their questions—and their eagerness to question—left him cold and . . . closed. He didn't like being around them, didn't like anything about them. But the reasons for his feelings were as much a mystery as his instant affection for Dominguez. Normally, Felix knew full well, he didn't notice people at all, much less have emotional reactions to them.

There is something very odd here, he thought to himself, glancing at the passage overhead. Something wrong. The drop itself . . . this bunker, these people. Me. Especially me. I feel. . . .

And that, of course, was it, he realized suddenly. He *felt*. He felt. . . .

"Ah, c'mon, what was it, Felix? Exactly how much combat have you *really* seen? How many drops?"

Felix looked at the man who had asked the question, disliking him at once. He was somehow too snide and too cynical and too . . . My God? Envious?

"This is twenty," Felix snapped without thinking, shouldering past the man and continuing his way down the passage.

It was very quiet behind him. He walked several steps, then considered stopping. He wasn't at all certain about where everything was and Shoen. . . .

Then she was there, by his side. "Here," she said, pointing to a cutoff he recognized as the lab hallway.

298 / John Steakley

He looked sideways at her as they entered the alcove holding their suits. She didn't speak. But she didn't seem at all displeased.

He glanced at his suit, a sudden revulsion surging at the thought of putting it back on and then . . . Just the thought of wearing it seemed enough. He leaned against the wall and lit the other cigarette he had brought from the squad bay.

"That was pretty good," she said suddenly. He looked at her. She was nodding with satisfaction. "Garrel Brunt is an ass."

He half-smiled, waiting patiently.

"I don't blame you a bit for saying that to him," she continued. " 'Course, he'll just go look you up now. He can do it, too—he's got the pull to check most records. And you'll hear from him again, loudly, no doubt, and in public, no doubt. He hates looking like a fool."

Felix got it. "You mean that last guy?"

"Right. Brunt. I loved that look on his face when you told him twenty drops." She laughed lightly to herself. "The rest, too. They didn't believe it either—but what could they say? What if it was true? Ha!" She laughed again, smiling at him. "I don't blame you a bit, really. Must get awfully tired of hearing that same question. Bet you've heard it a lot, huh?"

He shrugged. "Never so much as today."

"Really?" she asked. She looked thoughtful. "Maybe it makes sense. These guys would be awfully curious about combat, since none of them ever should've seen any. Or mostly none." She looked at him suddenly, grinning. "How many drops have you really had?"

"Twenty," he replied absently. "But what are they doing here if they. . . ."

He stopped when he saw her face.

Her voice was very deliberate. "Did you say . . . do you mean to say that you really have dropped twenty times? On Banshee?"

He nodded. "Counting this one."

"That's impossible."

He sighed, dropped his cigarette on the floor. "Okay."

"No. I mean it. That can't be."

"Why?"

"Because . . . Well, because it . . . it just can't be! How long have you been here?"

"Six months."

"Six *months*?"

"About that."

She stared at him, then looked away, staring still. "Garrel Brunt's going to drop dead when he reads that." She looked back at him, a wan smile trying bravely to rise. "He's going to wish he'd never even seen you, or even come here, for that matter."

"Colonel. . . ."

"Call me Canada," she said quickly.

He glanced at her, couldn't read what he saw. "Okay. Canada. Tell me. You said this guy Brunt, and most of the others, would never see combat? You mean if they hadn't come here?"

"That's right."

"Then what are they doing here?"

She shrugged. "They're here to see combat."

"I don't get it. If they don't have to fight, why would they want to?"

"They don't. Most of 'em don't. They just want to . . . well, see it. From the bunker."

"Oh."

She peered carefully at him. "Do you understand?"

"I think so." And maybe he did. Or was beginning to.

"Felix, I know you think this is . . ."

"Who are they?" he asked bluntly.

She blinked. "Oh. Well, that bunch you saw just now are liaison officers."

"Liaison officers . . . Observers?"

"Right. For . . . I don't know, different branches of the services. Subcommittees, that sort of thing."

He nodded. He looked at her. "And who are you?"

She blinked again. "I'm from Militar. Fleet Central."

He nodded again.

"But I'm no Observer," she added quickly. "I'm here because the bunker was partly my idea."

"Your idea?"

"Well, it came out of our office, anyway. Operations

Analysis. It was my idea to have the ants checked after each stage of the battle.'' She squared her shoulders. ''Those of us from *my* office have jobs here. We . . .''

''Us? Who else?''

''You saw some of them outside. Ali—Colonel Khuddar, he works with. . . .''

''That guy's second-in-command. He's senior on the command staff.''

''Right,'' she replied happily, pleased he had remembered—and totally unaware of his reaction.''

''He's never seen combat? Like the rest of you?''

''I don't think so,'' she replied, thinking. ''He's dropped before, though, I believe. No, I'm sure he has.''

''What are you people doing here?'' he asked in a calm controlled voice.

She looked surprised. ''I told you. We . . . Oh, I see what you mean. This *is* Banshee, after all . . .''

''It is.''

''Well . . .'' She looked very young suddenly. Childlike. Guilty? ''You have to admit, though, this is the best chance most of us are ever gonna get to see combat. I mean, it's perfect here.''

''Perfect?''

She looked impatient. ''You know,'' she insisted matter-of-factly, ''safe.''

Felix stood atop the bunker wall facing due east. Below him was the killing ground, its smooth, Siliconite-covered surface sparkling in the morning sunshine. The area looked to be every bit as large as Shoen had said it would be. It sloped gently down from the foot of the wall for several hundred meters before beginning a long gentle rise to the top of the ridge—everything else had been blasted flat by the engineers. rounded mogul-like humps just before the top of the distant ridge everything else had been blasted flat by the engineers.

To his right and south—and likewise to his left and north—it was the same story without the slope. The sand, flat and open, stretched directly away from the wall for half a kilometer. Some cover did exist, however. Starting from about one hundred yards directly off the southeast corner of the fort, and stretching all the way to the ridge, was a typical Banshee maze.

Made of three- to seven-meter high ridges meandering randomly in any and all directions—as well as the various wind-carved gulleys and arroyos separating them—the maze had been considered too great an obstacle to blast away. Besides, Shoen had assured him, it was so cramped and narrow as to be useless to the ants. They liked to attack en masse, in waves. The widest of the gulleys could handle no more than two or three ants abreast.

Scanning the area one last time, Felix had to admit that everything seemed to have been considered. The fort, with its back to the western sea, seemed ideally situated.

He turned his attention toward the inside of the walls. The last of the orange p-suited engineers were stepping onto the Transit platform. Both halves were being employed in the same direction to save time. They had been on Banshee almost three hours now. Soon the ants, even those still remaining inside the Dorm, would be warm enough for a full-scale rush.

Felix shook his head in awe. Only three hours. And they had a fort! Even with the bunker itself having been dropped pre-built, it was an astonishing feat. He would have thought the wall alone would have required at least a day or two.

A gust of wind rose quickly and fluttered past them. But no dust. Thanks to the Siliconite, their vision would never be obscured by rolling clouds of sand. Maybe they really had thought of everything.

Dominguez appeared beside him on the wall. "Do you know what the hell's going on?" he asked bluntly.

"What do you mean?" Felix replied.

Dominguez hooked an armored thumb over his shoulder toward the warriors in the courtyard, all two hundred plus of them, forming up.

"We're moving out, for chrissakes, Felix! Can you believe it?"

"Why?"

Dominguez shrugged, snorted angrily. "Ya got me, Man. They go to all this trouble to build this goddamned miracle out in the middle of nowhere, then leave it before it does anybody any good.''

"Have you talked to Can . . . Colonel Shoen?''

"Shit!'' snapped the sergeant disgustedly. "She's too busy hanging out with her chums up there to fool with anything as puny as life and death.''

Felix followed the other man's gaze to "up there,'' the Command Platform. He could barely spot her warrior suit amidst several others of equal or higher rank. He was about to offer to talk to her himself when a Lieutenant bounded up beside them on the wall and gestured to Dominguez.

"You're Dominguez, right? You and your squad are moving with my group. Get formed up.''

"Yessir,'' Dominguez didn't quite snarl. He dropped down to the courtyard to where the other warriors were already lined up for the leap-by-pairs over the forward wall. There was no gate. Only the ants would have required one anyway.

The lieutenent eyed Felix a moment. "Who are you, Scout?''

"Felix.''

"Oh,'' said the lieutenant. He watched Felix another few seconds, then bounded away without speaking.

Felix watched him go. Now what the hell . . .?

The command frequency chattered into life with the order to move out. The leaping began. Felix watched in silence as almost the entire complement of warriors exited the fort. In seconds, only he, the cannon crews, and the brass jamming the Command Platform were left. Felix glanced back toward the bunker itself. The liaison officer Observers—or tourists, as he had privately labled them—were nowhere to be seen. He assumed they were waiting to see that it was, in fact, as safe around here as it was fun. Or perhaps they weren't even grounded. Felix knew there was another Transit area inside the bunker itself. He had seen the sign for it.

He watched the two lines of the warriors working up the forward slope toward the ridge. The leading edge of the formation was already passing through the moguls and out of sight over the ridge. Within another few minutes, the entire troupe would have reached the Dorm itself, only a quarter of a kilometer or so past the ridge.

It was insane.

Shoen appeared on the wall beside him a few minutes later. "You ready?" she asked.

He nodded. What else?

They hopped over the wall and started up the long slope to the ridge. The bootprints of the warriors ahead of them left only faint impressions in the Siliconite-coated sand. Felix stared idly at them as he trotted along, listening intently to Shoen's chattering tone to hear the reason for everyone leaving the safety of the fort. But Shoen was concerned only with providing him with blow-by-blow details of power plays among the young officers of the Staff.

Suddenly, Felix realized they were the same thing. He stopped.

"Let me get this straight: We're going out to the Dorm because your friend Ali wants to prove something to the CO?"

She looked at him. "Well, Ali *is* in charge of all the warriors. And how's he going to be able to show what he can do with them inside the walls?"

Felix stared at her a moment, then resumed trotting without a sound. They were almost to the top of the ridge before she spoke again. Her voice was plaintive, defensive.

"Felix, you just don't understand how tough it is for one of us to. . . ."

"Shoen!" sounded sharply on the command frequency. "Hold up there for an extra hand."

They stopped and turned to face the now-distant walls. "I bet I can tell you who this is," said Shoen, sounding pleased.

A second later it was unnecessary. With the first sight of the huge blue warrior suit—larger by far than any other Felix had ever seen, and infinitely more impressive—there was no doubt in his mind as to who it had to be: Nathan Kent. He began by bounding, with ease, over the forward wall as if shot out of a cannon. He was running as he struck the sand some thirty meters down the slope. A second later he had already begun climbing up the ridge toward them at an easy gentle lope—and a speed Felix knew he could never hope to achieve.

He was awesome.

And beautiful, Felix thought, watching the blue suit hur-

304 / John Steakley

tling toward him. The combination of state-of-the-art armor and athletic magnificence was a sight overshadowing everything else; the war, the ants, the man alone—nothing else had to do with the vision of excellence but the vision itself.

"Felix," Forest had told him, "it wasn't even close."

Felix believed her.

Kent arrived. There was no indication that he was even short of breath. Shoen introduced them. They shook hands. Felix started to say something, decided against it. Not the time, he thought, turning and leading them the rest of the way.

Once over the ridge, the terrain became once more Banshee-like. A smaller maze covered the last few hundred meters to the Dorm. In silence, Felix led them through it, following the tracks of the preceding warriors. He never once turned to look at the two following behind. He knew about Shoen, he thought. And he could almost feel the presence of Kent.

He would have to tell him about Forest, about that last time with her—that was certain. But how to go about it? He had debated that with himself on and off from the first moment of meeting Kent in the drop bay. What to tell Kent about Forest . . . There was much to tell.

For one thing, Felix thought her to be the best armored fighter he had ever seen, himself included. And besides her skill, there was her bravery—no less considerable. Her value as a companion was no doubt well-known to Kent already. And though Felix doubted Kent would find the topic boring, however often it was discussed, there was much more to say. Much, much more.

She was very proud of you, friend Kent. On top of that she respected you—for what you really were inside. And something else, Friend Kent. Forest loved you.

Yes, she did. She loved you. The way it should be done and for always. Forever. To the very end. I know, for when she died saying so, it was in my arms.

My God! he thought suddenly, feeling the tears on his cheeks, *I'm crying!*

"How weird!" he blurted out loud, stopping short.

The other two wanted to know what he meant, what was going on. They weren't at all satisfied with his "Nothing."

And as they resumed the trip, he could sense their uneasiness.
But he didn't care about theirs. His was plenty for the moment.

What the hell was happening to him?

The maze parted at last, revealing the warriors deployed in
the classic Fleet semicircle. Less than forty meters beyond
their positions, the roof of the Dorm itself shone in the sun.

Awfully close, Felix thought. Awfully damned close.

Shoen raced past him to the knot of warriors around her
friend Ali.

"Is that it?" asked a shy and gentle voice from over his
shoulder.

He glanced at Kent briefly. "That's it," he replied.

Kent was watching the Dorm. "I don't see any ants," he
offered.

"Good."

"Felix!" Shoen called, waving him toward the group. Two
of the other five scouts were already there. "You're being
drafted," she explained. She indicated the other scouts. "Ali,
Colonel Khuddar, wants you three to make a scan around the
far side of the Dorm."

Felix nodded to the other scouts. "Right now?"

"Right now," she replied. "Report on Command Prime
Frequency."

"Okay." He started off with the others.

"See you later, Felix," Kent called cheerfully.

Felix paused, regarded the huge blue suit. "See ya," he
managed.

They found nothing new on the scan. The Dorm was
situated in the middle of a large depression on a relatively flat
plain between several sections of maze. It looked to Felix as
though it had recently been unearthed from a covering
windstorm. He couldn't see much more than the roof without
approaching to the lip of the crater. One of the scouts suggested they do that very thing. Felix stared him into silence.
It was plainly evident that neither of the other two scouts had
seen Banshee, or ants, before. In fact, he soon discovered,
none of the six scouts on the drop, besides him, had ever seen
Banshee. None had ever worn scout suits before either. They
were all from Militar, all green, and all thankful to Canada
for getting them this chance to see "the real action."

Felix groaned. He sent them back to the colonel after the brief sighting and went to find his own squad. He found them arranged at the southern end of the semicircular deployment, crouched behind a short bluff of a dune that made up the farthest extent of the ant's unearthing efforts. Shoen wasn't there. Curiously enough, Kent was.

So was Dominguez, looking fretful even through his faceplate.

"Too goddamned close, Felix," he said at once.

"Hello again," offered Kent in the same pleasant tone as before. Felix nodded to Kent, agreed with Dominguez. He regarded the overall deployment.

"What's the idea, exactly?" Dominguez demanded.

Felix shrugged. "They want to see if they can contain the first charge right here using our own crossfire."

Dominguez stood up. "You're joking!"

"No."

"What's wrong?" Kent wanted to know.

"What's wrong???" Dominguez snapped angrily. Then, seeing it was Kent who had asked, he continued in a softer tone. "What's wrong is that we're too damned close to be just sitting here waiting for them."

"We've got 'em in our crossfire," offered Kent hopefully. No one replied.

"Well," insisted Kent, "don't we?"

Felix nodded reluctantly. "We do."

"But what've they got us in?" added Dominguez sourly. He regarded Felix. "This whole deal gives me the creeps." He gestured behind them. "No other cover either, see?"

Felix looked behind them. It was open for some fifty meters to their rear. The closest obstacle was the edge of the maze, a smooth sheer wall five meters high. Not too high for powered legs to clear, of course. And there was a gap there, he noticed. It was wide enough for a couple of warriors to use at one time. Still, all that open space to get there made it. . . .

"Maybe we ought to pull back a bit."

"I'm for that," said the Sergeant.

"But Canada told us to stay here," protested Kent.

"And I meant it," said Shoen, appearing from down the long line of warriors. "What's this talk about pulling back?"

"We're too damn close, Colonel," said Dominguez firmly.

"Too close for what?" She waved toward the Dorm. "Dorm's don't have any artillery."

"How do you know?" Felix asked.

She looked at him. "You ever heard of them having it?" She looked at Dominguez. "Have you?"

"No," they conceded in unison.

"Then there's no reason to expect any." She paused, sat down in the sand. "Colonel Khuddar knows what he's doing."

Felix snorted. "False, Colonel. For one thing, he's never done this before. And for another . . ." He looked at her. "Your Ali is just a bit too eager for me."

She met his gaze. "Maybe he hasn't had much actual on-the-spot experience. . . ."

"Any, you mean."

She ignored him. "But he's had the full benefit of all Fleet research on Dorms."

Felix laughed bitterly. "Fleet research thought these things were supply dumps the first time they dropped me. We stepped from the ship straight into six marching rows."

It was quiet for several seconds while they digested that.

Then, "When was that?" Shoen asked.

"The Knuckle," Felix replied in a dead voice.

There was a sudden movement beside him. He turned to find Kent's massive blue helmet looming over him.

"You . . . You were at the Knuckle, Felix?" he asked, his voice an almost inaudible whisper.

Damn, Felix thought. Damn! Not this way.

"Yes . . ." Not Kent. Nathan. "Yes, Nathan. I was there."

He lifted a gloved hand to rest on the great shoulder. . . .

And the first explosion went off. Several more erupted immediately afterwards, a staccato barrage of noise and flying sand. Dominguez's order for all to hit the sand and stay flat was lost in the rolling thunder of the concussions and the bone-chilling screams of surrounding warriors.

In seconds, it was over, as abruptly as it had begun. Recall chimes sounded immediately afterward, filling the heavy silence.

"That's it!" shouted Dominguez to one and all. "Let's hit it home! C'mon!"

Felix, half-buried by the cascading sands, dragged himself out and up to his feet. Around him everyone was fleeing wildly toward the maze. Everyone who could. A dozen steps away, a warrior's suit arched stiffly before suddenly bursting outward. He shuddered and turned away.

Kent was there, standing still as a statue and looking over the rise. Felix turned to follow his gaze and froze himself. A solid wall of ants was boiling up and over and down toward them.

"Let's move it," he shouted. He grasped Kent's armored shoulder and tried to shake it. It was like trying to budge the bunker itself. "Come *on*," he all but screamed, standing with his faceplate before the other man's. Still, Kent wouldn't move.

Felix glanced over his shoulder; the ants were almost there.

"Godammit!" he raged at the blue suit. "Move!!" And he slapped his hand against the side of Kent's helmet. Apparently without thinking, Kent hit him back, a backhand to his chest. Felix somersaulted backward into the sand.

When he shook himself alert once more, Kent was gone. He looked up. The ants were not.

"Dammit!" he groaned and started running, just beyond the outstretched reach of the first of many, many claws. Ahead of him, he saw the blue suit reach the first wall of the maze and vault over it. Five meters over it. Awesome, he thought again.

But then all thoughts were lost to his flight. The ants had almost cut off his retreat. He bore down hard, slamming his boots into the soft footing and accelerating at ultimate intensity. He crossed the last few meters to the maze in seconds, mere steps ahead of the closing mass. He darted through the gap in the first ridge blindly, clipping an edge of the wall in his haste, sending him tumbling off-balance. Still careening, he slammed into the next wall. "Idiot!" he grumbled furiously to himself.

And then he was up and running again, no less blindly. For the ants were through the gap almost as quickly and piling up against one another in their attempts to follow him down the gulley. He kept on, not bothering after that one glance over his shoulder to check their progress. He followed that gulley until it came to a dead end and leaped over the obstruction. He followed another gulley awhile, leapt again, leapt some more. Ran. . . .

At last he reached the killing area where he could achieve full speed. Ahead of him, the last of the others were already clearing the walls of the fort into safety. Behind and above him, the ants were boiling into sight over the top of the ridge and down the long smooth runway to the bunker.

Felix ran like hell to beat them to it.

Twenty last steps away, he noticed one of the gunners pointing a cannon just over his head at the ants he knew were just behind him. The gunner looked too damned itchy. . . .

He pointed a shaking finger at the figure above him. "Hold your fucking fire!" he screamed at the top of his lungs.

The gunner's hands jerked, as if stung, from the triggering keys.

Felix took two more steps and launched himself for the top of the wall. Too hard, he realized in the air. "Dammit!" he cursed as he glided ungracefully past his target and crashed onto the smooth hard surface of the inner courtyard.

Two large warrior's hands hauled him roughly to his feet. Dominguez.

"You in a hurry?" asked the sergeant dryly.

Felix laughed shortly. "You still here?"

Dominguez shrugged. "It's a living."

"Fire!!" blared out on Command Frequency. "Fire all cannon!!"

They looked at one another, then bounced back up onto the wall. Most everyone else was already there. Felix had to wedge himself in between warriors to see. He almost wished, a few seconds later, that he hadn't. He had seen slaughters before— primarily at the Knuckle, but often since. Nothing had prepared him for this sight.

The cannon were cutting the ants in half. From one end of the killing area to the next, ants were being litterally cut in two by the huge beams of coherent light. It happened too quickly for them to hide—even if such would occur to them. It happened too quickly for them to regroup or dodge and dart or, ultimately, threaten the fort in any way. The three cannon on the forward wall arced back and forth against the front ranks of the teeming horde with breathtaking efficiency. Piles of dead and twitching ants began to grow, to jam up the ones racing up from the rear. Because of the blockage in front, the gunners began directing their fire farther back into the ranks. Secondary piles began to form.

Thousands of ants, enough to cover the entire killing area, the entire runway of it, had stormed over the ridge towards them. Two or three thousand at least, Felix estimated. Perhaps as many as five. In a very few moments, all were dead. All. They never had a chance.

Never cared about one, he thought, watching the last few on the fringes of the mass being obliterated. Even the last stragglers had been intent on but one thing: attacking.

"Incredible," said a young warrior beside him. He turned to Felix. "I had no idea it was like this," he added.

Felix smiled coldly. It isn't like this, he wanted to say. At least it's never been before. And what . . . What if it really isn't now?

"Hold your fire!" sounded at last.

The cannon stopped, the people crowded even more tightly along the wall to see. There was a pause, and then a long ragged cheer erupted from the ranks. Felix found himself standing next to Dominguez once more. The sergeant hooked a thumb toward the mass of dead.

"How about that?" he asked.

Felix shrugged. "You really think it's all going to go like this?"

Dominguez nodded, understanding. "But there it is," he offered.

"Yeah," Felix replied. "There it is."

Ten minutes later the second wave appeared over the ridge. The order to fire was delayed until, once more, the runway was covered with their rush.

Then the same thing happened. Once more, in moments, it was over.

A five-minute delay occurred before the third wave. It, too, went as before.

The ants waited a full fifteen minutes before the fourth

wave appeared. It did them no good. Again, thousands died. Quickly, easily, distantly.

When it was all over, the warriors stood staring at the mass of corpses and pieces of corpses before them. They shook their heads in amazement. How stupid the ants were, they said, to be willing to let so many be wiped out.

Felix listened, but heard no one remark on what it meant that the ants were willing to let so many die. To them it was merely stupidity. To Felix, it was . . . something else. Something alien. While it made the others laugh, it made him . . . what?

He realized, after a moment, that it frightened him. Terrified him, in fact, in a way that nothing before had.

"They just don't care," he mumbled to himself. No one else heard. No one would have paid any attention, he knew, if he had.

So ended the third hour of the drop.

Shoen's squad formed on the southeastern corner beneath the cannon platform. It had been forty-five minutes since the last wave. She was afraid to wait any longer. The number of ants still seen to be twitching in the piles was rapidly shrinking.

"We want the ones still alive if we can find them," she admonished the team. "Or just recently dead."

They nodded. With Felix in the lead, the five of them went over the wall.

They were lucky. The first pile they reached had ants still jerking spastically. Felix and Dominguez stood watch while Shoen directed Ling and Morleone where and what to cut.

"Damn!" gasped Dominguez, staring at the carnage before their eyes.

Felix agreed. "Damn."

When they headed back, Felix saw that Shoen's face looked pale behind her faceplate.

Good for you, he thought.

The fifth hour began with the rotation of several groups back into the bunker for rest. All the scouts were in the first group. They were going out again, Felix was told, as soon as they returned. Felix eagerly accepted the opportunity, finding to his surprise that he had been looking forward to a shower all along.

Later, he sat dripping in the head, smoking and watching himself in the mirror. You sure got used to this in a hurry, he thought.

He found the mess with little trouble. He sat on a bench and sipped a mug of hot tea given him by an enthusiastic galley tech. At the next table several young warriors discussed their first-ever sight of ants. Some were beginning to feel a delayed reaction of nausea at the experience. Two said they wouldn't look the second time it happened. One said he felt sorry for all those poor ants. "I think I would have mutinied if I'd been one of 'em," he offered. Felix left.

He wandered the passageways until he found the main hall. It was the largest room he had found by far. In it, several techs were aligning hundreds of seats and benches. On the far wall, a huge blank screen hung before the rows of empty seats. One of the techs explained that the Old Man was planning to address everyone later.

Felix picked a seat at random and sat down to smoke and think. He stared at the screen. He thought some more. He finished a cigarette and lit another. He thought. What was wrong with him?

His mind told him this was wrong. This was a lie. And his guts, his instincts, told him the same thing—there was a frailty here not yet seen.

But he couldn't get excited about it. He couldn't get . . . scared enough.

His thoughts drifted to Kent. He hadn't seen him on the wall watching the slaughter. Embarrassed, he figured. A lot was expected from "everybody's hero," but that didn't include a perfectly normal reaction to a perfectly abnormal dose of horror. He thought back to the easy tones he had heard from the man and of the handsome face he had met earlier in the drop bay. All of it fitted with what Forest had told him.

"No Engine in that guy," he muttered to himself unconsciously. "Too gentle. Too nice."

Again he thought of Forest and of how to best explain to

Kent what had happened and what it had meant. What she had meant. If he could just show him how much she had. . . .

"Dammit!" he gasped suddenly. He was crying again! What the devil was going *on* here? Come to think of it, what had been going on. . . .

Because it had been happening for a while now. Ever since . . . when? Michalk, of course. Ever since Michalk.

He had screamed when he had seen what they did to Michalk. Twice, he had screamed. Twice. Not in fear or pain either. But in surprise and, face it, the anguish of loss. He had liked Michalk, even in the short time he knew him.

But how?

And what had that bit in the ship been about, anyway? Refusing to fight as if . . . as if he had a choice. As if he had somewhere else to go and something else to do. As if he were a real live person again.

Since being at the bunker, too, he had acted strangely. He had laughed with Dominguez. He had cried with the memory of Forest. How? How was he able?

He shook his head. He lit another cigarette. He had thought all such feelings long gone, long beyond his reach. But here he'd been, feeling like mad. Laughter and tears and . . .

And more. He had to admit it. There was more. The memory was returning. Of Her. Lately, he had caught himself . . . well, not exactly thinking about Her directly. Nothing so deliberate. Nothing so daring. But he had seen Her a couple of times. She had appeared, without conscious effort, full-blown and clear before his aching brain. All at once, She had been there. Maybe . . . Angel.

Then the pain hit him. It clutched at his middle, doubling him over in agony. He pitched forward in his seat, dropping the mug clattering onto the floor. The searing anxiety shot bolting up and down his spine. The pain, the Pain! As if no time had passed and nothing had happened.

Desperately, he forced his thoughts to blank. He must hold them there. Blank. Blank. Empty. Think of nothing. Don't, don't, *don't* let It out. . . .

In a few minutes of long controlled breaths, he was safe. He could move. He stood up, ignoring the cup at his feet and the stares of the techs arranging the chairs. He headed back to the squad bay. Back to another shower.

Afterward, his face was pale and shaken in the mirror. It had been very close. Too damn close. It made him angry.

"Fool!" he growled at himself. "Idiot!"

With a snort of disgust, he shook his head, shaking off the beads of water from the shower that were maybe tears as well. He stared angrily at his own reflection, stared hard. He must concentrate. Psyching. . . . Psyching. . . .

After a while, he felt it start to happen. He felt himself dropping away. Dropping back to nothing, to the nothing he had been and to the nothing he still needed to be. But he couldn't get all the way. He couldn't quite get back to where he wanted.

He couldn't quite get back to the Engine Felix. But he would, he told himself with bitter certainty. He would.

He'd better.

Felix slipped carefully through the center of the maze toward the ridge and the Dorm beyond. He had left the walls ten minutes before with the rest of the scouts.

"Find out what's what," a Major Aleke had told him. "We don't want any surprises."

Felix had nodded and, finding himself in loose command of the other five scouts, had simply lined them up at quarter kilometer intervals and sent them off. He had ended up, by virtue of this system, with the center of the maze. He cursed at the effort involved. The others were surely far ahead of him by now. Railsmith, for instance, had the smooth edge of the killing runway and. . . .

"Help! Help! Oh shit!" sounded from somewhere. From someone . . . Was it Railsmith? That would make it to his left.

"Help! Help! Blasters! Look out!"

Felix controlled the command prime band. He keyed it and spoke, trying to sound controlled.

"Who is this? Railsmith? Is that you?"

"Felix? Felix! Yes, it's me! Help!"

Felix cut him off. "Where are you, dammit?"

"At the Dorm! I'm here with . . . Oh, shit! We're coming back!"

"Well, do it then," he snapped angrily. Stupid jerk!

He paused a moment, considering. Railsmith was to the left. He'd probably come straight back down the edge of the runway, sidestepping the piles of dead ants. Felix headed for the killing area to cut him off.

Other voices sounded alarms all up and down the lines. He interrupted their exclamations long enough to shout "Scouts in!" Unnecessary, of course. From the sound of them, they had been retreating when it had happened.

Cursing eloquently, he clambered over the last three walls of the maze onto the edge of the runway just as Railsmith and another scout appeared over the ridge in panicked flight. The other scout . . . Jiller, maybe, damned near died at Felix's abrupt appearance right in front of them. He dropped his rifle and skidded to a stop on his butt.

"Pick that up," growled Felix. Then, to Railsmith, "What is it? Blasters?"

Felix's calm appeared to offend Railsmith deeply. "Hell, yes, blasters. They've all got 'em. Everywhere! Never seen so many."

Felix resisted pointing out that Railsmith had never seen any before. Instead he tried getting something in the way of coherent details.

But that's when the heat ray struck them.

"Holy shit!" screamed Jiller, jumping three meters straight up.

"C'mon, dammit," Felix snarled, dragging them sideways into the cover of a gulley. The two scouts started tearing down the length of it. "No, no!" Felix shouted. "Shoot them! Like this!"

Rifle in hand, he leaned around the edge of a dune and fired at the half dozen ants coming down the runway. All, he noted grimly, carried blasters.

"What's with you?" demanded Railsmith angrily. "You're so damned brave, are you?"

Good point, Felix thought. Then, "So let's get the hell back to the fort." He stepped back onto the runway. More ants had appeared over the ridge, firing blasters. "This way," he waved.

Railsmith stared. "They can shoot us that way! There's no cover! I'm going back through the maze."

Felix grabbed and held him. "C'mon, you idiot. The blasters can't stop us in time. They aren't blazers, dammit! Besides," he added, indicating the maze with a gesture, "they'll catch up to us in this shit."

Railsmith looked hesitant. Jiller looked frozen.

"C'mon," Felix repeated, waving them forward again. "I'll cover."

He stepped out around the dune once more and fired at the hurtling ants. The first seven crashed instantly to the sand, piling up the others behind. He waved the other two scouts on. "Run, dammit, while they can't shoot."

The scouts obeyed at last, streaking past him onto the Siliconite-packed runway. Felix provided another couple of seconds of covering fire. The ants were too jammed up onto themselves to require much more.

So eager, he thought grimly. *They want us too much to even look where they're going*.

Then he followed the other two. As fast as he could run.

Felix sat on a stool atop the Command Platform working the wand over the relief holo of the area between the bunker and the Dorm. Where he touched the tip of the wand to the surface of the screen, a star would appear, symbolizing every place the scouts had reported contact with blaster-carrying ants.

The brass standing over his shoulder as he worked moved quickly forward when he put down the wand. Somebody gasped when the full extent of the sightings was seen.

"Well, hell," said somebody Felix hadn't met, "they've got every approach covered."

"I didn't even know Dorms carried blasters," said somebody else, a captain, looking accusingly at Felix.

"They didn't tell me either," he replied dryly.

Major Aleke spoke up. "That's not the point. The point is: what are they trying to keep us from seeing. What are they hiding?" He looked around at the others. No one responded.

Colonel Khuddar was insistent. "Well? Anybody got an idea? Felix?"

Felix considered a moment. "Maybe nothing," he said at last. "They may just want to keep things tight while they bake reinforcements."

"I still think we'd better have a look," said the Major. He looked then, as did everyone else, toward the CO, Brigadier Hammad-Renot.

The Old Man was silent, as he had been since Felix's arrival. Felix found little hope in that.

"What do you say, Felix," insisted the Major. "How about taking a look?"

Felix met his gaze. "They don't like me," he replied carefully.

"Ah, c'mon, Felix," barked Khuddar heartily, slapping Felix's shoulder with gusto. "Those blasters are puny things. You know how long they gotta focus on the same patch of armor before the plassteel goes?"

Felix's voice was wooden. "How long?" he asked.

Khuddar hesitated briefly. "A long time," he said at last. "Believe me, a long time."

"Perhaps if the colonel would demonstrate the first run . . ." Felix suggested in the same wooden fashion.

He missed the colonel's angry reply. He was watching the major instead, who had sidled up alongside the Old Man. The others turned to watch as well. After a few seconds of the armored version of whispering, the major got his response: a short, decisive nod.

"All right, Felix," said the major. "Go."

Felix stared at him. "Are you kidding?"

"Now just a second there, Scout . . ." began somebody.

The major cut him off with a gesture. "Go, Felix. Right now. That's an order."

Felix stood up. He sighed. "It would be," he said.

Felix had decided to use the gap in the ridge they had used to flee the Dorm that first time. He couldn't make the best sighting from there, he knew. But neither could he make the best target.

He clambered over a wall, pausing before dropping to the

gulley on the other side. He looked back instead. The network of the maze sloped away from him. It looked like
something rats should be running through, not people. Almost,
he thought with a shudder, as if the ants had planned it that
way. He dropped over the wall into the next gulley. He
examined the next crusted wall of sand, as always, higher
than the last one. He sighed. He figured he had no more than
two or three more to climb before he reached the gap.

He leaped, without further hesitation. No sense waiting for
them to sense his presence, assuming they hadn't already.

Two walls later he got lucky. The last wall, complete with
gap, was below him. Through it he could see the top of the
Dorm itself. There was an ant there, too. He unclipped his
blazer and killed it, then dropped into the gulley and looked
through the gap.

An ant looked back at him.

Felix gasped and leaped back, firing from the hip. The ant,
and two more behind it, were blazed down. The edges of the
gap were immediately illuminated by bursts of blasterfire
coming from the direction of the Dorm. He couldn't, wouldn't,
take a chance on looking through it now. Perhaps if he leaped
quickly to the top of the wall itself?

From opposite ends of the gulley, ants appeared firing
blazers. He fired in both directions, slicing them apart. More
blasterfire struck him, this time from the top of the wall he
had just exited. How the hell did it get up there? he wondered
wildly, firing. That's where he had just been.

More blasters erupted from the ends of the gulleys. There
didn't seem to be any place else to go. Felix leaped back up
onto the next wall alongside the ant's body. The gulley
beyond was filled with them, all carrying blasters, all firing
upward.

He unclipped a blaze-bomb and dropped it amid them, then
tore off running down the top of the wall as it blew. The wall
ended suddenly. He leaped to the next. It collapsed beneath
his weight, needlessly cushioning his fall and half-burying
him in the process.

Blasterfire hit him from all directions, the ends of the
gulleys, the tops of the walls . . . Shit! They were following
him along the tops of the walls!

He threw blaze-bombs in all directions. He fired at a lone ant blasting at him from what he hoped was the direction of the killing area and home. His blazing cut the ant in half. He hopped, running, over both halves and ran wildly past them.

Twenty seconds later he had managed the smooth killing area. He ran down the runway, sidestepping the thousands of bodies, toward the fort. It took him another twenty seconds, but he was soon safely behind the walls.

No one liked his report. He could understand that.

The colonel eyed the pitifully meager data Felix had added to the screen. He tapped an armored finger on the surface. "It looks bad," he commented thoughtfully.

Felix leaned forward and tapped his finger beside the colonel's. "Better here than there," he said pointedly.

They sent him away. Gruffly. Angrily. They said they would call him when they needed him.

Felix said he was afraid of that.

An hour later he was back in the maze, perched atop a wall some hundred meters or so into it. The sighting was only slightly more extensive from this point of view than from the walls of the fort—and considerably more dangerous—but the brass had insisted.

"We want all the extra warning we can get," the Colonel had told him.

That I can get, he amended. But only to himself.

Fatheads, Felix thought from his perch. What was the point in building the goddamn bunker in the first place if they were going to send people out of it every chance they got? And for what? He was able to scan maybe thirty approaches more from where he was than the lookouts on the wall could see. But the nature of the maze screened at least that many. They could be close and coming from almost any direction without him seeing them.

Shit, he thought. *Fatheads.*

Still, he had to admit he enjoyed talking to them. Needling them. He was worried some about damage he might be doing to Shoen's career. But not enough to stop it. Frankly, he thought with a grin, he was having too much fun.

He caught himself. Fun???

What's got into me, anyway?

"Ants," reported a voice he didn't recognize—one of the other scouts similarly perched. "Southeast from the bunker. Anybody else see 'em?"

Felix did. He said so. They were halfway across the maze and coming fast. "Looks like some of 'em are sweeping for a southerly assault."

He stood up unsteadily, tracking the bouncing skullheads in the distance.

Major Aleke cut into the frequency. He sounded breathless. "Felix?"

"Felix."

"Ants?"

"Ants."

"What else?"

Felix barely hesitated. "Just ants so far. Scouts in!"

With that he cut the circuit and scrambled back toward the bunker.

Felix knew better than to report to the Command Platform in person. After gathering all information from the other scouts, he sent Railsmith along with it. Then he looked for a seat among the scores of alerted warriors scrambling along the wall to watch.

Dominguez appeared in front of him. He grabbed hold of Felix with both armored hands and held him still. He placed his faceplate against Felix's.

" 'Just ants so far?' " he echoed.

And they both began to laugh. To giggle, really. Helplessly, they collapsed together. They laughed and laughed.

What's got into me? he thought, trying to catch his breath.

Six hours and forty-five minutes into the drop, the second attack began. It came from two directions at once, without pause between the waves. The main runway held the bulk of the attackers. The southern wall fought off the rest. Altogether, there were half again as many ants the second time. Wave after wave after wave.

It didn't help. The ants were running into instant death, as before. It was brutal. It was ugly.

It was short.

Half an hour after the attack the order came to go out for another specimen. Some lieutenant brought the message. Like Kent, Shoen had been absent for quite a while. Felix and Dominguez went alone, leaving Morleone and Ling on the wall.

There were ample targets. They found several ants not only alive, but apparently uninjured. They were tangled in the bodies of their dead, strung like jungle undergrowth in their path. From this grotesque trap, they managed to collect six ideal samples and return to the walls in less than five minutes flat.

They sent Ling into the bunker with the spincs. Felix informed the gunnery crew chief about the live ants. Thereafter, warriors took turns manning the cannon for signs of movement. Great fun was had watching the ants extricate themselves painfully, only to have their exoskeletal hides boiled away after two steps.

The eighth hour order for "Scouts Out" meant, essentially, Felix and Railsmith. Since no activity—other than that among the dead and dying—had been sighted, they were sent ahead of the other scouts on a "quick run" up the runway itself to the ridge for a sighting.

Felix was automatically dubious. But he followed the prede-termined route, leading Railsmith up the slope between the piles of dead and the edge of the maze. He took a lot more time than the brass had wanted, however. Surprises meant a lot more outside the fort than just a report to the Command Platform.

He needn't have bothered. They found nothing at all until they reached the Dorm itself, and little there. Only a handful of ants were in sight, wandering aimlessly about outside the entrance. Felix was sure they were spotted, but, though three of the ants carried blasters, no effort was made to attack them.

"Hard times in Antland," commented Railsmith with happy relief while Felix reported the situation.

"Stay put and watch," was the word that came back to them minutes later. They obeyed without comment, sitting down side-by-side against a dune less than a hundred meters from the perimeter of the Dorm.

Soon they were joined by five warriors bearing shovels, Siliconite cylinders, and a case of blaze-bombs. Felix and Railsmith got out of their way.

Ten minutes later, Forward Observation Post One was ready. It consisted of a curved, sheltered bowl from which sightings could be made in safe, seated, comfort. Then the five warriors left to build Ops Two and Three farther down the line.

"Looks like that's it," remarked Railsmith when they were alone once more.

"What do you mean?" Felix asked.

"The ants are finished," He replied. Then, when Felix was silent, he added: "Don't you think?"

Felix considered a moment, said: "No."

"Ah, c'mon, Felix! After all this?"

Felix nodded. "And more."

Railsmith was astonished. "You really think there's something to worry about?"

"I don't know," Felix admitted after a moment.

Maybe I'm just tired, Felix thought and keyed a stimule. Railsmith was probably right. Almost certainly. But. . . .

Was it just too easy? Was that it? And what was wrong with it, if it was? They were sure due!

Still, he felt uneasy. And oddly depressed.

"Well," said Railsmith after a while, "we're sure as hell killing 'em! Doesn't that count for anything?"

Felix sighed. "It never has before," he replied blandly.

He began a four-hour rest period at the ninth hour. By 9:05, he was inside the bunker, outside his suit, and under the shower.

Dominguez was just reaching the squad bay when Felix emerged, dripping and smoking.

"Did you see all those people coming down?" the sergeant asked him.

Felix shook his head. "Who are they?"

"Dunno. Not warriors. Just p-suits. Allsize p-suits at that."

Felix nodded. "Volunteers."

"For what?" asked Ling from the far bunk.

Felix shrugged, smiled. "Well, we're out of ants. . . ."

Shoen found him in the mess, stuffing his face.

"You'll get fat," she warned. Her face was glowing.

He smiled. "That's a deal."

"Look at this," she said and slid a two-dimensional hard copy of a computer holo under his nose.

"Lovely," he said.

She punched his arm. "Bastard. It's an x-ray of a snip."

"Okay."

"It's from that last batch you collected." She leaned over and pointed with her index finger. "Note these striations along the core. Here, too."

He nodded. "It looks cracked. Broken."

"Uh, huh. As though badly healed. But it's not. It's badly *grown*!"

He got it. "It's working?" he breathed.

"Yep."

He looked at her smiling face. "It's really working!" he exclaimed.

She laughed. "It really is! Let's celebrate."

He laughed as well. "Walk on the beach? The poison is lovely this time of drop."

"I've got a better idea. Let's go to the Old Man's press tour. It's in the main hall. I've just been there. Felix, you should see it. It's jammed with reporters."

He stared, remembering what Dominguez had said about the visitors. "You're joking. Here? On Banshee?"

She gestured about them at the bunker walls. "Well, hardly on Banshee. Come on!"

He did.

There were over three hundred people in the main hall. There were the Liaison Officers he had heard so much about but never seen, warriors rotated back inside for rest like himself, all manner of techs—and reporters. Reporters everywhere. They ran up and down the aisles between the vast sea of well-scrubbed faces and freshly cleaned jump-suits shaking hands and gossiping. There were hearty greetings and heartier reunions.

Felix found that it bothered the hell out of him.

Shoen had found them seats up front, just behind the top brass and assorted VIPs. She plopped down beside him only after several cheerful exchanges with superiors she didn't bother introducing to him. He thought it was just as well. He didn't feel like meeting anyone. It all seemed a little too eerie to concentrate.

She waved an arm in a broad gesture which indicated the vast throng. "Fleet's finest!" she proclaimed.

"I believe you," he said seriously.

Too seriously. She glanced sideways at him. "What's wrong?"

He frowned. "I'm not sure."

She was irritated. "You're not still sneering at us, are you? We *did* it, didn't we? What else do we have to do to prove our competence?"

He met her bitter gaze. "It's not that," he tried.

She sniffed. "I should hope not. Let me tell you something, Felix. Some of the finest minds of man are in Fleet. Some are in this room now."

Somewhere deep within him a bell rang. He sat forward in his chair. *"That's* it!" he whispered excitedly.

"What's it?" she asked suspiciously.

"That's the point. What are they doing here? What are they doing in *Fleet*?"

She blinked. She was completely bewildered. "For such a good fighter . . . Felix? Are you antiwar? I mean . . . are you a pacifist?"

A pacifist?

Was he?

He thought back.

He shook his head a few moments later, said: "No."

She still wasn't happy. "It took you long enough . . ."

He looked at her. "It was a long trip for it."

Then the lights went down and the screen grew bright with the warm and winning smile of Brigadier Hammad-Renot.

*　　*　　*

Half an hour later, Felix decided the Old Man should have become a vid star instead of a soldier. Though when he really thought about it—about the stone-silent and unhelpful figure on the Command Platform—there was little evidence that he was a soldier at all.

In any case, the man handled the tour brilliantly. He had a genuine gift for using the vid. Moving about through the bunker with the monitors in tow, explaining what this was or that did, sliding jokes in and out without a scratch, he projected the model image of the humble soldier forced by his own excellence up through the ranks. He was terribly handsome as well, his huge screen face somehow capable of intimacy despite the vastness. Paternal, brotherly, and grand at will, he was, at the same time, The Commander, favorite uncle, wiseman, king, drinking buddy, and Dad. Sexy, too, Felix assumed, glancing at Shoen's upturned and attentive face.

When the tour was almost over, the star was "surprised" with a plaque of gold, silver, and plassteel for which all personnel had supposedly contributed. Felix had not, to his knowledge, contributed a thing. No one had asked him to. Perhaps, he thought ruefully, they solicit during briefing— another thing they hadn't bothered him with.

He glanced again at Shoen. There was nothing wrong with her. It was just Banshee. On impulse, he reached over and patted her hand. She smiled, trapped it with one of hers, and smiled warmly, scaring him.

"Want to go to a party?" Shoen asked him when the show was over. She had left him briefly to huddle with her colleagues. She returned with an impish expression.

"Where?"

"A party, Felix. There's a terribly festive, incredibly illegal party going on even as we speak. Shall we?"

He laughed. It was perfect. Of course these people would have a party afterward! He should have expected it.

Before he'd go, he insisted on returning to the main seal and to the monitor banks beside it. The techs on duty before the screens assured him no trace of ant activity had surfaced.

Further, there was no indication that any would appear. Felix nodded, allowed Shoen to lead him to the fete.

In truth, he hadn't expected trouble. He would have been greatly surprised had there been any. But that wasn't why he had gone to the monitors. He had gone to the monitors to warn himself.

Banshee. Ants. Death. Still.

Don't forget it, he thought to himself. He sighed. Was he being foolish? Was he. . . . What the hell *was* he?

He tossed the thoughts aside with another sigh and hurried to keep up with Shoen, anxious to rejoin her friends and the glowing novelty of this, their very first, really and truly, official, Antwar Campout.

The party was indeed festive and most illegal and therefore a great success. It was held in a sealed-off section of the second floor, an area housing most of the Liaison Observers and other Fleet Names. Technically, it was for the press only. In reality, it was for Kent. It was a ceremony, a rite, held in his name for all. The high point of the evening, Felix soon learned, was to be the awarding to Kent of his first battle ribbons.

Felix loved the very idea of that. He noticed his own wide grin only when he caught himself laughing out loud at the sight of the forest of brass spread about the room awaiting the ribbon ceremony. His mysterious recklessness had returned, he noted dimly. But it didn't seem to matter. Not here.

"Everyone who is anyone is here," he said straight-faced to Shoen, only to find that she had left him to join a gaggle of the like-minded.

He shrugged and walked over to the bar and had a drink— his first since . . . Since when? Since that last night before. That first night Before. As he tasted the first sip of beer, the knowledge that he must return to duty in a mere four hours— and the horror of the chance he was taking—seemed not only distant and irrelevant. It was macabrely funny.

He forgot those thoughts, too. Half an hour later he was mildly drunk. He didn't care. He was having too much fun enjoying the crowd.

The food, too. Beside the bar was a long table covered

with decorative knickknacks and, more importantly, many goodies. He had, on very first sight, officially designated the table as his all-time favorite Fleet Thing. He had remained within arm's length of it since that moment, sipping and munching and patting his happy tummy.

Not that the chow aboard the *Terra* was bad, because it really wasn't. It was famous, in fact, for being the very best to be had—aboard warships. Felix accepted this oft-repeated accolade without examination, though the image of gourmets making a culinary pilgrimage between warships did not come easily to him. On the other hand, he conceded, it was no sillier a use for faster-than-light than rending exoskeleton.

Even Hammad-Renot made appearances. Every half hour he would stop by just long enough to receive his due before assuming the truly perfect expression of the great leader who, though at heart a fun-loving fellow, was nevertheless far too dedicated to allow his personal needs to come before his noble suffering 'neath the awesome burdens of command.

"Wish I could play hooky and stay," he would remark with a twinkle before leaving to return to unspecified duties.

But then, almost exactly half an hour later, he would return and do and say it all again. Felix wondered what the man did in the meantime. Watch the clock, probably. It made him a bit queasy at first. Later, he enjoyed even this.

But more than anything else, he loved watching Kent. He hadn't seen him since the trouble at the Dorm. He had assumed this was because of Kent's embarrassment at freezing up under fire. If so, he seemed to Felix to have gotten over it. Warm and friendly to all, tall and handsome, exuding twin auras of good will and unintentional physical intimidation, he really *was* everything Forest had said he was. The shyness was there, too, broadcasted by his pained efforts to conceal it. It was a genuine attempt, Felix knew, to be what everyone seemed to need him to be: the lion he resembled.

Felix smiled and sipped. He knew a thing or two about lions. And Kent wasn't in it. Nowhere near arrogant enough. It was Felix's firm conviction, furthermore, that it was no loss. None at all.

"Gentle is better," he whispered, tilting his glass at the

handsome features across the sea of admiring officers and press.

Then Kent saw him looking and everything changed.

At first Felix thought it had been his imagination. Kent's sudden paled expression couldn't be due to recognition, he thought. How would he know me outside my armor? It soon became apparent, however, that Kent did know him, knew, in fact every move he made through the crowd. Every few seconds or so, Felix would catch Kent watching him. He would always look away when their eyes met. But he would be looking again a few seconds later. Looking and drinking. He drank a hell of a lot, even—or especially—for a well-tuned athlete. Felix was becoming alarmed and he wasn't the only one. The first time Kent staggered, the entire horde seemed to bow with the shock of the sight.

Felix hated it. He wasn't equipped for it. He wasn't adequate. Not now. Not anymore. He left quietly, sliding unobtrusively out the door as the ribbon ceremony began.

Shoen caught him outside in the passageway.

"Where you goin'?" she wanted to know.

He said something about being on duty in two more hours and too much to drink and such.

She took a step closer and rested a hand on his shoulder.

"Have you forgotten how to have a good time?" she asked.

He ignored the sinking feeling in the pit of his stomach. He smiled badly. He said he hadn't forgotten.

Shoen eyed him suspiciously. "Are you sure that's true?" she demanded.

He paused. "Sure it's true," he exclaimed. He smiled again. He patted her on the shoulder. He walked away.

And it was true, he said to himself as he entered the lift. He did remember. He did. He just wasn't sure that was enough.

He smoked and dripped, watching himself in the mirror on the far wall. He watched without passion. Numb. Tired. Suspended between. Somewhere out there were so many, many things. The horror of the ants. The legions of their dead strewn about on the sand. The memory of how it was done

and of how it had been done in the past. The past. That was
out there, too, hovering between the laughter of the child-
warriors and their party and visions of killing ants one by
black-bleeding one.

Kent came in. They stared at one another in the mirror.
Finally, Felix indicated a spot on the bench before him and
Kent sat there. He was holding a bottle. He offered it. Felix
drank. Then he spoke. He told Kent about Forest. He told it
straight through, without pause, without emotion. His voice
echoed hollowly in the empty chamber. Kent began to cry.
After a while, Felix did, too. But he didn't stop. He finished
it. He emptied it out of himself with his voice.

Then Kent hit him.

No! No! he thought as he crashed backwards over the
benches to the floor. It couldn't have happened! It wasn't
possible! He peered uncomprehendingly upward at Kent, his
mind racing desperately for an alternative.

There was none.

"I know what you think of me," groaned Kent, his voice
rasping mercilessly. "You think I killed her because I . . . I
didn't kill her. Who cares I loved her too maybe . . . Not like
maybe I . . . I didn't . . . You bastard!" he screamed, and
slammed his foot into Felix's side. "It doesn't mean I'm
small!!!"

Felix cried out in pain, sharp, strident. Helpless again.

He fainted.

Dominguez found him and questioned. Felix told him too
much to drink, he was fine though. Dominguez watched his
face a long time before answering.

"Sure, man," said Dominguez and helped him to his feet.

Felix was once more at Observation Post One when, at
twenty-seven minutes into the thirteenth hour, the third attack
began. It was pitiful.

The ants were, quite literally, pale imitations of their former selves. Their hides appeared unformed, almost translucent.
Their awkward gait was barely sufficient to carry them up out
of the darkness toward the waiting warriors. Fewer than two
hundred ants appeared.

Felix glanced at the dozen warriors inhabiting the vastly enlarged OP with him. He decided their make-work project of expanding the OP might come in handy.

He tongued the Command Frequency and told them about the attack. Then he told them he and the dozen warriors could handle it on the spot.

The reply was lost to him the first time. It was the Siliconite, he had been told, that was responsible for the gradual deterioration of communication. He waited a couple of seconds and tried again.

This time the voice from the Command Platform came through. Distorted, but coherent enough. "Go ahead," a bored voice advised him.

Suddenly, another voice grated onto the circuit. Felix recognized Major Aleke's businesslike tones.

"Don't attack! Repeat: Don't attack! Let them through. You hear me, Felix?"

"I hear you, Major. You want us to let them through?"

"Right?"

"Why?"

But there was no answer. Static, possibly. He told the others.

As they gathered up the gear and prepared to pull out, one of the warriors turned to Felix. "How come, Scout? What's the point of not killing 'em now?"

Felix said he didn't know. But he should have seen it.

It was the press. They had already taken vids of the battlefield, carpeted with blasted ants. They had gotten the warriors, too. And the bunker and the walls and, recently, Kent's ribbon ceremony. Now they were going to get a real-life ant slaughter.

Felix and Dominguez stood side-by-side on the wall among the jumble of reporters and tourists and watched the cannon crews toy with the last of the enemy.

"Holy shit!" Dominguez exclaimed suddenly. He slapped an armored hand against Felix's back. "We beat, 'em, Felix!" he said, amazement in his voice. "We beat 'em."

"By God," said Felix as it also dawned, "you're right. We did. We really did."

The two of them thought about that in silence awhile until Shoen appeared beside them.

"I want a sample or two as soon as possible," she said.

Dominguez laughed. "Hell, Colonel, it's possible right now," he said and hopped over the wall. The battle, such as it was, was still going on and for one heartstopping instant, Felix thought the man would get a cannon in his back. But the crews spotted him in time and held their fire. Then Dominguez proceeded to take three samples of ant spines before the eyes of mankind. There was much cheering when he hopped back over the wall carrying the snips. Reporters converged on him as if magnetized. Felix and Shoen laughed, applauding awkwardly with plassteel palms.

Felix spent the early part of his fifteenth hour of the drop on a solo scan of the area surrounding the Dorm. He found no ants, no signs of them. He was alone. On his way back he found an ant blaster. On impulse, he retrieved the heat weapon.

Inside the fort, the reporters went crazy over the alien instrument of terror. The brass, seeing the possibilities, decided to debrief their scout while surrounded by vids. Felix went along, telling before the crowd what he had just finished saying to the brass alone: no ants. He was amazed at how many different ways Major Aleke used to draw the session out. But he played along. "No ants" was reported many ways.

Later, they wanted an interview inside the bunker. Felix knew better than to expose his face. He declined, answering questions in his suit instead. The first interrogator sought patriotism.

"I bet you'll be glad when Banshee is ours, won't you."

Felix said that would be good.

"Aren't you excited by the prospect?"

"I guess." Felix replied. "But I wouldn't want to live here. Would you?"

"Living here afterward is hardly the point of the fighting, soldier."

"I hope you're right," replied Felix with apparent earnest.

Another reporter wanted to come along on the next scouting mission. Felix asked her if she wanted to die.

"What do you mean?" she scoffed. "There aren't any more ants, are there ?"

"I didn't see any," he corrected. 'But you're wearing a p-suit. You don't need ants to get killed in that."

"Huh?"

"You could cough a hole in that."

She looked alarmed. She fingered the material with concern. "You really think so?"

Felix really thought so. "It's a towel," he assured her.

She walked away looking fretful.

Given an hour off, he went indoors and took another shower. Shoen was there when he stepped out. They talked while he dried. It was only when he started to go that he saw it.

She blocked the door. "You knew what I was up to at the party, didn't you? That's why you ran off."

He didn't know what to say. He didn't. . . .

"I had thought it might be a little war injury or some such," she said with a cackle, blatantly eyeing his nakedness.

He looked at her, becoming conscious for the first time of her appearance. Blonde hair, blue eyes, beauty. Canada. He touched her face.

"Before that," he said gently.

Then he shuffled quickly past her, unwilling to summon more.

"Again?" he asked.

"Again," Colonel Khuddar assured him. "We've already got the OPs manned. But we want another run at the Dorm itself. You've got the experience. You've got the job."

"Yessir," he replied. Why not? There was nothing else to do. And they wouldn't be leaving, the Old Man had announced, until the eighteenth hour.

"Our job here," he had announced with classic drama, "is done."

Evidently, Felix's was not. He hopped over the wall and trotted the length of the runway to the ridge. When he reached OP One, he was given the unsurprising news that nothing had happened. Khuddar had told him to check in when he reached the OP. He did.

"Very good, Felix," said the Colonel with great deliberation. Even through the grinding static, Felix gathered they had an audience. The press, he figured. "Now make another turn around the Dorm perimeter, if you please."

Felix was pleased to do that. Why not?

He reported again when he'd finished. Still nothing to see.

"Very good, Felix," sounded, crackling, once more from Khuddar. "Now if you would, I'd like an eyeball of the immediate area in front. Inside the crater."

Okay, he could do that. Why not? And he did. The area in front of the dark and gaping triangular entrance was absolutely smooth, absolutely flat.

Felix reported the neatness of the ants.

"Very good, Felix," intoned the Colonel one more time. Then, "How about taking a look inside?"

Felix shrugged. How about it? Just a quick little. . . .

He froze. He had actually taken a step to do it. He peered into the darkness looming over him. The bunker had been a good idea after all. The drop had been one of the easiest he could remember. The party had been fun. But no more. Not one step more.

Unconsciously, he backed to the edge of the perimeter, his eyes still riveted on the blackness, on the depth of it. Every instinct told him that first step through would be that one step too many.

Suddenly, the idea of doing it, of almost having *done* it, clutched him. His mouth went dry. He trembled.

He refused.

"What if I made that an order!" snapped the colonel, his voice fading slightly.

"Make it a threat if you like," Felix snapped back. "I ain't going."

There were several clicks and pops having nothing to do with the static. He assumed the press people were no longer eavesdropping. "Felix," said Khuddar, "go down that hole."

"Colonel," said Felix, "no."

There was a pause. A different voice sang out. "Return to the OP and stand by."

Okay, he thought. Why not?

It was the Old Man's voice, he realized at once. The

Brigadier. Hammad-Renot himself. And he was making it a threat after all.

"If I have to get someone else," barked the CO, "it'll cost you. I can promise you that. Now, I want you to apologize, publicly, to Ali . . . Colonel Khuddar, and carry out your mission. Is that understood?"

Felix sighed. "I know what you want, if that's what you mean. No."

A pause. "Mr. Felix, is that you're final word?"

"No, it isn't," he snapped. He was suddenly furious, livid with rage. "Old Man, you shoot some other hero down that hole and you kill him. I know. I know ants and I know Banshee and I know you do not. So listen."

"Now, you just shut your . . ."

"How many drops you had, Old Man?"

A pause. Felix went on. "I've had twenty. You send somebody else and you kill him. I know it. You should know it. And when he doesn't come back—and you can be sure he will not—everybody else is going to know it."

Another pause, longer. The circuit severed.

A few minutes later, the five warriors manning OP One were recalled. Felix was told to stay put in the same breath. No explanation.

Half an hour later, Colonel Khuddar called. Even through the interference, Felix could tell he was making great effort to control his anger.

"Since you're not obeying any more orders, Mr. Felix, allow me to 'suggest' you stay where you are until called. Which won't be, I'm reasonably certain, until our guests have departed. Can we expect your . . . cooperation?"

"Of course," replied Felix pleasantly. "When do they leave?"

"Hour eighteen."

"Fine."

"One last thing, Felix. A personal item."

Felix groaned. "Is it necessary?"

"I believe so," retorted the Colonel, his voice an icy whip. "This may be my last chance to tell you what I think of you. . . ."

"Aw, well, Ali," Felix drawled. "I was hoping it'd be about those warriors you lost at the Dorm this morning."

Another click. Decisive. He was alone again. He sat.

When he saw Kent coming, he checked the time. Amazingly, over an hour and a half had passed. He blinked, considered. But he could not recall a single thought he had had during that period. He stood for Kent.

The apology was stumbling, but sincere. Felix's acceptance was equally sincere. But Kent kept apologizing.

"Every time I think about what I did, I throw up," he said.

Felix laughed.

"Don't you believe me?" asked Kent stiffly.

"As a matter of fact, I do," said Felix. "It's you." He sat, motioned for Kent to do the same. "Forest would say it's the best of you."

"It's not the me I want," said Kent unhappily.

" 'You' want?" echoed Felix.

"Yes. Me. I want to be . . . more . . . Tougher, I guess."

Felix laughed again. "You were pretty tough a couple of hours ago."

Felix could almost feel the other man's face crimson. "You know that's not what I mean," said Kent.

"Yeah."

Kent shifted. "I want to be more like she was, I guess. Like you are."

Felix stared at a patch of sand between his boots. "Like her, maybe. Not me."

"You're a helluva fighter, Felix," insisted Kent. "You'd have to be . . . And, anyway, Canada saw you."

Felix laughed shortly. "Canada Shoen—combat vet?"

Kent laughed, embarrassed. "Well, she knows what she saw. . . ."

"No, she doesn't!" Felix heard himself suddenly snap. "None of you . . ." He stopped, paused. Kent had tensed like a spring, he saw. "Aw, well," he began again. "So you want to be a combat soldier and you feel bad that you haven't been."

"Why shouldn't I?"

Felix eyed him. He shrugged. "I dunno." He glanced away, toward the Dorm. He looked back a second later. "But did it ever occur to you that you're the only one of us to ever put this hardware to decent use?"

There was another pause after that. A long one. Felix spent it wondering how he could have lost an hour and a half.

"I want to be a real fighter," Kent said suddenly.

"Huh? What's that?"

"You know, against ants and . . ."

"Oh, ho," growled Felix, his voice sounding bitter even to him. "You want to be a killer." He stood up. He looked at the other man. "That's what I really am, Nathan. I'm a killer. I don't fight 'em. I kill 'em. That's how I've managed it."

Kent stared upward at him. "What's the difference?" he asked gently.

Felix found he could not look at him. He turned away. "I don't know," he replied, not at all certain it was true.

They were quiet after that. Felix's mind was blank. Flexed blank.

Shoen called at the eighteenth hour.

"I'm supposed to tell you two to stand at parade rest."

Felix cocked his head. "I beg your pardon?"

"Has the service started?" asked Kent.

"About to," she told him.

Kent turned to Felix. "They're holding a memorial service for the nine we lost at the Dorm this morning."

"Oh."

They stood, clasping gloves behind their backs. After a few seconds, Felix sat down again.

"What's the matter?" Kent asked.

"What do you mean?" Shoen wanted to know.

"It's Felix. He sat down."

"I'm tired," Felix said quietly.

They heard Shoen laughing. "Don't blame you, Felix. Lots of folks up here would like to lie down after all the partying they've been working at."

"Still?" asked Kent.

"Sure. Up to about half an hour ago." She giggled. "The whole place is drunk, if you ask me."

Kent sat down. Next to Felix.

"Uh, Nathan? Felix? The service is on Command Three if you want to tune in."

Felix shook his head. "I'll pass."

"Me too," said Kent.

She sighed loudly. "I don't blame you. Pretty dreary. Felix? Whatcha been doing all this time?"

"Policing the area," he replied dryly.

She laughed. Then, abruptly, she groaned. "My God!" she exclaimed. "What was that? Did you two feel that?"

"Feel what?" asked Kent.

"I don't know. I guess it was an earthquake . . . or Bansheequake. Oops! There it goes again."

Felix was already to his feet and moving. The fear rushed like burning tendrils down the back of his neck and across his shoulder blades.

"Don't you feel it, you two?" she persisted. "You should. You're only about. . . ."

"Canada!" Felix all but shouted. "Get to the. . . ."

"Well, dammit!" she continued without hearing. "I can't believe you didn't feel that one. . . ."

"Canada!" Felix barked. "Get inside. Get in the bunker!" He began to run toward the fort. Kent seemed to get it at the same moment. He barely hesitated before following.

"Canada!" Felix called again.

"Yes, Felix. I'm here. You don't have to blast my ears. . . ."

"Are you doing it? Are you going to the bunker?"

"Well, no. Why should. . . ."

"Damn you, Shoen," Felix snapped. "You want to die?"

"It's just a tremor, Felix. Get hold of your . . ."

"Shoen!! That's no quake! Remember where you are! Remember what lives here! What lives underground! Get everybody inside!"

There was no reply. "Canada?" Kent called. "Canada! Answer!"

Her scream began as a low whimper, plaintive and childlike, before swelling suddenly, horribly, across the spectrum until it burst forth as the bloodcurdling cry of a grown woman gripped by ultimate terror.

"Oh, God-Oh-God-Oh-God!!! Felix-Felix!!! Ants, *ants*, ANTS—*ANTS*!!!"

There was no one in sight as they streaked to the foot of the forward wall. Felix glanced briefly at Kent, rolling alongside. He had told the other man. . . . Nothing to tell him. Don't panic at what you see. Nothing else could mean anything. Kent had soaked it up like a sponge.

"Jump onto the wall, not over it," Felix cautioned him one final time as they leapt side-by-side into the air.

This is the only way home, He reminded himself.

He was unprepared for the sight. It stunned him. It staggered him. He could not, would not, believe it for the first precious idle instant.

Writhing slaughter swirled beneath them. It was jammed tight from wall to wall. It was a nightmare. *Thousands* of ants. . . .

"Oh, my God!" Kent gasped, as though wounded already. For the first few seconds it was hard to distinguish any detail. Then a warrior was spotted, then another. Over there a mob of fifteen or so wedged back-to-back and going down. Another smaller pack there . . . a group of fifty scattering . . . a lone suit, frozen in Traction Mode . . . another obscenely imploding . . . Blazers sweeping wildly, panicky, over their heads . . . The Main Seal was buried from sight behind the trembling horde fighting to enter it.

Wake up! he screamed to himself. React. Erupt!

But he only stared.

"There's thousands of 'em! How? How?" Kent wailed.

Felix shook himself. He scanned, pointed. There were three roughly circular holes in the northeast corner of the compound. Ants poured from each. Faded ants, he saw then. The tired ones they had fought that last time. Weak and . . . But so many! So many!

"C'mon," he said to Kent and rushed along the top of the wall to the corner. He unclipped three blaze-bombs as he moved. He dropped the first two in the first two holes. The third was partially blocked by a bright orange engineer's p-suit, being dragged-carried struggling down into oblivion.

Felix hesitated but a moment on a man he could do nothing for, then dropped the third bomb into the darkness where the orange had just been. Kent looked sideways at him, then back down as the bombs blew. Sand, dust, ants, and quite a bit of orange material vaulted up from the shadows before raining back upon the collapsing sides of the holes.

"Not much," Felix muttered, almost to himself. "Something."

Above him, the barrel of a blazer cannon pointed into the sky. Hey! He hopped up into the cockpit, stomping down hard on the swivel bar. It rotated smoothly to the right and stopped, pointing down the length of the outer wall. He tried the other direction. The barrel stopped again, just as before. A safety measure, of course. He kicked the turret as hard as he could. Then he hopped off. He tried adjusting the gearing directly. He tried altering the mechanism underneath. He even tried lifting the entire assembly from its anchor. But it wouldn't budge.

"Here," said Kent, shouldering him aside and grabbing hold of each end. With a single heave, he ripped the turret, the chair and the cannon right up out of the wall. "Grab that," added Kent, indicating the ruptured foundation rod with a massive nod of his great blue helmet.

Felix grabbed it, planted his feet firmly, and tried to keep from being thrown into the killing by the violent torque of Kent ripping the cannon free from the rest with a single twist of his armored wrists. Felix knew he'd have to take the time to be impressed by that some day.

"Where do I shoot? There're people in them and. . . ."

Felix pointed to an area just in front of the main seal. A defensive formation of sorts had formed. But there were so many ants and so many who didn't know what to do and so many more without weapons, only p-suits that seemed to be tearing whenever he saw them, ripping and flapping and. . . .

"Just there," Felix said shortly. "Protect the bunker door.

"But . . . but there's people! I'll kill them, too!"

"Yes."

Kent stared at him. Felix stared back, then pointed again.

He heard Kent sigh. But he pointed the cannon and pressed the key.

Nothing happened.

"Dammit!" Felix snapped. "We ripped the feeder loose, too."

"I can fix that," said Kent. "This suit of mine . . ." His voice trailed off as he concentrated his attention on something in a pouch under an armpit: A feeder line. He ripped the shattered ends of the other feeder free, then snapped his into its place. He touched the trigger key; a blue blazer beam shot forth. It was thick and bright and damn near as strong as the original.

From his suit alone! Felix thought in awe. Then he slapped the other man's shoulder and said, gruffly, "Shoot!"

Kent shot.

He hated it, Felix knew. And he groaned whenever the beam swept over a human form, which was often, but he shot. Slowly, the pressure on the mob before the Main Seal began to lessen.

But on the wall itself, it began to get tight. They were the only ones on the wall, the only ones providing any outside help. The only ones giving hope. The ants rushed over one another to kill them. Felix got very busy trying to keep Kent alive long enough to do any good.

They clambered upward at them, piling atop one another, straining, arching up to the walkway. As they reached it, Felix began killing them. He shot them in two, between their globular eyes or sections, toppling their top halves over backwards, the blood spewing and staining. He killed with efficiency and with dispatch. He killed with the touch of experience.

But he was killing alone. And slowly, slowly, he was becoming aware of it.

He shot to his left and to his right and between his feet and when the rifle began to heat up he punched the toe of his right boot at a head and . . . it . . . lopped . . . off. Weaker ants! Weaker! Cheaper just to do it that way and he did. He kicked them and punched them or swung his rifle stock, shattering and bashing them.

They died in bunches.

But they came in greater bunches and it was starting to get very very tight and scary. All of them swarmed at him now, the real threat, and not at Kent, whose destruction was distant and uninvolved. Gradually his rifle cooled and he could use it again and he did, wondering how much power was left within it. But there was no time to stop and check. They came at him from both sides and in front—all along the wall now and surging at him. And still he killed them. But he was doing it alone.

The Engine had not come.

It hadn't come all along, not since that first one at the beginning of the drop, that first one that had surprised him. The Engine hadn't been there either. Where was it? Where are you? Help me! Lift me! Erupt, dammit! Erupt!

But it wasn't there. He was alone with just his body and his fear and he hated this, hated it as he always knew he would. He turned his head toward Kent for . . . what? Assurance? Shit! He snapped his head back to the job. He was alone! Okay! Okay! And he killed some more until the rifle stopped working and then he used the heavy end of it to cleave and bash and . . .

Then he saw that Kent was no longer shooting, had dropped the cannon. He clouted his shin alongside a clacking mandible mouth, leaped over several outstretched claws, and trotted along the top of the wall to Kent.

"It was draining me!" Kent explained guiltily.

"Don't worry about it, dammit!" he growled, slapping the other's shoulder as he passed. "C'mon!"

He led them again to the northeast corner and around it. Below, the swarming ants swayed with the change of direction like waving grain before a gust of wind. They want us so bad! he thought. We gotta get inside while there still is one.

It looked like they might have a chance to do it. Kent's brief attack had been devastating for a while. The ants had thinned noticeably. Clear territories were beginning to develop in the shifting crush below. But the number of blazers still working—always heartbreakingly small—had likewise diminished. They were still being overcome by the ants, still being killed, still being pulled apart.

They were still losing and they were still going to lose. But if they could get inside and use the protected Transit Cone. . . .

He pulled them up short when they were even on the wall with the Main Seal. He turned to Kent.

"We've got to go down there in front of that seal and bust up that mob. Nobody can get in now. You see?"

Kent followed his gaze to the wedged bodies shifting below. Ants were swarming at them, dragging individuals away from the outer limits of the pack. The others seemed too panic-stricken to fight back They simply pressed closer to the seal itself, making it impossible for anyone to use it.

The only actual fighting being done was by the poor lost souls who were cut off in the surge of ants. They fought, mostly alone, and died, without hope of reaching the bunker itself. Yet the sheer numbers of ants these few drew to themselves could make it possible for the sheep at the seal.

"Okay," Kent said sharply, without conviction.

Felix paused the briefest moment and looked at him, peering through the clear faceplate to the pale face behind it. Kent was willing. But he . . .

This isn't for you, Felix thought.

Then he leaped off the wall into the compound. Kent followed.

At that instant, the fourth tunnel opened. Ants streamed up into the center of the compound five abreast.

The jamming horde before the Main Seal, now close enough for proximity band, seemed to fill their ears with a single mindless scream of horror.

"Felix! Felix, look!" Kent cried. "We can't . . ."

Felix knew what he meant; they were cut off. They'd never hope to reach the seal through this new surge. He pointed to a relatively clear space in the corner between the bunker's northern face and the northern wall. Not because he had hope or because he had a plan . . . it was simply a clear space and the ants were coming—so many! God! So many!

Kent followed him. There were perhaps three ants in their path. Felix carved through them with his speed and his forearms and his fear. He heard Kent grunting behind him with efforts of his own. And then they were there in the corner. But he didn't know what to do, where to lead them next. Up onto the walls once more? But here was the hope. Here was the only way home and he didn't know what to do. He didn't! And the Engine. . . .

The Engine would not come.

Dimly, he realized Kent was calling to him, pulling at him frantically.

"This way, Felix! This way, Felix!" he was yelling and Felix looked where he pointed and saw the squat little cube nestled against the outer wall of the bunker. A door? A hatch? Did it go inside?

And then the surge of ants hit them and he struck out at them, splintering their faded bodies and their poorly honed exoskeletons and their pale dead globular eyes—different somehow, shinier and slippery or . . .

"Felix! The hatch! Help me!" Kent shouted from very close.

He rocketed a fist through an eye into the brain case of the ant directly before him, killing it instantly, and jamming it up in the clattering hooves of the one behind it. He half-leapt into the air, scissoring his legs, and slammed first one then two boots up through the shattering hide of a gaping mandible. Then he spun about, his arms unfolding, and beheaded the one behind against his right wrist. Black blood gushed and sprayed high into the air.

But he was gone when it fell, jamming past the bodies of the dead and the reaching claws of the deadly . . . to Kent, who stood, miraculously, beside the open hatch, the handle of the hinged door in his hand. His other arm was out before him, blazing apart the rush with a pitifully translucent beam.

"Inside!" Kent yelled.

Felix nodded, already in the air. They dropped together into the darkness. The hatch slammed shut over their heads as they struck bottom, five meters below.

It was dead still. Absolute quiet. Absolute emptiness.

"Where the hell?" Felix asked.

"Don't you know?" asked Kent, bewildered.

"Just tell me, Kent! 'Cause nobody else has! Right?"

Kent hesitated, taken aback briefly. Then he hurriedly explained: "This is the concussion cellar. In case of artillery.

The air in here is supposed to compress instead of the walls of the bunker."

"Oh. Does it work?"

Kent shrugged. "It's new."

"Can we get inside the bunker from in here?"

"Huh? Yes! Yes, we can! I forgot! Here! Down the passage."

The chamber they were in was ten meters square. At the far end of it stood a heavy plassteel door. Kent reached to grasp its oversized handle.

"There's a passage behind here that leads to a . . . Shit!"

"What's the matter?"

Kent jerked at the door. "It's stuck."

"Perfect!" Felix snarled

"Wait a minute," gasped Kent. He took his glove from the handle and placed it flat against the door itself. Holding it so, he worked keys on the inside of his forearm with his other hand. Suddenly, he jerked back from it, banging into Felix.

"What's the matter?"

Kent looked at him. "Ants." He pointed a finger. "Behind the door. Lots of 'em."

Felix stepped up, placing a hand on the plassteel. "Trying to get through, you think?"

Kent shrugged. "I guess. *Some*thing's jammed it."

Felix dropped his hand. "Is there another way?"

"No."

"Shit."

From somewhere overhead, a thunderous blast rang out. The floor of the chamber rocked violently under their boots. Sand rained from the high ceiling.

"About goddamned time!" Felix snapped happily.

"Reinforcements!" gasped Kent with equal pleasure. "Those are concussion grenades. We use them in the . . ."

A second blast rocked them, followed by a third and fourth in quick succession. The floor trembled crazily. The walls bowed inward, shimmering. The falling sand became a continuous cloud.

Kent laughed uneasily. "If they're not careful, they're gonna . . ."

A searing, bursting shockwave slammed them to the floor.

The walls across the chamber buckled and split, spewing a huge chunk of plastiform into the ceiling. The ceiling, already bowing, split in turn. Great plastiform beams tore loose from their moorings and crashed to the floor all around them. Several holes burst open in the ceiling itself. Sand poured through in huge quantities, piling into cones that spilled toward them.

"Look out," Felix warned Kent as a chunk fell heavily to the floor just behind him.

"Oh God!" Kent screamed, pointing back the other way.

Felix turned to look just as the great plassteel door exploded from its hinges. Ants boiled out of the choked passage toward them.

And then it was happening again and he lashed out at them, bashing them with his forearms or boots or the butt of the rifle. But without the Engine and its strength. Alone still and knowing it. Only his experience and his fear and the knowledge of nowhere else to go . . .

Kent, no killer, was awesome still. He obliterated them with the thunderous sweeps of his fists. He lifted chunks of plastiform and threw them. He threw beams, too. And sand. And much, much fear.

They were holding their own for several seconds and more. But it was a useless struggle with only one outcome, only one end, with the swarming upon them, pulling and tearing and raking at faceplates and seams, exhausted last-ditch struggles using energy as well applied to the screams equally certain to come . . .

"The hatch!" Felix shouted. "We've got to get back . . . !"

Kent nodded. He heaved a long length of plastiform beam—so big Felix could not have lifted it—at the nearest swelling gang, flattening the first four outright. The two of them took advantage of the momentary pause to back up quickly to where the hatch had been.

When they got there it was gone.

"Oh, no!" Kent wailed.

In place of the hatch was a warped square of plassteel crammed awkwardly into a sunlit manhole. The grenades had blown their exit apart.

"Try anyway," urged Felix, shoving Kent forward. "Try

jumping up through it." When Kent hesitated, he shoved him again. "Try, dammit! Come on! You can see the sky there."

Kent nodded, flexed his knees to leap . . . And another explosion staggered them. More plastiform, more sand, cascaded from the walls and ceiling. Felix righted himself with difficulty. The sand was almost thigh-deep now and it hampered his movements.

It hampered the ants as well, but not nearly so much. One vaulted forward at him out of the raining-pouring sand, its claws hammering at his helmet, its pincers snapping audibly for his middle. Felix threw himself back, threw a boot up. The boot struck at the ant's pelvis joint, snapping it cleanly. But the upper ant grasped him still, raking and reaching. He brought his palms up lightning-quick from his sides and slammed them into the eyes. They exploded. The ant slid off as he turned once more to Kent.

"I'm gonna try it," Kent yelled. "It's better, see?"

Felix looked up. The plassteel hatch was gone. An uneven square of daylight remained. He nodded. "Go!"

Kent went. It was a sloppy, uneven jump. The sand packed about his legs threw him off-balance. But he made it, his arms darting up and grasping the edges of the hole and raising him up.

Another ant slammed into Felix through the sand. He tore its head off in his hands and threw it at the one coming behind. His boot touched something hard. He reached into the soft powdery sand between his boots and pulled out a helmet-sized chunk of plastiform. The second ant, hardly delayed by the skull, died instantly, beheaded, as Felix drove the chunk against and through its thorax.

"Felix! Come on!" Kent shouted.

"Right!" he called back. He stepped under the hole, aimed his leap. Another ant piled into him from the rear. He struck out blindly with his armored elbow, slamming it pistonlike against the great skull repeatedly. He felt the grip of the claws slip once, twice, then fall away. He should have jumped then, right then. But he turned around instead, wary and fearful of more to come.

They were coming. Four abreast staggered-stumbled forward, claws stretched out and working.

He should have jumped then, too. Right then. He should have tried for the only way out. He should have known better. The Engine would have. But the Engine was gone. And Felix, left behind, could think of nothing but running. And he did, away from the ants, away from the hole.

When it was too late, when he was too far away to go back, he stopped and tried. He and the ants hurtled toward each other.

The chamber, by now nothing more than a half-filled cavern, pitched suddenly sideways, throwing him off-balance to one side. He heard a deep tremulous grinding and looked up to see an entire section of the ceiling collapsing upon him. He jerked spastically away, rolling on his side in the cloying sand. The section crashed into the sand less than a hand's width away from his hip.

Get up! Get up! he screamed inwardly. Move!

And he did, rising quickly but unsteadily. Too much! Too much at once and the ants . . . God! I'm so sick of . . .

"Felix! Felix! Where the hell are you!"

"I'm here!"

"I can't see you!"

Nor could he make out the hatch. It was almost completely blocked by the debris. And the ants . . . ? Crushed, he saw a second later. Some of them. How close they had been!

Then he saw the sunlight. The hatch! he thought and lurched forward.

But it wasn't the hatch. It was a thin fissure opened by the shifting cavern. But it was far too small. He could never . . .

He spun about as more ants clambered toward him around the remnants of the ceiling.

"Felix!"

"I can't get there!" he heard himself screech. Damn! "Get me a blazer," he yelled in a more controlled tone. "Or something."

"You can't get back up?" Kent persisted.

"Ants!" he gasped, wanting simply to sink to his knees. The shouting exhausted him. "They're between us."

"Felix, I'm coming to help."

The blatant sham of the tone touched him. He drew himself

up sharply, feeling a hard and bitter grin tighten about his mouth.

No, you're not! But you've got to say it, don't you, Hero?

"Felix?" Kent called, from the sound not one bit closer.

"Yes, Nathan," he hissed.

There was a short pause. Felix used it to throw a chunk of masonry at an oncoming ant. The trouble was, he couldn't see at all. And the sensors were sharply localized by the Siliconite hanging in the air.

"Felix, do you want me to come?"

That too! He must let him off the hook as well! Great . . . Never mind. It's over. Do it.

"No, Nathan. They'd only get you, too. Save yourself."

"Well . . . If you're sure . . .?"

Felix threw his head back, cackling wickedly. Fuck you, Hero, he thought. Then he decided to say it.

"Fu . . ."

And again, the cavern pitched. The entire center support system collapsed during the rocking. A single beam, jutting up at a slant from the floor, was struck just right by a falling block. The beam see-sawed wildly, a fulcrum, vaulting up out of the soft sand. It flattened two ants against the remainder of the ceiling.

Felix shook himself. He realized he'd been just staring. There was something he should be doing instead of just . . .

"You fool!" he groaned disgustedly.

He'd been waiting for Kent to come anyway. "Fool! he said again. "Come on, damn you!"

He was urging no particular direction—he had no plan. He was just . . . calling the Engine. Beckoning. Beseeching.

He moaned as he tripped over something he couldn't see and banged his chin. It didn't hurt, of course. He wasn't hurt. He was just falling apart, cracking like the goddamned bunker.

More ants stumbled toward him. He turned away. Distantly, he heard Kent's faint voice calling. The debris and the Siliconite had finally cut him off completely. He tried once to understand what Kent was saying. But it was too faint. Too faint and too late.

He remembered the fissure. He turned his head. It was there. Small and narrow—too narrow. They'd catch him up there, he knew. Sure as hell, they'd come up and pull him down and. . . .

"Shut up!" he barked loudly. He stomped through the cloying sand to the sharp rays of sunlight. What choice was there? Sit and wait for 'em? Not these bastards, he thought angrily, as though he both knew and disliked them personally. He paused beneath the fissure. The first part looked possible. He leaped and grabbed the edges. He pulled himself up, wedging past the first bottleneck with considerable difficulty. The Siliconite again. It made it hard to shove through. The sand was firmer, less yielding. He looked up. It got narrower. He'd never make it all the way.

What else, then? Pop his suit when they came? Damn.

He planted his boots and wedged himself up past the second bottleneck. He stopped halfway through, caught. He'd hung up on something. He reached back and unclipped the culprit, his last blaze-bomb. He re-attached it on the other side.

Why'd you bother? he asked himself when he'd finished. Planning to end it that way? A blaze-bomb would do breathtaking things in this rathole, sure enough. Entomb him, for one.

"Dammit! Damn you! The goddamn ugly sky is right *there*. Move!"

And he lurched upward. He jammed himself up, kicking and twisting, carving ruts in the sand with the outline of his suit. In seconds he had to stop, exhausted. He looked up. He had come maybe two meters. He still had another seven or ten to go. He looked down. The ants had massed in place. Two were climbing atop others to try to reach him.

Which they would, of course. About sand, ants were practically overqualified.

Come on! Don't just watch them. . . .

He strained and shoved himself up some more, feeling a prolonged shudder of claustrophobic panic when the narrowness stopped him suddenly. He couldn't move. It felt, even through the suit—which was insane—as though the entire weight, the entire crushing mass of Banshee held him. The planet had him, pinned at chest and back, waiting for the mood to strike and the cavern to shift . . . The suit would resist, resist, crumpling more and more before the planet would grow bored and *slam* him flat like two palms. Would he feel it? What would he feel? His organs spewing through his mouth, perhaps?

"Damn you, Felix."

And he flung himself up once more, either to pop loose or to jam irrevocably. One or the other.

He felt something touch his foot. He jerked it up, looking down. An ant was just below. But . . . it seemed to be jammed as well. Experimentally, he lowered his foot again. The ant strained its claws upward and . . . grazed the sole of the boot. Nothing else. It couldn't reach him yet.

Not yet. But it would. It would work its way free. And soon.

He arched, bucked, warping his spine and dragging at the Siliconite sheen. He thought he felt something give. He mustered his energies for one major push.

The land, the cavern, the walls of the fissure—all shuddered with the sudden tremor. The walls closed in on him. Just a bit. They stopped, shaking. Then they closed in a bit more. And then some more. Then it stopped. The last movement, the last shifting. The last hope. If he hadn't been caught before, he was now.

I'm dead, he thought and rested his faceplate against the sand. He closed his eyes. Odd how he could hear nothing, even with the sunlight on him. Siliconite was a great tool, all right. Like those concussion cellars. He sighed. *I'm so tired,* he thought.

And then he thought: *Kent, you worthless, timid, everybody's hero bastard!*

Oh, but why not? Why the hell not? If it had been the other way around, he'd have done the very same thing.

Except, of course, he wouldn't have, he realized with a mournful groan. He would've helped; that's what hurt. For Kent, Fleet's Kent, Forest's Kent, he'd have hopped down that hole swinging. In a scout suit, no less. Never mind the awesome might of Kent's custom-built.

But why? Why? How had this happened? How had he folded so badly and . . . so quickly!

He glanced down. A second ant had joined the first. Not

long now. He glanced at the time, shook his head, looked again. He had been alone almost half an hour! He was sure of it, because he remembered looking before when he had to stop and transfer the . . .

What an insane idea!

Quickly as a striking snake, his hand reached down and snatched the blaze-bomb loose. He held it firmly pressed against his faceplate. Exhilarated, sweat broke out.

No way, of course, he thought, grinning delightedly. Still, it was nice to kill a few.

"Yup," he said to the bomb, "killing them is better than getting peeled. In fact, killing them is better than not killing them. Killing them is fun."

The narrow gap between the two beneath him would require a little delicacy. No good to have it get hung up on them. Plassteel was very nice. But two meters away from a blaze-bomb, it was about as protective as cotton.

"Of course, it *would* unstick me."

Maybe it didn't matter. Thus confined, even from so far away as the cavern floor, the bomb would almost certainly kill him. Either with the blaze or the compression or by shaking loose the pinning walls, driving them suddenly together to squash. . . .

"What the hell," he said, keying and dropping the bomb in a single motion. It fell cleanly between the two monsters. Well, that was something anyway.

The blaze killed the ants instantly. It also boiled their hides, fusing them into a single hurtling mass that rushed like an artillery shell up the fissure. Felix was aware of light, noise, and, finally, movement. Then all was dark.

Was he dead? It sure hurt.

He opened his eyes. The light streaming through from above was a searing on his retinas. His eyelids fluttered. He tried moving, found he could do that. So he looked and moved together and found out where he was—the last part of the fissure just below the surface. He was hanging—sagging—down into the crevice, too wide to slip through and fall. But . . . he had to have come that way.

The ants were everywhere, plastered to the sides of the fissure and, he noticed distastefully, to him. Mostly on his legs, but his back and hands and even his chest had ground ant packed on them. He was surrounded.

He propped a boot against the curve of each wall and raised himself erect. He examined the exit, glaring brightly and painfully. Not too far. He glanced again at that last narrow section between his boots. It wasn't wide enough for his helmet. He shuddered, turned back to the light. Better not to think about it.

It took him several tries to get a grip on the sides of the opening. The pain steadily increased in almost every area. And his muscles had begun almost immediately to tremble and knot.

Hurt bad, he thought dimly. Really, really, bad.

He began pulling himself up and knew at once he wouldn't make it. He was too weak. He was too tired. It hurt too much. He had no idea how much power was left in the suit—he couldn't read the dial. He tried marshaling a final effort. Nope. Falling. Colors flashed dizzily across his eyes, followed by rhythmic waves of feverish heat. Falling. Straight back, his grip going and lost down here . . .

Armored hands on his upper arms lifted him easily, miraculously, into the open air and sunlight. He squinted from side to side, vaguely recognizing the shapes of the warriors beside him. He nodded to them. He straightened up proudly. He crumpled, without warning, onto his heels.

Alive. Even now. Even this. No pity.

"Felix!"

He recognized the voice. Forest? No. Shoen. Canada. Her shadow blotted out the bright light as she leaned over him.

"Felix, you made it! You made it! We thought you were lost! Nathan thought you were lost! Oh, Felix!" And she hugged him, awkwardly. Painfully. He groaned and tried to pull away. But she wouldn't let go. She hugged him again. "Oh, Felix! They should give you a medal, too."

The second shadow before him was Kent. He saw it hanging on the front of the great blue-chest armor. Even though it wasn't there, he saw it. It glinted in the sun.

Perfect.

Now was the time to pop his suit, he thought in a wave of scalding bitterness. And with that thought, the dark and the cold and the strength of both returned at last, slamming in from all sides at once, protecting and separating him once more.

With a vengeance, the Engine had returned.

He slept.

Shaking pain. Shaking and pain. He awoke only because he had to and there was the psychotech, red-faced and shaking his shoulders and screaming.

"I'm so sorry! So *sorry*! Oh, God, I am! I *am*!!"

Two meditechs dragged him away. He struggled with them to get back. "You don't understand!" he shouted at them.

A doctor-type bearing white-haired authority appeared. He tried to soothe him.

"You don't understand," the psychotech pleaded. "It's my fault."

"Nonsense, son," purred the Doctor. "The ants did this to him."

Felix smiled.

"No, no, NO! It was me!"

A third meditech pressed something against his arm. Almost at once, the man began to calm. His shouting fell to unintelligible mutters. Soon he was slumped between the two meditechs. They hoisted him away.

"See to it that he's looked after," the Doctor called to them.

"Yes, Doctor," one of them called back.

Felix realized he was still lying in his open suit. They must've just brought him up. White-gloved hands appeared overhead and fiddled around him. He couldn't see their owners. Maybe there weren't any.

A second doctor-type, older and female, appeared beside the first. The emblem over her left pocket was huge and colorful.

"Sorry, Chief," the doctor told her.

"Don't give it a thought," she replied soothingly. "These things happen in war."

Felix smiled again.

The doctor turned to another woman, hurrying past. "Leclere," he called. "What happened here?"

Leclere was pretty. Not blonde, though.

She shrugged her shoulders. "That psychotech evidently worked with this man. He felt responsible for sending him down again and having this . . ."

Felix regarded the banks of flickering lights all around him. One of the magic gloves reappeared. It placed a clear nozzle into the suit beside his chin. It sucked and gurgled.

Leclere was still talking. ". . . screaming and shouting about how he'd already been through too much . . ."

"The psych?" asked the doctor.

"No," replied Leclere. She pointed a clipboard at Felix. "This guy. The scout. Said he'd already had four major medicals and some ungodly number of . . . Hey, he's awake!"

"*Four* major medicals?" echoed the older woman, the Chief. She looked at the older doctor unhappily. "How's that possible?"

"It's not," the doctor assured her firmly. "It's not." Then he leaned forward over Felix and became fatherly. "Son, have you ever been in Intensive Medical before now? Do you recognize this room?"

Felix couldn't speak. But the Engine could still smile. It did. It seemed to scare them.

Good. He slept.

It was perfect.

He recognized the voices because he had gone to sleep hearing them. He recognized their problem the same way. It seemed a great deal of trouble to open his eyes and since he could already enjoy their uneasiness without it, he didn't.

He was a computer glitch and it wasn't anybody's fault. Still, something had to be done. His group, his A-team, had been reported wiped out so he, Felix, was too. Only he wasn't—his number was still in there somewhere in the other banks and that's why they kept calling him because they called everybody from those outfits that weren't there—why take them out of the computer? But anyway, that's how it happened. It's a tragedy and unfair but what are we gonna do about it when they find out? It'll be our necks either way, you know it will, Chief.

Chief agreed. Something had to be done. But what? the doctor wanted to know. Chief had an idea and the doctor didn't like it but how did he think the Chief felt about it? It's just that their only chance was in the records themselves.

No option.

They decided to leave him with twelve drops instead of twenty. Five majors instead of thirteen. One major medical instead of five.

It was the only way.

Felix heard it all. He pronounced it perfect.

He became aware of days. Different meditechs came at different times and then all again. One day he awoke to a solid ceiling instead of the clear curved dome of Intensive Medical.

A meditech came to give him an explanation of his condition. There was a long list of injuries in it. Felix was enjoying watching the man's lips work—so elastic—when, suddenly, they stopped.

"You're not even listening," accused the irritated man. "Don't you even care?"

"Of course," replied Felix in a clear, strong Engine voice.

There was a commotion in the corridor outside of his room. He heard the name Kent and opened his eyes as the shaft of light crossed toward him. There he was, huge shoulders silhouetted. A meditech stood beside him.

Something odd. They had stopped talking. They were staring at something beside him. The meditech ran off in a hurry. Felix rolled over on his side and saw the crumpled psychotech, blood still pulsing from his wrists.

Felix rolled back onto his back and closed his eyes. He needed all his rest if he wanted to kill ants.

He had to work out in secret because the physitech didn't understand and would make him stop. The physitech had never dropped and he didn't know the shame of a body that just kept failing.

He visited his suit often. It was fine.

In his new squad bay—they were always new—all the kids could talk about was the Masao being aboard. It was supposedly Top Secret. But everyone seemed to have found out about it the instant he had arrived. It was hard to hide an Imperial yacht, of course.

The ones who knew almost nothing about the Masao, either the planet or the man, enjoyed great status while telling about it to those who knew even less. Felix soon learned that this pattern was unavoidable. Everywhere he went, the squad bay, the mess, even the gym, the same thing was going on: wide-eyed kids asking other wide-eyed kids if it was true what they said about the Masao. Did he really *own* the planet? That whole wealthy planet and all fifteen million people? Was it true they practically worshipped him? He could change *any*thing the regular government did just like that? What's a samurai? Was that the same thing as being from Japan and how come everybody on Masao practically was Japanese?

Did everybody have to call him Great One? Even the captain?

When they asked Felix about it, the way they asked him about everything else, he just shrugged. Like always.

The screen at the foot of the bunk finally gave in. It was time.

"Good luck, Felix," said one of the kids.

Felix smiled at him. Then he made himself get up and go over and pat him on his freckled shoulder and thank him for it. Only then would he let himself leave. He did, hurriedly, but feeling good about what he could do through the sheer power of his will.

It was worse than a minor drop. It was a token drop. The Masao, they claimed, wanted to see Banshee for himself.

Felix stood at the end of the line of thirty regulars listening to the briefing while awaiting the imperial presence. The mission was officially a probe placement. Felix had heard all he was told before. He knew the purpose of the probe: to measure the shifting magnetic patterns of Banshee. He knew why it was important: once man could learn how the ants were able to change the patterns artificially, they could program their missiles to adopt to it. He even knew the essential truth about the probes themselves: they didn't work.

The sergeant doing the briefing ended it the same way as always. "Just stay the hell away from the damn things and let the techs do their work. Right? Right."

All heads turned at the appearance of the man at the entrance of the Drop Bay. He was an Imperial Guard and an incredible sight. He wore bright red armor with the Masao's crest emblazoned across the chest in white. He wore a white silk scarf around his helmet where his forehead should be. He wore two swords, one short, one long. He was beautiful.

He spoke in highly dramatic, thickly accented, standard.

"Be all aware: His Royal Highness, Alejandro Jorges Umemoto, Supreme Lord and Great One of . . ."

"Enough, Suki," said a strong and gentle voice. "Just let me in."

Suki sounded upset. He waved a hand abruptly at the entrance. "The Masao," he said shortly.

There were a few giggles in the ranks at Suki's expense. They stopped when he walked in. The Masao was wearing gold armor. Not that it wasn't plassteel, too. Not that it wasn't strong and utilitarian. It was. But it was also gold. The collective sigh was almost unanimous.

Behind the Masao, in two sharply stepping files, entered the remainder of the imperial guard. There were eighteen altogether. All wore the red, the scarves, the swords. One carried an extra two: the Great One's.

The captain in charge of the mission immediately fell all over himself trying to show not only the proper respect, but also that he wasn't really that undone by it all. What he succeeded in displaying was his almost paralyzing sense of intimidation. The Great One rescued him. Charming, and friendly, making a great effort not to appear mighty—while making it clear to all that the effort was a genuine courtesy on his part—he did manage to calm them down a bit. He even insisted the captain merely call him "Sir," a gesture which visibly shook his guards, even through their armor.

Next he started down the line, shaking the hand of each and every warrior. Almost no one present was aware of the true purpose of the guard that accompanied him down the line: to kill anyone insufficiently safe, courteous, or impressed. He wasn't needed. All were awed.

He didn't make it to Felix, at the end of the line. The sudden appearance of the ship's Captain himself stopped the greetings. A brief ceremony followed, with the skipper loudly and dramatically bestowing his prayers, faith etc. on the Great One's journey. The Masao handled it as if he had been accepting even greater honors all his life—which he had.

Then it was time to go. The scouts were called to point. Felix was with them. He stepped out of the ranks and took his place in front. The noncombatants fled the chamber. Felix found that he was trembling. But that ended when the familiar pattern of Transit Lights began. He tensed forward eagerly. He was ready for this. He was ready for nothing else.

Then the lights went to green and he stepped forward. It would be his twenty-first drop.

And his last.

Fleet seemed to be getting the hang of it. They had said no ants and there were none about. Felix approved of the glimmer of profesionalism though personally, of course, he was disappointed.

He scanned the area. No wind now, but evidence of a recent storm was everywhere. There were no mazes. And what few dunes did exist were smooth sloping things rising and falling with gradual grace. The landscape rose gently eastward in broad, widely spaced humpbacks. In all other directions, vision was unobstructed for several kilometers.

It was a good team. The warriors spread out without having to be told, forming the defensive perimeter. The Imperial Guard was even better. Their circle around the Masao was completed many seconds sooner.

Felix found himself in the center of both rings along with the CO, the techs, and the Masao. He couldn't stand it. He offered to scout upslope while the first probe was being planted.

"Of course," replied the CO, as if he'd ordered instead of approved.

He went almost two kilometers. Nothing. No enemy, no ants.

"Shit," he mumbled and trotted back downslope.

He was perhaps half a kilometer away from the rest of the

team—they had just come into view below him—when he stopped short.

He didn't want to go back.

He turned around and looked back up the hill. That was where the ants were. Sooner or later. He looked back downslope. There was . . . what? Probes. A safe route, a quick route, then home. No ants. Just worthless readings and . . . and the Masao.

He didn't want to go back.

And he wasn't. He was actually turning away, toward Banshee and ants and oblivion, when the sudden bright glare off the gold caught his eye. He squinted. Then, seeing it, he gasped. His mouth went dry.

The Masao was coming up the slope.

There was another with him in a red suit. Suki, no doubt. Felix began to shake. The urge to flee was immensely strong. Anything. Anything! But not this. . . .

Yet he stood still where he was. Even when, at fifty meters, Suki stopped to let the Masao approach alone. Even then, knowing what it must mean—even then, he could not move.

The Masao halted a mere two steps away. And during the brief silence before he spoke Felix could feel the Engine shudder. Then: "Hello, Felix."

He sighed. "Hello, Allie."

Allie stepped forward to join in the embrace. Felix stopped him short by thrusting his hand forward. Allie paused, looked at the black armored hand offered him, then slowly took it in his own.

Felix shook briefly, then dropped his hand. He had to moisten his lips before he could speak.

"Didn't waste much time, did you?"

"That's if you don't count the two years it took to find you," Allie replied with a laugh. He gestured about him. "Besides, I don't much like this place."

"Who else knows?"

"About you? No one but me."

"And you won't tell 'em," Felix sniffed sarcastically.

Allie's reply was soft with gentle hurt. "I wouldn't do that Felix. You should know that."

"All right. What are you doing here?"

"I came to get you."

"And take me back to . . . to . . ."

"To Golden?"

"Yes. Golden."

There was a pause. Felix stared at the sand.

"Felix, what are you *doing* in this place?"

"Killing ants."

"I see," Allie replied slowly. He took a frustrated step to one side, then back. "Yes, I had heard that. You're good at it?"

"I am."

Allie strode forward and peered at him. "So tell me, old friend. Does it help?"

"Don't, Allie," Felix warned and took a step back.

"I don't think it does."

"Allie . . ."

"You couldn't even *say* Golden just now. . . ."

"Stop it."

"So I don't believe you dare *think* of the rest of it . . ."

"Stop!"

". . . or of her . . ."

And Felix hit him. It was not a deadly blow. It was not even hard—this was Allie, after all.

But Suki came running anyway, drawing his long sword. The blade glowed with the rich dullness of plassteel. Felix shoved Allie back and eagerly faced the charging guard.

"Who's the clown?" he called as belligerently as he could.

Allie threw up a golden arm. "Suki! Hold!"

The guard skidded to a halt. "But my Lord!"

"I am unhurt," assured his master calmly. "Leave us."

"You tell 'im, Allie," snarled Felix, spoiling.

Suki whirled to face him again. "You dare to speak that way?"

Felix pointed a blunt black finger. "You won't believe how quickly I'll kill you," he said flatly.

Suki raised the sword.

"Hold, Suki!" commanded Allie. "Put that away."

Suki stared helplessly at him. He obeyed reluctantly. "Lord, how can you let him behave so?"

Allie patted his armored shoulder. "Suki, a Guardian Archon behaves as he will."

"Don't call me that!" Felix snapped angrily.

"It is what you are," replied Allie firmly.

Suki had dropped to his knees before Felix. "My Lord Archon, please forgive me. I didn't know!"

Felix stared at him. "Aw, shit! Just . . . just go away!" Suki did not move. "I said 'Go!' "

"You know he can't do that now, Felix."

Felix groaned. Allie was right. He did know that. "You can do it, though. You tell him, Allie."

"And shame him further?"

"Damn you, Allie!" he snapped. He hesitated, then stood over the kneeling samurai. He looked at Allie. "I don't remember what to say."

"Oh, come now, Felix" Allie snorted disgustedly.

"I don't," insisted Felix.

Allie peered at him. "Truly?"

Felix shook his head. "I don't remember."

" 'Rise, loyal one, forgiven,' " Allie intoned.

Felix repeated it. Suki stood, bowed, and backed away without a sound. Felix watched him go. He turned back to his friend.

"Allie, you set that up. You set me up."

"Yes. I needed to know."

"Well, you found out."

"Yes. You buried it deep."

"Let it stay there, Allie."

"No."

The ominous tone touched Felix. He felt something tearing far inside. The Engine warped violently in and out of the shadows.

"Allie, please. . . ."

"Look at you! Look at what you've become. Wrapped up in that . . . that *husk* of yours. You look like a weapon."

"That's what I am, Allie!"

"Yes. But whose?"

"My own."

"That's not the way it works, Felix!" He raised his gold-covered hands and clenched them into fists before Felix's faceplate. "Goddamn you, Felix!" he roared. "You are *not* dead! Stop acting like it!"

Felix lurched back as if struck. He knew it was coming. He saw it in his friend's angry eyes. And he knew there was no way to stop it. There was no protection, no armor—not for this.

"Angel is dead," said the Masao.

Felix sank to his knees like a rag doll. "No, Allie . . ."

"She's dead. Angel died."

"No, please . . ." He was gasping, his arms folded tightly across his stomach. He couldn't breathe.

"She's dead. Your wife is dead. She died in a freighter accident . . ."

He vomited, tried to crawl away.

The Masao followed. "It was a freak accident. It shouldn't have happened but it did."

"Please, no . . ." Felix gasped.

"Yes! *Yes!* You know it. You found the freighter your-self . . ."

"Allie . . ."

"NO! You found the ship and you found her body! Or what was left of it after zero pressure had blown . . ."

"Noooooooo!" He rose back to his knees. His arms shot out from his sides, begging, beseeching. "Nooo-Noooo! Angel! Annngellllll . . .!"

And he screamed the scream again, that same scream from that same horrible ice-bloody sight. He screamed with his mind and he screamed with his soul and he could not stop, not to breathe, not to forget, not to live.

He fainted, the only way.

When he awoke, he was lost. He tried to rise but something held him fast. Something strong and gold—Allie! And it all rushed back in waves of pulsing agony and he wept as only once before he had. The golden arms curled around him, holding him, as his body jerked and heaved with each racking sob. He clung to Allie, trying to make it. And it helped. Even through the armor, it helped.

But he couldn't do it. He reached for the forearm panel to pop the suits. Allie's powerful arms, possessing all the leverage, clamped his arms too tightly. He struggled, but could not get them free.

"Oh, Allie, I want to die!"

"Is that all?" asked his friend gently. "Just die?"

"That's all."

"And so you came here?"

"I . . . guess so."

"But you forgot you can't 'just die.' "

"Why can't I?"

Allie held him tighter, cradling. "Because, despite it all, you are Felix and must be killed."

Again, he slept.

When next he awoke the sobs were much less devastating. His body could no longer support them perhaps. Soon they stopped. He lifted his helmet from Allie's golden lap and sat up. Several meters away, the warriors and guard were gathered into small groups, sitting and talking. And, obviously, waiting.

"I'm sorry," said Felix. "How long was I out?"

"Don't worry about it," Allie said gently. "You feel better?"

"Yes. I can't believe I could sleep. I just got up." He indicated the others. "Haven't they said anything?"

"Forget them."

"But the drop . . .?"

"Forget that, too."

"But. . . ." He stopped, seeing it. He faced his friend. "It was all a fake. The drop . . . all for me."

Allie nodded slowly. "Mostly," he admitted. "This is Banshee, however. And we are carrying probes. Of course they don't work."

"They never have."

"So I understand. Lovely war, this."

"How'd you do it? You said no one else knew."

"And they don't. No one here, except Suki, knows."

"Then how, Allie?"

Allie shrugged. "The master of the *Terra* was most cooperative. He gave me a drop of my own."

"He went along, without even knowing why?"

"I *am* the Masao."

Felix smiled. For some reason, he had always found his friend's astonishing arrogance endearing. He gestured toward the others. "And the CO?"

"Oh, much easier. Command Voice and all that."

Felix winced. "He's not a pet, Allie."

"Oh really? Then what's he doing *here*?"

He laughed, started to say something else. But it came again, without warning, doubling him over, grinding up and out. He wept and wept.

He had been sitting and staring at nothing, thinking of nothing. He was numb, exhausted, wrenched flat. And, he realized with amazement, relieved. He didn't know exactly what it meant. He didn't want to know. Or at least he didn't feel like examining it. Beside him, sitting patiently and waiting, with his back to all, sat the Masao. Felix smiled—he had his legs g-crossed Bhudda-fashion.

All his life he had known this man. He was closer to him than any other human. Despite the fact that they were from two different planets and two different cultures, they had managed to stay in touch since infancy. Most of the major events in their lives had been joint ventures. Allie had been Best Man.

But what really, he thought, did they have in common? Only that their recent ancestors had been rich enough and tough enough *and* egocentric enough to establish favorite monarchies on the two richest planets in known space. Even in that respect the two were different. Felix had been but one of twelve candidates for Guardian. The Masao had been the Masao from conception. He had always known it and always loved it that way. Whereas, Felix. . . .

Still, he loved him. In his short life, there had been only the two who had touched him. Now one.

He glanced at the time. Damn! Two hours here!

"Allie, we've got to get out of here. Call the ship."

"Suddenly you're in a hurry."

"I'm not. The ants are. They must've sensed us by now. They'll be coming."

"Fleet reports say no ants here. It's why I picked it."

Felix stared at him. "Fleet reports? I thought you'd been keeping track of this war."

"Hmm. I see what you mean. Fleet isn't here."

Felix laid a glove on his shoulder. "Let me tell you something, old friend. Fleet is never here. Call the ship."

"I can't. Well, I could, of course. But we need to go somewhere else to get picked up."

"Why is that?"

"Dammit, Felix. This is supposedly a probe placement. They pick us up at the end of the line when we've finished planting them."

"Where?"

"About ten kilometers, I believe."

"When?"

The Masao eyed him with distaste. "I think I liked you better in my lap."

"When, Allie?"

"About five hours. Plenty of time."

Felix stood up. "Let's get started."

"You trying to scare the Masao?"

"Allie, don't you understand? This is Banshee!"

"Oh! You mean *this* is Banshee. . . ."

Felix tried to get angry. He failed. "Come on," he urged.

"Relax, my friend. We'll have you in the Hall of Gold in less than. . . ."

"No."

Allie paused. He stood up. "You mean you won't go back?"

"Let's talk about it later. We've got to get these people moving."

"Very well," Allie agreed reluctantly. "For now. Suki!"

They were up and moving in seconds, a steady procession of two concentric circles. A good team. Felix only had one suggestion. He thought the probes ought to be left behind now that their purpose had been served. The CO treated the advise like an order. "Yessir," he replied respectfully and ordered the probes abandoned on the spot.

Felix stared at him. Now that he noticed it, all the others were treating him with equal deference. He caught them glancing his way occasionally, always taking care not to get caught gawking.

He accused the Masao.

Allie laughed. "I swear to you. I told no one. And Suki wouldn't dare."

"Well, I guess seeing that we knew each other . . ."

Allie laughed again. "Could be that. Could be your Command Voice."

"Buzz off, Allie."

"You can't still blame them," Allie insisted. "Besides, it wasn't their fault the freighter buckled."

Felix sighed. "It was their fault she was on the freighter in the first place."

They had been walking for over an hour. Allie had been on him the whole way. He turned his gaze to the others, marching steadily around them. No one had approached, no one had spoken. Their privacy was respected. Pure Masao, he thought wryly.

He realized Allie had been talking. "What?" he asked.

His friend sounded exasperated. "I said you can't go on blaming a whole people for a mistake made by a few."

"Allie, those few didn't just err, they defaulted. You know how long it took me to run away? Three months. I planned for three months and my bodyguards *still* almost caught up with me. Angel lost hers, without planning, in three minutes. That's a breakdown in commitment. The guards simply didn't care enough about her to do their duty."

"All right," Allie conceded. "Perhaps you're right. . . ."

"No 'perhaps' about it."

"Okay, okay. You made your point. But you're still blaming the planet for it?"

"Allie, the guards were just indicative. They never accepted Angel—no one ever did. They never gave her a chance."

Allie shrugged. "She was an Earthwoman. Your people resented it."

"Goddammit! My mother was from Earth! So was yours. They never had any trouble."

"That was a long time ago, Partner. They were there from the start. They were very old and revered. Mine still is."

He grinned, looked sideways at his friend. "Still beautiful, too?"

Allie laughed. "By Imperial decree."

"I always loved your mother."

"She loved you. She's missed you."

"Yes."

They were quiet for several steps. "Angel left me a note before she left. Did I tell you that?"

"Yes."

"She said she was afraid she was holding me back."

"Yes."

"She didn't know. Even then, she still didn't know how much I . . . I" His voice cracked. He fought the churning.

"Do you want to stop?" Allie asked him.

"No."

"We can. We've got plenty of time."

"No," he said firmly. "I'll be all right." He looked at Allie through his tears.

Maybe I will, he thought.

An hour later they had covered over half the distance. The landscape had gradually changed. They were on a long broken plain apparently unaffected by the storm. Crusted dunes were everywhere around them. In the distance, foot-hill-size drifts could be made out.

Allie tried patriotism.

"The people need you," he said.

Felix sighed. "They have a Guardian now. They have Tasp."

"You know about that? Well, you have bothered to keep up then."

"No. But who else could it have been?"

"You."

"Well, it wasn't."

"You would be better."

"What's wrong with Tasp? Don't the people like him?"

"Of course they do. He's a good Guardian."

"Well, then."

"But he isn't you." Allie stopped suddenly, looked at him carefully. "They wanted *you*."

Felix matched his gaze. "I wanted Angel."

*   *   *

Another hour. The team sat or lay sprawled around them in the sand. They were making very good time. Allie voiced concern about arriving early.

"If we have to wait two hours there, won't it be just as bad?"

"Aha," laughed Felix. "I *have* scared the Masao."

"Don't be impertinent."

Felix laughed again. "Yes, Great One." And he went on to explain that it was location, not timing, that counted. He was explaining about the three-hour safety margin surrounding Retrieval when it hit him. He stopped and stared at his friend, seeing him, really seeing him for the first time. And, more importantly, really believing he was here.

He sat forward and threw his arms around his chest and held him close. They were silent for several seconds. Then they broke away. Allie peered closely into his faceplate.

"You're back," he said.

Felix smiled. "Yes."

"This is really you again."

Felix laughed. "It always was."

"Some of you," Allie corrected.

He nodded. " 'Some of me' still, Allie. It's been . . . very bad."

"Whatever. I think it's incredible. In four hours—after two years of being . . . whoever it was you were."

Felix shrugged. "I was already on my way. He was dying."

"He?"

"The Engine."

"And that is . . . what?"

"Exactly. A what. As opposed to a who."

Allie shook his head. "I don't get it."

"Good. It's just something that . . . well, it kept me alive."

"If that's what you call living. The life you had is . . ."

"Allie, once and for all—I'm not going back. Never."

The Masao sighed loudly. He lay back in the sand. "All right." He tapped the toe of a boot against Felix's armor. "I hope your next suit is more fun."

Felix shook his head violently. "No. No more armor for me. I don't . . ." He stared at something in the distance, not seeing it, and wondered how he had possibly done it at all. He shook the thoughts away. "I don't know what I'd do if I had to fight again. No more armor for me."

Allie shrugged. "I wasn't talking about fighting especially. But it's still armor, whether you admit it or not. It's still something you hide in." He sat up. "Felix, you came here to hide in there. But everything you were hiding from was in there with you. That's the trouble with armor. It won't protect you from what you are."

"And what is that?"

"What you'll do."

"When?"

"When it counts."

Suki approached and bowed.

"Speak," said the Masao, standing up.

"Lord, the officer in charge reports the scout . . ." He looked at Felix, embarrassed. "That is, one of the warriors. He was sent ahead, over the next hill. He reported Retrieval Proximity."

"Hot damn!" said Allie happily, slapping his golden palms. "We're there."

"Damn near," Felix agreed.

"Lord? Then I can tell them we can begin at once?"

"Oh, yes. Yes, Suki, by all means. At once. Let's get the hell out of here."

"Yes, Lord!" Suki agreed happily, bowing and backing away.

Felix stood up too. Soon the procession was again on the move. They marched in silence over the hill. Soon each had the Retrieval Beacon flickering below his holos. Only a few hundred yards to go.

Allie matched steps with him, throwing an arm over his shoulders. "So tell me: what *are* you gonna do? How are you going to live?"

Felix grinned. "The Masao will be pleased to provide the necessary luxuries."

Allie's arm jerked away as if stung. "And what if he does not?" he demanded in mock outrage.

Felix's grin broadened. "Then I'll break his legs."

"Hmph," sniffed the Masao. "Said Felix the Scout."

Felix laughed. "Of course, there is always blackmail."

"Blackmail? You dare to suggest the record of the Great One is impure?"

"Personally, I would not," replied Felix humbly. "But Labella might."

"Labella!"

"Now there's someone your mother would *really* love."

"How could you do this to your oldest and dearest friend? You bastard! I was only sixteen."

"That's the best part. Seeing as how she was sixty-something."

"She was not. She was . . . thirty-ish."

Felix threw back his head and cackled. "Are you kidding? Her wrinkles had wrinkles. You could draw a line between her nipples and get her navel."

"That's unfair."

"Unlikely, is what it was."

"You're very cruel. Labella loved me."

Felix shrugged. "You were a big tipper."

"Now that *is* unfair."

"I always thought so. Considering the quality of her act."

"Felix, don't you start on her dancing again. You just never understood. She was a very artistic . . ."

"Grandmother?"

Allie started to speak, but the laughter burst through at last. They howled awhile. Then Allie became quiet.

"You know, I think about Labella now and again."

"I should think so. You were going to give up your title for her."

Allie sighed elaborately. "I did love her. I had such passion for her eyes."

"That's horniness. For her thi . . ."

"You have no romance in you, you know that?"

Felix laughed. "My karma."

"Your karma's jammed," said Allie sourly.

Felix laughed again. "Now, to the money?"

"Oh, very well. Even though it's against my principles. But only in installments. I don't want you running off on me again."

Felix touched an armored hand gently to the other's arm. "I won't. Never again."

Allie looked at him. His eyes shone. "I know," he said shortly. Then: "I brought you a ship. It's small, but . . ."

"You knew?" cried Felix, amazed. And delighted.

The Masao nodded. "Let's say I feared."

Felix stopped, put an arm out to stop Allie. Then he placed his faceplate against his. "Thank you, Allie. For . . ." The tears ran warmly down his smile. "For coming to get me."

Allie blinked, embarrassed. He shrugged elaborately. "I had some free time . . ."

Felix laughed . . .

And it began. So quickly, it began.

The wind first. It swept over them without warning, pounding against them with rhythmic, pulsing, gusts. The sand sizzled against their armor . . .

The Transit Cone symbol appeared on his, and everyone else's, holos . . .

The CO's voice barked on Command Frequency: "Everyone in from the perimeter! Prepare for Retrieval . . ."

The Imperial Guard materialized out of a gust, collapsing around their master . . .

"Damn this wind," shouted Allie. "Come on!" he shouted and started to run. Felix and the Guard followed . . .

The CO again. "Transit Cone sighted. Everyone in on me. On the double . . ."

Felix and Allie arrived at the back of a pack of warriors. Seeing them, the warriors parted to let them by. The Transit Cone, ten meters away, shimmered clearly before them . . .

The CO again, in front of them as a gust receded: "Sir? If you'd care to go first?"

"I would indeed," replied Allie, stepping forward and motioning Felix to do the same.

"What's that?" asked a voice. Felix was not paying attention.

"Looks like a mountain," said another voice. Felix was just following Allie.

"Where?" asked a third voice. Felix automatically looked around.

"There!" said the first voice. And Felix looked where the man was pointing and froze . . .

The warrior was pointing to a hive.

It was the biggest Felix had ever seen. Kilometers away, it must have been thousands of meters high. But he did not think of that then.

He thought of Hive! Knuckle! Transit Beam! The Hammer! The Hammer!

"Alllieee!"

The first blast was awesome. It threw him off his feet. He crashed into the sand on his side. He could see nothing for the sand. Screams piercing, whimpering, unbelieving, filled his ears. He couldn't find Allie and he yelled for him but there were too many people yelling already and too many forms on his holos. He stood up and rushed forward and the second Hammer struck, flattening him face-down into the sand. And there were more screams and with them horrible sounds coming from all over of wrenching plassteel and bone and pressure escaping. "ALLLIIEE!" he screamed but he could hardly hear his own voice, much less any reply.

Another blast erupted. And another and another. All around him. Homing in, he knew. Homing in on the Transit Beacon and the people and Allie and . . . More screams and something flew past him, crumpling as it went and he knew what it must be but he didn't care—he didn't!—it wasn't gold.

And there he was, suddenly, on the ground before him, the Cone flickering dully off the gold. He rushed forward and grabbed and tried to lift as another blast struck and more screams. . . .

"No!" Allie was screaming. "Let go!"

And he saw it then, saw the hole, saw the sand being blown out from between Allie's golden clenched fingers as they tried to hold it shut.

Seconds—only seconds—left!

"Allie! I'll carry you! Don't worry!" He reached down and tried to get a hold to lift the huge suit but it was an awkward position and he was so afraid of dislodging Allie's grip on the hole! The hole! My God, a hole!

Seconds! *Seconds!*

"I've got you," he said and the next blast struck—damned

close—and in that instant before he careened away he saw—
through the glare of the blast, through the blinding sand,
through the reflection of it all on Allie's faceplate—the fear.
Allie was afraid.

And then he was crashing and tumbling through the air and
the sand and bodies jounced obscenely past him and against
him and the world was filled with the sounds of their terrors
and their deaths.

Seconds—seconds—seconds. . . .

Somehow he was back and leaning over him again. There
was nothing else, nothing but this to do and this one to live,
to make it. To live! Allie!

But the glove on the rip was weakened and opening, the
head lolling inside the helmet.

"No!" he screamed! "NO!"

And he reached down and clamped his glove over his
friend's and gripped with all his might. With his other hand he
reached around and down and lifted him, weightless, up
against him as a mother does her child, pressed against her
chest and protecting. Allie's faceplate full on his own, Allie's
eyes darted slowly and rested on his and he opened his mouth
and ice formed immediately on his gums but he still managed
to say "Felix . . ." before he died.

Three steps into the Cone. Unhurt by the carnage. Untouched by it.

Transit. The patterned lights. The Drop Bay and people
everywhere rushing with waving arms and strident voices.
Someone tried to take the golden suit from his arms and for a
moment the urge to kill was strong and clear and pure.

But no. He relented, slid the shining gold to the floor and
walked away. It may as well have been an empty suit. Allie
was gone.

People pushed against him, shoving him back from the
growing center of alarm and accusations. He moved when
they pushed, stood still where they left him. He seemed to be
there a long time, facing without seeing the cascade of movement and emotion. Then someone took him by the arm and
led him firmly away. Someone big. In big blue armor.

Fine. He could walk. He could do that.

Through the corridors they went. They passed the door to

the armor locker. They took a lift. They transferred to another. They began to walk faster, urged by the big blue glove on his arm. They were in a part of the ship he had never seen. He recognized it from the briefings and the rest but he couldn't seem to place it exactly.

And he was tired of walking, tired of the suit, tired of the urgency he could not match in their strides.

They stopped. The blue arm let go. He stood in semi-darkness watching as a black and white jumpsuit, Security, rushed forward yelling about unauthorized and wearing armor where they should not and the blue arm whipped out tendon-taut and the black and white was on the floor.

What the hell?

He blinked and looked and . . . and Kent? Kent?

Kent was coming toward him again, the determined iron look on his face. He had seen that look before, once before and . . . "No!" he blurted and tried to push out to protect himself.

But then the great blue fist rocketed up at his eyes, *slamming* against the faceplate and as he fell, he relaxed and let go.

At last, at least, it was over.

PART FIVE

ARMOR

I

There was nothing more on the coil.

Holly kept checking, running it through as Lya and I sat there on our couches, stunned and staring. But it was no good. It was over and nothing could change it. Nothing could change the fact of it or the aura of obscenity it created.

Kent had killed Felix. Kent!

After all he had been through and all he had had to become and become again, after all the bravery and . . . talent . . . and . . . After being the toughest man alive . . .

Kent, everybody's hero, had killed him.

Holly gave up after a while and sat back down. The medicos came in and fussed with us. We took it without speaking, without thinking. They pronounced us emotionally and physically exhausted. They said we must get to bed at once.

And we did. Still without speaking, without saying goodbye or good night, we went. Lya, I remember, was weeping softly, almost silently. I could not. It wasn't sadness, I felt. Not exactly. Not remorse. It was disgust.

I stumbled back to my room, still dazed. Fucking Kent!

That one fact managed to say more about the whole filthy mess, the whole filthy war, than anything else. To me, it *was* the war.

I found my suite empty. I slid out of my clothes and stood there, wondering what to do. Then I saw the bed and remembered. I sat down on it. The mirror was across from me and I stared at myself without recognition or purpose.

Fucking Kent . . .

I slept.

And then I was waking, badly and slowly and still dulled. I looked up to find Cortez shaking me awake.

"Leave me the hell alone," I growled and turned over.

He shook me again. I spun around, lashed upward and snatched him by the collar of his Crew jumpsuit and gripped hard. His eyes bugged.

"It's Wice," he hissed. "Wice sent me."

I stared. "You? You're in on this, too?"

He nodded quickly. Like a squirrel. I sighed and dropped my hand. "Tell him later," I said tiredly. Then I noticed the clock. It didn't seem right. "What time is it?"

"Almost morning," said the squirrel. "And . . ."

"And what!"

"And the City is burning."

II

Project Security was on full alert. No one was allowed to leave or enter. All this from the squirrel.

"What're you gonna do?" he asked as we strode down a corridor.

I stopped, eyed him with disgust. "Go away."

He went. I made sure he wasn't following, though I couldn't imagine him having the nerve to try. Then I made for my exit. I went through the place, down more corridors, down a lift, and into the lab area without seeing a soul. I found the hatch next to the circuits I had rigged earlier. I could betray Holly twice from the same spot.

Though I wasn't thinking of it as that. I wasn't thinking of it at all, or of anything else, as I popped the hatch and slid out into the darkness. Just get across the river without being blazed in the back. I keyed the hatch to re-open.

The bridges were out, of course. The Security there was deep and alert. But they didn't see me slip around the corner of the dome and into the river. And if they heard my splashing, they weren't certain enough of its meaning to fire. I crossed without trouble; the water was warm.

The City was *not* burning. Too much plassteel and hull for a conventional fire. But the dark shadow of looming smoke meant that everything else was probably gone. I couldn't see much else. The approach I was forced to take led me through undergrowth and tall trees that blocked the outline of the Maze. It also blocked my view of the stars, any sort of trail, and tiny little bushes about ankle high that repeatedly jammed their nettles into my boots. I found a clearing by tripping and falling forward into it. God, but I hated the outdoors.

I was just rising to my knees when he appeared. He was tall as me, heavily armed, and wearing full open-air battle armor. A commando.

"Cale?" he whispered in my direction, then reached for his pistol before I could mumble the lie.

I kicked him in the face twice, in the forehead and right cheek. He dropped like a rock. I stood over him, gasping and waiting unnecessarily for his response. If I hadn't seen that armor. . . .

I knelt beside him and looted. He had all the goodies. Grenades, a comvid, blaze charges. It was Fleet stuff. It was Borglyn's stuff.

Today was the day, it seemed.

I took the pistol and a single charge. I clipped the comvid to the loop at my waist. On impulse, I reached over and drained the power from the armor. Then I threw the rest of the extra charges into the trees. It was as good as tying him up—that stuff was heavy.

I never considered wearing it myself. Never.

No one else popped up in the long half-hour it took me to make my way to the edge of the city. And after awhile I had managed a fairly decent rate of progress. More importantly, I felt sure I could retrace my steps.

The main square was apparently deserted. I hated the idea of strolling across so open an area but the Maze was made of less forgiving terrain than the woods and I knew only the one way to get to Wice. I took a deep breath rich with smoke and trotted across to the other side. Nothing happened.

Minutes later I had climbed the passage and the building at the end. The guard that loomed at me from the shadows acted like he was expecting me. He led me through the lair without speaking until we stood before Wice's broad door. He knocked in an obvious pattern and waited. The door opened.

"Crow," he said shortly.

The stooge at the door peered at me, nodded me through, closed the door behind me.

There were five of them in Wice's office. Or six, counting the poor fool lying moaning and bleeding on the floor. All but the fool turned toward me as I entered.

Wice nodded. " 'Bout time," he growled. "Again," he said to one of the others standing over the fool.

The man, huge and heavily muscled, was taking off a shirt soaked with sweat. "Okay," he said resignedly, dropping the shirt on the back of a chair. Then he leaned over and slammed his fist into the fool's kidneys. The fool warped like a beached fish and screamed.

"What the hell are you doing?" I demanded, striding forward.

The man without the shirt stood up quickly, warily on guard. I ignored him for Wice.

"If you ever showed up when you're goddamned supposed to, you'd know!" Wice snapped back angrily. "Borglyn's gonna. . . ."

"Wice!" I interrupted impatiently.

He stopped, looking at me, really looking at me for the first time. He sighed. "Where've you *been*, Jack?" he asked with evident hurt in his voice.

Incredible. Between us lay a man waiting to be tortured some more. But all Wice could do was pout. I remembered what he'd told me about being at my piracy trial, the pride he felt at being there. He gaped like a disillusioned child.

"Later," I said shortly with a brusque wave. I sank into the easy chair. "Tell me."

"Well, for one thing, today is the day we. . . ."

"I figured that. What's this?" I pointed to the man on the floor.

Wice shrugged. "Some pilgrim came in a coupla weeks back with a whole carton of rifles. The locals got 'em."

"How?"

He looked at the floor. "He gave 'em the rifles."

"To stop you?"

"Yeah."

"These people don't like you, Wice," I said on impulse.

It struck home. "I don't give a shit," he snarled unconvincingly.

I stared. A child. He *was* a child. He motioned the puncher forward. "Again, Lopes."

"Wait a second," I said to Lopes, then turning to Wice before he could protest, "Who is this guy anyway? The one with the guns?"

Wice shook his head. "No. But he knows where they are. He knows all of it, where the leaders are and everything. And he's gonna tell it all."

I stood up, forcing my muscles to laxness. "Wice," I began calmly, "this is only going to make it worse. They'll never accept you after. . . ."

"They'll accept Borglyn."

"But Borglyn . . ." I began and stopped, suddenly, seeing it all at last. "Borglyn was never just coming for fuel. He's coming to stay, isn't he? He's coming to take over."

Wice's mouth was open. "You didn't know? You really didn't know?"

I didn't answer. I was too busy wondering if I had known all along. It wasn't a Fleet planet, after all. It was Lewis's planet. Borglyn needn't fear the might of avenging starships. He could roll over the drunk—in his sleep—and he would own it all. Maybe he wouldn't even bother with Lewis. Or maybe Lewis wouldn't care. Maybe both.

It was the tension in the room that brought me back to them. They were all standing very, very still and watching me. I think they knew before I did.

Certainly Wice did. "Jack?" he said quietly. His voice was almost pleading.

I met his gaze, still not decided. Hell—still not truly conscious of the decision before me. I never was. But I reached for the blazer just the same.

I lived because I was fast and because Wice maybe hesitated an instant and because two of them didn't really believe I would do it until I had and because the two who did reach and fire were the kind of men who enjoyed watching torture and had waited to be fodder all their lives. I lived because they died, because I killed each and every one.

The fool on the floor had a name—Northrup. He knew a lot about the place. When he was able to move, he showed me Wice's secret exit onto the rooftops. He was very agile, darting from one oddly leveled crag to the next. He was also very happy. And talkative.

Just wait 'til he got me back to the others, was the gist of it. And how delighted they would all be when they found out I was on their side. Just knowing they'd be fighting alongside the great Jack Crow would be a big help.

I was silent, letting him think what he wanted. As far as I was concerned, I had done too much fighting already. Too damn much. The idea of switching sides, of *taking* sides as if there was doubt . . . No. It was over. I could give them some help though and I intended to. With a little advice: Run.

Run away, far away, and hide. Run now, right now. Don't think about it or consider or ponder or make any more speeches—move! Run!

Because Borglyn could not lose.

III

Eyes was beautiful in the starlight. It emphasized the richness of her hair, the soft delicacy of her skin, the Eyes, themselves.

She seemed determined to have all that and all else she possessed carved up.

"We have guns," she insisted for the thousandth time.

I sighed, dropped my cigarette and stepped on it. I glanced at the open hatch behind her, filled with dim light and the energetic sounds of the others arguing over whether or not I should be trusted at this late date. There was repeated mention of The Plan uttered with tones of faith better suited to a suicide pact. Which was what it would be. I wondered what they would think if they knew I couldn't care less.

I glanced back at Eyes. I did care about her, maybe. But dumb is dumb.

"You have guns," I conceded at last. "But they have blazers. Also concussion grenades and mortars and open-air armor. Have you ever *seen* what can be done with that? They can peel this building apart."

"Buildings don't shoot back."

I blinked. From one bizarre to the next. From one child to another. Madness!

"Neither do dead people!" I barked angrily.

She stared, looked away. Her foot tapped impatiently. This was all decided for her long ago.

"Look. You gather up all your little guns and put them in a pile. Then you all line up behind them out of reach and wait for Borglyn to come. Then you smile at him. Then you give him the keys to the City."

"Then what?" she asked sarcastically.

"Then he won't kill you."

She opened her mouth to speak but was interrupted by a particularly loud burst of arguing. She gestured toward the noise with a toss of her head.

"They don't trust you," she said.

"Fine."

She frowned. "I know what you're trying to do."

"I beg your pardon?"

"Oh, come on, Jack," she said with a conspiratorial smile. She squatted down in front of me. She put a feathery hand on my knee. "I know you're not as cold and hard as you make yourself out to be."

I stared at her. This was *not* happening.

"You haven't fooled me with this bit of yours—you never have."

"I haven't . . ." I echoed dully.

"Not a bit. I know you, Jack. I know that you care."

"Of course I do. That's why I'm trying to get you to. . . ."

"No, no. You *care*, Jack. You care about justice and you care about right and wrong and you care about this thing turning out the way you *know* it should."

She really believed it. I could see that. I thought I saw something else, too. She believed they would win, of course. Because they were in the Right, by God! But she believed in more than that. She believed we would all live to see it. Casualties, of course. Strangers, mostly. Or the enemy. But, basically, all—and I meant all—would be well.

She believed it would be easy.

She was dead.

I took her hand from my knee and kissed it softly. "Good-bye," I said, with as little emphasis as I could manage. Then I stood up and headed back the way I had come across the rooftops.

She raised up slowly, watching me go. I could feel it building behind my back.

"Damn you," she blurted it out at last. "You're going to be that way to the very end, aren't you?"

I nodded. "I've seen 'very ends' before."

The explosion of gunfire seemed to come from everywhere at once—the street below, the inside of the building, the surrounding rooftops. The answering blazers were silent but just as obvious in the eerie blue glows their arcing beams made on the plassteel walls across the way.

I had dropped to the deck with the first sound. So, thank God, had Eyes. The blaze aimed at her cut a neat hole in the top of the doorway instead of her nose. Two beams arced at me a second later, passing far too close overhead. I crawled over to a space underneath the protection of the meter-higher roof adjoining. More beams struck, from new and different angles, pressing my nose into the damp rooftop. Damn! They seemed to be everywhere.

The gunfire had cut the argument short inside. I heard boots stomping and the clicking of rifle business. I turned to the open doorway.

"Stay in!" I yelled to them.

No such luck. The idiots weren't convinced until their first three crusaders had been sliced apart. Eyes screamed as a headless torso plopped to the roof beside her. I thought she was a little late. Somebody offed the interior light, also a little late.

But still a good idea. I crawled rapidly through the darkness toward the entrance and cover. I found the way blocked. It was inconceivable, but the crusaders were using the cover of darkness to get out and fight.

I couldn't believe it. "You fools! You *wanna* die? We're pinned!"

They didn't even bother to acknowledge me. They simply crawled past, took up the first hint of cover in their way, and opened fire in every direction. Worse still was their reaction to the murderous crossfire that responded.

"There they are!" shouted a half dozen voices at the appearance of the various beams. Then half a dozen or more rose to charge each position, firing from the hip. Some of them actually yelled battle cries as they charged.

Some of them actually lived, too. But not many. It didn't matter. The doorway was positively choked with more storming out to take their places. Not once did they consider retreating. Not when twenty or more had died, not when the number of beams suddenly, inexplicably, doubled, not when the counter-charge was launched from all sides but one.

That one safe direction was for me. The building was at the very edge of the Maze proper. There was nothing between it and the woods but a handful of one- and two-story shacks. I figured the fall was worth it. The trouble was that I wouldn't actually be able to see where I would be landing. I could possibly fall the entire three stories.

No choice. I edged out onto the overhanging lip and paused for one last glimpse back.

It was horrible. The beams were coming from two dozen different directions at once. The crossfire was a solid mesh of maiming burning slicing . . .

Damn them! I thought. "Damn you!" I shouted.

Then I rolled over and dropped. I bounced on something three or four meters below but it was slanted and I fell some more, bouncing some more, badly and out of control and then I hit something very hard, hard enough to go out before the pain had a chance.

IV

I had many dreams, none remembered except the last, the nightmare. Borglyn was the source of it. His deep powerful voice was the instrument of his fear. I dreamed he was using it to describe in detail what would happen when the blazer he held to my temple was keyed. His voice rang with implacable superiority and with reasoned understanding of my fear and helplessness. He was almost sorry, he seemed to be implying, that he was going to kill me anyway.

It was horrible.

Then the pain woke me up and I found out most of it was true.

It was still dark, though without stars. Perhaps two hours had passed. No more. I was lying—I was crumpled, against a rusted sheet metal smokestack at the bottom of an even more rusted slanted rooftop. Almost everything hurt, but my head was throbbing with a ferocity all its own. I groaned and felt around to my crown for the lump I knew must be there, found it, groaned again. I tried pulling myself to my knees.

Borglyn spoke again, from millimeters away.

I started, thrusting blindly away from the sound and trying

388

to turn and face it at the same time. I fell again, hard. My chin snapped against the sheet metal with a rumbling thud, I groaned once more, wincing with the pain. I opened my eyes reluctantly, more to stabilize a wave of dizziness than to see.

But I saw. Borglyn was there, on the vidcom screen. I blinked, blinked again. It was the smallest I had ever seen him. It didn't help. Another voice emitted from the grille. Staring at Borglyn, and still groggy, I paid no attention to what it was saying. Then I recognized the voice as Holly's.

I sat up painfully and grabbed the unit soaking up every word. I didn't understand all the references. Much had apparently occurred in the time I was out, however. That was clear enough. For one thing, Borglyn's force was already on the planet, camped across the river from the Dome. For another, they were unopposed.

I glanced behind me at the kaleidoscopic jury-rigging of the walls of the Maze rising above my perch. There was no sign of movement anywhere along their length. No gunfire sounded. Either they had finally taken my advice and run away, or Borglyn had already gotten them.

Borglyn began to speak again. All the reasonableness from the dream was there. His tone was respectful, unhurried, and, still, implacably superior.

"I won't argue with you, Dr. Ware," he said with a patient and patronizing smile. "You and I both know your defense screens are gone. I suspect you even know how."

"I've a pretty good idea," from off screen, his voice a subtle mixture of bitterness and sorrow.

I felt like he had punched me in the stomach. I grabbed up the unit and fiddled with the dials. It was suddenly very important that I see his face.

"Yes," agreed Borglyn with a neutral nod of his huge head. "At any rate, you're helpless. And, as far as I can tell, alone."

I gave up the fiddling. Alone? No wonder he sent no image.

"But in a fort," Holly was pointing out.

Borglyn sighed. "True, Dr. Ware. Project Domes are forts. But without screens, medieval ones. You have no chance."

"We'll see," said Holly.

Borglyn sighed again. So did I. What the hell was going on? What could Holly be thinking of?

"Very well, Dr.," said Borglyn with a trace of impatience. "We will see. Or you will. Observe."

The image on the screen shifted. We were looking down over Borglyn's shoulder. Before him were arranged the numerous keys and screens of the Coyote's command console. Borglyn was still inside his ship, still in orbit overhead.

He turned toward the monitor and smiled a cold smile. "I trust you can pick up my screens on your own," he said, sweeping a hand along the console. "Let me identify them." He tapped a screen on the top row. "That is the planet, Sanction. This next one is the Dome from one thousand kilometers overhead." He dropped down a row. "The monitors relaying these images are at my commandos' camp—less than half a kilometer from where you are now." He worked a key. A screen showed a pan of the camp itself, an area newly blasted free of vegetation stretching at least one hundred meters from treeline to riverbank.

Every step had firepower.

"Those are the two hundred commandos that will come from you," Borglyn continued, pointing from screen to screen. "They are as well-armed as Fleet can manage. Those on the right are wearing open-air battle armor. There are thirty of them—each and every one an expert."

I doubted that, but was damned if I knew what difference it made.

"Those large instruments in the rear, Doctor, are medium-range mortars. They are out of line-of-sight of your tactical blazer cannon and will, in fact, obliterate them when I give the order. You already know something of the one on the left." He leaned forward and worked a key. The screen above it swelled as the monitor zoomed forward. "That is the hole it has already blown in your . . . your fort."

I was squinting at a tiny screen showing an even tinier image and still the hole was clear. It was that big.

God, Holly, get *out* of there!

The tour ended with Borglyn's terrifyingly off-handed inventory of his other miscellaneous killing tools. He listed the concussion grenades and the fully charged blaze rifles. But more than what he said, was the way he said it, as if they were just insignificant toys when he knew damn well they were a hell of a lot more.

And he knew Holly knew.

It was chilling.

"Still with me, Dr. Ware?" inquired Borglyn pleasantly.

"Yes," Holly replied shortly. Was that fear? Certainly respect.

But it sounded too much to me like fatalism.

Borglyn's smile dropped instantly. His manner became threatening. "And have you indeed *seen*?" he demanded, biting out each word.

Holly was too smart to answer that one. Or too scared.

Borglyn went on. "Well, I hope you do." He shrugged slightly; he appeared to be making an effort at maintaining his reasoned calm. But as he began to speak once more, it gradually slipped away to something ominous. Something ugly.

"I have been frank with you. Let me be more so. I want that Cangren Cell—you know that. I want it intact and working—you know that, too. But consider this: We are desperate people, Doctor. We have no fuel left for faster-than-light. Your refusal to cooperate means we must stay and fight you for whatever is left. And we will. One way or another, Sir, I *will* have you out of that Dome. Even if I have to land this ship myself and blast the can, the dome, the hillside behind it, and you, Doctor, to *glass*!"

Borglyn paused once more. He was breathing heavily with barely contained fury. His deep blue eyes, always incongruously troubling, shone with a depth of damn near tangible menace.

And one more time it reminded me of something I always seemed to forget when he wasn't around: he scared me. Not panic. Not quaking. But fear, yes. I genuinely feared the man, more than any other I had known.

I thought of Holly, in there alone and seeing it.

Or maybe he didn't see it. Maybe he didn't know enough to realize how utterly lethal Borglyn was. Holly was still in there, after all.

Borglyn was calm again when next he spoke. "You have

half an hour, Dr. Ware. Use it to . . ." His lips curled a cold smile. ". . . to assess. Then the real world will hit."

"I'll watch for it," blurted Holly suddenly. But it wasn't even faintly convincing. I felt that pain in my stomach once more.

Borglyn's voice went dead hard. "Then watch me kill you!" he roared and leaned up to key off the monitor. He stopped his hand. The cold smile returned. "No. You like to *see*, don't you?" he snarled. Then he keyed the sound off with a click and spun angrily away.

Damn.

V

I had to get him out.

And I had to go in there with him to do it. Holly knew what I had done. I doubted he would talk to me at all if he had any choice. I had decided not to give him one.

I stood up, ignoring my wobbly gait, and fell-jumped off the roof onto the soft ground below. I picked myself up about halfway, then had to sit down again. Vertigo. I had to blink my eyes several times before they would focus right. Damn! I didn't have time for a concussion.

I stood up slowly the second time and stayed up. I scanned the dark outlines of the trees before me. I could almost feel the commandos wandering through them. Too much weaponry and not enough targets. It would have to be the bridge route. Borglyn was sure to have them guarded, but anything was better than crowded woods.

I started off at an easy trot down along the outer perimeter of the Maze toward the river. The jumbled stacks of hovels looming over me were still silent and still. The City looked empty. Or beaten. Or both. Eerie. Where were the crusaders?

I had to slow down to a walk for a while to give my head a fighting chance. Fat lot of good to Holly if I conked again.

Damn Holly, I thought suddenly. What the hell was he doing?

He had a plan, of course. A Plan. There had to be one. Something suitable for a spindly over-romantic would-be hero to pull out at the last second, no doubt. Something the Evil villain would never suspect.

Or probably, in the case of Borglyn, notice. I had to get in there.

I tried trotting again. It worked after a fashion. Faster, anyway.

So. I had to get in there and make Holly see me, make him tell me the grand scheme, make him see it wouldn't work, plus make him leave with me—all in half an hour.

I tripped on something and slid down on my butt. It hurt like hell. I reached back around and pulled out the culprit. I had landed on the comvid.

I was rearing back to throw it against the side of a shack when it spoke to me in Lya's voice.

". . . oh please, Darling," she was saying, "it can't do anybody any good if you get killed."

She sounded awful. Her voice was hoarse, barely above a whisper. Despair and worry and fear, and exhaustion from them all, trembled within it. Then the screen flickered to life with her face and I saw it was even worse than it sounded.

I hit a key. "Lya? This is Jack."

She perked up. "Jack? Jack, where are you?"

"Outside the City."

Her eyes got wide. "The City? But . . . Oh, Jack. You've got to help Holly. He's in the Dome all alone and he won't come out and they're going to blow it up in just a few minutes. And he won't answer me."

"I'm going there now. Is he really in there alone?"

"Yes," she sobbed. "He's locked himself in and, Jack, the defense screens are down. He'll be killed."

I waited for her sobs to pass. "What happened? How did all this happen?"

She gathered herself together with effort, brushing back the tears and her hair and sitting up straight. Then she told me.

Most of it I knew, who Borglyn was and the like. And what he wanted. Other parts I had assumed. The ultimatum, the landing of the troops, the guarantees of safety for cooperative types. No one had believed Borglyn when he had first claimed to have "arranged" to sabotage the screens. The boards showed green.

Then had come the blast to match the hole Borglyn had already shown me. Shortly afterward, Holly had ordered everyone out. It wasn't until all were gathered in the valley at the Crew Quarters, that Lya had noticed he was missing.

"I called him at the Dome. And he said he wasn't coming and that he wouldn't let anyone else in and . . . and he hasn't spoken to me since. Jack, you've got to do something."

"I will. But why, Lya? Why did he stay? Did he tell you?"

She frowned and shook her head. "Just that he couldn't give in to that man, to Borglyn. Not after what happened to the Cityfolk."

I sighed. "What happened?"

"Oh, I didn't tell you that. I was so worried about . . . Well, they had guns, Jack! I don't know where they got them. And they attacked Borglyn's people."

"And got killed?"

"No! Well, yes, some of them. I guess a lot of them. God, Jack, those monsters have everything!"

"I know. What about the City?"

"Oh, well they all ran back there to hide. But Borglyn called them and told them to bring him all their guns."

"Did they?"

"Some did, I think. But most of them didn't. Then Borglyn said he was going to teach them a lesson and he started bombing them or . . . whatever he did to us."

"Mortars."

"Yes, mortars, He shot them all over the City. Said he was teaching them a lesson."

I frowned, looked up at the looming slums. Still ugly, but standing.

"Anyway," she went on. "Then they all came out with the guns and they took them, Borglyn's people did. But when they got back to the City, he started the mortars again."

"After they'd given in?"

She nodded. "He said the lesson wasn't over."

I looked again at the stacks. It didn't make sense. Then I reached the end of the perimeter and made the turn inward toward the main square."

"Goddamn!"

"What, Jack?"

I explained to her that I had just found the lesson.

There *was* no main square. The land was there. Even some of the puddle. But what made it a square, the buildings which surrounded and enclosed it, were gone. Gone. So was most of the far side of the Maze. A square kilometer at least. The only section still intact was the perimeter I had been following. And nothing, nothing at all, was moving. No one.

"Did he kill everybody?" I muttered.

"Jack?" called Lya.

I ignored her, still staring. Then I laughed.

"Jack?" she called again. "Are you laughing?"

"No," I lied, though I soon stopped. It wasn't funny, but . . . I had slept through it. It was too terrifying to be anything but funny. Damn, I thought next, I must have been in a coma. I felt the back of my head again. The lump felt bigger to my trembling fingers.

"Of course!" I cried, seeing what must have happened. "Holly decided to defend the Dome after this."

She nodded glumly. "That's right. Jack, can you . . . is there anything you can do?"

"I have a way to get in," I assured her. If Holly hadn't closed it, I amended to myself.

I started my trotting again. The small bridge across the creek-sewer was just ahead and intact.

"You've got to get in and stop him. You've got to make him listen."

"I'll try," I puffed, tromping loudly across the small span and on to the river.

"You've got to. He won't listen to me or anyone else from the Project. Lewis was the only one he talked to, and that was hours ago."

I snorted. "Lewis! Great!"

"Oh, no. Lewis is very concerned."

I had to stop. I leaned over and braced my hands on my legs. "I'm sure," I managed to reply.

"He is, Jack. You don't know. He's very worried. He said he'd rather give the planet away then have Holly killed."

"Then why doesn't he?"

"He tried. Borglyn wants the Dome. But Lewis did say he could have it—he didn't care."

I smiled. Now that I could buy.

I looked at the sky. Dawn was coming fast. How many minutes left? I forced myself to stumble ahead, clutching my stomach tightly with a forearm to keep it where it should be. I stopped when I heard the river. I lifted the Comvid and whispered into it. "I'm turning you off, Lya."

"What's the matter?" she all but shrieked.

I slammed the volume control. "I'm at the river. Guards will hear you. I'll talk to you again when I get across."

She probably said okay. I keyed off and dropped the unit to the ground. Then I crept slowly forward until I could just make out the outlines of the bridge. I didn't bother to locate the guards I knew must be there. Instead I cut off at a diagonal to the riverbank. The water was still warm. It seemed to clear my head.

Less than a minute later, I was sliding the hatch open.

It was very dark inside, much darker than the false dawn outside. I felt my way along slowly, my arms stretched out in front like a sleepwalker, until I found a wall to follow. I had gone maybe ten meters when lights, blaring and blinding, flashed into life overhead. I groaned, covered my eyes with my hands.

"What do you want?" said a stern voice from close by, Holly's.

I moved my hands and squinted enough to see the blazer pointing my way.

"Holly," I said as calmly as I could.

"What do you *want*, Jack?" he repeated.

"I want to know what you're doing in here."

"Why?"

"Why not?"

He stared awhile, determined to be firm and hard and angry. But he hated it and had to fight himself to do it.

He took a deep breath. "Get out," he said harshly, waving the barrel back toward the hatch.

"No."

His eyes widened. "I'll shoot you."

"Okay."

A beat. Another. The gun slumped with his arms. Tears pooled in his eyes.

"Jack, how could you?"

My own eyes began to sting. "I don't know," I said at last. And I didn't.

He looked at the floor. His chest shook. I thought I would die.

Something. Not "sorry." Not enough. Something. . . .

"Holly, one thing." He looked up at me as though he expected more bad news. I swallowed. "Holly, it was before. I couldn't have afterwards."

He understood at once. "Before?" he echoed uncertainly.

I nodded. He made a half smile. He waved me down the corridor. I followed behind him, wondering if from now on the rest of our lives would be divided the same way—before and after Felix.

VI

Holly had no plan. He did have an arrangement of sorts. He started my tour with the Master Ground Control room, the safest room in the Dome, located in its exact center. Holly had managed to get some of each essential packed into this tiny chamber surrounded by consoles and screens.

He had blazer rifles, of course. Two new cases were stacked in one corner between equally new cases of blaze-bombs on the left and concussion grenades on the right. Against one wall he had a long hospital table and lamp, complete with all the medikits and medipacks on a shelf above. Cases of food were littered everywhere, enough for a couple of months at least.

I found his confidence alarming.

Other nooks had other things, books, changes of clothing, every coil from both his and Lya's files.

"You've got everything in here but the suit," I commented.

He blushed. "The wheelchair wouldn't fit through the doorway."

I grinned. "You mean you actually tried it?"

"Sort of. Caught myself trying to jam it through without

remembering going to get it. Unconscious, I guess. Or driven mad from the pressure.''

I laughed. "I don't know. I wouldn't want it lost either."

Holly smiled his gratitude. "Where is it?"

He led us out of the control room into a large rectangular room easily as big as my suite. It had an extremely high ceiling with beams running out of the wall behind us, down the length of the ceiling, and into the next wall. There were more supplies stacked about. More weapons, more food, more medical things. Against one corner was a desk, Holly's desk. In the far corner, sitting in the powered wheelchair, was the suit. It looked like an alert pupil, head up, back straight, arms folded in its lap.

I shuddered. "Every time I see it again. . . ."

Holly smiled. "Yeah. Not like before though, you know?"

I nodded. I knew. We had always thought of the suit as Felix's killer.

"It wasn't a murderer after all," I mused.

Holly became thoughtful. "Wasn't it, though? I mean, what if Felix were still alive? Knowing what we do, knowing what it would do to him to wear it again, wouldn't we think of it as a murderer once more?"

I saw what he meant. "It is a murderer. Even Felix's murderer, given another shot. But it didn't do it!"

"You know, it *feels* benevolent. But only because it's powerless and we don't fear it. A killer with only one victim."

"And he got away," I finished.

"I don't know why *we* ever feared it so?"

I smiled sadly. "Probably the same reason he did. It worked too godamn well."

Holly looked at me. "Or he worked it too well."

"Yeah. That, too." I pointed at the ceiling. "Where are we, exactly? I don't think I've ever been in here."

"This is the Complex central core. It bisects the width of the rectangle."

"Okay," I said uncertainly.

He laughed. "This structure is a rectangle. Those eaves that jut out at the four corners are attachments."

"Those big curved wings are just plugged on?"

"Yes. And they're very unstable. Which is good for me."

"Why is it good to be in an unstable building?"

"I'm not. I'm set up here in the core. It's entirely separate from the rest of the surrounding rooms. It's built that way for . . . well, for situations like this one. Or in case of earthquakes. The core shields the Cangren Cell."

"All right, but why is it good to have everything else shaky?"

"Because they can't attack me from the long ends without creating a barrier of rubble six stories heavy. They have to come right down this line." He pointed along the overhead beams. "And they have to come from only one direction, the riverfront."

"Because of the hillside in back?"

"Right. And when they try to come through here, they'll find three walls in their way. Come on."

We went into the next room, even larger than the last. At the far end, it grew alcoves from each side, making a "T." Along the wall of the "T" were several consoles.

"That's the outer wall," explained Holly. "Those are stations for the blazer cannon. Now, back the other way."

We retreated into the second room. Holly closed and sealed the door behind us and pointed to a small console on the wall.

"If they should manage to penetrate the outer wall into the room we just left. . . ."

"Which they damn sure will," I pointed out.

"Well . . . if they do, I can come in here and hit these keys and seal off so thoroughly that that other room's ceiling could collapse and I wouldn't feel it."

"And then they'd have to start all over again?"

"Right."

"Minus the cannon."

"True. But their field of attack would be severely limited. They would be crowding into my killing area."

"You planning to open the door and shoot?"

He blushed. "There are other things. That room, both of these rooms and the control room alcove, are mined like crazy."

"They're in big trouble, all right."

He frowned. "I know they'll probably get through anyway. . . ."

"Surely get through anyway," I corrected.

He frowned again. "What else can I do?"

"Are you kidding? Almost anything. Run away, for a start."

"I can't do that," he replied miserably.

I examined his face. "Holly, you're not scared enough."

"Ha!" he cried, a wry sad smile curling on his lips. He leaned against a wall and slid down it to the floor. "I've never been so scared in my life. I didn't know you could get this scared!"

"All right! Let's get moving."

"I can't!"

"Why the hell not?"

"Because this is the only chance of stopping him."

I blinked, stared, sat down abruptly in front of him. "Is *that* why you're here?"

"Why else?"

I shrugged. "I dunno. Principle of some sort. Desire for hero role. Or martyr's."

"No. This is just the best way."

"This is no way."

Holly leaned his head back and stared into space. "He must have killed a thousand people in the City this morning."

"They're dead. Gone."

"But others live here. And more are coming."

"And?"

"He'll have to be brutal, won't he? After what he did?"

"After the mortars, yes. He'll have to maintain. Fear over the hate."

"So it will get worse and worse and on and on. I've got to stop him."

"Holly, do you really think you can?"

"If I can't stop him, at least I can drain his arsenal. I can make him use up irreplaceable munitions. There will be a chance that someone will be able to overthrow him." He brought his head back to level and met my gaze. "You know, Jack? You're the only one who came."

"You locked everybody out, didn't you?"

"I had to be secure. I asked for volunteers first."

"I hadn't heard that part."

He blinked. "You mean that's not why you're here?"

"Not at all. Borglyn's won. I came to get you."

"Oh. Well, I won't go."

"You can't, I know."

"But there just isn't anyone else!" He stared at the floor between his boots. "I wish there was. Anything, just . . ." Three tears plopped loudly onto the polished floor. He sniffed, wiped his nose with the back of his hand. "I'm sorry. I'm just so scared."

"Me, too."

He looked at me with such innocence and said. "Well, Jack, you ought to get started. It's going to start any minute."

I lit a cigarette instead of answering. I puffed and thought. Now what? He had a damn good point about the time. And he had a damn good point about what Borglyn would become. Dammit! I hadn't expected this. He didn't *want* to be a martyr. He had no interest in being a hero. He would have given up his role in a second, if . . . If there had been anyone else. But there wasn't. Only him. He was the only one who could make a difference. Not that he would. He wouldn't. He would die. But he was the only one who *could*, who *might*. He had to.

"I guess I'll stay," I said without thinking.

He looked surprised. I bet I did, too. "Why?"

I shrugged. "I won't leave without you."

"I could use your help."

"You sure could. You wouldn't have a chance alone."

"And with you?" he asked, smiling.

I shook my head. "Dead as dirt."

An overhead thunderclap, the first mortar, signaled the beginning. Holly leaped to his feet and ran to the door and unsealed it. "You know how to work a blazer cannon?"

"More or less," I answered without conviction.

There were six along the wall running across the top of the "T." Holly grabbed the third from the left. I took the fourth. I peered suspiciously at the console. A monitor, on the barrel most likely. I keyed the screen. It glowed brightly, receded, then coalesced on the river below. I grabbed the triggers and fired a burst at the water. It worked.

It worked on water. It worked on trees and on sky. But not

on mortars. Borglyn had told the truth. There wasn't a target in sight. Damn!

Meanwhile, mortar shells were ripping the hell out of everything. Great holes appeared out of the smoke along the riverbank. The holes began working their way up the slope to us. Closer and closer, seemingly more and more powerful. Distant concussions echoed from direct hits on the Complex.

Then they hit our wall, about five meters to Holly's right. The floor warped violently with the shock wave, tossing Holly up and back into the center of the floor. He bounced like a dead man. I rushed to him to see if he was as bad as he should be. He just rubbed his head and smiled. He was getting up to reman his cannon station when it just blew off the wall, console and all. We ducked no more than half a second after it had hurtled high over our heads.

It got worse. Four blasts slammed against the outer wall within three seconds. The warping floor bounced us like babies about the room. Chunks of masonry crashed to the floor from high above. The sound of it was . . . Godlike.

It stopped suddenly, all at once. We got to our feet. Holly rushed to a panel on the wall and read some dials.

"Uh-oh," he said quietly. And was silent.

"Don't *do* that!"

"Huh? Oh, I think we have a lacing split here."

"That's bad?"

"The lacing is behind two half-meter layers of reinforced plastiform."

"What's behind the lacing?"

He made a face. "Mostly paint."

"Holy shit!" I cried, grabbing him and dragging him back from the front.

"It won't collapse, Jack."

"It will when the grenades hit it."

"What grenades?"

"They stopped the mortar barrage for something!"

"Shouldn't we be shooting 'em as they run up to throw?"

"To do that, we would have to approach the guns. The guns are on the. . . ."

Wham! Two, three, four-five-six. Pause. Three more almost at once.

On the floor from the first one. Holding my ears. Opening my eyes reluctantly, sure of seeing blood.

Smoke and dust were filling the room—thick and black and brown and gray, but I saw through it for just an instant, just long enough to recognize the river through a two-meter-high, meter-wide, gash.

They had pierced the first wall.

On impulse, I grabbed a concussion grenade from one of the scattered cases. I threw it, without looking, out through the smoke. Screams followed its detonation. I grabbed up three more and threw them, too.

Now was the time to go to the cannon. "Wait here," I said to Holly who lay sprawled and choking dust.

"No. No, I'm fine," he lied and thumped awkwardly head-first into a cannon station.

My cannon had been where the gash was. I stepped one over and keyed it up. I had a target for maybe a second and a half. Once he may have been where my beam struck.

"Dammit! barked Holly. He took his eyes off of his screen and frowned in my direction. "You know, I'd like to shoot back at least once. But unless it's a tree, there's never any damn target."

Bingo! "Shoot 'em."

"Huh?"

"The trees?"

"Why?"

"They burn?"

'So?''

"They burn down."

We made a forest fire. It was quite an impressive blaze in no time at all. The far side of the river disappeared behind the wall of smoke. I decided to take a small chance. I stepped through the gash and looked around.

Chunks of plastiform were scattered all over the slope to the water. Much of it was from our wall, but the vast majority of the debris had been blasted from the walls on either side of the core. But no breaches, as Holly had promised. Instead of standing still for the punctures, and making an entrance, the other walls simply collapsed atop one another. One spot, repeatedly targeted, had a massive cone of masonry that seemed to have been torn through a good five meters. But the pile was right where the wall had been and just as obstructive.

I took another quick chance. I trotted around to the ground underneath an eave. Bootprints covered the entire area. This is where they stood when they threw the grenades and made the gash. I stood in one of the spots and pressed myself against the wall. Out of range.

After forty-five minutes of waiting for something to scare us, we decided to get a bite to eat. I was starving. I hadn't eaten since . . . I wasn't sure. Not today or yesterday or. . . .

Damn. Felix had been just yesterday. Damn.

Borglyn's programming was fun for a while. Mutineers and deserters weren't much at fire-fighting. They were damn good at trenches, though. They had two of them dug deep enough for the mortars long before the fire went out.

"Pretty far back, though," observed Holly.

He was right. Too far back to melt the barrels, anyway. Cannon are not made for distance. Then I saw what Holly meant. I didn't know much about artillery, but Borglyn had called them medium-range mortars. They were a kilometer away.

The question was answered as we watched. The crews began firing at us. We rushed to the outer room, ready to seal it off if need be. It wasn't necessary. It wasn't even dangerous. I sat in the gash, enjoying fresh air and a smoke and admired the splashes for half an hour. Not that they didn't have the range. They did. At least two shells whistled *over* the Dome. But no accuracy.

When the shakes came, an hour into the respite, I went to the head and sat them out. When I returned, I pretended not to see Holly having an even worse time. I could do that, had been doing it for him since it had begun. It was really getting to him. Too smart not to appreciate what could happen, he was also too sensitive to ignore it. A nice man.

An hour later, the fire was finally going out. I figured we had another hour yet to come. It was an exhausted, ragtag crowd across the river.

"You think it will matter to them?" wondered Holly aloud.

He was leaning against the wall as before, his head back and staring.

"Who?"

"The people who are left after."

"Under Borglyn?"

"Uh-huh."

"Depends on how well we do. On how much we make them work for it. There're only two of us, after all. Far as they might know, only you. If we make them treat us like an army, it'll be remembered."

"Do you think we can?"

"No."

"Why not? We've done pretty well."

"But we're out of trees."

He laughed shortly. "I would like this to count," he said wistfully.

"Well," I said encouragingly, "it would help if we could make them flatten the hillside. Or better still, land the Coyote."

"Should that be our goal?"

"Hell, no. We're either doing this to win, with the idea of trying to win, or it's masturbation."

"I'd still like to see the Coyote. You think we will?"

I had been pondering that. "We might," I said carefully. "But I don't think it will attack us. Nothing eats fuel like a Nova-blaze."

He nodded. We sat there, watching the smoke rise into the sunshine.

"Hey!" I blurted suddenly. "It's daytime."

Holly smiled. "Has been since it started."

I relaxed. "I suppose so," I mumbled.

What was I doing? Why was I here? I knew how it was going to end. I *knew*. But still I went along, on and on as if not really examining the madness would make it safer.

Holly. Sweet Holly. I knew why he was here. He felt he had to be. He felt he was the last hope and therefore responsible to try. I understood that. I understood those reasons. For him.

I did *not* understand those reasons for me. Yet here I was. Idiot.

There were a lot of things I didn't understand lately. Like that morning when I had. . . .

"What?" he asked.

"I guess I was mumbling."

"Tell me," he said excitedly, sitting up and leaning forward.

I smiled. "It's not as much fun as that."

"Is it bad?"

"Mostly."

"About what you did?"

"No. About something else I did. This morning."

"What?"

"I killed five people in the City."

He blinked. "Why?"

"I'm not sure."

"Why don't you just tell me what happened."

So I did. About Wice and about Northrup, the tortured fool. And about Lopes. About the other three.

"The thing of it was, I *knew* I was going to do it before I *felt* like doing it. Well, I didn't want to do it. I had no passion for that fight. But I knew I was going to do it because. . . ."

"Because it was the right thing?"

"Oh, shit. I hope not."

"Afraid of becoming noble?" he asked, his eyes twinkling.

"That, too. But basically, that's the worst reason I can think of for killing. That it's the right thing to do. You kill out of outrage or fury or to keep from dying or something like it, that's fine. Hell, kill them rather than bother with them—or be bothered by them. But if you're killing them because it's the 'right thing to do,' it's only because you've done so many wrong things up until then to make that spot. It's not the right thing to do. It's the best of the last of your choices."

"That's the longest I've ever heard you talk at one time."

"That's because you never ask me about my hair."

Later, I asked Holly about the eaves. He said fine. We set the last of the charges as the first bunch appeared from the right. I leaned out the hatch and shot one of them. The others flattened against the wall, out of range. Holly was all for blowing it right then. But I wanted to wait for the left-handers to show up, too.

When the first blaze-bomb rattled at us from the right, I acceded. Holly keyed the charge from the control room so we could see it better. It got everyone of them. But it kept falling and rolling, great chunks cascading over and over. When it had finished, we had a ridge of debris from the Dome to the river. It was five meters high at it's highest point.

"We've cut them off!" announced Holly with a cheer.

"No. They'll blow it open. But it got their attention."

We blew the second on the grounds that no one could be that stupid. It made another ridge. All the way to the river. Hot damn.

So ended the second attack.

Things started happening pretty fast after that.

The trouble was, the whole thing had been damn near a blur all along. From the beginning when the squirrel woke me up to Wice to . . . no more Wice and then no more Crusaders and then no me for a couple of hours. To crazy Borglyn to crazy Holly.

Now crazy me.

They came in the third wave moments later. They came to the ridges we had made by blowing the eaves down the hill. They didn't blast them, though. They just stood behind them, out of sight and out of range, and threw things at us. They didn't bother with catapults or launchers. They hauled out the people wearing that open-air armor. Their artificial muscles were plenty. They threw concussion grenades and blaze-bombs, which I had expected. And smoke, which I had not. Idiot.

They had us anyway. We had no place to go. Only one place from which to fight back. The smoke wouldn't hide us from them. But they could use it. And they did.

"Get ready to blow this first one!" I yelled to Holly as the first half-dozen blasts rocketed masonry along the front wall.

"Can't we wait?" Holly yelled back gamely, running to another cannon console.

"No!" I screamed back. "No! We can't stay in this forward room! We've gotta go back to . . ."

"Look! They're coming up at us!" he said, ignoring my cussing and firing away with the cannon.

But the smoke bombs hit then, cutting off most of our

effectiveness. And then the first of the grenades hit, rocking us back and rocking the wall itself. Through the dust and smoke coming in I saw it waffling back and forth on either side of the gash. It was crumbling and warping and shaking. . . .

And then coming at us as something hit it just right and a five-meter-wide section just folded back, just lifted up and folded back from the gash toward us. We were already down, blasted down and bouncing, me screaming for Holly to get back, goddammit, before . . .

Too late. That section of wall, folding and crumpling and collapsing, disintegrated from the force of another blast and then those pieces blew apart from the force of another and then one of those smaller pieces—a tiny one no larger than me—shot forward across the floor and over him.

"Holly!!"

And I leaped forward to help him, to get him back and get him away from the commandos I knew damn well would be coming up the hill from those ridges through the smoke. More grenades and blaze-bombs and then blazers and then hand-to-hand with that . . . Damn! With the ones wearing armor!

"Holly!" I screamed again and tried to get through the smoke and the blasts that wouldn't stop coming, wouldn't stop shaking me and throwing me about. The chunks of wall were rolling through now, from the gash and the inside of the wall and from the ceiling, falling and smacking horribly close by.

"Holly!" Then there he was beside me, the blood streaming and he lifted his head and gave me sort of a half-smile that he was all right but he damn well wasn't and I cussed at him or maybe at me and then they hit us face-to-face.

I shot one. Two-four-five. The cases of grenades were there and I grabbed and threw with such urgency and terror that I didn't bother to key them to blast, just threw them and heard them scream and saw them drop back out of sight. Then I had a second and I used it to key the next batch of three or four. I tossed the rifle to the side and grabbed for Holly. He moaned as I lifted him off the floor but there wasn't anything I could do about that right then. The people outside hadn't thought we were still in there that close and they were sure to drop back and throw much, much more.

And then the blasts were there, *right* there, at the area almost directly in front of the gash. Soon they would be coming all the way through. I tightened my grip on Holly's shoulder, ignoring his cries, and hauled him back, stumbling, toward the next inner door. We were almost there, almost through it all the way, when two or three or a thousand seemed to hit all at once and the blast threw us forward, punching us limply through the air and the doorway. I heard Holly scream again, knew what must be happening to him, felt the hurtling chunks rake across my back and shoulders. A small something tore across the back of my neck as I lifted up to key the door shut and sealed and safe. The blood, the screams and the pain, the pains. . . .

The door slammed shut, locked, and sealed itself automatically. For the moment, it was over.

Holly screamed as I dragged him the length of the second room to the Control room. The screams were strident and searing and they echoed off the floors and the ceiling and those beams. I ignored them and got him into the Control room and up onto the hospital table and slapped a medigrip on the worst of the spots, his broken-shattered leg where the bone was white and stark. Then I did something to put him out. He went. Then I collapsed.

VII

I was thinking of the funeral.

The funeral. The one with presidents and ministers and secretaries of this or that, representing these or those, all decked out and solemn in black and respect. It was the biggest funeral ever, somebody had said. Everyone who was anyone, everywhere that was anywhere, had somebody, a Somebody, in attendance. Nobody wanted to miss *the* funeral.

It was Kent's funeral.

Like most people I had watched it. It had been carried on the Fleet beam, no less, and perhaps had the largest audience for any event in history. Such a man! Such a hero! Everybody's Hero! I had felt pretty much the same way. I hadn't known any better.

What a man. . . .

Funny the things you think about when you're tired and scared and only have a second or two to rest.

Which was all I had. Half stimules and half painers, I had managed to get Holly and me pretty much fixed up. Medigrips and medipacks everywhere over the cuts and contusions and abrasions. There was a disquieting, and possibly crucial, amount of blood over us. But I figured we would live until they killed us.

Lya called. I was too numb to think not to answer.

She hated me, of course. And she blamed me. For Holly still being there, to begin with. Maybe for him ever being there. And I was a liar too, for not calling her back like I had said I would. True, true, all of it true. All of it and more. I smoked and listened in silence, staring not at her but at the view of Borglyn's console which he had so generously and sadistically continued to provide.

We were really screwed. They had the whole riverfront laid out, staked out. They were ready for us. They were waiting for us. They had us.

Shit.

Something in Lya's tone had changed, I realized distantly. I looked up to see the same tears and the same aching pain. But something else had been added. Resignation. Acceptance. Whatever we wanted to do. . . .

Huh?

". . . should have realized you would never give into them. And Holly . . . I guess I knew all along, from that first moment when we got here to the valley and he wasn't with us. He's just too good a man." She paused, whimpered, pulled herself together. She smiled weakly at me. "And you, too, Jack. You're both too good."

I stared. Then I mumbled something back about, well, t'weren't nuthin'. But I was thinking what I had thought long ago—how long ago? A month?—when she had first accepted me along with all the rest of the Jack Crow smoke.

You're a fool, Lya. Still a fool to trust me.

It made no difference that now, when it wasn't going to help, when it was far too late for that, that she could trust me. It made no difference that I would never leave him now. It made no difference that I was about to die with him and for him.

She was still a fool. So were we all.

I was about to key off when she said, no, there was someone else who wanted to talk to me.

Karen. Dry-eyed and stone faced and good-bye, Jack.

But *too* dry-eyed. *Too* stone-faced. It was on her, too. And because of that, I guess, as much as anything else, it sank upon me at last. It was over, over, over. We were dead.

"I lo . . . Good-bye, Jack," she said and I saw the tears coming at last.

I nodded, feeling my eyes heating up and leaned forward to key off. Her face became alarmed suddenly, and she asked one last thing. She asked me to tell her that I wasn't doing this for her in any way.

I said I wasn't. Straight-faced and not lying much. Then I keyed off.

Borglyn began to laugh.

I looked up, startled, then furious. He was back at the console. He had been listening in.

"A peeping tom now?" I asked him. Snarled at him.

He continued to laugh. It was a deep, powerful laugh. Like the rest of him.

It unnerved me. But I lashed out as if it didn't, about how he might as well listen in to me while he could and then in on others later because he sure as hell wouldn't have anybody of his own from now on. Not unless you count the daughter of somebody he was beating to death in another room.

"She'll do it, Borglyn." I was really rolling now. "She'll do it to keep Poppa alive but she'll hate you. She'll want to throw up when those fat pig hands and that fat pig body . . ."

He cut me off with his raging. I had hit something.

"Don't give this to me, Pig. Give it to her. But don't expect it to keep her from vomiting into those blue eyes. You're dead and gray and laid open and she'll see it."

He was very quiet.

"Is it worth it?" I asked him and smiled ugly through dry caked lips. "Is it worth what you've done to be what you're gonna have to be for the rest of your life?"

He was still quiet. And something else. I remembered the look he had given me that last moment in the ship when he had laughed with such bitterness about Banshee. I had thought Banshee was destroyed and he had laughed in that way that looked like it hurt.

But not now. No help from that now, godammit!

"And don't start on that damned war, Borglyn! A lot of people came through that war."

He was excited again. And angry. "You don't know anything about it, Crow!" he roared. "You . . . you damned adolescent! You don't know anything about what it was like, what it meant, how. . . ."

His voice trailed off.

"I know one thing, Borglyn. I know it when I see it. And it's you."

His eyes went wide, confused. Vulnerable.

"You're the damned war, Borglyn. You and your punks are now. You see any other ants around here?"

He was quiet for a beat or two. Then he leaned forward to the monitor and spoke in a dead voice. Bright red dead.

"You're gone, Crow. Gone. I don't care if you try to give up now or not. Either way, I'm gonna see you stretched and bleeding."

And then I was standing up from my stool and yelling at him and shaking my fist at the screen and saying there wasn't much chance of that when he was in orbit and safe and hiding and . . . and *still* running away from the fighting.

Borglyn screaming back that, by God, he oughta come down there and show me just what the hell fighting really was. . . .

And I shouted louder, shouted over his fury and outrage with fury and outrage of my own and more, with the fear the sight of him gave me. "You come down here, Pig, and I'll cut them off and bounce them on the bridge."

Goddammit! He was coming right *now*! And he yelled at somebody to take her down and then he whirled back to glare at me and together, against each other, we reached up and keyed off.

Men are so cute.

I woke Holly. Borglyn was sure to lighten a bit on the way down. And it was never going to be a case of dueling pistols anyway. I was going to have to get to him on my own. But he would be there! He would be on the planet and in range of some kind of chance, some kind of scheme. . . .

I laughed. The Plan had raised its throbbing head at last.

Holly refused unless he could play too. He looked at me with those bloodshot darting eyes and refused. He was pale and shaking and hurt. But still he wouldn't.

"You're gonna *have* to have some support fire, Jack. You haven't got a chance without it."

"Dammit, Holly! I haven't a chance anyway. Stay out of it. Just show me how to blow what's left of the outer room and . . ." I got a bad thought. "What about after that? Will I be able to get the door open once I've blown the bastards in front of it?"

He smiled weakly. "The door will spring," he assured me. "I'll do it for you."

I stared at him. "No need. Just tell me how."

"No."

Damn! So cute.

It took a lot more painers to get him going again. That and stimules. On second thought, I took a bunch myself. Why hold back now? I loaded up on other things, too. On blaze pistols clipped on everywhere. And a rifle with extra charges and a row or two of concussion grenades. Not enough to get me across the river to the Coyote—there weren't enough in the universe to do that alone—but maybe enough for my little Plan. Maybe enough to get to one of the commandos wearing that open-air armor. *Any*body could wear open-air. It wasn't like Felix's specially built black suit. And once I had that on, and with perhaps a break or two . . .

And then we were at the door, me loaded down with goodies and Holly equally burdened with two blaze-rifles and the medigrips piled around his leg and other places, making him walk bowlegged behind. I didn't want to waste any time on the off-chance that Borglyn would tell them I was coming out. I didn't think he would think of it. But still, I knew the people outside would *never* expect it.

I stood crouched before the door and nodded to Holly, by the panel. He keyed the blast. It shook the floor and the door. It blew, according to Holly, the outer room, floors and ceiling and gash *and* commandos down the hill toward or in the river. It was very loud.

"Now spring the door," I urged him. I didn't want to wait an instant for them to recover.

Holly nodded. He keyed the switch for "open." That's all it took. I snarled at him as I raced forward. He laughed and stumbled along behind.

The Plan was for me to rush out ahead to find cover. Then I would support Holly's exit against any resistance that might be left from the first blast. Holly could thereafter support my charge down the hill over the ridge.

We never had a prayer.

The blast had done its job well enough. There was no sign of the front chamber except for the huge chunks of masonry scattered about. As I leaped forward to the first boulder-sized one, however, I knew it was over.

They were waiting at the ridge, safe and secure and already firing, already filling the air with the arcing grenades. I spun around to yell at Holly to stop! "Stay where you are! Holly! I'm coming back in. . . ."

But then it was too late. The first blasts hit and we both went down. I saw him slammed against a jagged cornice and lay stunned. I tried crawling toward him but then the air was full of blue beams and dust from the blasts. I felt a surge of heat along my thigh and jerked it out of the open. I couldn't get across the open space to him. I was cut off. But he was exposed! He was open to their fire and the blasts, without any protection at all but a difficult angle up from the ridge.

The ridges. The other side opened up about then. And then from two sides the air was filled with beams and grenades and dust and slamming rocking noise. I tried crawling back to him, curled up around myself to ward off the dust and rock that rattled against the surrounding rubble. But it was no good. No way to get back without being struck by the flying shards. No way to stay. No way to do anything. So I crawled and stumbled forward and things crashed into me, cutting and tearing and crushing and I yelled to Holly that I was sorry, sorry, so sorry that I wasn't going to make it to help him, I was dying and sorry and Holly? Can you hear me?

Suddenly moving quickly, sliding roughly across the broken stones. Holly? But Holly was there beside me, sliding along parallel and . . . What the hell? I strained to lift my head, to see who had us by our collars. But then he no longer did. We were inside the second room once more and he had dropped us flopping on the floor and turned to re-seal the door.

It was Lewis. It was the drunk. He was sober. I remembered the hatch.

He didn't bother to take us all the way back to the Control-room table. He left us lying where we were and used the medical supplies stacked against the wall.

"Lewis?" asked Holly suddenly.

I turned, surprised and delighted to see he was still alive. "Holly! You made it!"

He grinned, winced from the pain. "Why not? You did," he asked.

Then we both laughed.

Lewis did not. He didn't speak at all, in fact. He tended to us in grim silence, darting back and forth from body to body with grips and packs and an air of urgency. We weren't much help. Too tired and too hurt and, come to think of it, too amazed at being alive.

When it was over and we were going to live for another short while, he sat us up against the wall and gave us some water. Then he hauled over a chair and sat down and lit a cigarette and looked at us with that same grim expression, of a parent furious with naughty children, and asked: "Why?"

Holly tried to tell him. About Borglyn using mortars on the Cityfolk again and again and about how horrible that was and what it meant. About how Borglyn would be so hated now that he would have to be even more brutal later on and how, no, we didn't think we could beat him exactly, but slowing him down would surely mean something. . . .

He interrupted once. In a cold tone he nodded at me. "All this for you, too?"

I nodded, feeling strangely embarrassed.

Holly seemed embarrassed, too. He went on, really wanting Lewis to understand.

"It has to be done, Lewis."

Lewis sighed. "It always does, Holly. That's no reason to do it."

"But all those people!"

"What about them?"

Holly frowned, stuck. He turned to me. But I couldn't think either. He turned back to Lewis.

"Lewis, there just isn't anyone else? Can't you see that?"

He stood up, walked a couple of steps. He puffed a puff. He looked down at us. "Shouldn't that tell you something?"

Holly faced him. "I just didn't see any way out, Lewis. I still don't."

Lewis frowned. "Don't you?"

"I don't," replied Holly in an odd tone.

I looked at him. Tears were starting from his eyes. I shook my head. What the hell was going on?

And then Lewis was there, right in front of us and crouched down and peering at us with eyes I didn't know he possessed and he said: "You can't? Neither of you? You don't see *any way* out?"

We shook our heads. And then Holly said, in a calm clear voice: "There isn't one."

Lewis dropped his face into his hands. He rubbed it hard.

But then, when he lifted it back up, the grimness had gone. It was replaced with . . . what? Reckless abandon?

He smiled. "I was afraid you'd say that."

Then he stood up and stripped off his jumpsuit. He was naked underneath. I heard a groan behind me. I looked and saw that Holly was openly crying now. He must have known then.

But I didn't until Lewis walked naked to the far corner of the room and did something that only one human creature in all the universe could do. He touched his open palm to that of the black suit—and it opened.

Felix.

VIII

It couldn't be.

"I want to know how come you're not dead!" I demanded idiotically.

Lewis/Felix laughed. It was that same carefree abandon as before. Then he winked at me. "You got a couple of minutes?" he asked, indicating the door to the outside.

That wasn't what I meant. I said so. Holly helped. He asked about Kent.

"Kent's dead," was the uncarefree reply.

"I know that. He died on Banshee. But what I . . ."

"He didn't die on Banshee. He died on the *Terra*."

We looked at each other. I went this time. "Lew . . . Felix? Is it Felix?"

He nodded. "Of course."

"We thought Kent killed you."

He frowned. "He saved me. They killed him."

"Who?"

"Fleet," he said in a dead voice and knelt down to fiddle with the suit. It had sprung, spread-eagled open, off the wheelchair onto the floor.

In a hurried voice, Holly told him what we meant, why we had thought what we thought. When he got to the part about immersing, Felix cringed.

"You really did that? You went through the whole thing with me?"

Holly said we had. "Except between drops. But everything in the suit."

Felix shuddered. "Still . . ." He shuddered again, made an effort to regain his former humor. "I hope you guys had more fun than I did," he said and laughed.

We didn't know what to say. We didn't *want* to say anything. But we had to know. Holly told him about being there when Kent had struck him and then everything going blank, the Alpha readings dropping out of sight.

Felix smiled. "I can see your problem. But all that happened was that Kent popped my suit when he hit me. I guess he was afraid I would struggle or something. As if it would have made any difference. Damn! but that man was strong."

We nodded, watching in silence as he continued to both talk and work the suit.

"Then he put me in a ship. It was . . . He'd stolen it from someone I . . ."

"From Allie?" Holly prompted.

Felix looked at him, surprised. Then he nodded slowly. "That's right. You know everything. The whole story."

I really wanted to disappear. But Holly didn't seem the least bit embarrassed.

"Everything in the suit," he said.

Felix nodded back. He took the cigarette out of his mouth and regarded it lovingly. Then he tossed it away.

"Kent put me on the ship and sent me off, still in his armor the whole time. When they tried to find out what was going on, he blocked them." Felix stared, remembering. His voice was very quiet when next he spoke. "I saw what happened from the port. They cut him in half." He shrugged, almost violently. "But I was long gone by then. To here."

"And all this time . . .?" I wondered aloud.

He smiled. "All this time. Have I got water? I notice I've got everything else."

Holly nodded. "Fully operational."

I looked at him. "Why?"

He blushed, looked at Felix. "I suppose you think that's sick."

Felix grinned, then laughed, then giggled wildly, almost falling over. "Holly? How the hell would *I* know?"

Then he lay down in the suit. And it closed over him. Then they both stood up.

It was terrifying.

"Is . . . is it all right?" Holly stuttered.

The black helmet nodded. The amplified voice was harsh and deep. It echoed loudly. "It hurts. I'm out of shape."

He walked loudly and heavily over to the seal and paused with a huge black finger poised over the panel. "Just key it open?"

Holly nodded.

I tried to pull myself up, slipped back down. "Felix . . .?"

"What?" boomed back, not unpleasantly.

"Uh . . . nothing. Later."

"Later," he echoed. I couldn't read it.

He sighed loudly, electronically. "I wish you could smoke in here." Then he pushed the key and the door opened and he was gone. We heard the blasts begin almost at once. The door, set to close behind him, cut out everything afterward.

"Come on," shrilled Holly, stumbling across the floor to the Control room. "I want to see."

I followed. So did I.

It took us a long time to clamber inside and get the panel working. Our own monitors were long evaporated by battle. And Borglyn had cut us off before. So we missed a lot of it. But Holly managed to jump into Borglyn's signal anyway. We tried several angles, but none of them got what we wanted.

Finally, we managed to get our old perspective, from the monitor over Borglyn's shoulder. We could see what he could see. It was great.

Felix was incredible.

He was everywhere at once. Borglyn couldn't keep track of him cleanly from his monitors. There were just scattered images. Bodies flying through the air . . . blaze-bombs or grenades exploding with no one around . . . blazers cutting off abrupty, shattered and bent . . . Felix steaming right at the monitor as he reached the edge of the river and *leaped* across it, all twenty-something meters of it . . .

Then the main camp scurrying about and the mortars going off and somebody yelling in a high-pitched strident tone of growing terror that there were no targets, where the hell was he and. . . .

"Omigod! There, there, *there*!"

Felix was great!

Borglyn, on the other hand, was terrified.

"Lift! Lift, goddammit!" he yelled to one and all and the Coyote began to rise.

One of his henchmen, in the Control room with him, said something about running scared and the sumbitch not being able to hurt a starship anyway.

Borglyn hit him, a loud back-handed smack across the face. "*You* said he'd never get across the river! Lift!"

But the ship was already rising, a few meters up already and then I heard Holly hiss beside me, "No!" as we both saw the black suit still coming, loping incredibly fast across the ground. And I knew what he meant. I knew what he feared.

And Borglyn knew what to do.

"All tacticals," he yelled to unseen crew around him. "Discharge them all at once. Now!"

On the screens the wall of fire blocked the sight of everything as it swept down across the camp, boiling the mortars and the commandos and the land and everything else.

Then the view was eclipsed by interference as the Coyote vaulted suddenly upward into Sanction's sky.

I just sat there.

But Holly evidently could not. He began to furiously work the keys, trying blindly, desperately, to restore our view. He almost got it a couple of times, though not well and not clearly. And our fix on the monitor we wanted was clearly lost. We got random snowy pictures from all over the ship, corridors and bulkheads. No sound. No pattern. And no hope. The ship was pulling out of our range.

But that was the least of it anyway. I reached a hand over

and lay it gently on Holly's. I couldn't stand to see him torture himself, or me, by trying for. . . .

He went stiff when the screen went sharp and clear.

I looked where he looked.

The image was from the outer portside monitor. It showed the length of the outer hull illuminated against the backdrop of daytime Sanction. And silhouetted against that, right in the center of it. . . .

The black suit had one plassteel hand gripped vise-tight on a warp bleeder conduit. The other was clenched into a black fist that hurtled toward the monitor's single eye.

And then all was dark.

EPILOGUE

We have never found the Coyote, of course.

Sure, it took us a long time before another ship came and we could even begin the search. And space is big and the ship was out of fuel anyway, so it doesn't make much difference.

But still we looked.

So do the people from Golden. Yes, they showed. About a month later. Reluctantly, we told them the story from the beginning when we found the suit until the end when we lost it. And we said we understood how reluctant they must be to want to spend much time searching for the remains of the dead and fuel-less hulk. That we would be staying and if anyone ever reported anything we would be sure to let them know.

They looked at us like we were crazy.

"The Archon was not seen to die, is that not correct?" the representative asked Holly.

Holly said that, yes, that's true, but . . . There was no *fuel*. Not to mention the terrible damage the ship undoubtedly underwent. "I mean," Holly blustered on, red-faced, "There was a battle we didn't even *see*."

The Rep eyed him coolly. "But the Archon was not seen to die?" he asked again.

Holly looked at me and shrugged. "Well, no," he replied.

The rep nodded. "So. We shall continue the search."

And they have. They stop by here now and again.

A couple of other things:

We're not a part of Fleet any longer. In no way. They're mad about it. Fuck 'em.

We traced the rumor about "Lewis's" rich-kid past to—surprise—Lewis himself.

We have a growing colony. A government. Holly and I are on what they call the Council of Elders. But they don't call us much.

Lya is pregnant with her second. Her first is a girl with her looks and Holly's brain.

Karen is not pregnant and won't be. Yes, we're still together. But we are not, repeat: *not*, happy. But I guess we'll keep at it anyhow.

I never saw Eyes again.

The Antwar continues.

What about me? Besides the fact that I'm getting fat and thoughtful? Not much else. Both traits are, understandably, fulfilling.

What I eat is everything. What I think about . . .

The past, of course. My life and what it's meant and what it will mean from now on. And Felix. I think about Felix a lot.

And about the Masao and what he said, about there being no protection from what you are and all. And I think I may have something to add:

There is no protection from what you want.

Hell, they keep searching, which is dumb enough. But when I think about the certain look in that Rep's eye, in all their eyes when they drop by to question again and again. And when I think about all of it—from Golden, to Banshee, to Sanction . . .

When I think about it, I wonder.

Dammit, I cannot *help* but wonder:

Are you there, Felix?

Are you there?

DAW

**THEY WERE THE ULTIMATE ENEMIES,
GENERALS OF STAR EMPIRES FOREVER OPPOSED—
AND WORLDS WOULD FALL
BEFORE THEIR PRIVATE WAR...**

IN CONQUEST BORN
C.S. FRIEDMAN

Braxi and Azea, two super-races fighting an endless campaign over a long forgotten cause. The Braxaná—created to become the ultimate warriors. The Azeans, raised to master the powers of the mind, using telepathy to penetrate where mere weapons cannot. Now the final phase of their war is approaching, when whole worlds will be set ablaze by the force of ancient hatred. Now Zatar and Anzha, the master generals, who have made this battle a personal vendetta, will use every power of body and mind to claim the vengeance of total conquest.

☐ **IN CONQUEST BORN**   (UE2198—$3.95)

DAW

SCIENCE FICTION MASTERWORKS FROM THE INCOMPARABLE
C.J. CHERRYH

The Chanur Series
- [ ] THE PRIDE OF CHANUR   (UE2181—$3.50)
- [ ] CHANUR'S VENTURE   (UE2183—$3.50)
- [ ] THE KIF STRIKE BACK   (UE2184—$3.50)
- [ ] CHANUR'S HOMECOMING   (UE2177—$3.95)

The Union-Alliance Novels
- [ ] DOWNBELOW STATION   (UE2227—$3.95)
- [ ] MERCHANTER'S LUCK   (UE2139—$3.50)
- [ ] FORTY THOUSAND IN GEHENNA   (UE1952—$3.50)
- [ ] VOYAGER IN NIGHT   (UE2107—$2.95)

The Morgaine Novels
- [ ] GATE OF IVREL (BOOK 1)   (UE2257—$3.50)
- [ ] WELL OF SHIUAN (BOOK 2)   (UE2258—$3.50)
- [ ] FIRES OF AZEROTH (BOOK 3)   (UE2259—$3.50)
- [ ] EXILE'S GATE (BOOK 4)   (UE2254—$3.95)

The Faded Sun Novels
- [ ] THE FADED SUN: KESRITH (BOOK 1)   (UE1960—$3.50)
- [ ] THE FADED SUN: SHON'JIR (BOOK 2)   (UE1889—$2.95)
- [ ] THE FADED SUN: KUTATH (BOOK 3)   (UE2133—$2.95)

NEW AMERICAN LIBRARY
P.O. Box 999, Bergenfield, New Jersey 07621

Please send me the DAW BOOKS I have checked above. I am enclosing $_____
(check or money order—no currency or C.O.D.'s). Please include the list price plus
$1.00 per order to cover handling costs. Prices and numbers are subject to change
without notice.

Name _____

Address _____

City _____ State _____ Zip _____

Please allow 4-6 weeks for delivery.

DAW

A GALAXY OF SCIENCE FICTION STARS

Attention:

DAW COLLECTORS

Many readers of DAW Books have written requesting information on early titles and book numbers to assist in the collection of DAW editions since the first of our titles appeared in April 1972.

We have prepared a several-pages-long list of all DAW titles, giving their sequence numbers, original and current order numbers, and ISBN numbers. And of course the authors and book titles, as well as reissues.

If you think that this list will be of help, you may have a copy by writing to the address below and enclosing one dollar in stamps or currency to cover the handling and postage costs.

DAW BOOKS, INC.
DEPT. C
1633 Broadway
New York, N.Y. 10019